For Philly

PROLOGUE

Alone with the memory of your lies, it took three murders to show me who you really are.

You must see who you are too: the brutality and the cruelty, the suffering caused.

Right here, right now, I promise you this: whatever else happens, I will bring light from your darkness. I will turn you to face the consequences of your crimes.

I will find grace in your weakness. And mercy in your sins.

Sophie McKenzie is the author of best-selling crime novels *Close My Eyes*, *Trust in Me* and *Here We Lie* as well as over twenty books for children and teenagers including the multi-award-winning *Girl, Missing* and *Split Second* series. She has twice been longlisted for the prestigious Carnegie Medal. She lives in London.

Find Sophie online at www.sophiemckenziebooks.com, on twitter at @sophiemckenzie_ and on facebook at www.facebook.com/sophiemckenzieauthor.

THE
BLACK SHEEP

SOPHIE MCKENZIE

SIMON &
SCHUSTER

London · New York · Sydney · Toronto · New Delhi

A CBS COMPANY

First published in Great Britain by Simon & Schuster UK Ltd, 2017
A CBS COMPANY

Copyright © Rosefire Ltd, 2017

1 3 5 7 9 10 8 6 4 2

Simon & Schuster UK Ltd
1st Floor
222 Gray's Inn Road
London WC1X 8HB

www.simonandschuster.co.uk

Simon & Schuster Australia, Sydney
Simon & Schuster India, New Delhi

A CIP catalogue record for this book
is available from the British Library

Paperback ISBN: 978-1-4711-3322-0
Trade Paperback ISBN: 978-1-4711-3321-3
eBook ISBN: 978-1-4711-3323-7

Typeset in Sabon by M Rules
Printed and bound by CPI Group (UK) Ltd, Croydon, CR0 4YY

MIX
Paper from
responsible sources
FSC® C020471

Simon & Schuster UK Ltd are committed to sourcing paper
that is made from wood grown in sustainable forests and support the Forest
Stewardship Council, the leading international forest certification organisation.
Our books displaying the FSC logo are printed on FSC-certified paper.

OUR FATHER

Friday 8 January 2016–
Friday 15 January 2016

FRAN

1

I drew Ruby closer as the music faded away. Oasis. 'Don't Look Back In Anger'. One of Caspian's favourites from years ago, before we met. Ruby wiped away her tears and looked up at me with trembling lips.

'Okay?' I whispered.

She nodded. On my other side Rufus sat rigid in his chair. A stranger might have thought he wasn't feeling anything, but I could see the strain behind that blank expression in every muscle of his face. He was thirteen. Ruby just nine. And this was their father's memorial service. For the thousandth time I wondered if, despite what everyone said about 'structure' and 'ritual' and the chance to 'say a proper goodbye', they were too young to be here. I put my hand on Rufus's and, for the first time in months, he didn't shake it off.

'Are you all right?'

He nodded.

'That's it, we can go now.'

The relief on his face was unmistakable. A wave of guilt washed over me. He said so little these days it was impossible to know how he really felt about being here – but I strongly suspected he was putting up with it all because he thought he ought to look after me, not as a helpful part of remembering, or mourning, his dad.

My own father appeared in front of us, solid and grave.

'Francesca?' He offered me his arm. A typically formal yet thoughtful gesture. I glanced at Rufus again. 'Lucy'll take him,' Dad said.

Sure enough, my sister was already steering Rufus out of his seat.

I stood up, Ruby clinging to my side, and linked my arm through Dad's. The touch of his silk suit was soft, yet the material strong. A new song began – some classical piece I didn't recognise, chosen by Caspian's parents. My thoughts drifted momentarily from Rufus to my husband. My late husband. At the way he would have demurred over that descriptor – 'you're the one who tends to be late, darling' – at the way he would have meekly submitted to his mother's snobbery in insisting on a string quartet for his funeral 'even though the only music she ever listens to is Cliff Richard', at the way it was his dependable arms I wanted around me right now.

Grief, raw and fierce, clutched at my throat, twisting it tight. A sob rose through me and I stumbled. Dad caught me, pulling me close.

'I know,' he breathed in my ear. 'I know, sweetheart.'

He meant Mum of course. Lost suddenly, like Caspian, though in an accident brought on by her diabetes nearly five years ago: prosaic compared to the horror of Caspian's murder – a knife attack on a sunny September morning the year before last, as he walked from his car to the hospital to begin an early shift.

With a jolt I realised we were outside, the low winter sun in my stinging eyes. I turned from Dad and wiped my face. As I turned back my sister and Rufus joined us, then Dad's wife, Jacqueline. After the stillness of the hall the outside world seemed harsh and brash. Cars zoomed past. People milled by. Across the tarmac I spotted Dad's older brother, my Uncle Perry, deep in conversation with Caspian's parents. I couldn't see anyone else I knew. Ruby's arms were still around my waist. I stroked her hair, wishing I'd never agreed to the service. It was true that Caspian's funeral had been a blur – the shock of his passing too great and too recent to make any sense. But this, today, was just raking all the pain up.

'It's a milestone, sweetheart,' Dad said softly, clearly reading my mind. 'Something for you and the kids to hold on to.'

'Though I'm never sure how helpful these things are without a religious structure.' Jacqueline sighed. 'I'm sorry, Francesca, that came out wrong. I know Caspian's parents were just trying to honour his ... his ...' Her voice faded away.

I focused on the top of Rufus's head. He was growing

fast. Four inches since the start of the school year. Already up to my shoulders.

'That's right,' Lucy said softly, squeezing my arm. 'Mr and Mrs Hoffman were just trying to do what Caspian would have wanted.'

I shot my sister a grateful look. These days Lucy carried her Catholicism with a gentle touch. She was devout, no doubt about it, her entire life revolved around daily mass, regular prayer groups and the endless work she did for the church, but she never overtly pushed her faith on anyone else. As usual she was dressed in white, with a long cream jacket over her trademark floaty dress. Jacqueline, in contrast, wore a snappy dark-blue suit and swung a Prada tote from her arm. *Her* religious credentials were a bit like that handbag: something for occasional public display that was stored out of sight at home.

No, that wasn't fair. Jacqueline was trying to live according to her faith, just as Lucy did. My stepmother might have had a tendency to be prudish and controlling but she was fundamentally kind and certainly brilliant at coping with Dad's intense personality.

Dad and Jacqueline wandered across the tarmac to join Uncle Perry while Lucy turned to speak to one of the other guests.

'Can we go soon, Mum?' I had to bend down to hear Ruby's whisper. Next to her Rufus leaned in. He wasn't looking at either of us but I could sense he was as eager as his sister to get away.

They weren't the only ones. I couldn't wait to leave

myself. I'd never wanted this service. The whole thing had been Caspian's parents' idea and the hall was full of their friends. Well, several of Caspian's colleagues were here too, thanks to a notice his mum had displayed in the hospital, but I had deliberately kept my invitations to family and a few close friends. And not just because it was hard on the kids. I'd had enough of dealing with strangers who didn't know what to say to me. At the thought a lump lodged in my throat. Once Caspian and I saved each other at parties. But Caspian had been dead for a year and four months and I couldn't remember the last party I'd been to.

Across the gravel a tall man with a long narrow face wearing a dark overcoat was leaning against the wall, not talking to anyone. He was watching me closely; too closely. I looked away. Another reason for not doing this – being the focus of attention was something I loathed.

'*Mum*?' Ruby repeated.

I glanced down at both children. They gazed back at me with miserable faces. Not for the first time I felt a throb of rage that I'd been left a single parent. It wasn't fair. Not on me.

And certainly not on either of them.

'We can leave soon,' I said. 'Though—'

'Hey, guys.' My cousin Dex materialised in front of us. 'I was wondering where you'd got to, I don't know *anyone* here.' He gave the kids a broad grin then hugged me. Lucy, he simply nodded at. He wasn't being mean, Lucy just wasn't in the slightest bit tactile, especially not when there was an audience. Even the kids sensed it. In a setting like this it would have felt like an invasion of her privacy to touch her. The last time she and I had held each other in public had been at Mum's funeral five years ago.

'Uncle Dex,' Ruby said, hurling herself into his arms. She adored him; both the kids did. Frankly, Dex was hard to dislike: he emanated warmth and was as charming as he was good-looking.

'Are Rubes and Rufus staying on for the food in the hall?' Dex asked.

'I said we'd play it by ear,' I said, grimacing to indicate that I'd far rather we could all leave straight away.

'Well, if you guys want you can come home with me.' He smiled at Ruby and Rufus. 'I've got the boys this weekend. I'm picking them up in half an hour.'

'Yay!' Ruby clapped her hands together. 'I'm gonna beat last time's keepy-uppy score.' Dex saw his children every other weekend – his marriage had ended years ago, buried under the weight of his many affairs – and we often spent the day together when they were around. Ruby was just a few months older than Dex's eldest, who shared her love of football. While at seven and a half, Dex's younger son was already an expert enough gamer to give Rufus a run for his money.

'That okay with you, Dumpy?' Dex asked, using his old pet name for me from childhood. He'd bestowed it on me when we were just eleven. Dex was already taller than me then and came up with Dumpy mostly as a way to wind me up. To get my own back I started calling him

Scab Face – after a nasty injury he'd sustained in some fight at his boys' school. We both went to single-sex, private Catholic schools. But of course Dex's scab fell off after a few weeks and the name no longer fitted, whereas I was still – and forever – short.

'Please, Mum?' Ruby added. 'Can we go to Uncle Dex's?'

'Sure.' I shot Dex a grateful smile. 'Thanks. I'll join you as soon as I can.'

We had always understood each other, Dex and I, like siblings from the start and especially close after his dad – my Uncle Graham – left his mum just after Dex's twelfth birthday.

Dex walked away across the gravel, holding Ruby's hand. Rufus hurried after them. As usual, every woman present turned to watch Dex as he strolled along. The effect he had never ceased to amaze me. To me he would always be the boy with the gappy teeth and the cowlick, though I had to concede that he looked cool today in his sharp grey suit: all chiselled jaw and bright-green eyes, oozing charisma.

My sister tapped my shoulder. Though several years younger than me, Lucy had been taller since she was thirteen. Like our mother she was heavy-breasted with long, slim legs while I was more evenly proportioned and, of course, far shorter.

'How are you doing?' Lucy asked.

She had buttoned up her jacket and the formality of the stiff wool above the flowing crepe of her dress underneath made her look older than usual. She turned thirty just a couple of months ago, but regularly got taken for a teenager. It was partly the lack of make-up and jewellery and partly the innocent, almost angelic, fragility that radiated off her in waves.

'I'm fine,' I said.

It wasn't true of course, but since Mum died, there had been a distance between Lucy and me that I didn't understand and was at a loss to know how to deal with. We talked, but only about superficial things. Or, rather, only about things superficially, as if our outlooks on the world prevented us from really understanding each other. I guessed it had something to do with the things we didn't share, like her having a faith and my having children. Whatever it was, Caspian's death hadn't brought us closer together. Don't get me wrong. Lucy was brilliant – always on the phone asking if she could help out with the kids or if we wanted to come over for supper. Just that I never really felt we connected. I certainly didn't understand the choices she'd made – she was smart but had dropped out of uni and still lived in our childhood home with Dad and Jacqueline. She didn't work – she didn't need to, thanks to the trust fund she received from Dad – unless you counted her voluntary efforts for the Legion of Mary and her various prayer groups. Most strange of all, despite being staggeringly pretty in a simple, natural way, she had never had a proper boyfriend.

Still, perhaps there were good reasons for that: she'd been seduced when she was fifteen – raped, basically, though typically she refused to see the encounter that way – and fallen pregnant. She'd had an abortion, which I'd helped arrange without our parents' consent. They'd found out years later and Lucy's shame and humiliation over both the original 'episode' as she referred to it and the subsequent exposure had reinforced her introvert tendencies.

Shy as ever, Lucy slipped away as a paunchy, middle-aged man with thinning sandy hair strode over and planted himself in front of me.

'Francesca, it's so good to see you.'

I blinked, startled. The man was vaguely familiar, but . . .

'Simon Pinner.' He held out his hand and we shook. 'Colleague of your husband's. Good man, Caspian.'

'Hi,' I said, still struggling to place him. 'Are you a gynaecologist too?'

'Another gynae surgeon, yes. For my sins.' He smirked, as if he'd said something funny. 'We actually met briefly at a dinner party two or three years ago. It's good to see you again, though I'm sorry it has to be under such circumstances.' Simon's thin lips stretched into a wet, pink line.

'Oh,' I said. 'Thank you.' Had Caspian liked him? Respected him? I couldn't remember.

'What a lovely service,' Simon went on. 'Well, not a service really, I suppose.'

'It was what Caspian would have wanted, what his parents wanted,' I said, wondering if Simon caught the slight note of resentment in my voice.

'Quite,' he said.

13

There was a short pause. Dex and the children had vanished. My sister was across the tarmac talking to Dad and Jacqueline. Auntie Sheila – Dex's mum – had just joined them. As she planted a brief kiss on Jacqueline's carefully powdered cheek I caught sight of the tall, dark stranger with the narrow face. He was on the edge of the crowd, still watching me. It was too much. I badly wanted to leave.

'I'd love to take you out to dinner,' Simon said.

What? I stared at him, taking in his face properly. He was in his fifties, I guessed, with weather-beaten skin and watery-blue eyes. Not remotely attractive, but not hideous. Recently I had started guiltily to fantasise about dating again. Nothing serious, not with the kids, just to hang out with someone new, someone who didn't see me solely as Caspian's widow or the mother of bereaved children. I missed the conversation. The being held. The sex.

Still, there was no way I was going anywhere with someone who thought it was okay to ask me out at my husband's memorial service.

'Thank you,' I said, floundering for the right way to say no. 'But I have the kids ...'

Simon waved his hand dismissively. 'I'm rather a simple sort ... simple Simon, you might say ...' He chuckled to himself. 'But I know a thing or two about fine French wines and I've got a definite sixth sense for a decent menu.'

Though not much of a sixth sense for a brush-off, I thought to myself.

'I'm afraid I can't,' I said, more firmly.

'Can't or won't?' Simon smirked. 'Ah, well. I'm sure we can work it out.'

What did that mean?

Simon waved his fingers at me and walked away. I was alone. I felt cold, though the winter sun was still shining brightly. Simon Pinner was definitely not a potential date, but maybe I should go for dinner with *someone*.

The idea of it scared me, but it also felt exciting.

Not that I wasn't still mourning Caspian. Every day I missed him, while every week brought a new aspect of living without him, from dealing with the car – which had always been his province – to the suspicions constantly rearing that when Rufus grunted at me or Ruby persisted in wanting to play football 'like boys do, Mummy', it wasn't just hormones but unprocessed grief that was being acted out.

'Francesca?' Dad materialised in front of me. 'They've laid out some food in the memorial hall. Shall we go back inside?'

Eating was the last thing I felt like doing, but I let Dad take my arm, bracing myself as we returned to the hall. Two large tables had been set up at the end of the room, each one covered with a white cloth and a selection of silver platters containing meats and salads. A waiter offered me a glass of white wine. I took a sip. It was warm.

A moment later I was hugging Caspian's parents, who were keen for me to meet various guests. I spent the next fifteen minutes shaking hands and accepting condolences from people who clearly had only known Caspian as a child or very briefly and superficially as an adult.

It was exhausting and I was grateful when Lucy whispered in Dad's ear that I was tired and he, in turn, drew Caspian's mother to one side and said in his usual forceful manner that he was going to take me home in a few minutes. Such protective actions were typical of them both – indeed Dad's overprotectiveness had driven me mad when I was younger and rebelling against his Catholic strictures – and though there had been many times over the past year when I'd felt over-whelmed, even suffocated, by their attempts to look after me, right now I was grateful.

I caught sight of Simon Pinner again, edging towards me past a table laden with bread rolls, and I hurried off to the ladies. I took my time, emerging a few minutes later with a fresh layer of make-up. Simon, thankfully, was nowhere to be seen. I headed over to the long coat rail to the right of the exit, intending to get my coat and make my goodbyes. As I ran my hand over the rough wool jackets hanging from the rail a male voice said my name.

Heart sinking, thinking it was Simon again, I turned.

The tall man with the narrow face I'd noticed earlier was standing in front of me.

'Hello,' I said, bracing myself. Was this another col-league of Caspian's?

'Harry Dunbar,' the man said, holding out his hand. He had a flat-vowelled Manchester accent. 'I'm so sorry for your loss.'

16

I smiled as I shook. There was an endearing intensity about the man. He was better looking than I'd realised too: not in Dex's league, but his eyes were a deep chocolate brown and there was a masculine elegance to the slope of his nose and the curve of his cheekbones.

'Did you know Caspian?' I asked.

'No, not really.' Harry hesitated. 'Well ... we met at a conference just over a year ago, just before he ... that conference in Paris.'

I nodded, remembering. 'It was the last trip Caspian did,' I said.

'I know.' Harry hesitated again. 'Look, I'm sorry turning up like this but I've been abroad for work and I didn't know Caspian had died until I read about the memorial service in the hospital newsletter a couple of weeks ago.'

'Oh.' I gazed at him. 'Are you another gynaecologist?'

'No.' Harry smiled and the effect transformed his face, making him seem almost mischievous. 'I'm a sales rep for a small company ... Devora Pharmaceuticals. Look, that doesn't matter.' His face grew solemn again. 'Truth is that I hardly knew your husband, but I had to come here today to let you know what he told me.'

'Sorry?' Most of the room was hidden from view by the coat rail. I could see Dad out of the corner of my eye. He was looking around, presumably for me. 'Sorry, I'm not sure what—'

'Caspian and I met in the bar of the conference hotel,' Harry interrupted. He looked awkward now, his forehead creased with a frown. 'We were in a group,

17

drinking, then the two of us got talking, then ... then Caspian said something. He was tired, a bit drunk. His guard was down. I guessed from what everyone said that you had – have – no idea ...'

My heart lurched into my mouth. 'What are you saying?'

'I'm saying that my understanding is that everyone including the police think your husband got caught up in a random knife attack, a mugging gone wrong or something.'

'Yes, but—'

'It wasn't random. At least, I don't think it was.'

The chatter in the room whirled around us. I kept my gaze on Harry's soft brown eyes. 'Why ... why would you say that?'

'No one was ever caught, were they?'

'No.' The police's investigation had stalled early on thanks to the lack of witnesses and DNA evidence. A hooded man had been seen on CCTV getting into a stolen Vauxhall Astra on the next street shortly after the stabbing but he'd never been identified and the car had never been found, though a burnt-out Astra – number plates removed – was discovered in an Essex wood two weeks later. 'Why are you saying it wasn't a random attack? Whoever it was stole all the cash from Caspian's wallet.'

'Yeah, I read that when I looked up the story. *Murdered for £150*. That was the headline, wasn't it?'

I nodded, wincing at the memory. 'Why do you think different?'

'Because your husband told me in that bar he was being threatened.'

'*Threatened?*'

'He hadn't said anything to you because he didn't want to worry you, but sometimes we tell strangers things and he told me he thought his life was in danger.' Harry paused.

'What else?' I asked, sensing he was holding something back.

'He said that the threats were coming from someone specific.' Harry held my gaze. 'From someone close to you both.'

2

The light streaming through the window from the fierce January sun dimmed and the chatter of the busy hall faded to a background hum. For a split second my breath caught in my throat. Then the absurdity of what he was saying struck me. I laughed out loud.

'What *are* you talking about? The police didn't ... No one has said *anything* about threats, let alone someone *close* to us.'

'I know.' Harry hesitated. 'Look, I realise this is a lot to take in.' He fished a piece of paper out of his pocket containing a scribbled number and handed it to me. 'This is my mobile,' he said. 'Call me when you've ... I'm really sorry, I know this is a bad time, I just didn't know how else to find you ... to tell you.'

'Wait,' I said. 'Who is this person "close" to us? Did Caspian give you a name? Or a reason?'

'He thought the threats were something to do with his work as a doctor ... carrying out abortions.'

We stared at each other. Caspian had performed terminations ever since I'd known him. They were part and parcel of his duties as a gynaecologist, as a surgeon. We'd talked about the ethics of abortions many times during the first year we were together. It had been such a huge and emotive subject in my own strictly Catholic upbringing: firstly with me arguing a pro-choice position from my early teens and later, when I helped Lucy arrange her termination. Our parents were furious when they found out. Mum took it personally that Lucy and I had gone behind her back, while Dad channelled his anger into *Shield*, a pro-life campaigning organisation which dominated his free time for years.

I couldn't believe it when I met Caspian and discovered abortion surgery was part of his working life. Caspian himself was characteristically logical on the topic. He didn't much like carrying out the procedure but refused to disqualify himself as many other doctors did.

'How can I turn my back?' he used to say. 'It would be hypocritical. The women making this choice aren't doing it because it's easy. It's hard for them too and if I support the intellectual idea of it I can't run away from the application.'

We even argued about it in the months after Rufus was born when – ironically – the pro-life lessons that had been drummed into me as a child reasserted themselves with a short-lived but fiercely felt intensity that shocked me, even at the time. Caspian stayed calm in the face of my tears as he repeated his belief that if abortions were legal he was obliged to carry them out. As usual, he won me over with his implacable reasoning and the steady, solid way he made his arguments: nothing ever loud or emotional.

Having had my own children the years passed and my revulsion at abortion subsided again. No, that's not quite right. I was never revolted at the thought, merely upset. Which Caspian always said he was too. Intellectually I agreed with him. Always. It was just that for a time the prospect of getting rid of a foetus appalled me – a visceral reaction which had never wholly left me since and which Caspian, I'm certain, never shared.

'Your family is Catholic, isn't it?' Harry asked, his voice low and intent.

'Ye-es,' I acknowledged, my anxieties rising. 'Why . . .? What are you saying?' Was Harry implying the person 'close to me' who was threatening my husband was a member of my own family?

Harry hesitated.

'What did Caspian actually tell—?' I started.

'Francesca?' Jacqueline was waving a leather-gloved hand in my direction. 'Francesca, the car's ready.'

I stared helplessly at Harry. He gave his head the tiniest of shakes, then leaned forward so I could feel the brush of his lips against my ear.

'Call me,' he whispered. 'I'll tell you everything I know.' He turned and hurried away.

'What was that about?' Jacqueline asked, glancing after Harry.

'Nothing,' I said.

But as I got into the car with my family, all I could think about was Harry's claim. The more I thought about it, the more preposterous it seemed. For a start, I couldn't imagine *anyone* threatening my husband.

Threats belonged to a more dramatic world than the one solid, dependable Caspian lived in. And if somebody *had* threatened him, why wouldn't he have told me about it? In fact, why on earth would he have confided in a stranger in a bar? Caspian was reserved. Definitely not in the habit of revealing personal information to people he didn't know.

On top of all that, why hadn't Harry gone to the police and let them deal with it? Why had he come to me? Harry's words echoed in my head.

The threats were coming from someone ... close to you both.

Was that why he'd come to me? To warn me?

A shiver snaked down my spine. Preposterous or not, I needed to know more.

As soon as I got home I called the number Harry had given me.

'Hello?' I could hear the smile in Harry's voice. 'Is that Fran?'

'Yes,' I said. 'I need to know exactly what my husband told you.'

I paced up and down Ayesha's living room the following morning, waiting for Harry to arrive. He had suggested we met in central London, but when I'd called Ayesha to look after Ruby while I was gone – Rufus already being out at a friend's house – Ayesha first winkled the whole story out of me in typically persistent fashion, then insisted I invited him round to her flat.

'Far safer, girl,' she'd said in her no-nonsense way.

'Me and Lori will be in the house too, in case he turns nasty.'

I wasn't sure how much protection Ayesha and her teenage daughter would really offer, but Ayesha wasn't a person you argued with. We'd been friends since we met at Newcastle University seventeen or so years ago. It had been the first proper week of lectures. I was miserable, away from home for the first time and realising that the outspoken, go-getting teenager I'd found it easy to be in the small, white, narrow world of school was totally intimidated by the daring, drug-experimenting girls in my shared residence. I'd escaped to the library and was doodling, pretending to read a psychology text book and seriously contemplating getting the next train home to my parents and Lucy.

I heard Ayesha before I saw her. She was shouting at the librarian for some act of perceived pettiness. I don't remember the details, just Ayesha's wide, appalled eyes and the force with which she made her arguments. She was dressed in something asymmetric and flowing, with red and orange ribbons wound through her hair. The librarian, a frowsy woman twice her age and several inches taller, was gaping. Because despite her intense manner, the smile never left Ayesha's face. I remember thinking she was beautiful – all shiny black hair and caramel skin – and that whoever she was, she looked capable of ruling the world. And then the librarian nodded and Ayesha leaned forward and hugged her – which really took my breath away. As she flounced out she paused by the desk where I was working.

'You look interesting,' she said. Still smiling, infuriatingly haughty and utterly charming. 'Let's get coffee.'

My jaw dropped as Ayesha swept my books into my bag and marched off. I followed in her wake, as baffled by my own compliance as I was, already, completely under her spell.

We talked for two hours straight in the university café. Ayesha, it turned out, was not only flamboyant and direct – but also a fantastic listener. She constantly gave advice, but never in a way that felt undermining. And her reaction to my sudden outpouring of homesickness was characteristically brief:

'Sucks, girl. We need to dress you up and get you out. Like to a party.'

I agreed, with only a small show of reluctance. I'd seen myself as a rebel at home and school, a big fish. But so far at uni I'd been docile . . . a plankton. I longed to party. And I sensed, rightly, that Ayesha would know exactly where to find the most fun on campus.

All that seemed a long time ago as I carried on pacing across Ayesha's living room.

'Hey, Mum, can I go with Lori for ice cream at Mariner's?' Ruby bounded in, breathless and wide-eyed.

'I guess,' I said, as Lori herself appeared in the doorway.

Lori was Ayesha's only child – a sweet-natured doll of a girl who, if she lacked her mother's verve, had certainly inherited her generosity of spirit and her beauty. She was almost sixteen and in her GCSE year. Not that exams figured largely in her thinking. Lori had been saying since she was six that all she wanted to do was look after children and, right now, she was applying for jobs at local private nurseries.

I opened my mouth, but before I could speak Ayesha butted in. 'She knows, don't you, Lori?'

Lori nodded. 'Be careful of strangers, hold Ruby's hand crossing the road and only one scoop of ice cream or you'll spoil your lunch,' she said with a grin. Despite her softer, calmer nature there were times when she strongly reminded me of her mother.

I grinned back, gave Ruby a hug and watched out of the window as the girls skipped off down the road. Mariner's was in Putney, only a short bus ride away. In truth I was glad Ruby would be out of the house for Harry's visit.

'No sign of the handsome stranger?' Ayesha asked.

I shook my head.

'I told you you should have let me come to the memorial, I could have checked him over for you.' Ayesha flumped down on the sofa with a groan. Her furniture was old, but covered in flame-coloured silks and wools. She had a fabulous knack of combining colours which I totally lacked and often added a new throw to her collection of burnt oranges and hot pinks.

'I didn't say he was handsome,' I said absently.

'Bet he is though.' Ayesha snorted. 'Beware of strangers bearing bad news, as they say.'

'Actually they say beware of Greeks bearing gifts.'

'That's a bit racist.'

'Don't start.'

This low-level bickering characterised the friendship which the two of us had established that first term at uni. We'd been close ever since, keeping in touch all through the following spring and summer when Ayesha moved to London to pursue her dream of becoming a dancer – she was talented, but had started too old and was never sufficiently disciplined. She came back to Newcastle that autumn with her tail between her legs to pick up her degree. And almost immediately discovered she was pregnant with Lori after a random one-night stand.

There was never any question in Ayesha's mind that she might not have the baby. She still thought then she might get involved in the dance world somehow. After we left uni – me with my degree, Ayesha with Lori – we moved into a shared flat in Southfields, west London – one of Dad's many property investments, where we stayed for a nominal rent. I watched as Ayesha grappled with the demands of single motherhood and gradually let go of her dance world ambitions and took a job in hospital administration.

I moved out when I met Caspian to whom she introduced me in the pub near the hospital where they both worked. 'Great,' she said, once it was clear Caspian and I were a serious item. 'I can see I'm going to be hoisted to homelessness by my own matchmaking petard.' But Dad wouldn't hear of it. He was always incredibly caring towards Ayesha who, as he put it, had made the right choice for her baby by going through with the pregnancy instead of succumbing to the 'easy and foul temptation' of an abortion. Dad insisted that Ayesha and Lori should stay on in the flat – and they still lived there, just five minutes around the corner from my own house.

A sharp rap on the front door made me catch my breath. Ayesha sat bolt upright, hands theatrically extended in front of her.

'You get it,' she said. 'I'll be upstairs if you need me.'

My heart thudded as I opened the door. Harry stood in the porch, a smile on his face. There was an openness in the way he carried himself and in the warmth of his dark eyes that instantly reassured me. It was raining lightly outside and Harry dusted the drops from his hair, sleeking it back off his angular face.

'Come in,' I said.

As Harry followed me into the living room all the questions I'd been trying not to think about for the past twenty-four hours zoomed around my head.

'I'm glad you got in touch,' Harry said. He looked around, taking in the purples and pinks of the couch under the far window. 'This isn't your place?'

'No.' I hesitated. It was hard, now I was face to face with him, to plunge straight into the conversation we needed to have, but no way could I manage any small talk either. 'Er, look . . .' I grimaced. 'I'll get straight to the point . . . the things you said yesterday, about my husband . . .'

'Mmm.' Harry nodded intently, a sympathetic look on his face. 'It must have sounded kind of ridiculous.'

He paused. 'And yet I'm guessing you found you couldn't stop wondering about it?'

I looked away, not wanting to reveal how accurate his words were. I cleared my throat and forced myself to face him again.

'I just need to know exactly what you meant ...'

Harry perched on the scarlet armchair, removing the heart-shaped cushion and placing it on the floor. I took a seat opposite.

'Okay,' he said. 'Let me tell you exactly what happened. As I already explained, I met your husband in the bar of the conference hotel. He'd had a few drinks so ... well, I'd say he was gently pissed. Everyone was. It was a long and, I have to say, fairly dull day.'

'I know,' I said. 'I spoke to him both nights.'

'He and I got chatting,' Harry went on. 'He said how he hated these sort of conferences, especially when they were abroad ...'

'He did.' I smiled, remembering how resentful Caspian would get about having to travel to places where he only ever saw the inside of meeting rooms and conference halls.

'... And how he missed you and the kids.'

A lump stuck in my throat. Unable to speak, I nodded.

'So ...' Harry hesitated. 'I said he sounded happily married, that I envied him.'

'You're not happily married?' I asked.

'Not married at all.' Harry smiled and I wondered, fleetingly, what was behind that smile. I couldn't

imagine he had any problem attracting women. 'So ...
I asked what the secret was.'

I leaned forward.

'Your husband said he had no idea, he'd just been
lucky, then he laughed and said, "Though I guess
communication is important, like everyone tells you."'

'Caspian said that?' It didn't sound like the sort of
thing my husband would come out with, especially not
to a total stranger.

'As I said, we were all a bit pissed.' Harry smoothed
his still-damp hair off his face. 'Then Caspian went
on ... "Not that I tell my wife everything."'

My stomach tightened. 'Oh,' I said.

'Of course I made a prat of myself and gave it large
with some joke about him having a girlfriend at every
conference, which is when the whole conversation takes
a turn and your husband gets all serious and ... well,
at first I think he's really offended because he's shaking
his head and going, "No, not like that, not that at all."'

'Okay,' I said. This sounded more like Caspian. If
he had a fault it was a tendency to earnestness and the
missing of jokes, which generally led to him putting
a dampener on whatever fun was happening around
him.

'Then your husband lowers his voice and whispers
in my ear: "I'm being threatened," he says, "I've had
messages. I've destroyed them but ... they were threats
against my life."'

I shook my head. 'Sorry,' I said. 'But it sounds so ...
so ...'

'So melodramatic?' Harry nodded. 'That's what I thought too. In fact, at first I think he's joking,' Harry said. 'So I laugh. But he doesn't join in. He frowns and then he says: "I'm serious." So I stop laughing and ask if he's told anyone and he says no and repeats that he'd destroyed the two separate notes he received.'

'He never said anything at all to me.' I drew back. Surely there's no way that any of this can possibly be true. After all, why wouldn't Caspian have said something to me? We didn't live in each other's pockets but we told each other all the important stuff.

'I know he didn't tell you,' Harry said. 'Like I said before, he didn't want you to worry.'

There was a pause. Caspian was always very protective, sometimes annoyingly so, but it's hard to accept he really wouldn't have confided in me. Not unless there was a good reason.

I look up. 'Go on.'

Harry shuffled in his seat, looking uncomfortable. 'So the next bit is going to be hard for you to hear, but I swear it's what Caspian said. He says: "It's Paul ... I think it's Paul."' Harry glanced up. 'That's what Caspian said. Do you know anyone called Paul?'

'No.' My mind raced. I couldn't think of anyone either Caspian or I knew with that name. 'Did he say Paul who? If it was a first name or a surname?'

'No.' Harry frowned. 'The only other thing he said wasn't meant for me at all.'

'What was that?'

'He said it as he was turning away. Exact words:

"I think Jayson Carr got Paul to do it, it was Jayson's Paul.'"

I froze. 'Are you sure?'

Harry nodded. 'That's why I came to you and didn't go straight to the police.'

There was no guile in his expression.

And yet how could what he was saying be true? I realised I was gripping the edge of the sofa and released my fingers. Jayson Carr was many things: a man of powerful personality and strong faith, albeit far less rigid in his beliefs than he used to be; he was a public figure with a string of successful businesses and, in more recent years, his prison rehabilitation charity. He was a good man. A moral man.

Above all, he was my father.

3

Harry's words catapulted through my head. Could Dad have ordered someone to kill Caspian? No. It was impossible. 'That's crazy,' I insisted. 'Apart from the fact that my dad *adored* him, there's no way Caspian would have told a total stranger my dad wanted him dead. It doesn't make sense.'

Except maybe it did, murmured a little voice inside my head. Maybe it explained exactly why Caspian turned to a stranger instead of to me. After all, how could he have told me he suspected my own father wanted to kill him?

Harry said nothing.

'You must have misheard,' I protested. 'Or else . . .'

'I'm not lying.' Harry met my gaze. He looked sincere, his eyes full of compassion. 'Think about it. What reason could I possibly have to lie? I just wanted to pass on information, it's up to you what you do about it.'

I sank back into my chair. Ayesha poked her head around the door. 'Everything okay?'

'Fine,' I said. No way was I going to tell her. It wasn't just my disbelief that Dad could be involved in murder, it was my shame at the discovery Caspian had spoken his fears to a stranger, that he hadn't felt able to talk to me.

And my total lack of any clue about what to do now.

Ayesha slipped away and Harry leaned forward in his chair.

'I understand that you don't want to believe this, but is there any chance it could be true? That your dad threatened your husband? Got someone to carry out those threats?'

I shook my head. Quite apart from the impossibility of the idea, I'd never heard my father mention anyone called Paul, neither as a first nor a last name. Which meant nothing, of course. I didn't know all his friends, let alone all his colleagues. How could I? But Dad was a good, decent man. Too driven and short-tempered when we were growing up, of course, but he'd mellowed since then, especially after Jacqueline came into his life. I couldn't remember the last time I'd even seen him raise his voice. He was surely incapable of hurting anyone, let alone the son-in-law he doted on.

'Are you sure you didn't misunderstand what Caspian was saying?' I asked. 'It must have been noisy in the bar ...?'

'No.' Harry met my gaze. 'I'm sorry, but there's no way.'

There was a long pause.

'What do you want to do now?' Harry asked.

'I don't know,' I said. 'I need to think.'

'Of course. I'll leave you in peace.' A few minutes later Harry was gone with a promise to call me later.

Ayesha bounded in as soon as he'd left, demanding to know what he'd said. I played it all down, making no mention of Dad and stressing I thought Harry was making too much of what he'd heard. We stopped talking about it when Lori and Ruby came home and the four of us sat down for lunch – a typically disorganised Ayesha affair of random vegetarian dishes, finished off with runny ice cream that Lori and Ruby had brought back from Mariner's and which no one had thought to put in the freezer.

I took Ruby home afterwards, picking Rufus up on the way. All three of us were on edge. I wasn't sure why. Ayesha and Lori seemed to have such a charmed relationship, their personalities dovetailing perfectly: Ayesha was flamboyant but too chaotic to be controlling while Lori was docile and biddable, happy to let her mother take the lead in everything. By contrast Rufus, Ruby and I were like three knives in a drawer, constantly clashing. I'd thought when Caspian died so suddenly that the loss would show itself over time in the misery of his absence. No dad there to help with homework or cheer at football matches or offer up behavioural boundaries and hugs. I'd thought Caspian not being there would be a hole that I would have to work doubly hard to fill.

But it wasn't like that at all. Or rather it was, but it was so much more as well. Without Caspian's steadying presence in the house it was as if the magnetic force that kept us in harmony alongside each other had vanished and we were unable to control our interactions.

Sometimes this meant we existed too much in isolation, separate and unknowable to each other; or else, to go back to my knives in the drawer comparison, we lived in a clash of metal, taking tiny cuts out of each other as we tangled, all sharp and hard and pointed.

Right now, for example, I had forced the children to sit down to dinner with me, which had involved tearing Ruby away from her football magazine and Rufus from his computer game.

In the old days, this would have been a normal and expected occurrence. But now it involved tears and shouting from Ruby, 'You're so mean, I just had two pages to go', and an absolute refusal to engage whatso-ever on Rufus's part. All I got from him were grunts.

By the time I had wrangled them into their seats at the kitchen table I was exhausted and in no mood for the cottage pie I'd heated up from the freezer. All I really wanted to do was think about what Harry had told me earlier, but the children needed me to make more effort than that.

Rufus sat glumly, merely picking at his mince and pushing all the potato to the side of his plate. Ruby shovelled in her food as fast as possible, tear tracks glinting on her cheeks.

'So do you still want to start Power League, Rubes?' I asked.

She looked up at me. 'Course,' she said. 'I think I'm going to be a striker but maybe attacking midfield, it depends ...' She chattered on, still munching away. Her earlier hysterics had passed. I nodded whenever she paused for a response, but inside I couldn't help wondering if she would be so committed to football in another year and, if she was, whether there would be other girls her age eager to play with her. Already the friends she had once been surrounded by were dropping away. I often saw them look at her then turn to each other and whisper and giggle. Was Ruby aware they thought her odd? Losing her dad had already set her apart from the others. Some, of course, had divorced parents but none of her friends had experienced the trauma of bereavement.

I knew a little what it was like to stand out. My own father's prominent role in the Catholic community, combined with his strict rules about our dress and behaviour, caused me no end of frustration as a teenager. But not beforehand, when I was Ruby's age. Back then church on Sundays was simply part of our normal routine, my faith as familiar and comfortable as the teddy bear I cuddled in bed every night. I certainly would never have flipped out over being called to dinner while I was reading. It was only as I reached puberty that I started to rebel, when I realised not everyone shared my parents' views on abortion and stem cell research and the rest.

'I've finished.' Rufus's tone was defiant. And no wonder, he'd left half his plate.

'Fine,' I said, too weary to fight him.

Mollified, he hurried off upstairs. Ruby scampered after him. I cleared the table on autopilot. Harry's words were a splinter lodged under my skin:

I think Jayson Carr got Paul to do it.

It was preposterous. And yet I couldn't stop thinking about it.

Could Dad have had anything to do with Caspian's death? Perhaps there was some connection he wasn't even aware of? For months, now, I had accepted that Caspian's murder was a random affair, telling myself that though of course I wanted my husband's killer punished, simply knowing their identity wouldn't bring him back just as seeing them behind bars wouldn't help me accept his loss.

But now it seemed there was a chance – albeit the slimmest, craziest of ones – that my own father might in some way be linked to the killer. I had to talk to Dad directly, ask him straight out about this Paul person.

I had to find out the truth.

It was just past 3 p.m. the following afternoon, Sunday, and the dark sky was threatening rain as I hurried Ruby onto the portico of Dad's four-storey Kensington house. Rufus hadn't wanted to come and in order to avoid a big argument I said he could stay home alone for a few hours. As I rang the doorbell my eyes lit on the nick in the brickwork where the old latch used to catch when the door was slammed, as it often was during my teenage years. It was always weird, coming back to the place where I'd grown up but hadn't lived for many years. A house that both did and didn't feel like home.

Lucy still occupied her old bedroom. My old bedroom was now just one of the house's many spares. Jacqueline had redecorated it of course. She'd redecorated every-where. Which was fine. I'd have probably done the same thing in her position. Anyway it didn't matter; Mum was still here, infusing every corner, even five years after her death. She died in this house after passing out from her diabetes and falling down the short flight of stairs from the kitchen to the utility room.

Afterwards Dad walled in the steps, which meant no more utility room until he moved Jacqueline in less than a year later, which seemed fast to me and Lucy. But then Dad, for all his fiery forcefulness, was the kind of man who was lost without a woman to anchor him. Jacqueline shifted the entire kitchen to a larger, lighter room on the other side of the ground floor. It was a good idea, I had to grudgingly admit, but typical of the way Jacqueline (she hated her name being abbre-viated) took over the house, not to mention Dad's life. She never failed to ask if Lucy and I minded when she removed curtains and painted walls and sold, stored or commandeered furniture, but there was always something slightly haughty in her manner as she did so. She was an ex-lawyer with her own money, super-organised about everything – and the polar opposite of Mum, who was a bit of a dilettante, dipping her toe into all sorts of creative projects, none of which ever came to anything, from novel-writing to life-drawing to dress-making.

But the biggest change Jacqueline made to Dad, for which I was prepared to forgive her all other trans-gressions, was to encourage him to be gentler and less rigid in his views. As a result Dad decided to step down from his chairmanship of the prominent pro-life group *Shield* that had dominated his life for years, ever since he found out about Lucy's abortion in fact. Instead he took a senior post with a prison rehabilitation charity that was much more suited to his persuasive skills. Instead of arguing the philosophical case against abortion he was able to campaign with all the force of his personality for better facilities for ex-offenders.

For me, the softening of Dad's religious beliefs changed everything. It allowed us to reconnect properly after years where we'd been semi-estranged. We'd argued for years over my lack of faith, but at last our different perspectives became an area of our lives where we could simply agree to disagree. As I'd told him many times, there was no way I was going to change *my* mind on religion. Apart from Lucy's confirmation, Mum's funeral and a couple of weddings I hadn't set foot in a church since the April after my eleventh birthday when I saw on the news that a tropical cyclone in Bangladesh had killed over one hundred thousand people and I solemnly told both my parents I thought if God existed he must be a mean old man to kill for no reason like that. Mum and Dad insisted, of course, that natural disasters were all part of God's plan and divine mystery but I wasn't buying what I saw as vague, meaningless claptrap any longer. I pronounced myself an ex-Catholic and, though I never went as far as to call myself an atheist, one of the reasons Caspian was so attractive to me was his absolute and certain disbelief in any kind of deity.

Jacqueline's housekeeper let me in and took Ruby through to the kitchen for cookies. Warning them both she wasn't to spoil her appetite for tea later, I hurried upstairs to find Dad. As I reached the first-floor landing I heard his deep, measured voice coming from the master bedroom.

'You look lovely, darling,' he was saying. It was impossible to miss the note of weariness as he spoke.

'You say that about everything, but I think this makes me look fat.'

Great. My dad and his wife were in the middle of a minor domestic. Of the things Jacqueline had a tendency to be controlling about, her own appearance was by far the greatest. Lucy and I had long learned to offer simple statements of support about how she looked, avoiding getting drawn into discussions on the detail of her obsession with her saggy neck and tummy tyre – not that there was much evidence of either.

I stood outside the bedroom door, my hand raised, hesitant. Part of me knew I should walk away, but I needed to ask about Paul. I wouldn't be able to rest until I could put Harry's claims out of my head once and for all.

'Of course you don't look fat,' Dad said, his voice now calm and soothing. 'It's the perfect choice: smart but demure, and the blue brings out the colour of your eyes.'

I didn't hear Jacqueline's reply, just the low murmur of her voice. Hoping this meant she was reassured I knocked on the door, then walked inside.

Dad and Jacqueline were standing on opposite sides

41

of the bed. Jacqueline was wearing a shift dress with a beaded trim. It was indeed a beautiful blue – and fitted Jacqueline's slender form perfectly. She was in her mid-forties, just a decade or so older than me, but she could easily have passed for younger. Sharp-boned and skinny where Mum had been all soft curves, she was as groomed and elegant as Mum had been untidy and free. Dad was knotting his tie – also blue and probably hand-picked by Jacqueline to tone with her dress.

He looked up and beamed at me. 'Hi, darling, I didn't know you were here.'

'Hello, Francesca.' Jacqueline smiled into the mirror.

'Hey,' I said. 'Could I have a quick word, Dad?'

'Course.' Dad walked over and gave me a hug. 'What's up?'

'We really don't have much time, Jayson,' Jacqueline warned from her dressing table. 'We're late as it is. The tea starts at four.'

Dad winked at me. 'We've got a couple of minutes. Are Rufus and Ruby here?'

'Ruby is.' I nodded. 'She's downstairs.' I squeezed his hand. 'Before you say "hi", I just wanted to ask one question.'

'Go on,' Dad said, resuming his tie-knotting.

'Do you know anyone called Paul?' I asked. 'A friend? Colleague? Someone with strong anti-abortion views?'

Across the room, Jacqueline stiffened slightly. Was that because she knew someone? Or just because I was introducing a subject that had once been the cause of such argument between Dad and me? A look of consternation flitted across Dad's face. Then a blank mask descended and he shrugged. 'I don't think so,' he said. 'Why on earth are you asking?'

I hesitated. Repeating Harry's claims out loud seemed melodramatic.

'Someone ... a guy at the memorial service. He said he thought Caspian might have ...'

Dad frowned. 'What?'

'He thought Caspian was being threatened just before he was killed.'

'*What?*' Dad now looked appalled.

'For goodness' sake,' Jacqueline gasped.

'According to this guy, Harry, he was at the same conference as Caspian in Paris and ... Caspian told him there were threats.'

'Wouldn't Caspian have told *you* if that were true?' Dad asked, echoing my own initial thought.

'Apparently he didn't want to worry me,' I said.

'Jayson—' Jacqueline began.

'Harry says the threats came from someone you know called Paul.'

Dad stared at me. He blinked, clearly shocked.

'Do you know a Paul?'

Dad shook his head. 'I don't, darling. I'm sorry but I think this Harry person must have got the wrong end of the stick.' He took my hand. 'I know it's hard, but you have to remember the police did a thorough investigation. If there was a trail of threats I'm sure they'd have found them last year.'

I nodded, relieved. Dad was right. I should have

thought of the police investigation myself. Harry *must* have misunderstood what Caspian said. It was the only explanation that made sense.

'We really need to go,' Jacqueline said, picking up a handbag – a navy Chanel clutch as opposed to her Prada tote from the memorial.

Dad pecked me on the cheek. 'Try not to worry.'

I nodded again and followed them out of their room. I waited at the top of the stairs as Dad's heavy thud and Jacqueline's stiletto-light tap sounded across the parquet in the hall. Dad made a beeline for the kitchen and a second later I heard Ruby's excited squeal and delighted giggle.

I smiled to myself. Never mind how strict and distant Dad had often been when I was a child. He was all gentle playfulness with his grandkids, nothing like the busy, driven man of his younger days. He couldn't possibly be linked to any kind of anti-abortion-inspired killing, let alone involved with my own husband's murder. I was embarrassed to think I'd considered it possible even for a fraction of a second.

Dad and Jacqueline left and I settled down in their kitchen with Ruby and my sister, who had just come back from mass and was baking a batch of brownies with her niece – with a promise Ruby could take some home with her later. I murmured that what with the biscuits earlier, Ruby had already had quite enough sweet things for one day, but Lucy just winked and said she'd put them in something airtight so they'd last through the week. The two of them had always been close. When Rufus was born, Lucy was upset that Caspian and I didn't want him to be baptised. But by the time Ruby came along she'd accepted our rejection of the Catholic faith and, though she did sometimes tell Ruby bible stories, she was careful never to criticise our decision.

We left for home as soon as the brownies were done. I didn't want to leave Rufus on his own any longer. He was in the living room when we got back but disappeared up to his room, merely grunting a 'yes, fine' when I asked if he'd been okay alone in the house.

'Any final bits of work for school, Ruby?' I asked with a sigh.

'No, Mum, I *told* you earlier,' Ruby shouted, morphing abruptly from sweet-natured child into proto-pubescent monster. 'Stop going *on*!'

She stormed up the stairs and slammed the door of her bedroom.

I was about to follow her up and demand an apology for her rudeness when the doorbell rang. The man's dark head was bowed as I peered through the spy hole. Was that Harry, seeking me out? The thought of seeing him again knotted my stomach with anxiety – and excitement. I would have to talk to him, to tell him he must have misunderstood what Caspian had said to him. In spite of the potential awkwardness, the prospect of speaking to him again was appealing. Which meant what?

I was just acknowledging the unfamiliar feeling that I

fancied him ... that I was attracted to a man after over a year of sexual shutdown, when the head was raised and I realised that instead of Harry it was watery-eyed Simon Pinner standing on the doorstep.

My heart sank as I let him in. Caspian's old colleague was the last person I wanted to talk to right now.

'Hello, there.' I forced a smile onto my face.

'Long time, no see. Ha, ha.' Simon beamed as he held out his hand to shake. His limp palm in mine was damp. In fact everything about him seemed a little wet, from those watery eyes to the thin smile on his tightly stretched lips. 'I got your address from Caspian's parents,' he said. 'I was just passing ...'

That was a lie. He even blushed as he told it. No way had he been passing. He'd come here deliberately to see me. Cursing my parents-in-law I ushered Simon into the kitchen where the remains of our breakfast dishes were still on the table.

'You're having dinner ...?' Christ, was he after an invitation?

'Not just yet, but, er, it's a school night for the kids,' I said, hoping he'd take the hint.

Simon nodded. 'I like to eat early too.'

'Er, right.' I wanted to ask what he wanted, but couldn't work out how to express that without sounding rude. Had I always been this useless at dealing with men I wasn't interested in? I hadn't been on a date since meeting Caspian. I'd been a bit of a party girl up to that point, with a propensity for one-night stands. I'd never gone out with anyone for more than a few months.

Caspian was older and possibly the calmest, steadiest person I'd ever met. There was no way he was only up for a fling, no way our relationship together could ever be framed in casual, purely sexual terms. And I was ready to give up my protracted adolescence and settle down. We'd been together less than a year and had just got engaged when I fell pregnant. Life soon revolved around babies and work. There'd certainly been very little time for romance once Rufus was born: Caspian worked all hours and, anyway, he had never been the romantic type. Sex had been infrequent for years before he died, which didn't bother me much. I was busy with the kids and my job as a fundraiser. I never strayed, though there were plenty of opportunities. And it was always impossible to imagine Caspian himself wanting an affair – or ever needing the excitement an illicit liaison might bring.

I focused on Simon, still smiling hopefully across the kitchen table. 'How are you?' I asked.

'I'm fine,' Simon said. '*Particularly* fine since seeing you at the memorial.'

I looked away, embarrassed. Surely I'd made it clear I wasn't interested in having dinner with him then.

'I realise I was rather presumptuous,' Simon went on. 'Wrong time. Wrong place. That sort of thing.' He chuckled.

I turned back. He seemed older than he had at the memorial. The bright kitchen light highlighted the lines on his weather-beaten face.

'It was nice to see you,' I said, trying to sound polite but neutral.

'It certainly was.'

'I don't . . . that is, I hope—'

'I know,' he said. 'You've got the kids and it's only been just over a year. I'm not looking for a relationship either.'

'Oh,' I said, slightly taken aback.

Simon took two long strides, closing the distance between us. He put his hand on my arm. 'It's just I sensed something . . . I was certain you'd felt it too, in spite of what you said.'

Was he serious? My mouth gaped again. Simon clearly took my shocked silence as a sign of overwhelmed bashfulness.

'You're very attractive, Francesca.' He pointed to the mirror propped on the kitchen counter which I'd used to apply my make-up that morning. 'Look at yourself.'

I turned and caught my reflection: a tousled tumble of dark hair framing a pale face. As usual, my eyes looked too huge, my chin too pointed. I'd lost weight since Caspian died, rarely eating other than when I forced the kids to sit down for a meal.

'It's very kind of you but—'

'I'm not being kind.' Simon traced his finger down my sleeve, leaving it for just a second too long before taking his hand away. I had the strong sense that it was a move he had rehearsed. It felt put on, inauthentic, like something from the opening scene of a porn movie.

'Shall we sit down?' Simon took a seat at the kitchen table.

Irritated at being invited to sit in my own house, I perched on the chair opposite. An awkward silence fell.

'So tell me ... how did you know Caspian?' I asked, hoping this mention would remind Simon I was in mourning.

Simon studied me for a second. 'We met a few times through mutual friends,' he said. 'On and off for years. And a couple of times at obs and gynae conferences.'

My chest tightened. 'Were you at the Paris conference?'

Simon shook his head. 'But I did see Caspian briefly just before he went. Last time I saw him, in fact.'

'Right.' Caspian's words, as reported by Harry, circled my head again: *I think Jayson Carr got Paul to do it* ... The splinter under my skin shifted, its point hard and uncomfortable. 'I don't suppose Caspian said anything about ...' I gulped, unable to stop myself from asking. 'Did Caspian ever mention anyone called Paul?'

'In what context?'

'Not anything good.' I hesitated, uncertain how much to give away. It struck me that even though Harry had clearly misunderstood the reference to my father, Caspian might still have received threats from someone called Paul, unrelated to Dad. 'It's just I heard ... I mean it might not be true but ... someone told me Caspian was being threatened by ... by a man called Paul.'

'God, really?' Simon asked. He reached for my hand but I shifted away. 'How awful.'

49

'You don't sound particularly surprised,' I said, struck by his even tone.

'No, well . . .' Simon shrugged. 'It's just that Caspian and I, well, as doctors who perform abortions, there are enemies. But I'm sure if the police thought PAAUL had anything to do with his death . . .'

'What are you talking about?' My heart lurched into my mouth. 'You're saying you know who Paul is? Someone who targets abortion doctors?'

'No, that is . . . not a "someone",' Simon explained. 'PAAUL is an organisation from the States. It stands for *Pledge to Avenge the Assassination of Unborn Lives.*'

'An anti-abortion organisation?'

Simon nodded. 'One that sanctions violence against people who have and perform terminations.'

'Oh, God.' Was it PAAUL Caspian had been referring to when he talked to Harry? I had no idea how this organisation might be connected to Dad, but it was easy to understand why a bunch of anti-abortion extremists might target a gynaecology surgeon.

'Hey.' Simon's chair scraped across the tiles as he stood up and walked around the table to stand next to me. 'Don't get upset, please. PAAUL operate in the States, and their MO is firebombs and shootings, not individual stabbings that look like aggravated muggings, like happened with Caspian. I'm sure they didn't have anything to do with his death. The police never suspected anything like that, did they?'

I shook my head, barely listening.

'Oh, Francesca.' Simon put his arm around my

shoulders and tried to pull me towards him. I stiffened, drawing away.

'Please don't.' I stood up.

'So ... like I said ... I don't think you really mean it about not, er, hooking up.' He grinned. 'My GCSE in body language told me as much at the memorial.'

Jesus, was he for real? A coil of irritation unfurled inside me, replacing my embarrassment.

'I'm afraid I *do* mean it,' I insisted. 'I told you, I'm not ready.'

'I can wait.' Simon raised his eyebrows slowly in a way that suggested he thought he was being very sexy.

'Please, Simon.'

'Mmm.' He moved closer. 'I like the way you say that.'

Anger bubbled up inside me. This was too much, especially coming on top of what he'd just told me about PAAUL. I jumped up. 'I think you should go.' The words blurted out of me, hard and fierce.

A tense silence filled the room.

'Right.' There was a new tightness to Simon's voice. 'You're a bit of a tease, aren't you, Francesca?'

'Please just go,' I repeated.

'Of course.' Simon's voice dripped with bitterness. 'Whatever you say, Francesca. And I apologise unreservedly if you feel ...' He paused, his mouth curved into a sneer. 'If you feel put upon in any way.'

I pressed my lips together, irritation building.

'Just go.'

'There's no need to be rude.' Simon took a step away,

his eyes hardening. 'By the way, if you're really interested in PAAUL you should ask your father about it.'

I stared at him, blinking. What did that mean? 'My *dad*?'

... it was Jayson's Paul.

A nasty smile replaced the sneer on Simon's face. 'Sure. Your dad knows all about PAAUL. Everything there is to know.' He strode to the door.

'*What?*' I gasped. 'Why would you say that?'

Simon reached the doorway and turned. Eyes hard and narrow, he gave a dismissive sniff. 'Because according to all the rumours, your father, Jayson Carr, is the secret head of PAAUL in the UK.'

4

I sat motionless on the couch as the sound of the front door shutting behind Simon Pinner echoed through the house.

Your father, Jayson Carr, is the secret head of PAAUL in the UK.

Now what was I supposed to think? Surely there was no way my upstanding father would ever condone violent extremism, let alone order people to commit acts of terror? He'd been a prominent force in *Shield*, the pro-life charity, of course, but he'd had nothing to do with that for years.

No, the entire thing was inconceivable. Simon Pinner must have been making up Dad's association with PAAUL in order to punish me for not wanting to date him.

'What an arse,' I muttered under my breath.

'Ooh, Mum, you said arse.' Ruby, having come back downstairs without me hearing, scampered into the room. Back to little-girl mode, she did a cartwheel across the rug.

'Not indoors,' I said absently.

'Whatever.' Ruby hurled herself onto the sofa

opposite me, mimicking a goal-saving keeper with a roar. A nearby vase wobbled on its shelf.

'Careful, Rubes.' I pressed my lips together. No way was I going to give Simon's stupid lies about Dad any credence. I would try not to even think about them and I definitely wouldn't tell Dad. Or Lucy. She adored Dad as much as when she was a child. I sat back. If only Mum were still alive. I could have talked to her. She would have been horrified and sympathetic. Above all, she would have reassured me that there was no way Dad could have wanted anyone dead, let alone my husband.

The evening wore on. I managed to chivvy both children into bed without too much trouble, then I sat down with a glass of wine. I tried to read but, despite my best intentions, I couldn't keep what Simon had said out of my head. In the end the clamour of Simon's claims joined with Harry's until both echoed through my head and I sat on the edge of my bed at midnight, my laptop in front of me, feeling sick with fear and apprehension.

I put *Pledge to Avenge the Assassination of Unborn Lives* into the search engine, then studied the first page of hits. As Simon had indicated, there were several reports of bombing campaigns and at least two occasions in the past five years where lone gunmen had mown down staff in abortion clinics. But all these atrocities took place in the United States, the only UK-based incidents were a couple of protests and a bomb scare from last year that proved to be a hoax. PAAUL didn't claim involvement in either of these, so there was no way of knowing if the organisation had anything to do with them.

With trembling fingers I typed my father's name into the search engine alongside PAAUL's. Just a couple of relevant hits, both occasions when Dad had spoken out *against* the use of extremist violence and named PAAUL as an agent of evil.

The speeches were given six years ago, when Dad was still head of his pro-life charity. So much had happened since – Mum dying, then him meeting Jacqueline and joining the prison rehabilitation charity – he'd probably just forgotten about PAAUL.

Which was encouraging. Wasn't it?

My mobile rang. It was Harry. I glanced at the time. It was very late for him to be calling.

'Hello?' I said, feeling wary. 'What's up?'

'I'm sorry, I know this is a stupid hour to be ringing you but . . .' He sounded fraught. 'But I just found out something and thought you should know straight away.'

'Yeah?' I sat up straighter. It felt, I realised, as if we'd known each other for far longer than a couple of days. 'Go on,' I said.

'I had to tell you . . . It's your father,' Harry said. 'On the net, there's stuff about him . . . rumours that he's the head of this organisation, PAAUL.'

I sat stock still, my heart beating fast. 'I know,' I said. 'That is, someone told me there were rumours, but I've looked online and all I've seen is a couple of mentions in speeches from when he—'

'You need to check out the forums.' Harry told me how to access them and I entered the murky world of the illicit internet, where users with names like *Wrathbaby* and *Gabrieltheavenger* and *FireAngel* swore vengeance on those who had committed abortions. Within a few minutes I'd found plenty of references to PAAUL, mostly from mad-sounding people talking about the 'abortion holocaust' and 'Satan's perfect sacrifice' and the mass murder of innocent pre-born life. Some spouted statistics about the 'millions' of souls lost since records began. Others quoted from Corinthians: *If anyone destroys God's temple, God will destroy that person; for God's temple is sacred and you together are that temple.* Others still referenced speakers and philosophers I'd never heard of who argued points of faith and linguistics.

All of them used their material to justify their belief that whatever it was permissible to do to protect a live child should be done to protect an unborn one.

In other words, to justify murder.

'So where's the stuff about Dad?' I asked.

'Scroll down.' I did as Harry directed and soon came to a thread of innuendo and rumour that basically suggested Jayson Carr had stepped down as chairman of the legitimate *Shield* organisation in order to build up PAAUL's network of underground operatives, ready to assassinate doctors who carried out abortions.

I blew out my breath, shaken to the core.

'Just because people think it might have happened

doesn't mean it has,' Harry said. 'But putting everything together there are a lot of people out there who believe that PAAUL's campaign has already begun, your husband's murder is part of it and . . .'

'And that my dad is right at the centre of the whole thing.' I cleared my throat. 'Why do you think PAAUL hasn't publicly claimed responsibility for all those murders?' I asked. 'I mean, if that's their plan then why kill abortion doctors and not boast about it?'

'So they can keep operating under the radar for the time being?' Harry suggested. 'I don't know, but it's at least possible, don't you think?'

I said nothing.

'I'm so sorry, this must be awful.'

'Did you find out anything else?' I asked, trying to keep my voice even.

'Just one more thing. Scroll a bit further down the page you're on, about halfway.' I did as he asked, squinting at the screen which was dark, with white writing in a handwritten-style font that was hard to read.

'What am I looking for?'

'Look for "Suffolk".'

I found the word as Harry spoke it:

It's in Suffolk, I'm telling you. The PAAUL HQ, where they're coordinating all the assassinations. Place called Aldeburgh.

'Do you know if your dad has any connection to Aldeburgh?' Harry asked. 'There's another thread on another forum, similar kind of stuff, that mentions a place called Lanagh as the specific HQ, but I don't know if the two are connected ...'

'Oh, Jesus,' I gasped.

'What?' he asked. 'What is it? *Does* your father have a connection to Aldeburgh? To this Lanagh place?'

'Yes,' I said, my head spinning. 'It's where he's from, where his older brother, my Uncle Perry, still lives. Lanagh is their family home.'

Harry and I drove to Aldeburgh the following morning. It was a dull day, the sky grey and heavy with rain that drummed down on the roof of the car like tiny stones. Harry had insisted on coming with me as soon as I told him I wanted to check out Lanagh.

'Are you serious?' I'd asked him, genuinely shocked that he was prepared to give up his time.

'I kind of feel responsible,' Harry had admitted. 'I mean, I turn up and drop a bombshell out of the blue. The least I can do is help you deal with the fallout.'

'You still don't have to come all the way to Suffolk with me,' I said.

Harry shrugged. 'Would you rather I didn't? Is there anyone else who could help you?'

The answer to both questions was 'no'. The last thing I wanted was to drive all the way to Lanagh and explore it on my own and I couldn't imagine confiding my suspicions to anyone I knew – I could barely admit them to myself. But Harry already knew everything. And, anyway, with his disarming smile and his easy, direct manner, it was impossible not to trust him.

I set off as soon as the kids had left for school, driving to Dad's where, thankfully, no one was at home. I let myself in and made straight for the spare keys to Lanagh. I removed them from their hook, checked in the drawer beneath for the Lanagh house alarm code and headed outside again. I picked up Harry near Highbury and Islington tube station and before too long we were on the A12. This was the third time we'd met in person and as he jumped into the car, his long face lit up with a smile, I wondered how on earth I could have thought for a second that he wasn't attractive. His features weren't even and regular like Dex's, but to me he seemed far sexier. There was something so expressive about his face – his eyes full of fun with just a tantalising hint of danger around the edges. I wanted to ask him questions about his life, especially if there was a girlfriend in the picture, but I felt suddenly and ridiculously self-conscious.

For the first half an hour or so, Harry kept the focus on the connection between Lanagh House and PAAUL. He was intrigued by the idea that the property might be being used as PAAUL's headquarters and wanted to know about Uncle Perry – Dad's older brother – who still lived there.

'He's a bit of an old fogey,' I explained. 'Comes up to London all the time and stays at his club in Mayfair.'

'And he's there now?'

'Yeah, arrived on Friday for Caspian's memorial service. He usually stays at least five days.' I fell silent again. The plan was for Harry and I to explore Lanagh while it was empty. I'd fixed last-minute play dates after school for both kids – with Ayesha as back-up in case of emergency. My mind whirred around the prospect of trying to identify the most likely places where information on PAAUL might be stored. I couldn't really believe that Dad – or indeed Perry – could be involved with PAAUL, but doubt still hung over me, its shadow long and dark.

'So how come you're not at work today?' Harry asked.

'I'm part time,' I said absently. 'What about you?'

'Oh, I'm supposed to be catching up on paperwork,' Harry explained. 'Do you like being part time? I've always imagined it's easy to end up going over your hours.'

'Yeah, it can be. I went down to three days a week after Caspian ... it seemed the best thing for the kids. I'll probably go back to full time when Ruby's at secondary school.'

'It must have been unbearably hard for them,' Harry said gently. 'Losing their dad so suddenly. *Still* be unbearable, I mean.'

I glanced out of the window, a lump in my throat. We were drawing nearer to the coast and the rain was growing heavier. I felt terribly aware of how close Harry was, how comfortable I was in his presence.

How was it possible for me to still feel such grief about losing Caspian, yet also this fluttering in my stomach at having Harry here, in the passenger seat, right next to me?

'Do you have kids?' I asked, slowing as we reached a roundabout.

Harry shook his head.

'You said before you'd never been married,' I went on, feeling suddenly nervous. 'What about a girlfriend?'

'Not for the past six months,' Harry said with a grin. I turned the steering wheel to the left. 'Basically what I've got is a long trail of relationship debris.'

I laughed out loud, keeping my gaze on the drizzle that gleamed on the road ahead. I was struck by the warm glow of pleasure I felt at the news he was single. Today was, I realised, the first time I'd been anywhere with a man I didn't know since Caspian had died. Not that this was remotely like a date. Having made the turn onto the road to Aldeburgh, I snatched a glance at Harry. He was studying his phone, his dark hair falling over his eyes. Even his nose – which by any objective measure was too long – suited his face. Not that it mattered. He wasn't interested. And neither was I. Not really. It was just nice to feel faint stirrings that one day, perhaps, I might be.

We drove on.

I was stiff from sitting still when we finally pulled up outside Lanagh House, the wheels of the car scrunching over the damp gravel.

'Wow,' Harry said. 'This is a mansion.'

I followed his gaze, across the ivy-covered brick and Georgian pillars of the large detached house in front of us.

'Imagine growing up here.' Harry glanced across

at me. 'Still I guess you don't have to, you grew up in a huge house in Kensington, didn't you? What's that worth? Ten million? Eleven?'

I shrugged, embarrassed. I was used to people being shocked – even envious – of my privileged background, but Harry didn't sound resentful. I hadn't met anyone so open, so frank since I was at uni. Caspian in particular had always been careful never to mention money. I'd appreciated that when I met him, though later I sometimes got frustrated with his habit of shying away from any conversational topic that was remotely awkward.

'So where did *you* grow up?' I asked.

Harry raised his eyebrows. I blushed. Had I sounded sharper than I intended?

'Tiny two-bed flat on a council estate in Manchester,' he said. 'We lived on benefits and my mum's cleaning work. There was damp in the flat and piss in the lift and the police were always there on a Saturday night busting someone or other for drugs. I worked on building sites for cash from when I was sixteen all through uni until my first proper job in sales.' He paused. 'I have no idea what it's like to feel I'm owed a living.'

'I don't feel like that,' I protested.

'I bet you have a trust fund as well, don't you?' Harry asked with a chuckle. Again he didn't sound resentful, merely like he was stating facts. 'Lots of people would say that a private income is the definition of entitlement.'

'Have you got a problem with that?' I asked, digging in my handbag for the keys to Lanagh to cover how flustered I felt. I did, indeed, have a small trust fund from Mum's estate. Lucy had one too, in addition to her money from Dad. Of course, unlike my sister I also worked for a living. 'Because I have a job which I need and two kids I support, so—'

'I'm not bitter about it,' Harry said quickly. 'I just think it's important to remind the rich that life's tough without money.'

'Okay ...' I opened the front door. '... but life can be tough whatever,' I said, hurrying into Uncle Perry's gloomy hall. The alarm beeped its warning. I scuttled to the alarm panel and punched in the code as Harry found a light switch.

We stood, side by side, in the eerie silence of the shadowy hallway. It struck me again that Caspian would never have helped me like this. Steady and reliable, he would have refused to explore Lanagh House without Uncle Perry's knowledge or permission.

'Are your dad and your uncle close?' Harry asked, as I led him across the hall towards Uncle Perry's study. I'd already decided that this was where we were most likely to find evidence of PAAUL. The rest of the house was Spartan and minimalist – not in the chichi designer sense in which Jacqueline kept Dad's house but as if a monk lived here.

'Very close,' I said. 'Uncle Perry has dinner with Dad at home or his club on most of the nights he's in town.'

'Was it always like that?'

'I don't know,' I admitted, pausing at the door of the study. 'Uncle Perry is much older – like eight years or so. He looked out for Dad when they were kids, protected him from bullies, that kind of thing.'

'And now?'

'Kind of the other way round. Dad's been really successful in everything. Work, women, health. Perry's had a harder life. He never married and he's had problems with his back ...'

'Do you think Perry might be part of PAAUL too?'

'I don't think either of them are part of it, not really.' My words sounded hollow even to my own ears. After all, if that were true what was I doing here? 'I just want to be sure,' I went on lamely.

'Of course.'

We walked into Perry's study. It was dominated by the large picture of St Francis of Assisi which hung on the wall opposite the door. A huge leather-topped desk stood in front of the window, laden with papers. To the side of the desk a row of hefty oak bookcases groaned with files and folders.

'Bloody hell,' Harry said.

'I know,' I replied. 'It's a lot to look through, but I don't have to be home until seven or so, we've got a good four hours.'

'Leaving everything as we find it,' Harry muttered, rolling up his sleeves. 'Let's get on with it, then. Er, what exactly are we looking for?'

'Anything connected with PAAUL.'

'I don't see a computer, do you know where it is?'

'Perry doesn't have one,' I said.

'How can anyone exist without a laptop?' Harry asked, looking genuinely shocked.

'Perry's not at all tech-savvy, not compared to Dad

and definitely not compared to most people nowadays. He only has a mobile for emergencies.'

'Right, so if there are any notes or records about PAAUL meetings you think they'll be on these shelves?'

'Yes, assuming the PAAUL meetings are really held in this house,' I said.

We each took a shelf and worked our way along it, pulling out every file in turn. Most of the information here was to do with Perry's long-standing interest in the lives of the Catholic saints, which I knew he'd inherited from his mother, though we also found some bank and investment portfolio information too.

'He might not be worth as much as your dad,' Harry said at one point, 'but he's not doing badly.'

I shrugged. Maybe Harry didn't believe it but I knew how lucky I was to have not only emotional but also financial support from my family. Dad had helped me buy my first flat – a big part of the deposit for the house Caspian and I later purchased – though, more recently, I had rejected his offer to pay for childcare for Ruby on the two days when I worked past the end of the school day.

I flicked through a folder containing reviews of books on sainthood – there had to be more than fifty of them, some curled and yellowing with age.

'So Perry's an odd name,' Harry said, breaking the silence as he replaced the last file on his shelf. 'At least it is compared to Jayson and ... there's another brother too, isn't there?'

'Yes, Graham. My cousin Dex's dad. Actually it's Graham who's the odd one out, name-wise,' I explained. 'Perry is short for Perseus, from Greek myth. And Jayson is from Jason and the Argonauts.'

'Blimey.' Harry raised an eyebrow.

'Their dad was a classics scholar,' I said. 'Graham's first name is Hercules, but he never uses it.'

'I can see why.' Harry grinned and pulled a large green file off the next shelf. 'Do your dad and Perry get on with Graham?'

'They don't see each other very often,' I said. In fact there was little love lost between Uncle Graham and the others. They'd barely spoken in years. Still, it felt disloyal to say so.

We worked on in silence.

'Why are you so interested in all this?' I asked. 'I mean, I get what you said before, about trying to help me deal with the "bombshell" you dropped, but you seem to really care and you didn't even properly know Caspian.'

'Oh well . . . people are fascinating and I'm basically very nosy.' Harry hesitated. 'Actually, if I'm honest I feel bad I didn't pass on sooner what your husband told me at the conference.'

'Why did you come to me instead of the police?'

'I told you.' He met my gaze. 'I thought it was only fair that you had a chance to process what might be happening first . . . with your dad . . .'

We searched on. After an hour it was obvious there was nothing about PAAUL here.

'Okay,' I said. 'If this really is the PAAUL head-quarters then they only use it to meet up, not to store anything or keep records.'

Harry stared at me. 'Or the records are somewhere else in the house.'

'I can't think where,' I said. 'There're not many places you can store stuff. Perhaps they just make plans and don't write anything down.'

'Mmn.' Harry sighed.

'I guess we could take a quick look round the rest of the house, just in case?' I set off upstairs, leaving Harry to explore the living room, the dining room – with its polished oak table – and kitchen, which hadn't been properly updated since my grandfather died and left Perry the house. I wandered through the four bedrooms upstairs. Perry still slept in his childhood room, leaving the larger master bedroom for guests. If I hadn't known which was which I wouldn't have been able to guess. All four bedrooms were decorated with floral wallpaper, polished wood wardrobes and pale-blue curtains at the windows. I stopped for a second in the smallest room, which I knew from previous visits had been my father's when he was a child. I tried to imagine him as a small boy, eager to keep up with his two older brothers. There was no sign of that boy in this room.

'Fran!' The urgency in Harry's voice roused me from my reverie.

I bounded down the stairs. 'Did you find something?'

Harry was in the hallway, eyes wide as he peered into the under-stairs cupboard. I frowned, following his gaze to the row of coats that hung on pegs on the far wall and the boots and shoes lined neatly underneath them.

'There's nothing here,' I said. 'And there wasn't upstairs either.'

'Look,' Harry urged. 'Behind the raincoat.'

Shaking my head I pulled back the mackintosh at the end of the row. To my surprise instead of the wall I expected to find, there was a door, the brass handle clearly exposed. I rattled it. The door stayed shut.

'Locked,' I said, meeting Harry's gaze.

He held up a bunch of keys. 'I found these in the kitchen,' he said, offering them to me.

I chewed my lip. It was one thing ransacking Perry's files, but blundering into a room he clearly wanted kept secret somehow felt like crossing a bigger line.

'You need to see,' Harry said. His dark eyes were calm, but intent. 'Don't you?'

I nodded, turning my attention to the keys. I found the one that fitted on the second try.

With a click, the door creaked open. I fumbled along the wall of the dim space inside and found a switch. The light illuminated a set of narrow stairs leading down, presumably to some sort of cellar.

'I didn't know this existed,' I breathed.

'Come on,' Harry said.

I took a deep breath and led the way down.

5

The stairs were steep as well as narrow and the dim light above them cast shadows across the stone floor to which we were descending. I realised I was holding my breath as my feet echoed across the large flags of what appeared to be some sort of cellar. It was cold and shadowy down here: an empty room with a single door at the end.

'What's through there?' Harry asked. I could hear the tension in his voice.

My heartbeat quickened as I opened the door and flicked on the light.

Inside was a storage room, full of boxes and old furniture. Some of it looked like it had once been ornate and expensive – a pair of now-threadbare brocade armchairs with matching footstools, a set of tarnished brass doorstops, a chipped oak sideboard stood on its end. Unlike the austere house upstairs, this place was a mess.

'Jesus, look at all this,' Harry breathed, opening the box at the top of the pile stacked against the wall opposite. 'Do we have time to go through it all?'

'Probably not.' I turned to the cardboard box nearest me. As I lifted the lid I glanced around the room.

There must be thirty or forty containers here. It would surely take us another two or three hours to check them all – and I had to make a start back to London by four thirty at the latest.

I rummaged through the box. Tax returns, insurance forms and sheaves of notes and correspondence on the headed notepaper of Perry's old surgery. Which made sense: Uncle Perry was a recently retired doctor. I sighed. Across the room Harry had yanked open the top of another box and sifted through its contents. We worked in silence, careful to replace everything exactly as we found it. Hardly any of the boxes were labelled. Disheartened, I tugged at a small box buried at the back. It had the words *P. CARR PRIVATE* scrawled across it in capitals.

A naked male torso met my eye. I frowned, picking the creased page up. It had clearly been torn from a magazine. Plenty of others lay beneath it – then whole magazines: *Attitude*, *Gay Times* and an American publication called *Black Inches*. All old and crumpled. Mostly from the eighties and nineties. My mouth gaped as I flicked through a few copies, then sifted the many, many photos underneath. Some were soft porn: just low lighting and an oily sheen on bare muscle. Others were hardcore, showing male-on-male penetration.

I stared at the pictures as the realisation settled in my head: my ascetic, God-fearing, extremely proper uncle was clearly secretly gay. This was his old porn stash. I closed my mouth. It all made sense, now I thought about it. Perry was unmarried and I'd never known him be in a relationship. I felt stupid as I reflected how I'd always, naïvely, assumed he had simply never met the right person. Perry seemed asexual rather than repressed. Anyway he was a devout Catholic, almost as observant as Lucy in his strict attendance of daily mass. I'd heard him speak out against homosexuality in a 'hate the sin, love the sinner' way a million times. It had never occurred to me he might be gay himself.

'Fran?' Harry's voice broke into the silence.

I shoved the magazine I was holding back in the box and flipped down the lid. No need to tell Harry about all this, it clearly wasn't connected to the secret meetings that we suspected had been taking place here.

'What?' I turned. Harry was holding up a sheet of paper, his dark eyes shining in the bright overhead light.

'This is it, Fran,' he said. 'Loads of stuff on your dad's anti-abortion work. It's all here, there's got to be something on PAAUL, on the assassination plan.'

'Really?' Still reeling over Perry's secret, I hurried across the stone floor and took the paper from his hand. As Harry reached into his box and drew out an A4 file marked *Shield on PAAUL Report 3*, I read what he'd given me. It was a report covering PAAUL activities during 2011. Dad had been passionate about his work for the pro-life charity both before and after that time. I well remember him hurtling like a bull into his first *Shield* campaign when he found out about Lucy's abortion. It was almost as if there was some way he could make up for her transgressions by trying to prevent other women making the same choice.

Had all that fervour really allowed him to justify killing abortion doctors? Including Caspian? I still couldn't really believe it.

I skimmed down the lists of protests and bomb scares. I'd read about several of the more violent ones online already. It was all US-based. I turned the page. And came face to face with a report headed:

Possible UK targets, 2012.

The first item read:

Underground crusade against abortion doctors.

'Oh my God,' I breathed.

'Look at this.' Harry shoved another set of papers into my hands.

I scanned the top sheet: another report, this one entitled *Psychological profiles of potential PAAUL recruits, UK.*

My stomach twisted into knots as I gazed at the notes in the margin, all written in Dad's looping handwriting.

'It looks like some sort of recruiting document,' Harry muttered. 'There's a paper here about "qualities of likely recruits" and another called *Top ten targets* of which the third is a list of prominent UK gynaecologists.' He looked up. 'Your husband's name is on the list.'

I leaned against the wall, unable to believe it. Up to this minute I'd not seriously believed that Dad or Uncle Perry could really be involved in PAAUL. But now ... was it possible my own father was some sort of secret extremist vigilante? It beggared belief. And yet why else had he lied when I mentioned the name PAAUL to him?

With a jolt I remembered the look Jacqueline had shot him when I'd asked him what he knew. Was she in on the secret too?

'There's a list of abortion clinics here,' Harry said, his voice hollow. 'Do you think it's another target list?' He glanced across at me. 'Do you think your stepmother or your sister know about this? They're big-time Catholics too, aren't they?'

'Mmm ... they're both religious but there's no way either of them would sanction anything violent.'

'What about pro-life stuff?'

'They're both against abortions, if that's what you mean.' I looked at him. Did he know about the termination Lucy had when she was a teenager? Was that why he was asking? No, I was being paranoid. It was almost eleven years since that had been in the press, you'd have had to search for it to find out about it now. Harry couldn't know. 'I've never actually heard Jacqueline talk about it but I'm sure being pro-life is part of her Catholic baggage. But Lucy I do know. She's pro-life in the same way she's anti-gay marriage. It's what she thinks, quietly. It's just a belief she has, she doesn't *act* on it or campaign about it, like Dad used to.'

Harry looked at me, a sceptical expression on his face. I felt a flash of resentment that I was being pushed into defending my entire family.

'Seriously. Lucy's more into her church groups than anything else,' I carried on, wondering why on earth I felt I owed Harry any explanations. He had an uncanny way of holding back that almost compelled me to talk. 'There's the Guild of the Blessed Sacrament on Saturdays and she goes to the Legion of Mary on Sunday afternoons . . .' I trailed off.

'What the hell is the Legion of Mary?'

Before I could reply the sound of footsteps echoed down the stone steps from the hallway. Harry's eyes widened. I spun around as a middle-aged woman appeared in the doorway.

'Francesca!' The woman clapped her hand over her mouth.

'Mrs Grayling.' I turned to Harry, who was speedily shoving the list of abortion clinics back into its box. 'Harry, this is Uncle Perry's housekeeper.'

Harry raised his hand in awkward salute. I smiled. Mrs Grayling had been with Uncle Perry ever since I could remember, though I hadn't seen her for years.

'Oh, Francesca,' Mrs Grayling gasped. 'I'm so sorry if I gave you a start, but I was afraid it were burglars.'

'No, we're the ones who are sorry,' I said, my heart sinking as I realised there was no way we were going to be able to carry on exploring the remaining boxes now. 'I didn't think anyone would be in. I'm sorry we gave you a fright.'

Mrs Grayling's brow knotted. 'What on earth are you doing down here? Perry didn't say anything about you paying a visit. He's still in London.'

'I know,' I said, thinking fast. 'I actually didn't talk to Uncle Perry about it, which I see now was thoughtless.

It was a spur of the moment thing, I was looking for, er, for some old stuff I thought might be here. My friend Harry came with me to help.'

The idea that we might have driven two-and-a-half hours from London in pouring rain on the spur of the moment sounded crazy even as I said it, but Mrs Grayling was thankfully more concerned with replaying her reaction to our presence in the house than analysing my explanations.

'I'd just got here,' she gabbled. 'And I thought it was strange the alarm wasn't on but Perry does sometimes forget and I was just doing a bit of housekeeping for when he's back tomorrow, you know ... clearing up, making sure he'll have a meal he can heat up. So ... I was cleaning the fridge and thinking about doing maybe a chicken chasseur, when I heard voices. I didn't know what to think.' She paused. 'Did you find what you were looking for?'

'No, it's fine, it was just some silly toys and stuff from childhood I thought might have ended up here.' I remembered the box of gay porn mags. I was never going to be able to look my uncle in the face again.

'There's a lot of stuff down here, I'm always saying he should have a clear-out, but he's so busy. If he hadn't been out today, I wouldn't have been so worried when I came in earlier.'

Mrs Grayling bustled about the kitchen, making us tea and going over her version of events again as the light faded outside.

*

We talked about what we'd discovered all the way back to London – well, everything except the porn, which I couldn't bring myself to mention. It wasn't the porn per se, more the hypocrisy of my uncle's life I didn't want exposed. Things looked bad enough as they were, with Harry insistent that everything we'd heard and found added up to proof of Dad's involvement with PAAUL.

I still couldn't believe it, though the evidence seemed overwhelming. Harry had an answer for all my objections.

'But Dad *left* the pro-life organisation he worked for years ago,' I protested. 'He only joined it in the first place because of what happened to Lucy. He's anti-abortion, sure, but it was never a big issue for him.'

'People change . . .' Harry pointed out.

'Yes,' I agreed. 'And the way Dad changed was that he realised his work for *Shield* wasn't really right for him.'

'Or else he became more militant so he decided to leave moderate *Shield* and go underground with extreme PAAUL.'

'No, you don't understand,' I protested. 'Dad changed *generally*, not just over that. It was Jacqueline's influence. He met her and he . . . he softened . . .'

'Or else she helped him see that if he wanted to go violent on anti-abortion he needed to take on a less public role so he wouldn't draw so much attention to himself,' Harry countered.

We slowed at a set of lights. Everything Harry said was logical, yet it was still, surely, impossible that Dad could be any kind of terrorist.

'The point is,' Harry went on more gently, 'are you one hundred per cent sure, or do you have doubts?'

I said nothing.

'And if you have doubts, don't you deserve the truth?'

I glanced over. 'You think I should talk to my dad about all this?'

Harry shrugged. 'That's your decision. I just know what it's like when you want answers . . . it's impossible to rest until you get them.'

It was dark, the windows misting with cold, by the time I dropped Harry in north London. I picked up Ruby and Rufus from their respective play dates and made my way home. By the time I'd sorted dinner and ushered them upstairs to bed I was exhausted. I knew I should call Uncle Perry – if for no other reason than to explain why I'd let myself into his house and rummaged through his storeroom – but I was putting it off.

To be honest, I was surprised he hadn't called me himself yet. I was certain that Mrs Grayling would have spoken to him by now. However, it was still a shock when the doorbell rang at ten fifteen that evening and I opened the door to find Dad and Uncle Perry standing on the doorstep. Though roughly the same height, Perry looked every bit of his additional eight years. His face was lined and his white hair thinning, while Dad was broader and more solid, his hair still thick and dark, just a little grey around the temples.

'Hello, darling,' Dad said, a strained smile playing about his lips. 'You went to Lanagh today?'

I stared from him to my uncle, the front door still open in my hand. Perry's mouth was set in a thin, angry line. 'May we come in?' he snapped.

I nodded, quaking, and led them into the living room. As soon as the door was shut, Perry turned on me.

'What on *earth* did you think you were doing?' he demanded with a furious scowl. He spoke slowly and emphatically, as always – but there was a sharp edge to his voice. 'Mrs Grayling said you and "a male friend" let yourselves in—'

'. . . with my spare key which you took without asking,' Dad added, sounding deeply concerned.

'And that you were rummaging about in my basement, going through boxes looking for *toys for the kids*?' Perry italicised the last few words, making it clear he didn't believe my excuse for being there.

The cover of a mid-nineties copy of *Black Inches* flashed into my mind's eye. I couldn't look at him.

'What were you really doing, Francesca?' Dad asked. He sounded genuinely bemused, a frown forming a deep ridge between his eyebrows.

'Why all the subterfuge?' Perry added.

Panic rose through my stomach, up into my throat. Should I lie? Or should I confront them?

'I think your uncle deserves a full explanation.' Dad's voice was more pained than angry. 'And I have to say I'm really worried about you.'

'Okay, er . . .' I stammered. Earlier I couldn't imagine how on earth to bring up the subject, but now *not* to say anything would surely be harder. Plus Harry was right, I needed to know the truth.

'I'm really sorry I didn't say anything to ... to either of you but, d'you remember, Dad, when I asked you if you knew about an anti-abortion organisation called PAAUL?'

A look of confusion passed over Dad's face. 'I remember you asked if I knew a *person* called Paul.' He turned to Perry. 'Some nutcase came up to Francesca and claimed this "Paul" person had been threatening Caspian before he died.'

'Which has got *what* exactly to do with my basement?' Perry demanded.

'Was the man who told you about PAAUL the same man you were with at Lanagh today?' Dad asked.

They both looked at me expectantly.

I nodded. 'We ... I ... I found out Paul is really P.A.A.U.L., which stands for *Pledge to Avenge the Assassination of Unborn Lives*. It's a terrorist organisation that ... that operates mostly in the US but it's possible it started carrying out assassinations of abortion doctors in the UK a few years ago.'

Dad and Perry exchanged a look.

'I still don't—' Perry started.

'But you already know about PAAUL, don't you?' I fixed my gaze on Dad.

He nodded.

'So why didn't you say so when I asked you?'

'I didn't want to upset you so soon after the memorial service,' Dad protested.

Was that true? Dad looked sincere enough, and he'd always had a tendency to be overprotective; it was something we used to fight about when I was a teenager.

'Anyway,' I went on. 'There's stuff . . . speculation . . . on the internet about you and this organisation, PAAUL, and links to Uncle Perry's house, to Lanagh being some sort of HQ.' I glanced at Perry, who was gaping at me, then back to Dad. 'Harry and I started looking into it.'

'Into a bunch of internet rumours?' Uncle Perry's voice dripped with contempt.

'It's not just online.' A vision of Simon Pinner's mean, watery eyes as he hissed his own suspicions flashed into my head.

According to all the rumours your father, Jayson Carr, is the secret head of PAAUL in the UK.

'It's . . . there are people out there who believe PAAUL is targeting abortion doctors and that you're involved,' I said.

'With *terrorists*?' The colour drained from Dad's face. 'You actually think I might be capable of—'

'I don't think anything.' Guilt at his consternation pricked at me. 'Harry and I were just looking for information. We read about the connection with Lanagh so we . . . we went there.'

'Unbelievable,' Perry muttered.

'I was desperate to find out the truth,' I stammered. 'Caspian was my husband. If PAAUL had him killed I need to know.'

Silence fell.

'You really think that your uncle and I might be capable of hurting your own husband ... my grand-children's father?' Dad's face crumpled.

'If there'd been any suspicion at all the police would have investigated us,' Perry added. 'And they didn't. As you know.'

I hung my head. I was handling this all wrong. Dad was devastated. Of course he wasn't capable of order-ing Caspian's death. And yet there had to be some explanation for the threats Caspian received and for all the rumours that connected Dad to PAAUL.

'This is ridiculous,' Perry spat.

'So what did you find in Uncle Perry's basement?' Dad asked. It looked as though it was costing him a lot to speak.

'Things ...' I stopped, picturing the gay porn again. It was impossible to look Perry in the eye so I kept my gaze on Dad. 'Things about PAAUL.'

'Of course you did, you stupid child.' Perry gave an exasperated sigh.

My head jerked up. What did that mean? 'Dad?'

'Oh, Francesca.' Dad sounded close to tears now. 'All those reports were done when I was working for *Shield*. You must have seen that from the headings, the dates.'

I nodded.

'There was ... a concern about some of the anti-abortion rhetoric we were hearing via our outreach programme ... concerns that PAAUL in the US was considering setting up an operation here. Perry and I did – well, we organised some investigating.'

'Investigating?'

'Yes, I ordered various bits of research during . . . I'm not sure exactly when, probably 2011 because I left the year after.' Dad frowned, clearly trying to remember the details. 'There was a report on activities and . . . and a list of abortion clinics we thought might make likely targets for PAAUL. Er . . . we looked at whether some sort of crusade of violence directed at individuals was probable, plus we tried to get a sense of possible PAAUL agents, their typical profile, that sort of thing.' Dad leaned forward. 'We were trying to find out about their activities, if they were attempting to recruit through our churches . . . not *help* them.'

'Oh.' I sat back, reeling. 'So *do* you think they killed Caspian?'

'No, sweetheart.' Dad blew out his breath. 'All our research showed that PAAUL was staying US-based and using bombs and, in some cases, gunmen to attack clinics. We found no evidence that they had or were planning any sustained campaign against individual doctors, certainly not in the UK.' He shuddered. 'It doesn't lessen their evil, but there was no evidence of any plans to bring their horrific violence over here.'

'Precisely,' Uncle Perry snapped. 'As we would have told you if you'd asked either of us instead of blundering about in my basement with a total stranger.'

'Oh.' My head spun. 'But ... but perhaps they started targeting UK doctors *after* you did your reports. Caspian didn't die until September 2014.'

'I'm sure that hasn't happened,' Dad said gently. 'I might not be involved with *Shield* on a daily basis but I often see people who still work there. Nobody's mentioned any new developments along those lines.'

I looked down.

'People will write anything when it's anonymous,' Dad said bitterly. 'One bit of misinformation leads to another and hey presto our secret investigations appear sinister.'

'And what about the threats Caspian told Harry about?'

'For goodness' sake,' Uncle Perry said with an angry hiss.

'That's enough, Perry.' Dad shot him a warning glance. 'Poor Francesca's been taken advantage of.' He leaned forward and patted my hand. 'I'm so sorry, sweetheart, but this Harry person either misunderstood what Caspian said or he's making it up.'

'Whichever it is, you should stay away from him,' Perry snarled.

I thought of Harry's handsome, narrow face, a smile crinkling around his eyes. 'You don't know him. He was just trying to help.'

Dad raised a sceptical eyebrow. 'He sounds like bad news to me.'

A tense silence filled the air.

'You've certainly let him get you all worked up,'

Perry snapped. 'Not surprising, I suppose. You're highly emotional and particularly vulnerable at the moment, especially without faith and prayer to help you.'

My jaw dropped. Pompous pig. 'How dare you—'

'Your uncle's just upset.' Dad shot another warning look at his brother. He turned to me again. 'Though he does have a bit of a point, sweetheart, you *are* vulnerable. And you have always been very emotional. Remember how you were as a teenager? Impulsive ... easily led by your peer group into dangerous behaviours? Don't you think breaking into Lanagh with a stranger is exactly that?'

Irritation roiled inside me. And yet, at the back of my mind, something told me Dad was at least partly right. Since Caspian died, I'd felt like I was in limbo, treading water, waiting for real life to begin again. And Harry's arrival had brought with it an explosion of real life. Maybe I was coping with the shock as I had done when I was fourteen and realised how sheltered my life really was. I'd wanted to act out, to defy my parents, particularly Dad. Were all my suspicions about him now really a way for me to regress to my rebellious teenage self?

Dad stood up. 'We should go,' he said softly. 'It's late. Thank you for being so open and honest with us.' He hesitated, his hands trembling slightly as they squeezed mine. 'I love you so much and I do hope we've reassured you.'

Tears pricked at my eyes. Talk about vulnerable. For

all his height and heft and commanding presence, Dad was one of the most sensitive men I'd ever met. His expression of dignified sadness made me feel ashamed. Whatever else had happened, there was no way he had hurt Caspian. No way at all.

'Thanks, Dad, you've really helped, I'm so sorry I upset you,' I said, hugging him. 'And please don't hate Harry for this, like I said, he was just trying to help.'

'All right, sweetheart.' Dad smiled, relief on his face. He kissed my cheek. 'Come on, Perry. Let's leave Francesca in peace.'

Perry leaned on the arm of his chair to help himself up. He seemed distracted as he followed Dad out of the living room. As he reached the door he turned to face me. *Sotto voce*, he said:

'Er, did you find anything else in my basement, Francesca?'

I met his gaze and in that moment I knew that he knew I had discovered his old porn mags. And that Dad had no idea about his being gay.

'Not a thing,' I said.

An hour later I was lying in bed, exhausted but too wired to sleep. I had been such an idiot, letting Harry get me carried away with his rumours and innuendos. Like Dad said, the internet was full of trolls and as for the threats Caspian received ... perhaps Harry mis-heard. Or else Caspian himself had got it wrong.

I would call Harry in the morning and explain everything. For now, I just wanted to put the whole business out of my mind. Easier said than done: I lay tossing and turning under the duvet, the bed too big as it had been for the past year and four months. Into the silence, my mobile rang.

It was Harry. My heart skipped a beat. Was he just calling to find out if I'd spoken to my dad? Because once I told him I was sure Dad was innocent, we'd have no reason to speak any more. Or was he concerned about me? About how I was doing with all the revelations of the day? He'd said he'd told me about the threat against Caspian out of a sense of duty. Was that still what was motivating him?

Maybe it was more.

I hoped it was more.

'Hi,' I said, glad he couldn't see the blush that burned my cheeks.

'Fran.' He sounded upset. Worried. 'Did you hear? It was on the news.'

'Hear what?' I sat up straight in bed.

'Another abortion doctor's been murdered. A stabbing. Somewhere in Surrey. Similar profile to your husband's death.'

I gasped, all the reassurance I'd gained from my conversation with Dad vanishing in an instant. 'Do you think it's PAAUL?'

'It fits.' Harry paused. 'I also think you know the man. I recognised his picture from the memorial service. I think he might have been a friend of your husband.'

'What was his name?' I held my breath.

'Simon Pinner,' Harry said. 'Wasn't he . . .?'

'The first person who told me about Dad being head of PAAUL?' I said, my voice hoarse. An image of Simon's doughy face with those thin, wet lips flashed into my head. 'Yes, he was.'

6

My doubts had reared up again, leaving me in an agonising state of uncertainty. Whether or not Dad had been involved in Caspian's and Simon's deaths, there was surely a strong possibility that PAAUL was behind them both. And believing that changed everything. It meant that Caspian wasn't killed in a meaningless attack but deliberately targeted for his beliefs. It meant he'd been hunted down like an animal, by a highly disciplined and effective organisation. It meant I had, at last, someone to blame, a place to direct my own anger, a chance to get justice for my husband.

I don't know what I would have done next if I'd been left to my own devices but, after tossing and turning all night, then waking late and rushing the kids to get ready for school, I arrived back home to find a man ringing my doorbell.

'Hello?' I said, hurrying along the path.

The man turned, holding up a police badge. 'Francesca Hoffman? I'm Detective Sergeant Chris Smart.' He had a nasal edge to his voice, and deep-set, wary eyes. He was tall but wiry, his ill-fitting suit too broad for his shoulders. 'Do you have a moment? Not rushing off to work or anything?'

'No, I'm working at home today.' The sun was shining but I shivered. Had something terrible happened to Dad or Lucy? There was nothing in the officer's manner that suggested crisis or calamity.

'I'm hoping to ask you a few questions about Simon Pinner,' DS Smart went on. 'I understand you spoke to him at the weekend?'

I nodded, my blood running cold.

'I'm not sure if you've heard but he passed away last night.'

'Yes,' I said. 'I know.'

DS Smart gazed at me. His dark eyes had a piercing quality that made it seem as if he were looking straight through me.

'May I come in?' he asked.

'Of course.' I took DS Smart into the living room. He sat in the armchair by the TV. What was coming now?

'So your father is Jayson Carr?' he asked.

'Er, yes.' I frowned.

'He's the head of that prison charity committee. Chief Super's on it.' DS Smart grinned, revealing sharp, pointed teeth. 'Gave me the third degree about minding my Ps and Qs when I interviewed you.'

'Right.' I fidgeted nervously. I was used to Dad having powerful contacts and used, when I was younger, to find his privilege and influence profoundly irritating. But right now all I felt was an uneasy fear. What did Dad knowing the Chief Super have to do with the investigation into Simon Pinner's murder?

'What, er, did you want to ask me?'

DS Smart consulted his notebook.

'I understand from your father that you spoke to Mr Pinner at your husband's memorial, but that you hadn't met him before?'

'That's right. At least, Simon said we'd been introduced years ago at a dinner party, but I didn't remember him.'

'We know that he was asking around for your address after the memorial service. And an examination of Mr Pinner's phone suggests he did indeed come to your house on Sunday afternoon, just over twenty-four hours before he was killed.'

'I see.' I gulped. All my suspicions and here was an actual detective, sent to my door. Should I tell him what Harry had told me? Should I pass on my suspicions about PAAUL killing Simon – and Caspian? Should I confide my agonies about whether Dad was involved?

DS Smart sat forward. His eyes were not just set deep, but also too close together, giving him the appearance of a wolf sizing up its prey.

'Is something wrong?' he asked.

'No,' I said. 'It's just ...'

DS Smart waited.

'It's just I've been wondering about Simon ... about him being killed. It seems similar to Caspian ... my husband, the way he was killed.'

DS Smart frowned. 'Not really,' he said. 'The methods, places, times of death were quite different.'

'But they were both doctors.' The words blurted out of me.

DS Smart tilted his head to one side, his frown deepening.

'Abortion doctors,' I went on. 'You know as well as I do that there are some violent, extremist anti-abortion groups out there. Surely it's possible one of them is . . . is on a campaign to kill doctors that carry out abortions.'

'Did Mr Pinner mention such a group had threatened him?'

'No,' I admitted. 'But he knew about one. It's called PAAUL. Based in the States. *Pledge to Avenge the Assassination of Unborn Lives*. I asked him about it, because I think PAAUL might have been behind my husband's murder.'

DS Smart drew back. 'You're saying you think Simon Pinner *and* your husband may have been killed by a violent anti-abortion group from the US?' he asked, an eyebrow raised. 'What's made you think this?'

I gulped. 'Somebody told me at the memorial service that Caspian told them he was being threatened by this group just before he died.' I stopped, unwilling to mention the possible connection between Dad and PAAUL.

I hadn't meant to say this much.

'Somebody told somebody who told you?' DS Smart pursed his lips. 'I'm sorry but I looked at your husband's file before I set out and there's absolutely nothing to suggest his death was anything other than a random attack.'

'I know, but . . .' I stopped again. There wasn't much more I could tell the detective without bringing Dad into it.

DS Smart cleared his throat. 'Let's start again,' he said. 'When you spoke to Simon Pinner on Sunday, did he give any hint about being in fear for his life? From this organisation, PAAUL, or anyone else?'

'No,' I conceded.

'Did he seem worried, or anxious, as if he were being threatened but was too scared to say?'

I shook my head.

'What *was* the nature of your conversation?' DS Smart persisted.

'He said he'd liked talking to me at the memorial service and . . . and he asked me out.' I paused. 'I said no and . . . and he left. I think . . . I got the impression he thought I liked him . . . and he was a bit pissed off I didn't want to go on a date . . .'

'I see.' DS Smart sighed. 'Doesn't sound like he was in the grip of any distracting anxieties then.'

'You don't know that,' I said.

'True.' DS Smart shut his notebook. 'But what I do know is that Mr Pinner gave no indication he was being threatened. He certainly didn't tell the police. Just as your husband didn't.'

'Okay, but it still seems like a weird coincidence that I find out my husband was possibly being threatened by an organisation that clearly had a reason to attack him. Then a colleague of his dies in a similar attack just over a year later.'

'Mmn.' DS Smart wrinkled his nose. 'To be honest the connections don't look as strong to me. Yes, they're both abortion doctors, but the attacks happened in totally different places and at different times and – I'm sorry to be graphic – but the weapons used weren't the same and nor was the pattern of attack. Anyway, no organisation has come forward to claim responsibility.' He paused, straightening up and adopting a more formal tone. 'We did look into motives for killing your husband very thoroughly when it happened. I wasn't on the case, but I remember it. We found no evidence of any extreme anti-abortion organisations wanting to kill him or any other doctors.' He sighed and offered me a sympathetic look. 'I know a random death is hard to accept, but sometimes there is no rhyme or reason to these things. Just someone in the wrong place at the wrong time.' He paused. 'Is there anything else you wanted to tell me? Like where you got this idea of your husband being threatened?'

My stomach twisted into an uneasy knot. If I gave Harry's name, then Dad would inevitably get dragged into the whole thing. Anyway it was obvious DS Smart thought the idea PAAUL might be behind Caspian's and Simon's deaths was preposterous.

Perhaps it was.

I sat back. 'No, that's everything.'

DS Smart left. I went to ring Harry but found instead a voice mail from him explaining he had to go to Manchester to visit his sister and would be out of town until Friday. It was a good thing, I reflected.

I was probably being hysterical, putting two and two together and making fifteen. A complete stranger like Harry was the last person I should be confiding in. Still, I badly wanted to talk everything that had happened through with someone.

Ayesha was at work. I couldn't imagine she'd have any more patience with my theories than the detective had. There was Dex, of course. But my cousin would probably just tease me as a drama queen for imagining a covert US-based conspiracy against Caspian and Simon Pinner.

Lucy was definitely out of the question: my sister would be devastated at the idea anyone could connect Dad with two murders. Lucy had always been super-sensitive. She would be upset for days if she found out what Harry claimed Caspian had said. What I really wanted was to talk to someone who knew Dad well enough to disregard the supposed threats he'd made to Caspian but who would take seriously the threat from PAAUL.

Of course. A smile spread across my face. I knew exactly who I should speak to.

I did a few hours' work – I'd make up the time that evening – then picked up Ruby from school and went straight to Auntie Sheila's house. Sheila was on her own when I arrived, dusting her tiny living room. It was funny: Mum's home had been cluttered and chaotic while Jacqueline's version of the same property was minimalist and organised to within an inch of its life. Auntie Sheila's house managed, somehow, to be both neat yet crammed with stuff. Every surface was covered with meticulously placed china ornaments. They ranged from a couple of beautiful and expensive pieces Mum and Dad had given her to chipped, well-worn dolls from her childhood and mementoes from her holidays in Italy and Spain.

When we were kids, Dex used to complain that they only ever went to places where there were Catholic churches to visit.

'At least you get actual holidays with planes and beaches after you've been round the churches,' I remember complaining back. When I was little Dad was always too busy to get away from the UK and Mum didn't like to travel abroad without him, so Lucy and I spent many summer holidays staring out of rain-spattered windows, wishing we could go abroad like other families to play in the sun.

Mum and Sheila had always been very close and their friendship only intensified after Uncle Graham left home. I can still remember the thrill of Sheila and Dex's arrival in the middle of the night after he'd gone – the adults all hushed and appalled and poor Dex shaking from the trauma. The split had been a long time coming – Graham had hit Sheila several times before they finally separated, not that I knew that at the time.

'Come on in,' Auntie Sheila said, beaming from me to Ruby. 'What a lovely surprise.'

I told Sheila I needed to talk to her, then settled Ruby down on the sofa in front of the iPad to watch *Brave* yet again. She'd viewed the download about fifty times and showed no signs of tiring of the movie yet. I wondered if her obsession with the film was normal or something to do with losing her dad. My psychology degree had taught me that any parent in my position was likely to view normal developmental foibles through the prism of bereavement. Or, as Ayesha, who was generally my go-to person for parental advice, had put it: 'Stop sweating the small stuff. Kids act weird sometimes. And they change. All the time. Whether or not they've lost a dad.'

Auntie Sheila bustled about the kitchen, fetching and carrying an orange juice to Ruby next door, then settling herself down in front of me at the kitchen table. Like the house around her, she managed to appear both excessively neat – everything tidily tucked away – and yet wildly over-decorated, with all the colours and patterns of her clothes clashing. Today she was wearing a floral shirt with a pink-and-white striped cardigan, while a polka-dot headband kept her helmet of grey hair off her face.

'What's the matter, dear?' she asked, wide-eyed. 'You look like you're carrying the weight of the world.'

I gave her a rueful smile. Now I was here it was harder to begin than I expected. Sheila was in her own way as much of an innocent as Lucy, eager to see the best in people, especially men. She had loved Mum deeply and treated Lucy and me as the daughters she'd never had, but she practically hero-worshipped Dad and had always adored her only son, refusing – despite knowledge of at least one of Dex's affairs – to lay any of the responsibility for his marriage breakup on his shoulders.

I came to see her most Sundays after she got home from mass. Had done since Mum died. I often brought a box of macaroons, which Sheila loved, and we shared them over cups of weak, milky tea and the gossip from Sheila's bridge club. Today, however, was a Tuesday. Not my normal day to visit. The scent of meat roasting drifted towards me and I wondered, vaguely, what she was cooking.

'It's about Caspian's death,' I started. 'The way he died ...'

Sheila made a sympathetic face. 'Such a terrible loss.' Her kitchen was all stripes and flower patterns with a large dresser crammed full of crockery. I stared at the row of prayer cards in front of a large, leaf-embossed platter, trying to frame what I wanted to say next.

'Your father told me some ex-colleague of Caspian's has been getting you het up.'

My head shot up. 'Dad told you?'

Why would he have mentioned Harry's claims to Sheila? Was he trying to warn her to be careful what she said to me? The thought popped into my head before I could stop it.

'He's concerned about you,' my aunt said with a soft smile. 'He knows we speak ...'

'Right.' I pressed my lips together, feeling unsettled.

'He said you'd heard rumours about an extreme anti-abortion group, about him being involved.' Sheila sighed. 'Maybe you've forgotten, dear, but your father resigned from *Shield*, which is a *moderate* pro-life—'

'I know he resigned from *Shield*,' I interrupted, irritated by her patronising tone. 'Theoretically it's possible that he decided to leave a moderate group because his views got *more* violent, not less.' My voice rose, the words tumbling out of me. 'Theoretically he could have wanted to start a secret murderous crusade against people who carry out abortions. Including my husband.'

My cheeks burned. Where on earth had all that anger come from? Sheila's mouth gaped.

'I'm sorry,' I said. 'I didn't mean to shout. Or say those things about Dad. It just ... what Harry told me really upset me.'

'I know, dear. Er, I need to baste.' Looking flustered, Sheila rose from the table and opened her oven. As she prodded the lamb joint inside I wondered who she was cooking for. That leg of meat was surely too big for one person.

'Francesca, I've known your father a long time,' she said. 'I met him the first time your Uncle Graham took me home, forty years ago. Jayson was in his early twenties then and I can assure you that in all the time since I have never seen him commit or advocate a single act of violence.' She paused. 'In fact the only time I ever saw him really angry was over that business with Lucy. That did change him, but not in the way your Harry person is suggesting.'

'You don't need to remind me,' I said. 'He was furious with me for going behind his back and organising the termination, remember?'

'Not really, dear.' Sheila shut the oven door and came back to the table. 'He was mostly angry with the reporter who wrote the story. And with himself. He thought it was his fault ... both the abortion and the fact you kept it from him. He felt he should have been stricter over everything that had gone before, you know: what you wore, how you behaved when you went out ...'

'Seriously?' I snapped. 'Because I don't see how he could have been any bloody stricter.'

Sheila shrank back in her seat.

Shit.

'Sorry.' I took a deep breath. 'But I honestly don't think Lucy ended up getting pregnant because Dad wasn't strict enough. If anything it was the opposite. He made it impossible to be normal, forcing us either to rebel or repress ourselves.'

'No, dear.' Sheila looked scandalised. 'I'm sure that's not right.'

'It *is*,' I insisted. How on earth had we got on to this? I'd come here to talk through the emotional trauma of the past few days and instead I was arguing over ancient history. 'Lucy's problem was that she wasn't worldly enough. Too trusting. That was Dad's fault.'

'Am I interrupting?' said a caustic male voice from the doorway.

I tensed as Uncle Graham walked into the kitchen. What was he doing here? Dex's dad was – had always been – the black sheep of the family. Unlike my father, who used his inheritance to build a successful business empire, Graham had gambled and drunk his money away. Even though he was bankrupt, alcoholic and violent, I'm not sure Sheila would have ever left him but after the third or fourth time he beat her Dad and Uncle Perry took matters into their own hands. They insisted Uncle Graham moved out and got treatment for his alcoholism. Graham, unreasonably affronted by this, chose to leave London entirely. He didn't see his family for several years, a devastating shock for Dex and a source of deep, unleavened shame for Sheila who – Mum used to say with great sorrow – never really recovered.

He had been a volatile occasional presence in our lives ever since. I hadn't seen him myself since Mum's funeral. He was rude to Dad at the wake, which had been the last straw as far as Dad and Uncle Perry were concerned. I was fairly certain they hadn't had any kind of meaningful contact since. Dex, I knew, had only seen his father a couple of times since Graham went bankrupt for the second time eighteen months ago.

'Hi,' I said, feeling desperately uncomfortable.

Graham scowled at me from the kitchen doorway. Had he just let himself in? What the hell was he doing with a key? Sheila scurried over to the oven, her face bright red.

'I wasn't expecting you so early ...' She opened the oven door and prodded aimlessly at the leg of lamb again. Was she having dinner with her ex-husband? Did Dex know they were in touch?

Graham shrugged. He was still glaring at me, swaying slightly. With a sinking heart I realised he was drunk. Sheila had told me a few months ago that she'd heard he was in recovery, though Dex expressed doubt it was true. 'Last two times I took the kids round he was in the pub across the road,' he'd said with a snarl. 'Selfish bastard.'

'I heard you mention your father,' Graham said. 'Whatever you think he's done, I'd be pretty sure it's something worse. My little brother's a fucking hypocrite.'

'Oh, Graham,' Sheila protested.

I stood up. 'I should go,' I said. I was used to my uncle's resentment towards Dad. There was no point arguing with him, he never listened to anything logical, especially when he'd been drinking.

'But you only just got here,' Sheila protested.

'Don't worry, I won't take it personally.' Graham offered up a mirthless chuckle.

I kept my gaze on Sheila's face. 'I need to get to the shops.' Lame, even to my ears, but I didn't care. I just wanted to get away. I scuttled to the door, wishing I hadn't come.

An hour later, back at home with both kids, I braced myself for another round of temper tantrums when I called them for tea, but in fact neither child made a fuss. Ruby bounded in from the garden to eat, then disappeared upstairs to read one of her many football-related stories. Rufus was quiet throughout the meal, toying with his food again and staying at the kitchen table long after Ruby had rushed away.

'Everything all right, Ruf?' I asked.

My son looked at me with a solemn expression. 'I'm looking after you now, Mum,' he said firmly. 'You don't need to worry.'

Tears pricked at my eyes. Had he sensed my anxieties over the past few days? My first impulse was to tell him I wasn't worried about anything, but my psychology degree had taught me denying a true emotion was never a good idea.

'Thank you,' I said. 'And I'll look after you too.' I hesitated. 'It's all going to be all right, you know?'

Rufus met my gaze. 'You don't know that,' he said, sounding more like thirty than thirteen. 'Nobody does.'

He sloped off to his room and I put the kettle on, feeling both touched and troubled. As it came to the boil my cousin rang.

'Hey, Dumpy!' Dex's cheery voice brought a smile to my lips. 'Mum told me you came round earlier and that you were upset. What's up?'

'Your dad was there for dinner,' I explained, unsure how to broach my fears about my own father. 'I'm worried for Sheila.'

'I know.' Dex groaned. 'I think she's seen him a few times, but there's nothing I can do. Dad hasn't actually been violent since they split up and Mum still holds an effing candle for him.'

'Nightmare,' I said sympathetically.

'So what were you upset about?' Dex persisted.

I told him.

And once I started, I couldn't stop. I told him

everything. In typical Dex fashion he took it all in his stride. But as I repeated what Harry and I had discovered, I found myself getting churned up again.

'And now I just don't know what really happened to Caspian and it's got all muddled because of Harry and ... and Dad ...' Tears bubbled up into my eyes.

'Whoa, calm down there, Dumpy,' Dex said, his voice warm and gently mocking. In spite of my upset I grinned. I should have talked to my cousin in the first place. Dex always knew how to make everything seem lighter, more bearable. 'For what it's worth, I can't believe your dad would ever sanction anything violent. He's worth ten of mine, the useless drunken bastard.' He paused. 'Anyway, never mind *my* loser of a father, let's go back to how Uncle Jayson is a terrorist leader.' He laughed.

'I know that part of it's stupid but ... but I still think it's possible this organisation, PAAUL, killed Caspian and—'

'So? Even if they did, it won't bring him back,' Dex said with characteristic bluntness. 'I'm sorry, but there's no point torturing yourself over it. What about Harry? How d'you feel about him?'

'I ... I don't know ... I guess I like him ...'

'That's what I thought.' Dex gave a knowing sniff. 'I reckon he's only pushing all this stuff about PAAUL to get inside your pants. D'you want him there?'

'Jesus, Dex.'

Dex laughed again. He had always been my go-to guy for advice on boyfriends, right up to the moment I met Caspian and knew, from our first conversation, that he was perfect for me: steady, loyal but quiet and unchallenging. 'All the best bits of your dad without any of the alpha male dramatics,' as Dex had commented at the time.

'Do you think it's too soon, after Caspian?' I asked.

'It's been over a year.' Dex paused. 'Hey, maybe we should do a double date or something?'

I frowned. 'That kind of adds to the pressure.'

'Okay then, well, how about drinks on Friday? I'm meeting some friends in Revelations. Bring Harry along. Lucy and Ayesha too if you like.' He winked. 'If he can cope with all that, maybe he'll be able to handle you. And don't worry about your dad. Or PILL or POLL, or whatever it's called.'

'PAAUL,' I said.

'Whatever. I'm sure there's nothing in it.'

'Okay,' I said.

There was a pause, then Dex chuckled to himself. 'So bring Harry on Friday and ... top tip, Dumpy. Don't be yourself, you'll scare him off.'

'Cheers,' I chuckled back. 'And by the way, screw you.'

The following day I headed to the office, though it was hard to keep my mind on my work. Harry called mid-morning to say he would be back from visiting his family in Manchester on Friday afternoon. To my relief he didn't mention Dad or PAAUL, just said that he'd like to see me, that we should talk. He agreed readily to the drinks Dex had lined up for Friday evening.

I checked in with Ayesha, who was all up for a night out, then called Lucy. She had just been to one of her prayer groups and agreed to a quick lunch in a local café. We settled ourselves into a corner table. I ordered a cappuccino and a salad, while Lucy sipped at her customary peppermint tea.

'I guess I could come out for a bit on Friday night,' Lucy said, with a frown. 'It's nice Dex thought of me. Just let me know where and when.'

'You sound worried,' I said.

'What would I be worried about?' Lucy rolled her eyes. 'Course I'm not worried.'

I didn't believe her. Lucy had always been a lousy liar. One time, when she was sixteen or so and I was home from uni for a few nights, she stole a favourite top and some high-heeled shoes of mine – things Dad had made it clear he hated. I was convinced she'd taken them to stop me wearing them and prompting yet another argument – especially when the items reappeared in my wardrobe the following day. Lucy denied the whole thing, of course, but unlike Mum, who insisted I must have simply mislaid the clothes, I wasn't for a second convinced by Lucy's tearful howls of protested innocence.

'You just seem a bit apprehensive. Is it going to a bar full of heathens you're worried about?' I persisted. 'Or is it that you don't like the sound of Harry?'

'For goodness' sake, Francesca, I'm not worried. Stop being such a therapist.'

'I'm *not*.'

'You're analysing me and I don't like it.' Lucy scowled.

This was a source of conflict between us that dated back to my psychology degree, one that Mum always used to somehow smooth over, telling Lucy to make allowance for my desire to rationalise and explain and me to respect her faith.

'I'm sorry,' I muttered.

Lucy sighed. 'I didn't mean to snap. It's just . . .' She hesitated. 'I actually met Harry before you did, at the memorial service. He asked me to point you out, said he'd met Caspian briefly. I . . . I didn't realise you'd been . . . seeing him.'

'Oh,' I said, taken aback. 'Well, it's very early days, we haven't been on a date yet or—'

'Right.' Lucy looked away.

What wasn't she telling me? I'd been very careful not to mention my suspicions about PAAUL's possible role in Caspian's death so there was no way she could know the turmoil that Harry had brought into my life.

'Lucy?'

'It's just I liked him, okay?' Lucy turned to face me, her cheeks flushing. 'I only spoke to him for a minute but he seemed nice and . . . really handsome. He was taller than me, too, which doesn't happen every day eith— Oh, for goodness' sake.' She curled her lip as I tried in vain to suppress the giggles that burbled up inside my throat.

'I'm sorry,' I gasped, now feeling guilty. 'I didn't realise.'

Lucy shrugged, sinking back into her seat. I took a swig of my coffee, now feeling mildly irritated. This was so typical. Lucy had shied away from men all her adult life. It was understandable, I guess, after the horrible way she got pregnant at fifteen – an older man plying her with drink in some hotel bar then taking her up to his room. She always said she'd lied about her age, pretending to be eighteen, and had agreed to the sex – but it was still rape as far as I was concerned. The pregnancy led to the abortion which led in turn to her deep regret for, as she saw it, killing her baby. In my darker moments I suspected that at some level she had never forgiven me for organising her termination and then going on later to have two kids of my own. Lucy had never taken the risk of being in a proper relationship but I had. I'd fallen in love with Caspian and he'd been ripped away from me and our children. And now, just as I was starting to think about opening myself up to someone new, here was Lucy raining on my parade.

'No one on the horizon for you then?' I asked with a smile.

'No way. Harry's the only guy I've seen in the last year that I've even fancied.'

This news slapped the smile off my face. 'Shit, Lucy.' My mind filled again with guilt. Should I back off Harry? Lucy so rarely expressed any interest in men. Except Harry approached me and started a conversation with me and appeared to be interested in me.

I let my breath out in a sigh. Whatever I did or didn't

do now, surely I didn't have anything to be guilty about?

'Don't make it a big deal,' Lucy said irritably. 'He's probably not even Catholic.'

I frowned. Was I making it a big deal? Surely all I was doing here was responding in a very natural way to my sister telling me she was interested in a man I had made it clear I liked. Lucy hadn't needed to do that. She could have just kept her mouth shut.

I sipped at my coffee, remembering Mum's counsel: 'Your sister finds it hard to express her vulnerabilities, so sometimes her sadness comes out sideways and makes it seem like she's being selfish or pushing others away, but it's the very people who behave like that who most need our compassion.'

'So you don't mind me being a bit interested in this guy?' I asked tentatively. 'And you don't mind coming along when he'll be there on Friday night?'

'No, I'll come,' Lucy said. She offered me a shy smile. 'Just remember, Francesca, it's not *that* long since Caspian. You're more vulnerable than you think.'

This last sentence stayed with me long after we'd parted and gone home. Dad had said much the same thing. Maybe he and Lucy were right. Just because I was attracted to Harry didn't mean I was ready to stop mourning my husband. Late that night, after the children were both in bed, I found myself in front of Caspian's laptop for the first time in over a year. When he died in such a sudden, shocking way, I had put his computer away. It was just too painful to look at. Now

I scoured everything I could find: documents, pictures, files and folders of all kinds. I had no idea what I was looking for now – though at the back of my mind I wondered if I might find a reference to the threats he'd told Harry about. I got sidetracked for at least an hour poring over his music – our tastes had never been in sync. I even checked over his emails, something I would never have dreamed of doing while he was alive. There wasn't much work stuff on the laptop – all that was on his PC at the hospital – but lots of the department secretaries' emails were copied to both his professional and personal addresses.

I searched for the details about the Paris conference from the week before he died and soon found the email he'd been sent. The delegate list was attached. I'd looked at it once before, in the first throes of my grief, staring at Caspian's name as if it would somehow bring him back to me. Now it occurred to me – with a tiny thrill of pleasure – that I would find Harry's name here. I searched the list, looking under both 'general' and 'pharmaceutical'. But Harry's name failed to appear. I looked for his company, Devora Pharmaceuticals. It was represented at the conference, but not by a Harry Dunbar.

I sat back. What the hell did that mean?

7

Revelations was a strange choice of bar, I thought. Dex loved the place, with its wrought-iron furniture and pseudo-religious erotic iconography dotted around the walls. To me it seemed both over-ornate and trying too hard to be shocking. Not that I really cared where we met. What mattered was trying to put everything about PAAUL and Dad and Caspian's death out of my mind and seeing if Harry and I had any kind of potential future.

I wandered over to the bar, my eyes flitting over the smattering of customers to see if anyone else was here yet. Maybe Dex was right about Harry liking me – it certainly explained why he'd tried to help me investigate PAAUL. But I was still wary. I hadn't seen myself as a sexual being for such a long time it was hard to believe anyone else might. Plus I needed to know why Harry's name hadn't been on that list of conference delegates. And I also had to factor in Lucy's interest in him. I sighed. Dex would say I was getting ahead of myself, overthinking it. But it was hard to know what to do.

I vaguely recognised a few of Dex's friends across the room but neither Harry nor my sister and Ayesha were here yet and I decided to stay by the bar until they arrived. Dex himself wasn't present either but then Dex was habitually late for everything. As I ordered a white wine spritzer my phone beeped with a text from Lucy explaining she was running late. Ayesha, I knew, was still on her way from work. I settled into the nearest booth and sipped at my drink. Madonna's 'Papa Don't Preach' gave way to Bruce Springsteen's 'Hungry Heart' in the background. They were weird choices for such a trendy bar, weren't they? Or had we stumbled across an eighties night?

'Hello.' Harry appeared at the end of the booth, eyes twinkling, a bottle of beer in his hand. He was underdressed for the bar, in jeans and a faded blue T-shirt, but the clothes looked perfect on him.

'Hi,' I said, my throat tightening. I gestured to the seat opposite and Harry slid into it.

'How've you been?' I asked.

'Hard at work,' Harry said.

'At Devora Pharmaceuticals?' I realised my fingers were digging into my palms and released them. 'They let you wear jeans?'

'Dress-down Friday.' Harry smiled, but there was something guarded in his expression. I hesitated a fraction, then ploughed on.

'You don't act like a sales rep.'

'How so?'

'You don't seem ... I dunno ... slick enough.'

Harry laughed.

I frowned. 'Slick' wasn't exactly what I'd meant, but I

111

couldn't put my finger on what that was. There was an air of adventure about him, a recklessness. Which meant what? A sense of foreboding shivered through me.

'Not slick is good, no?' he asked.

I shrugged. What was the matter with me? I should just come straight out and ask him.

'I ... I was going through Caspian's things and I found the programme from the conference you were both at.' I looked straight into Harry's dark-brown eyes. 'Your name isn't on the list of delegates.'

'I know,' he said, without missing a beat. He rolled his eyes. 'Conference admin cocked up. They were very apologetic.'

We looked at each other as the music swirled around us. Another track came on, a tune I'd heard on the radio recently but couldn't name. Was Harry telling the truth? He had answered me fast. Which surely meant he hadn't had time to make up an answer.

Unless he'd already prepared one.

No, that was taking me to insane levels of paranoia. I gave myself a shake. I had to stop seeing subterfuge and lies at every turn.

'What's this about?' Harry asked. 'I understand you're on edge because of what we found, but ... don't you trust me?'

'It's hard to trust anyone, not in a world where people get taken away from you in the blink of an eye.' I looked down. For goodness' sake. I sounded hysterical, more like Lucy than myself.

There was a long pause, then Harry reached for my

hand. 'Hey,' he said. 'I'll tell you whatever you want.'

His fingers felt warm on mine.

'Just tell me the truth,' I said.

'Okay.' Harry didn't take his eyes off me. 'This means something ... being here with you.'

My heart bumped in my chest.

'And maybe there are things ...' He hesitated. 'Things I haven't said but I want you to know that—'

'Hey, guys!' Ayesha loomed over us. I snatched my hand away from Harry's but I could see from the look in her eye that Ayesha had clocked our linked fingers. 'Having fun?' She grinned, sliding into the booth beside me. She was dressed in a silky red dress and high heels, a slash of scarlet on her lips.

'Where's Lucy?' I asked, hoping the dim lighting was concealing my blush. A new song rang out. This one was a Hozier track. I knew it because Rufus played it constantly.

'Bar.' Ayesha's gaze flickered sideways to where Lucy was drifting across the half-empty room towards us, an ice bucket containing a bottle of white wine in her hand. A young waiter followed behind with a tray of glasses.

My sister was dressed, as usual, in white. Her dress was made from a soft fabric, similar to Ayesha's, that clung to her, floating around her as she walked. The effect, however, was very different. Next to Ayesha with her sexy curves, Lucy looked positively angelic – far younger than her years. As she set down the ice bucket she shot a shy glance at Harry, looking up at him coyly through her eyelashes.

I remembered what she'd told me about fancying him and felt both guilty and annoyed. Had she seen us holding hands? Should I care if she had?

'Franny?'

I realised Ayesha was speaking and turned my head.

'How's work?' she asked.

'Fine,' I said absently. God, it was too much: my worries about Dad and PAAUL had given me enough grief this week without all the additional turmoil over whether or not I should get together with Harry. Surely, if it was the right thing it would feel simpler. I glanced up. Harry was still looking at me, an infuriatingly sexy and mischievous smile in his eyes. Desire surged through me.

And hope. Maybe everything was going to be all right? Dad was innocent, I was sure of that. And Dex was right that knowing who killed Caspian wouldn't bring him back.

If Harry liked me, I should give him a chance. Lucy would surely understand.

'How 'bout you, Harry?' Ayesha went on.

'I'd rather hear about Fran's work,' he said, raising his eyebrows as he gazed at me. 'I realised earlier I don't really know what you do.'

'I work in event management,' I said.

'She's basically a fundraiser,' Ayesha added. 'Ace at getting money and promises out of people.'

'I'm sure she is.' Harry smiled. 'What kind of projects d'you work on, Fran?'

'It's all business to business: conferences, product

launches, award ceremonies.' I shrugged. Work was the last thing I wanted to talk about, I'd certainly paid very little attention to the project I was supposed to be progressing this week; distracted when working from home on Tuesday, then coasting through a series of meetings in the office today and yesterday.

'How did you get into that?' Harry went on.

'After Mum died I thought about being a therapist for a while. Even started a course in bereavement counselling – my degree's in psychology so I was always interested, but it wasn't for me.'

'Mmn, I guess bereavement counsellor might be a bit of a downer at parties,' Harry said. 'People telling you about their losses over the canapés.'

Ayesha laughed then turned to help Lucy with the wine.

'You're probably right.' I smiled at Harry. 'Like being a doctor and hearing how the man with BO who you've just met has a rash.'

'Or an estate agent and hearing from the attractive woman in the low-cut top that she has a house wanting a valuation.'

'Actually that sounds like it might work. For the estate agent, I mean.'

Harry laughed. 'Well, don't worry,' he said. 'I haven't been bereaved. Ever. Unless you count a couple of hamsters when I was a kid.'

'Both parents still living, then?' I asked lightly.

'Sure. Well, my mum is. I don't know about my dad, he legged it when I was six, haven't seen him since.'

'Wow,' I said. 'Tough.'

'I don't really think about him to be honest. Not any more,' Harry said. 'I think my sister got the worst of it ...' He sighed. 'She's had one bad relationship after another.' He lowered his voice. 'In fact Mum and I think she's depressed. That's why I spent the past few days there. She's really down. Didn't want me to go, but there's only so much compassionate leave I can take.' He cleared his throat. 'To be honest with you, I called earlier to check on her and I'm a bit worried that she hasn't rung back yet.'

'I'm sorry.' At the other end of the booth Lucy was deep in conversation with Ayesha. The music surely made it impossible for them to hear what we were saying, but even so I lowered my voice. 'I worry about *my* sister sometimes, she's so ... so other-worldly and ...' I stopped, feeling disloyal.

'She's the black sheep of the family, yeah?' Harry gave a rueful smile. 'I can relate to that.'

'Actually I've always thought *I'm* more the black sheep in my family,' I said. 'Apart from my Uncle Graham, who's estranged from almost everyone. The rest of them are these diehard Catholics. Well, not my cousin Dex, but he gets on with everyone anyway. Whatever, if you'd known me as a teenager you'd definitely have seen me as the outsider.'

Harry's dark eyes twinkled. 'Maybe *everybody* thinks they're the black sheep. Maybe—'

Ayesha's squeal cut through our conversation. I turned to see Dex himself at the end of the booth wearing a stylish, slim-fitting suit and a big grin. Lucy, as ever, hung back shyly while Ayesha gave Dex a massive hug. I scrambled out of the booth feeling awkward. Harry was really opening up to me. And I liked it. I glanced at Lucy. She was still standing back, head hung. She looked miserable. My heart sank. Was that because of Harry?

'More drinks, ladies?' Dex asked.

Lucy pointed to the bottle of wine, still half full, in the middle of the table.

'Oh, we can always do with more,' I said. 'I'll come with you to the bar.' I took his elbow and led him across the room. I was intending to ask him how to handle Lucy's interest in Harry; Dex was good at things like that – he certainly had plenty of practice at dealing with lovesick admirers. But as soon as we reached the bar Dex was surrounded by three of his workmates and shooed me back to Harry with a tsk.

Feeling troubled, I returned to the booth where Lucy was still sitting with her head bowed as Ayesha and Harry chattered together.

Ayesha was laughing, teeth gleaming against the scarlet lipstick. That dress was perfect for her. She had a great trick of never revealing too much flesh, but always looking sexy as hell. A flash of jealousy roiled through me, hot and hurtful. I told myself not to be ridiculous.

'So, Manchester?' Ayesha asked.

'Yeah, that's right,' Harry said.

'City or United?'

'City,' Harry said. 'Though I don't get to many matches these days.'

'Oh, that's a shame,' Lucy said, too intently.

The others looked at her.

'London has compensations,' Harry said with a twinkle, glancing up at me.

Lucy blushed. I sipped at my wine, waiting for Dex to join us. He would understand. He would help me.

A few minutes later and Dex flopped into the booth beside Ayesha. He said something about the bar and the conversation shifted to the painted icon opposite of a heavily made-up Virgin Mary cradling a bottle of vodka.

'Actually I think it's blasphemous,' Lucy said softly.

An uneasy silence descended on the table. Around us glass tinkled, voices chattered and music thundered. Ayesha rolled her eyes at Lucy, who reddened and hurried off to the loo.

'Got the kids this weekend?' I asked Dex, mostly to change the subject.

'Nope,' Dex said. 'And I can't stay long 'cos I'm on a promise with the blonde bob over there. The one with the legs.' He jerked his head in the direction of a pretty woman at the bar. She was wearing an extremely short skirt and thigh-high boots.

'She looks like Marla,' Ayesha said.

'That's Dex's ex-wife,' I explained to Harry. 'She's a model.'

'*Was* a model,' Ayesha corrected. 'She's a stay-at-home mum now.'

'She's a black bloody hole sucking all creative and meaningful life out of the universe,' Dex said with a snarl. 'Still arguing over maintenance payments even though we agreed the court order over a year ago.'

Harry raised his eyebrows. 'How did you meet a model?' he asked.

'She was on an early morning beach shoot in Sydney. I happened to be walking past on my way home from a club.' Dex gave a lascivious smile. 'I was travelling in Australia. You know how it is. All that free time when you're a student.'

'Not really.' Harry grinned. 'I worked on a building site the whole time I was at college.'

I suppressed a giggle. Most men were a little intimidated by Dex with his expensive suits and breezy self-assurance, but Harry didn't seem fazed at all.

'Whatever.' Dex shrugged. 'Looking back, I'm certain Marla only wanted me for the visa. But at the time I was young and naïve ...'

Ayesha snorted.

'Really?' I laughed. 'Was this before or after your "I only sleep with married women" phase?'

'Dex is a commitment-phobe,' Ayesha added.

'What?' Dex widened his eyes in mock protest. 'I got married, didn't I? I stuck it out for years, the whole thing: nappies, listening, fidelity.'

'Yeah, right.' Ayesha rolled her eyes.

'Give us a break, Dex,' I said. 'You hated changing nappies, complained constantly that Marla moaned all the time and you stuck at the fidelity thing for about five minutes.'

Ayesha roared with laughter and high-fived me.

Grinning, I looked across the bar. There was no sign of Lucy. She must still be in the ladies. I felt a pang of concern. Was she all right?

'At least I did kids the conventional way,' Dex countered. 'Not like single mum over there . . .' He pointed at Ayesha, then turned to me, '. . . and shotgun wedding over here.'

'You got married 'cos you fell pregnant?' Harry asked me. 'How old-fashioned.'

'It wasn't really like that,' I said, feeling awkward. 'We were already engaged.'

I hadn't been sure how I felt about falling pregnant at the time – I hadn't envisaged having a baby that young – but within a few weeks it seemed like it was meant to be. Caspian had seemed the perfect choice to be a father: loyal and steady. Everyone said he'd be a great dad. Everybody liked him. That is, nobody *disliked* him, though Dex and he didn't really have much in common. In fact I saw very little of my cousin for the next few years. We reconnected when his younger child was born, when his own marriage was already in difficulties.

'See you guys later.' With a wink, Dex wandered back to his friends. Ayesha headed to the ladies, from where Lucy still hadn't returned, and Harry and I were alone again.

'I've been thinking about Simon Pinner's death,' Harry said, leaning forward and lowering his voice. 'It's got to be another PAAUL assassination. It's surely too much of a coincidence otherwise, after your Caspian dying in such a similar way.'

I stared at him, surprised by the sudden change of conversational tack.

'That's what I told the police,' I said. 'But they weren't interested.'

'Right.' Harry hesitated. 'Fran, there's something I need to tell you.'

'Okay.' I swigged my drink, feeling emboldened. 'Spill.'

Harry hesitated again. Across the room Dex had his arms around the leggy blonde. They were swaying in time to the music, their eyes locked. Dex was smiling, clearly enjoying the way her hips were moving under his hands. I looked away, wondering again what Dex had that made him so successful with women. I had never been jealous of anyone he'd hooked up with – Dex was like a brother to me and I had never thought of him in that way – but sometimes I felt envious of the ease with which he picked up women.

I turned back to Harry. He was watching me and, as our eyes met, I felt a pulse of electricity thrill through me.

What was I waiting for? I took a deep breath.

'This thing you've got to tell me?' I asked. 'Could you tell me at my home?'

Harry stared at me, and I watched, suddenly full of confidence, as the realisation of what I was suggesting dawned in his eyes and a slow smile spread across his lips. I sipped at my drink, enjoying the thrill of my own impulsiveness. It had been a long time since I'd done anything remotely spontaneous. Caspian liked to plan everything in advance, from holidays to shopping trips, and since he'd died I'd tried hard to give the kids what everyone seemed to think they most needed: steadiness and routine. As for sex . . . I could barely remember the last time.

Oh, God. I was going to have to be naked in front of Harry. I looked up, suddenly gripped by anxiety.

'Of course,' I started, 'if you don't want—'

'I do,' he said. And there was such warmth and strength in his voice that my anxiety vanished.

A moment later Ayesha's high-pitched giggle announced her arrival back at the booth. Lucy was with her, smiling gently as Ayesha gabbled away, full of some incident they'd just witnessed in the ladies. Lucy seemed fine. Feeling reassured and wanting to make a move before they had a chance to sit down, I set my glass on the table and stood. 'I think I'll be off,' I said, edging out of the booth.

Ayesha stopped talking. She and Lucy stared at me.

'Me too, I have mountains of work,' Harry said, following me out of the booth. 'Tricky client. Needs a lot of stroking.'

Ayesha's jaw hung open.

'Brilliant evening,' I said, hugging her. 'But I promised the babysitter I wouldn't be late.'

'I'll see you out,' Harry said.

I turned away to kiss Lucy on the cheek. Unlike Ayesha, who looked openly shocked, Lucy had covered her initial confusion with a smile, though she didn't meet my eyes.

I waved at Dex as Harry and I passed the bar. He winked at me, then turned back to his blonde.

I started to feel nervous again as Harry hailed a cab. He talked about his sister as the taxi drove us to Southfields, how concerned he was that she hadn't answered when he'd called earlier, how he didn't want to miss her if she rang back.

He only fell silent when we reached my house. I dealt with the sitter, then offered him a drink. Butterflies zoomed around my stomach as I gave him a glass of wine and went up to check on the kids. They were both fast asleep: Ruby curled tightly into a ball in her bed, Rufus flat on his back, making soft snuffling noises like a small animal. I drew the covers over his shoulders. He looked so young still when he was asleep, so innocent. Like the small boy he had been until very recently.

I came downstairs. It wasn't too late to tell Harry I wasn't ready to sleep with him, that perhaps we should go on a proper date, just the two of us, first. Hopefully I wouldn't need to spell it out. If I held myself back, maybe he'd get the hint, finish his drink and leave.

It was past eleven as I walked back into the kitchen. Harry was standing in front of the sink, his drink on the counter beside him, untouched. His eyes gleamed – all dark heat under the dimmed lights.

'Don't you want your wine?' I asked. My throat felt dry.

'I want you.' He said it in the same straightforward way that, I realised, he said everything.

'I'm scared.' The truth slipped out of me without warning. I felt myself blushing and looked down.

'Me too.' He said it so simply that my breath caught in my throat.

And I knew then without a doubt that I wanted him to stay.

Afterwards I couldn't work out if it had been good because it was us or because it had been such a long time since anyone had touched and held me. I hadn't been with anyone except Caspian since my early twenties and, though I felt guilty for thinking it, my sex life with him had always been a bit dull, even at the start.

What I didn't feel guilty about, much to my surprise, was sleeping with Harry in the bed I'd once shared with my husband. Strangely, that felt like the most natural thing in the world. I curled up in his arms, enjoying the sensation of his skin on mine, and we spoke softly of our families. Harry stroked my hair as I told him how much I missed Mum and how ill-prepared I was for Caspian to die so suddenly just three years after I lost her. Harry, in turn, spoke of his own mother's cancer and how he and his sister had been devastated by the possibility she might die.

'Mum's in remission now,' he said. 'But the doctors made it clear the cancer could come back. I think my sister finds it really hard. I mean, we both do, but my sister leans on Mum a lot because of the kids.'

'It's the uncertainty,' I said softly. 'The loss of control. Particularly hard when there's only one parent left.'

I tried to imagine life without my own father. He

had dominated my childhood – his brooding presence changing the atmosphere at home every time he walked through the front door. We'd moved to the house in Kensington when I was just twelve and Lucy six and a half. I had few proper memories of our life before then. I knew that Dad had made a lot of money, allowing for the purchase of the house and private school for me and Lucy plus the swimming pool and music lessons and all the other upper-middle-class trappings we enjoyed. But he was also strict – insistent that we remember our good fortune did not make us better than anyone else and putting a premium on good manners, modest dress and decorous behaviour at all times.

'I was such a rebel,' I told Harry, smiling to myself as I remembered the endless round of teenage arguments with Dad over music and make-up and clothes, with Mum always trying to negotiate a peace between us. At the time I was trying hard to be as different from my father as possible. Now I could see that his existence defined mine. 'At least with Dad I knew where I stood. He was always rigid in his morals.' I glanced at Harry, his suspicions about my dad and PAAUL flitting into my head. 'I know you think differently, but—'

'Wait, Fran,' Harry said, disentangling himself and sitting up in the bed. 'There's something I need to tell you before we talk any more about that. Remember? I mentioned it at the bar?'

I nodded. 'Go on.'

Harry hesitated. He reached for his boxers and put them on.

I watched, confused. 'Are you going somewhere?'

'Just to the bog, though maybe I should leave before morning. I don't want to confuse your kids.'

'Was that what you wanted to talk about?' I asked, feeling more and more bemused. 'The kids?'

'No.' Harry made a face. 'I'll be back in a sec, then I promise I'll explain.' He disappeared into the en suite and I had a sudden flashback to Caspian doing the same thing, every morning, for a shower and a shave. Again I felt no guilt whatsoever. Which was surely a good sign – a good omen.

Grinning to myself, I lay back against the pillows, wondering idly what Harry wanted to talk about. The sound of his phone softly ringing drifted up from the floor by the bed. It was coming from his jeans pocket. I glanced at the bathroom door. It was shut, the water running from the sink tap clearly drowning out the ringtone. I reached down and drew the mobile out of the pocket. The screen said:

Alexandra calling.

Was that Harry's sister? He hadn't, I realised, told me her name.

I stared at the phone as it rang a third time. He'd said he was expecting her to call him back and I'd got the impression she would be upset if he didn't answer. Perhaps I should take the call, then ask her to hold while I fetched him.

Without thinking about it any further I swiped the screen and put the phone to my ear.

'Hello?'

126

'Where's Harry?' a taut female voice snapped. She sounded posh and totally in control of herself. Not a trace of anxiety or indeed a Manchester accent like his.

'Hi there,' I stammered, feeling self-conscious, already sure this wasn't his sister. 'Harry's in the bathroom, he'll be out in a second.'

Silence on the end of the line.

Shit. It hit me like a slap.

He *was* married after all, in spite of what he'd told me.

This was his wife. Had to be.

Shit, shit, shit.

'Er, may I say who's calling?' I stammered.

Still silence. It was definitely a wife. Or at the very least a girlfriend. And then the woman spoke and my world turned upside down.

'Tell Harry it's his bloody news editor asking: where's my effing story on Jayson Carr?'

CIPHER

Friday 15 January 2016–
Sunday 17 January 2016

HARRY

Harry was having a great time at the bar until Dex turned up. Not only was he enjoying his three extremely attractive drinking companions; each of them appeared to be enjoying him too: Ayesha was hot and mildly flirtatious while Lucy was coy but clearly interested ... if things had been different who knows what might have happened. Not that Harry was bothered about either Lucy or Ayesha. Still, it was flattering to feel them watching him, knowing he could go there if he wanted.

Of course, above and beyond all that, there was Fran: hot and beautiful and with the sexiest smile he'd ever seen.

She was the reason he was here.

She was the reason he was feeling so nervous.

And she was the reason he was going to blow open his cover story.

He was just waiting for the right moment but it was hard. Talking with Fran was great. And easy. And fun. All of which the truth would change – at least temporarily. Still. It had to be done ... every time he mentioned any aspect of his Harry Dunbar legend to her he felt horribly uncomfortable in the lie. Which had never, ever happened to him before.

It was as if he had known her for ages, like he could look into those almond-shaped eyes of hers and see what she was feeling. The more they spoke, the less interest he felt in the other women. Ayesha became brash and obvious while Lucy looked more and more like the angel off his mum's Christmas tree: pretty but insipid.

Fran, on the other hand, seemed alight with life. She intrigued him. Wherever she was he wanted to look. Whatever she said he wanted to hear. Whenever she moved he wanted to follow. Harry had never met anyone – male or female – so effortlessly cool before.

But then, all of a sudden, bloody Dex was there, standing at the end of the booth with his slightly wild hair and piercing green eyes and his expensive suit with the sleeves hitched up just enough to reveal a tattoo of a yin-yang symbol on the inside of his forearm. Within seconds, all three of the women changed their behaviour, as if Dex was a sun that had pulled them out of Harry's orbit and into his own.

With Ayesha this meant she redirected her flirting. After an ear-splitting squeal she'd breathed a 'Hey you' at Dex, giving him a white-toothed smile then virtually batting her eyelids at him, glancing over even after he went to the bar and talking about him to Harry in breathless tones. 'Franny's cousin ... *such* a charmer ...'

The sisters' reactions to their cousin were just as strong as Ayesha's though not in any way sexual, at least as far as Harry could make out. Lucy just seemed shyer than before: sitting silently with her head bowed and definitely no longer hanging on Harry's every word.

But it was Fran whose reaction was strongest. She hurtled out of her seat to envelop Dex in an enormous hug, then dragged him off to the bar without a backward glance.

'Christ, but he's handsome,' Ayesha had said with a smile, watching Dex cross the room.

For God's sake, Harry growled silently. What was the man's bloody secret? He glanced over at the bar. Dex and Fran certainly looked good together. They had that upper-class secret of knowing how to wear clothes so they looked effortlessly thrown together. Fran was in an elegant green top and a black pencil skirt that curved tantalisingly over her hips. She leaned into Dex as they spoke, surrounded by a bunch of other equally beautiful people.

Harry frowned. The two of them were clearly close, but he wasn't getting the sense they were sexually interested in each other. Anyway, in Harry's experience, men who were keen to get a woman into bed didn't usually address them as 'Dumpy' in that brotherly teasing way Dex had. Still, he'd noticed Dex at that memorial service *and* the way women's heads turned as he walked past. Harry had never spoken to the man but he was certain he knew the type: privately educated and posh as a test cricketer's armpit but eager to give the impression that they were men of the people. On the surface they were all charm and politeness, but Dex must have seen Harry was at the table ... how much passive aggression had been in that 'Drinks, ladies?' and the fact that he hadn't even looked at Harry directly.

'Ooh, look!' Ayesha's attention had wandered from Dex and she was now pointing to the man in the booth across the room. 'Do you think that's a toupee?' she giggled.

'Definitely,' Harry said. But he was only pretending to look. He was still watching Fran, who was on her way back from the bar – without Dex – and with a deep frown across her forehead. Had Dex put that there? He looked like he didn't have a care in the world: surrounded at the bar by beautiful women, laughing and chatting. Harry felt a stab of jealousy as Fran returned to the table, clearly preoccupied.

Ayesha started talking about London versus Manchester as places to live. A minute later Dex rejoined them and the conversation shifted to the artwork in the bar, which Harry thought was okay but overdone. Then Lucy suddenly came out with the fact that she thought it was blasphemous, which put everyone on edge.

Harry felt lost. As Dex held court his resentment built. And then he looked across at Fran and saw she was looking at him and suddenly he knew what was really bothering him.

He couldn't lie to her any longer.

He built up to his revelation, his stomach twisting into knots.

'There's something I need to tell you,' he'd said at last. But then Fran had held him with those caramel eyes and invited him back to her house and there was no way Harry was going to turn that down. He would tell her *afterwards*.

And as he walked out of her bathroom several hours later he was, finally, ready.

Except by then, of course, it was too late.

Fran was holding up his phone, her face stricken.

'It's your news editor,' she breathed.

'Shit.' Harry could hear Alexandra Spencer's curt, upper-crust voice shrieking his name. He hurried to the duvet and took the mobile.

'Not now,' he growled into the phone, before switching it off, not caring that this was the kind of brush-off guaranteed to spin Spencer into a total fury.

He shoved the phone back into his jeans pocket, then hurriedly pulled his clothes on. The atmosphere in Fran's bedroom was taut with tension. Harry fixed his gaze on the soft grey blinds at the window, at a loss for what to say. The room was unfussy and elegant, much like Fran herself. Harry was overwhelmed by how much he liked her. And how comprehensively he had screwed things up.

Fran's mouth was open in shock. 'Who are you?' she asked.

'I was about to tell you,' he said, squirming inside. 'I've been meaning to tell you.'

Jesus, could he sound more pathetic?

Fran's eyes hardened.

'Tell me then,' she said.

'My real name is Harry Elliot and I'm a freelance reporter,' Harry confessed. 'I do a lot of stuff for the *Record* and ... and I've been investigating rumours about your father.'

Fran blinked. 'Rumours?'

'That he was head of PAAUL, that they were using his family home in Suffolk as a headquarters, that he'd sanctioned a new campaign of assassinations against individual doctors ... all the stuff I showed you on the dark net.'

Fran gasped. 'You *knew* about all that before you came to see me at the memorial?'

Harry nodded, a dull weight settling in his gut.

'So if you're not a sales rep, then you weren't at the Paris conference and you didn't talk to Caspian at the bar ...' Fran gulped. 'Did ... did you ever actually meet my husband?'

There was a long pause. Harry shook his head.

'And the threat he supposedly told you about ... that whole conversation between the two of you ... it was all a lie?'

'Yes.' Harry held his breath. Shame filled him, tightening his chest, flooding his face with heat. He sat down on Fran's bed. She got off it and backed away, across the room.

'Fran ...' he started.

'Bastard.'

'Fran, I know I made some things up but it was so you'd find things out more gradually, more gently,' he said quickly. 'If I'd come straight out and said I was a journalist who thought your dad was involved in your husband's death then you'd never have spoken to me.'

'That's not the point,' she snapped.

'At the time it was the only way,' Harry went on. He had the horrible sinking feeling that he was digging his way deeper and deeper into a hole, but he was desperate to make Fran understand. 'You know how your family hates journalists, your dad especially. He's famous for it.'

'Of course he is,' she snarled. 'When Lucy's abortion came out in the press it might have looked like a ... a passing "pop" of interest to you, but it was a massive bomb for my parents. And Lucy. And me. It *exploded* in our lives, changed *everything*.'

'I get that it's awful I lied,' Harry said, still intent on explaining. 'But you have to see that if I'd told you everything I knew straight off you'd have cut me off and warned your dad. You'd certainly never have taken me with you to the house in Suffolk. And we both know that all the evidence we found there, added to everything else, suggests I'm right.'

'I don't know that,' Fran snapped. Her breaths came out in angry heaves. 'All I know is that you've lied to me. That all your crap about being scared and how this – you and me – meant something ... you just said all that in order to fit in a quick shag before going back to—'

'No.' Harry's head spun. 'No, it wasn't like that. I like you. I was planning on telling you everything so that we could … I was *about* to tell you at the bar before … before …'

'Get out.'

'You mean far … far more to me than the story,' Harry persisted. 'I swear.'

'Get out!' Fran's voice rose. She reached behind her and picked up a stone Buddha that stood on the dressing table.

'I'm sorry,' Harry said, backing to the door.

Fran's mouth trembled as she raised her arm, ready to throw.

Feeling worse than he ever had in his life, Harry had no choice but to turn and leave.

Fran

I sank onto my bed as Harry's footsteps echoed down the stairs, across the hall and out of the house. Silence fell.

He had lied to me.

Lied and lied ... about meeting Caspian, about Caspian being threatened, about Dad ...

I put my head in my hands. I had been such an idiot, I'd actually led Harry to all those reports on PAAUL at Uncle Perry's house and he'd added to them with other bits and pieces of information, twisting everything we'd found to make Dad look guilty. It was all a set-up. Harry was a liar. He had used me to manipulate his way to a story on Dad. And then, to add insult to injury, he had tricked me into bed.

And I had *liked* him. *Really* liked him. It had been my first time with *anyone* since Caspian died. My first time with anyone *other* than Caspian since my early twenties. And it had been *so* good. Better than I ever remembered the sex being when I was married.

A wave of guilty misery washed over me. Sex with

Caspian might not have been very exciting, but at least Caspian had been reliable and dependable. He would never have lied to me like Harry had. I doubled over, sobbing into the duvet. The soft cotton felt cool against the heat of my face. I sat up, wiping my damp cheeks, as a furious anger grew inside me, dark and knotted in my stomach.

Harry had screwed me over in every conceivable way. Dad and Uncle Perry *had* simply been investigating PAAUL, just like they'd both said, and I'd doubted their word purely because Harry had put the poison of mistrust into my head. I gritted my teeth, twisting the duvet in my fist.

And then another, even more terrible thought struck me. I couldn't believe it hadn't occurred to me before: suppose Harry had already gathered enough material to write an article? He had said I meant more to him than the story, but suppose that had been yet another lie? He had clearly known all about PAAUL from the start. What if I had unwittingly supplied him with sufficient additional information for him to twist into a false story about Dad?

What if he was on the verge of making that story public?

Even if Dad denied it or sued for libel some of the mud thrown would stick. Poor Dad had already gone through the hell of Lucy's termination being exposed in the Catholic press almost eleven years ago. The scandal had nearly destroyed my family – and in that instance, the information made public had been true. I couldn't

140

allow a false story to destroy everything Dad had built up for himself in the decade since then. Especially when I'd inadvertently helped to create that false story.

My tears dried. My rage subsided. An idea began to form. I picked up my phone, clear-headed, determined and focused. Everything depended on what I did next.

The following morning – Saturday – I dropped Rufus at a friend's and Ruby at football club and drove into Kensington to Dad's house. He and Jacqueline were waiting for me. After their initial shock about Harry, they were as keen as I was to carry out the plan I'd suggested over the phone last night.

'We can't reason with him or trust him,' I'd explained, 'so we need to frighten him off his story – threaten him with lawyers if he goes ahead, that sort of thing.'

'Ready?' I asked, walking into the living room.

'Oh, yes,' Dad said.

'Absolutely.' Jacqueline nodded. She turned to Dad. 'I'm thinking you should put on your new Gieves and Hawkes jacket.' She looked down at her own black crepe dress. 'I'm going to add some pearls to my Jil Sander.'

I suppressed a smile. Dad just nodded, absently. They both looked tired – I was guessing they hadn't had much sleep – but determined.

Lucy was in the room too, though she didn't say anything. Dad must have told her what Harry had done because she was hovering white-faced in the corner. She was dressed in one of her floaty white skirts, her long fingers twisting anxiously around the hem of her baggy cardigan.

'I don't believe this is happening again,' Dad muttered, grim-faced. 'Sodding reporters.'

'I know.' I glanced at my sister. She was peering out of the window and gave no sign of having heard us. 'I'm so sorry, Dad.'

'It's not your fault,' Dad said, offering me a sympathetic smile.

Across the room Jacqueline cleared her throat. 'I think you should call Harry now.'

I scrolled to Harry's number, putting the phone on loudspeaker. He answered on the first ring.

'Thank God,' he said. 'Fran, I'm so pleased you've called.'

'Hi.' I hesitated. I had to get my tone right. Not too conciliatory but not too furious either. 'I've been thinking.'

'Of course,' Harry said. 'Do you understand now why I had to find a roundabout route to the truth?'

Across the room Dad gave a low growl.

You mean 'lie'? I bit the words back.

'Not really,' I said. 'I mean, I get why you didn't want to bombard me with accusations about Dad early on, but why lie about everything else?'

'I didn't,' Harry said eagerly. 'Everything I told you was true. Including about my family. My mum had cancer last year, my sister's struggling to cope—'

'But you never met my husband?' I persisted. 'You lied when you said he told you he was being threatened?'

'Yes,' Harry admitted. 'But honestly, I wanted to tell you the truth a million times. Remember last night at the bar? I said there was something and you said I should tell you later but once we—'

'I really need to talk to you about all this,' I interrupted, not wanting him to mention how we'd made love while I was on loudspeaker with Dad and Jacqueline listening. 'I'm so confused. I don't know what to think any more.'

'Of course,' Harry said. 'Shall I come over?'

I glanced at Dad. He nodded. Jacqueline gave me a thumbs-up. Lucy was still turned away, looking out at the street.

'I'm at my dad's house,' I said. 'He's not here right now, but he'll be back later. I was wondering if you could come here, to my dad's, explain everything to me. Then maybe we could talk to Dad together?'

There was a pause and, for a moment, I thought Harry might be about to smell a rat. But then he spoke and I heard the relief in his voice.

'Okay,' he said. 'I'll be right over.'

Harry turned up three quarters of an hour later. He must have raced out of the door to get here so promptly. I opened the front door and, in spite of myself, my heart skipped a beat as I saw his face: handsome and smiling.

'I'm so pleased we're doing this,' he said, those chocolate-brown eyes shining with pleasure. 'Because I really don't want to stop seeing you. I need you to believe what happened last night meant a lot to me.'

Was that true? Seeing him face to face – his expression of total sincerity – I wavered. *Did* I mean anything to him other than as a way to build a story about Dad? I stood in the doorway as the soft drizzle misted on Harry's hair and on the shoulders of his grey jumper. A dull ache settled in my stomach. Whatever Harry said now was irrelevant. There was no way I could trust him any more. The skies overhead were dark and gloomy, the perfect reflection of my mood.

'Do I mean more than your story?'

'I told you already: yes.'

'So are you prepared to drop the story?' I asked.

I watched him closely, expecting him to fudge and wheedle.

'Yes,' Harry said, meeting my gaze. There was no guile in those brown eyes. 'I promise I'll give the whole thing up.'

My mouth fell open. I hadn't expected him to be so direct. So absolute.

Or was this another lie?

'I mean it,' Harry said. 'I know you want me to talk to your dad with you. You must be desperate for the truth. And I'll do that if you want. But what we do with all the information . . . on your dad, on PAAUL, on your husband's death, that's up to you. *Totally* up to you.'

I nodded, my throat too tight to speak. My mind whirred. This was a massive promise, if it was genuine. Did it change what I'd planned with Dad and Jacqueline? Surely it had to. For a second I fantasised about grabbing Harry's hand and racing off down the street with him. Because if he was serious about dropping his story then what we were going to do was overkill.

And then, as I hesitated, Dad's voice drifted towards us. 'It's taking too long,' he was muttering. A second later he strode out of the living room.

Harry's jaw dropped. He met my gaze. 'Fran?'

'Get inside the house,' Dad ordered, his fists clenched. '*Now.*'

'You said your father was coming back *later*,' Harry spluttered.

'An expedience.' Dad's eyes flashed. 'It seemed the best way to deal with you. Now come here.' He grabbed Harry's arm and yanked him into the hall.

I gasped. Harry shook him off, wide-eyed. 'Fran, what is this?'

Dad stood, his breath coming in furious jags. He looked like he was barely able to stop himself from punching Harry.

'I ... I ...' My voice faltered. I hadn't seen Dad this angry in years.

'Don't you dare appeal to her,' Jacqueline snapped, emerging from the living room. 'You've already hurt her enough.'

Lucy fluttered into the doorway. The ends of her long cream cardigan swung back and forward as she fidgeted from side to side.

I stood frozen. Dad pushed Harry against the hall wall.

'How dare you spread lies about me and my son-in-law?' he hissed. 'Caspian was a wonderful man. The idea I might want to hurt him ...' He prodded Harry, hard, in the chest. My guts twisted into a knot. 'You're going to leave this family alone, do you hear me?' he ordered, spit flying from his mouth. 'And you're going to drop your pathetic, made-up lies about me.'

Harry's gaze flickered from Dad to me and back again.

'Just to be clear ...' Dad snarled. 'If you don't drop the story we'll get an injunction. If you ignore the injunction we'll sue you for libel.'

'We have very good lawyers,' Jacqueline snapped.

'Never mind the effing lawyers.' Dad prodded Harry again. 'If you write one word about me, I will *personally* make sure you are fired from your job and never get another.' He paused. 'It shouldn't be hard to completely discredit you.'

'You don't frighten me.' Red-faced, Harry pushed Dad away from him. 'And you won't be able to discredit me if it's the truth.'

'But it isn't the truth,' Dad said, squaring up to him again. 'Which is how I know that you have no proof and you never will have any proof.'

Harry looked at me again. Bewilderment and anger filled his face. I steeled myself. I'd thought this moment would make me feel triumphant and elated. But right now all I felt was confusion and misery.

Harry walked towards the front door, Dad following him. I turned to go back into the living room. As the front door opened, I could hear Dad talking again, his voice low and threatening, then more footsteps on the parquet. Harry's voice rose up, loud and scathing.

'This is ridiculous. You can't do this.'

I hurried out into the hall again. To my astonishment, Detective Sergeant Smart was standing with Dad and Harry.

'Harry Elliot, I'm arresting you for harassment ...'

'What? I *didn't* ... It wasn't like that.' Harry's voice drowned out the rest of the police officer's speech. My mouth gaped. Arrested for harassment? When had *that* become part of the plan?

'Dad?'

Dad spun around. Harry looked up. He caught my eye.

'Fran?' he appealed. 'I'm so sorry, I never—'

'I didn't know.' The words flew out of me, guilt suddenly overwhelming me.

'Get back into the living room, Francesca,' Dad ordered.

A set of trembling fingers found mine. Lucy. I hadn't even realised she was standing beside me. I let her tug me back into the living room.

A second later the front door shut. Harry appeared through the window, DS Smart at his side. They walked along the pavement and out of sight. Harry was talking, gesticulating wildly. He didn't look back at the house.

'I think that worked,' Jacqueline said as Dad strode back into the living room.

'When did you set that up?' I demanded. Now that the shock of Harry being arrested had subsided, I filled with anger. This was so typical of Dad: taking over, thinking he knew best, all drive and fire. 'I don't think what Harry did was exactly harassment. It was lies, but—'

'Don't make excuses for him,' Dad interrupted. 'I had a word with the Chief Super, that's all. Solid chap. I know him from the prison rehab committee. He's just getting one of his lads to put the frighteners on. Same guy who spoke to you about Simon Pinner, he said.'

'But . . .' I stared at Dad, overwhelmed with frustration. It was *me* Harry had tricked. Surely it should have been my decision whether or not to go to the police.

'Your father's just trying to help,' Jacqueline interjected.

I shook my head.

'It's a favour to me,' Dad said. 'It won't go anywhere. They'll just shake Harry up for a few hours, then let him go.'

'It does make it more likely he'll drop his story,' Lucy said softly.

'Did you know Dad was having him arrested?' I turned on my sister.

She shrank back, shaking her head.

'Come on, Francesca,' Dad said, his voice suddenly soothing. 'I'm just doing what needs to be done. To make sure this is over.'

'And at least you'll never have to see Harry again,' Jacqueline added.

I met Lucy's gaze. She knew I'd left with Harry last night. Had she guessed I'd taken him home and made love with him?

Even if she had, I was certain she wouldn't have mentioned it to Dad and Jacqueline. Not that my sex life mattered in all of this.

I let out a juddering sigh. They were right, all three of them. That is, Dad had gone over the top with the arrest, in typical Dad fashion. He should have consulted me about that – but at least I could be sure now that Harry was truly out of my life for good. Even if Harry had meant it about putting the story behind us, I would never have been able to trust him. It was better this way.

I still didn't feel triumphant.

Beside me, Lucy drew her cardigan tightly around her chest. Tears welled in her eyes. I met Dad's gaze. He raised his eyebrows, his expression reflecting the same mix of concern and irritation that Lucy's behaviour engendered in me. Why on earth was she getting so emotional? Okay, so she'd confessed to finding Harry attractive – and that was probably a bigger deal than I realised, considering Lucy's lack of romantic experience – but she'd barely spoken ten words to the man.

A beat passed, then Jacqueline tactfully backed out of the room murmuring something about being late for a facial and leaving the three of us together.

Lucy brushed away her tears and gave Dad and me a rueful smile.

Dad walked over and stood beside her. He glanced at me, to include me in what he said next:

'I'm so terribly sorry you've been put through this.'

'I'm fine,' I said, more pointedly than I meant. After all, it wasn't Lucy's fault she was so fragile. 'I'm just sorry I let Harry make me think ... all that stupid stuff about you and ... and PAAUL.'

'It was Harry's fault.' Dad shook his head sorrowfully. 'The devil has all the best tunes.' He put his hand on Lucy's shoulder. She shook him off with a shudder. 'Hey, sweetheart.' Dad caught my eye. 'Help,' he mouthed.

'Lucy?' I said. 'Are you okay?'

Lucy nodded. 'Like Daddy says, at least we know the truth now ... that everything Harry said was a lie,' she said, with a sniff.

'Exactly,' Dad said, a note of relief creeping into his voice. 'All lies.'

Is that really true? a small voice in my head whispered. *Just because Harry lied about some things doesn't mean he was wrong about everything. He might have made up all that stuff about Dad threatening Caspian, but even if Dad didn't have anything to do with PAAUL, Caspian could still have been killed by the organisation.*

No, I told myself. *Harry was manipulating me from start to finish. It's over.*

I waited again for the sensation of triumph to wash over me, but it didn't come.

HARRY

Harry had taken an instant dislike to Detective Sergeant Chris Smart. After arriving at the police station, Smart had made Harry wait for over two hours before, finally, taking him into an interview room.

Right now they were sitting across a table from each other. Harry's emotions were barely in check: his anger at Jayson Carr was only outmatched by his guilt over Fran. Smart, on the other hand, looked as if he'd never had an emotion in his life. A weasel-faced man with dark, sharp eyes set close together, Smart's wiry frame was tensed against his seat as if, any second, he might leap up from it. The man was a master in an art Harry had pretty much perfected himself: that of asking a shedload of questions then keeping quiet and allowing the person you were speaking with to fill the silence and, in so doing, give themselves away.

Much as this made Harry want to clam up completely, he knew that he needed to talk.

'I think we both know that harassment is a stretch,'

he said. 'There's no way you can charge me for telling a few lies.'

What he wanted to say was that he was bloody certain he had only been arrested because Jayson Carr had powerful friends and something to hide. The look on Fran's face when he'd been frogmarched out of Carr's front door suggested that she hadn't known in advance that her father was going to pull the arrest stunt. Not that it mattered. Fran had still tricked him into going round there. Which meant she was still furious with him for lying to her.

And with good reason.

Smart sat without speaking for a while. He shifted in his seat. 'I take it some of those lies you told concerned a fictional meeting you had with the husband of one of Carr's daughters ... er, Francesca?' He looked up.

Harry fought with himself. This was the perfect opportunity to pass on what he and Fran had found out about the Carrs' interest in PAAUL at the family home. Not to mention all the internet rumours that suggested Jayson Carr had left moderate pro-life organisation *Shield* in order to pursue a more violent, extreme and secret anti-abortion crusade as head of PAAUL in the UK.

'I was doing my job,' Harry said, playing for time. Should he tell the detective? He'd already promised Fran he'd drop his story. Passing on information to the police was a different matter from writing a news article, but he doubted she would see it like that.

And yet what was the point in keeping quiet? Fran was never going to trust him.

'Oh, and which bit was your job? Lying to the Carr family? Passing yourself off as a sales rep? Ingratiating yourself with a vulnerable woman?'

'It was all about investigating Carr. Ask Alexandra Spencer at the *Record*.'

'Oh, I have,' Smart said with a sneer. 'I've had a long chat with Ms Spencer about you.'

Great. Harry could just imagine how delighted his news editor had been about *that* conversation.

'So you know that there was nothing personal in what I did,' he pressed on. 'It was an investigation, which speaks against the harass—'

'I can assure you that any investigation *I* carried out wouldn't involve conning my way into the affections of the daughter of the man we were looking into.' Smart curled his top lip.

'Yeah?' Harry snarled. 'Tell that to the Pitchford Inquiry. I'm not taking any lectures on undercover work from the bloody Metropolitan Police.' He stopped. He was in the wrong. There was no point arguing with Smart over it. 'The truth is I'm really sorry Fran got hurt. I didn't mean for that to happen. I was going to tell her everything, but ... but ...' A vision of Fran as they made love filtered into his head. He couldn't bear the thought he'd never be able to see her again. It wasn't just the sex, either, amazing though that had been. Harry had only felt like this once before, in his last year at uni. He'd fallen in love with a girl who had seemed to love him back, right up until the moment that she dumped him. Heartbroken, Harry had vowed never to allow himself to be that vulnerable again. And yet, somehow, Fran had slipped past his defences, winding herself into the core of his being so emphatically that, as he sat here in this dingy interview room, he knew that getting her to speak to him again was more important than writing a damn story or passing on rumours and scraps of unsubstantiated evidence to the police.

He pressed his lips together. He would say nothing else.

Smart left the room, keeping Harry waiting for almost another hour. When he returned, he sat down with a sigh.

'Okay.' Smart tapped his long fingers on the table, considering Harry carefully. 'As I understand it from speaking to Mr Carr and his daughter, your evidence against Jayson Carr and his brother Perry amounts to a series of reports which you weaselled your way into finding at Perry Carr's house and which both brothers have explained. I might add that if they *were* guilty, bringing you to our attention would not be the cleverest way of avoiding an investigation.'

Harry kept silent.

'I'm not going to charge you, Mr Elliot,' DS Smart said with a sigh. 'But I am going to give you a bit of advice: Jayson Carr is *not* a good man to piss off so don't aggravate him any more. Now, get out of here and for God's sake, do yourself a favour and stay away from the Carrs, especially Francesca.'

Harry stormed outside where the light was fading and rain drummed onto the pavements. He stomped to his car, feeling drips trickle down the back of his neck. What a frigging disaster.

He'd lost Fran before he'd even properly got to know her.

On top of which he had almost certainly screwed up his career: he could just imagine how angry Alexandra Spencer would be with him, especially when he told her there was no story on Jayson Carr. Which, strangely, didn't bother him half as much as it should have done. Because he didn't care about the story – even though he was a journalist to his fingertips. There would be other, better stories.

But there wouldn't be another Fran.

He didn't even care about the ethics of a situation where a guilty man might walk free because Harry stopped trying to expose him.

All he cared about was Fran.

Out of the rain and inside his car, Harry switched on the engine and sat, watching the wipers clear the windscreen. He couldn't stop thinking about her face: first soft and vulnerable as they'd made love last night and then, later, shocked and stricken. Why on earth hadn't he told her the truth *before* they slept together, like he'd planned? He had to try and talk to her again, to explain why he'd gone undercover in the first place, how he had wanted ... started several times in fact ... to tell her the truth ... how his feelings for her had developed and deepened. How he hadn't told the police

SOPHIE MCKENZIE

anything. How he had dropped his story. How he was prepared to destroy every scrap of information he held about PAAUL and her father.

Would she listen? Would she give him a second chance?

Harry had a horrible feeling that she would never speak to him again. He let his mind drift once more over the memory of the time they'd spent in bed together: the feel of her skin, the curve of her hip, the dark sexiness deep behind her eyes.

He had to do something. DS Smart was right that most of Harry's information had come from internet reports. There were lots of these, far more than the few to which he had led Fran. He'd been researching this story for months, after all. He needed to make Fran see that though his methods had been wrong and hurtful he had genuinely thought that her father *was* the head of PAAUL, guilty of ordering the death of her husband. Under such circumstances he had, surely, been duty-bound to investigate. More than anything, he needed to convince Fran that he had never intended to cause her pain and that he was sorrier than he could say that he had.

The rain grew stronger as Harry drove off. By the time he reached home he knew exactly what he needed to do.

FRAN

'It's just so humiliating,' Lucy said in a miserable voice. 'But we have to remember that Harry needs our prayers. I'm going to ask my prayer group to say a Hail Mary for him *and* a Novena.'

'Right,' I said with a sigh. 'Great.' It was several hours since the showdown with Harry and I was desperate to get back home to the kids. But Dad and Jacqueline had gone out to a prison rehabilitation charity function and I had promised Dad I would hang on with Lucy until she seemed a bit less depressed.

DS Smart called to ask for more details about Harry 'harassing' me so I left Lucy in the kitchen and slipped outside to speak privately on the patio.

'Mr Elliot isn't saying much, mostly a load of bull-crap about a story on your father and how very sorry he is you got caught in the crossfire,' DS Smart said. I heard the rustle of his papers. I shivered, and not just because it was freezing out on the patio and I'd left my coat indoors.

Clearly, the so-called evidence linking Dad with

PAAUL amounted to nothing more than a few internet rumours. But Harry had believed them and had lied to me in order to get more and better proof. To him, the ends had justified the means. Was he really sorry now for conning me?

Through the kitchen window I could see Lucy fingering her rosary, her long hair falling over her face. I gave the detective an outline of Harry's lies, leaving out the embarrassing detail that we'd actually slept together, then I rang off and came back into the kitchen.

'Shall I make a cup of tea?' I asked, hoping to rouse Lucy out of her stupor.

'Sure, thanks.' Lucy gave me a weak smile. 'Sorry I'm so down, I just feel devastated that Harry tricked us.'

'Come on, Luce,' I said, wondering if maybe I needed to deploy a bit of tough love. 'It was *me* Harry was trying to trick.'

'I know, I know. I'm sorry, I'm sorry.'

I bit back my irritation. I was the victim here. *I* was the one Harry had duped. And yet here I was, just like Dad, once again falling over backwards to look after poor, fragile, vulnerable Lucy.

Of course, as soon as I'd thought this I felt guilty.

Trying to gather myself I wandered across the kitchen to fill the kettle with water. I wanted time to think through everything that had happened and it was impossible with Lucy taking up all the available emotional space.

It would have helped if I'd understood why Lucy was taking the news about Harry's duplicity so hard.

It surely couldn't be because she'd fancied him, could it?

I put on the kettle and fetched two mugs from the cupboard. Mum's kitchen had been full of mismatched, brightly coloured cups and saucers. Jacqueline's mugs were all the same tasteful shade of beige.

I still hadn't told Lucy about sleeping with Harry. Our failure to communicate about this stuff was typical of the emotional distance between us. I didn't even know if Lucy had ever even had sex – apart, of course, from the older man who made her pregnant when she was fifteen. I couldn't imagine her getting close to any man; she lived like a nun.

'Will you get the milk?' I asked.

'Sure.' But instead of standing up and walking to the fridge, Lucy started working at her rosary again.

For Pete's sake. Perhaps it was her lack of experience with men that made her reaction to Harry's lies so extreme. Or maybe, I thought meanly, she was just attention-seeking. Times like this seemed to push us back into our childhood roles: me the level-headed one, and Lucy the frail innocent. Dad played up to these roles without noticing he did so.

I fetched the milk myself and set it down by the kettle. My eyes lit on the knife block: French oak with a silver trim. The knives inside it were all brand new, Jacqueline's purchases. But the knife block itself had been Mum's, kept on by my stepmother, presumably because it was simple, unusual and extraordinarily expensive. Typical of Mum's random but often exquisite taste. In that moment I missed her desperately. For a start, she would have known how to deal with Lucy. She always did. While Dad and I had floundered in the face of Lucy's emotional outbursts, Mum knew exactly what to say and how to say it.

But it was more than that. Harry had made a fool of me – and I felt like an idiot. Mum would have laughed my blues out of me in that no-nonsense, flamboyant way of hers. And she would have found a way of knitting Lucy and me closer together, rather than leaving me with the stark awareness of just how estranged from my own sister I really was ... in the heart, where it counts. Because I didn't understand her. Why did she have to take everything so hard? Be so bloodless and fearful? Was it really because of her abortion all those years ago? Or because of the way it came out, causing such scandal and upset in our family? Or was it just Lucy's intrinsic nature: too many parts veal calf, not enough vim?

I made the tea, returned the milk to the fridge and set Lucy's mug in front of her. The doorbell rang just as I took my first sip.

'Who on earth's that?' Lucy looked at me over the rim of her mug.

'I'll go,' I said, tamping down the irritation that rose in me again.

Leaving my mug on the counter, I hurried along the hallway. Uncle Perry stood on the doorstep.

'Ah, Francesca,' he said, not meeting my eyes. His voice was terse. Angry. 'Been at the club. Your father rang, asked me to come over so you can get back to the kids. Said Lucy's taking it hard.' He tutted. 'Ghastly business. What a shower, this Harry fellow.'

He still wasn't looking at me properly.

Was that because he knew I'd found out he was gay? Or because of the secret porn stash?

Quite possibly both. Not that I could be bothered to worry about any of that now.

'It's awful,' I agreed. 'Lucy's still upset though.'

'Right.' Uncle Perry now sounded resigned as well as cross.

'You'd think her faith would help her through,' I said, 'but it doesn't seem to.'

Uncle Perry's head jerked sharply up.

'It's just . . .' I frowned, feeling guilty again. 'She just takes things so hard.'

'You can be a self-righteous little madam, can't you?' Uncle Perry snapped.

What? I stared at him. Perry pushed past me into the hallway.

'If you had ignored what the stupid man was saying in the first place we wouldn't be in this position,' he went on, tugging angrily at his scarf, unwinding it from his neck, his face reddening.

'I don't think that's fair,' I said.

Perry shucked off his long cashmere overcoat, the same sort that Dad wore. 'You're such a Martha, Francesca. Always complaining.' He hung the coat on the stand, folding and tucking his black leather gloves fastidiously in the pocket.

161

Was he serious? The bible story of Martha and Mary was familiar to me from my childhood: resentful Martha, running around and working hard, rebuked by a visiting Jesus for criticising her quieter sister who simply sat and listened.

No way was that me.

Was it?

'I'm not complaining,' I insisted.

'Please,' Perry snorted, turning to face me. I could see nothing but contempt in his eyes. 'This whole situation is your fault. Your father and I *told* you Harry was making things up, we warned you to stay away from him. It's very hypocritical of you to—'

'*I'm* not the effing hypocrite,' I snarled.

Uncle Perry blinked, taken aback. 'I don't know what that's supposed to mean but—'

'You know what I found in your basement,' I hissed, unable to stop myself. 'You know who you really are.'

Perry's face was now purple, his eyes blazing. 'I don't know everything that's down there,' he blustered. 'People have dumped things there over the years.'

'Sure,' I said. 'But probably not in boxes marked "P. Carr. Private".'

Silence fell. My uncle and I stared at each other.

Lucy's voice floated out from the kitchen, quavering with unhappiness.

'Who is it, Francesca?'

I snatched up my coat and handbag. No way was I staying here a minute longer. 'It's Uncle Perry. I need to get back to the kids.'

And without giving Perry another glance, I stormed out of the house.

I stayed angry all the way home but as Saturday wore on my resentment at Perry subsided and I ended up having a lovely afternoon with the children. I got both of them outside to kick a ball around together. Caspian used to do this all the time with them, organising games of soccer, French cricket and dodge ball at the drop of a hat, but I hadn't played with them outside since the summer.

Ruby and I made a team together against Rufus who, I noticed, was far gentler with her than he used to be, making allowance for her shorter legs and eager desperation to score. We stayed outside until the wind whipped up and the skies darkened. Once inside, Rufus and Ruby elected to play separately up in their rooms and I sat alone in the living room, a darker mood creeping over me. Outside the streetlights came on but I didn't get up and put on the lamp. My thoughts turned to Harry again. I felt hurt and stupid for trusting him, but that was only part of it. I'd wanted two things: to stop Harry pursuing his story, and to make myself feel better by punishing him for deceiving me.

I hadn't succeeded in either aim. In fact I'd made everything worse. Harry was gone for good. Uncle Perry blamed me. Dad and Jacqueline probably did too. I tried to reason myself out of my funk. But, as I'd learned during my short-lived attempt at therapy, knowing my state of mind was of little help in altering it. Nothing seemed to help … not even reminding myself that the kids needed me, that soon I would have to rouse myself and make tea for them, that Rufus and Ruby were still, as they had been since Caspian died, my biggest reasons to get up in the morning.

Indeed, all I could think was that there would be years not that far in the future which would be worse, when neither of them would be here on a Saturday night and I would be sitting in this living room, alone in the dark with no one to look after and nothing to do and no point to any of it.

A tear trickled down my cheek. I wiped it angrily away, now furious with myself for being so self-pitying. A soft tap on the front door sounded. I peered through the window; the shutters were still half-open to the darkness outside. A man was on the doorstep.

Harry.

I froze. What on earth was he doing here? Another rap, louder this time. Ruby's feet pattered down the stairs.

'I'll get it, Mum,' she sang.

I jumped up to stop her but before I could call out she had already opened the door.

'Hi.' Harry's voice sounded like he was smiling. 'You must be Ruby.' I steeled myself, waiting for him to ask if I was in. But instead he said: 'So, Arsenal, is it?'

'Yes,' Ruby said shyly.

She must be wearing her Arsenal football shirt. She was a very half-hearted supporter, only paying lip service to her tribe. She'd asked for the shirt for her last birthday. It had surprised me at the time, but Ruby was adamant, even though her interest in football had always been playing it, not watching the professional game.

'Why Arsenal?' Harry asked.

'It was my dad's team,' Ruby said, sounding more confident.

I stood, listening, now transfixed. What on earth did she mean by that? Caspian had never shown an interest in any sport, not the entire time I'd known him.

'Your dad?' I could hear in Harry's voice that he didn't know whether to refer to Caspian's death. It was a problem lots of adults had, of course, not wanting to upset the bereaved by mentioning their loss, especially when the bereaved were children.

'I think it was his team, anyway,' Ruby went on. 'It's the nearest Premiership team to where he's from. Hampstead. I looked it up.'

My mouth gaped. Had Ruby really made all those connections, all by herself? Tears pricked at my eyes.

'I lost my dad when I was about your age,' Harry went on.

'How?' Ruby asked.

'He walked out on me and my mum and my sister. Just vanished one day. But he supported Man City, which is why I support them. Like you with your dad's team.'

'Man City.' Ruby considered this for a moment. 'They're a good side.'

'They are,' Harry said. 'They should be too, all the

money they have. Wasn't like that when I was your age, I can tell you.' He hesitated. 'Er, is your mum here?'

I pulled myself together and hurried out into the hall. As I walked to the door, tight-lipped, Ruby slipped away and back up the stairs.

'Great kid,' Harry said. God, he looked handsome. His face was pale from the cold, and he had stubble on his chin with a dark wool coat over his grey jumper.

Anger surged through me. What the hell was he playing at?

'Didn't you get the message? You need to stay away from me and my family,' I snapped, reaching for the front door.

Harry put his hand on my arm. Unbidden and unwanted, a thrill of electricity pulsed through me. I shook him off, avoiding his gaze.

'That was your dad talking,' he said. 'Listen, please, I just came to apologise again, properly.'

'I'm not int—'

'And to tell you that though your dad had me arrested, I did not talk to the police about him. And that I absolutely meant it when I said I wouldn't pursue my story, that I'll do whatever you want me to.'

I stared at him.

'I also came to give you this.' He picked up a slim black bag. 'It's got my laptop, the password is written down. All my work is on there. And there's a memory stick too, which pulls together all the research I did on your dad.'

'I don't want it,' I snapped. 'All I want is for you to go away and leave me alone.'

'I understand,' Harry said. 'But I want you to see I had good reason to investigate your father and your husband's death.' He set the bag down inside the hall.

'Do you really mean it about dropping your story?' I asked. Not that it mattered how he answered. I wouldn't trust him, whatever answer he gave.

'If that's what you want.' Harry's voice was soft, almost pleading. His eyes were fixed on mine: dark and soulful.

My heart gave a little skip. 'Go away!'

'Okay.' He hesitated. 'Call me when you've looked at it all. Please.' He hurried off along the path.

I shut the front door and picked up the computer bag. A slim laptop was inside plus, as Harry had said, a USB stick. I took them into the living room and sat, staring at them as the darkness in the room grew thicker and heavier.

I spent the next hour or so making the kids' tea but all the time I kept thinking about what might be on the laptop. Could there really be more information about Caspian's death? In the end I had to look. It was impossible not to.

A quick scan showed me that the computer was crammed with stuff, though much of it was clearly unrelated to Harry's investigation. There were news stories he'd written going back years, the opening of a sci-fi novel which he seemed to have abandoned about ten months ago, plus pics of his family and friends.

I wondered at him giving me the thing. He must know I was angry. Of course everything would be backed up, but I could easily destroy the laptop itself. It was an act of trust. Which meant what? That he cared about hurting me, as he'd said? That he wanted to convince me he had been sincere about his investigation into Dad, if not honest in his methods? That he really was prepared to drop the whole thing?

I plugged in the USB stick. There was one file. It had my name on it.

My throat felt tight as I opened it to find a video showing Harry leaning forward in a chair. His face filled the screen. I pressed play.

Hi Fran, he said, *firstly thank you for watching this.* His eyes burned through the screen; he looked so handsome in his sweater and stubble. *Secondly, please feel free to read everything that's on my laptop. I promise it's all there, every bit of work I've done looking into your husband's death and your father's potential involvement.*

I peered more closely. He seemed sincere. He was certainly photogenic, though there were lines around his eyes and his expression was strained. *I understand why you're angry with me. It was wrong to lie about meeting your husband.* Harry ran his hand through his hair. *Worse than wrong. It was cruel. But I did it because I had a lot of information and I thought that if I just presented it as my own research you would dismiss it out of hand.*

So, here it is ... I'm certain and I have been for weeks now that PAAUL began a secret crusade against abortion doctors in the UK soon after your father ended his official involvement with Shield. I know you think this happened because his second, his current, wife – Jacqueline – influenced him to change direction, but it's a big coincidence, don't you think? Because that same time is when the rumours began about your father going underground to lead PAAUL UK from Lanagh House.

So what is PAAUL's precise UK strategy?

Harry cleared his throat.

It comes down to this:

PAAUL's aim is to assassinate doctors who perform late abortions.

Starting in 2012, one abortion doctor has died every autumn for the past four years, your own husband being the third in 2014. Each of these four doctors regularly performed abortions after twenty weeks. Simon Pinner's death last week fits the same bill as the rest but, of course, represents an escalation of the attacks.

The murders (and you'll find details of all of them in the folder marked CASE FILES) all look like random attacks, they all happened outdoors and all involved knives or beatings.

The police refuse to see the connection for several reasons: Firstly, the deaths are all different, not the pattern of a serial killer. Also, the men were killed in different parts of the country and had different ages and backgrounds. And finally, it is very unusual for a terrorist organisation to commit atrocities and not want everyone to know they are responsible.

I nodded to myself. These were all points DS Smart had made.

On that last aspect I'd say PAAUL is being clever. All the organisation cares about is saving those unborn lives. Making sure the deaths look like accidents is a way of staying under the radar. As for the differences in the deaths: the head of a prison rehabilitation charity meets a lot of ex-convicts, some of them violent ...

Which brings me to your father.

Harry's gaze was fixed on the camera, but it felt now that those dark brown eyes were looking straight into mine.

I may have lied when I told you that I spoke with your husband – but I have talked to plenty of other people. Nobody is prepared to go on the record – another reason for the police not believing me – but all those anonymous interviews (in the file marked SOURCES) on my laptop amount to the same thing: Jayson Carr is in charge of PAAUL and 'cleansing' the UK of doctors prepared to kill unborn life. He is probably using a roster of different criminals to carry out the crimes, but I'm certain he's behind every one.

I stopped reading, feeling sick to my stomach.

All the doubts about Dad which uncovering Harry's lies had blasted away now surged back, stronger than ever. Could Dad be the head of PAAUL UK after all? On the one hand Harry's research amounted to a huge pile of data that spoke against him. On the other, it was still all supposition. Anyway, how could I trust anything Harry said or did any more?

I turned back to the closing seconds of the video:

You are free to do what you want with this information, including destroying it all. I have wiped all my back-ups including in the Cloud, so this is, truly, everything.

Harry leaned forward again, his eyes intense.

What I want more than anything, Fran, is to see you again. To keep on getting to know you. To hopefully have you some day forgive me for my behaviour and ... and my lies.

Call me when you've thought about all this. I'll be waiting.

Harry's hand reached forward and a second later, the video ended.

I stared at the frozen screen for a few seconds then went back to the laptop and read the CASE FILE and SOURCES files. They were exactly as Harry had said. More, the research was thorough, far more extensive than the scant few reports he had led me to on the net earlier in the week. I pored over the files on the other doctors who had been killed: John Paterson, Rashid Ali, Christopher Carson and, of course, Caspian Hoffman.

It was easy to see why Harry had connected their deaths. And yet the police hadn't done so – were clearly still refusing to do so. Which meant what? That PAAUL – and therefore Dad – weren't behind the murders after all? Or that they had covered their tracks so well that they'd fooled almost everybody?

It was almost four in the morning before I fell asleep and past ten when the kids woke me shouting about whose turn it was to use the iPad. By the time I'd sorted them out – my head still going over and over Harry's files – another hour had passed.

My mobile rang. *Auntie Sheila calling.* Shit, I had completely forgotten that it was Sunday, my regular day to visit her.

'Sorry, Sheila,' I said, snatching up the phone.

'I thought perhaps you wouldn't come as you were here on Tuesday.' Auntie Sheila sounded wounded. 'But I baked macaroons in case you'd been too busy to buy any.'

I groaned inwardly. Going to visit her was absolutely the last thing I wanted to do, but Sheila seemed upset. Mum's voice echoed in my head: 'Be kind to those in pain and trouble, try and put yourself in their place, feel their fear and misery.'

'I was just leaving,' I lied. 'Be with you in twenty minutes.' Bundling two complaining children into the car I hurried off. Harry rang as we drove. The last thing I needed was to talk to him. I ignored the call.

Traffic was mercifully light all the way to Fulham. Once we were at Sheila's Ruby and Rufus settled themselves down in the living room, as usual, while Sheila and I headed into her kitchen. Sheila was full of horror at the news about Harry's infiltration into my life.

'I can't believe the audacity,' she said, sitting very upright and nibbling on the edge of a macaroon.

I looked around, desperate to change the subject. The surfaces were clear, no sign of any lunch being cooked. I remembered the roast – and Graham's arrival – from earlier in the week.

'Not expecting anyone for lunch?' I asked.

'No, dear.' Sheila blushed.

'Not even Uncle Graham?' I raised my eyebrows. 'I didn't know you were seeing so much of him. You never said.'

'I never lied about it.' Sheila bristled. 'And he is the father of my son.'

'He's not treated you very well in the past,' I pointed out.

Sheila set down her macaroon, two bright red spots appearing on her cheeks.

'I don't think, Francesca dear, after the way that wretched journalist tricked you, you are really in a position to lecture me about being poorly treated by anyone. Believe me, I'm well aware Graham is no angel, but he is my husband.'

Wow, I'd never heard her sound so snippy.

'*Was* your husband.' I couldn't resist making the point.

Sheila looked wounded and immediately I felt guilty. 'I'm sorry,' I said, 'I know it's none of my business, I'm just worried about you. I don't want you getting hurt again.'

Sheila pursed her lips. 'Graham's a good man, when

he's not drinking. All the Carrs are basically good men.' She tutted. 'Talking of which ... I hope you haven't let that journalist influence you against your own father. I know that's how they work: all lies and manipulation.'

'Are you really so sure everything he was claiming is untrue?' I couldn't stop myself from asking. 'I've seen a lot of stuff that suggests otherwise.'

'It's just rumours and ranting on ... on the inter-web ... and people with an axe to grind,' Sheila said, her voice suddenly shrill. 'For goodness' sake, Francesca, your father is one of the best men I've ever met. He looked after me when Graham left, when I had days when I couldn't get out of bed.' She was almost shaking with emotion now. I stared, horrified. I hadn't seen her this upset since Mum died. 'Your father is a *saint*. Do you hear me? A *saint*!'

'Sheila, I'm sorry, I just—'

'Your mother would be ashamed of you, thinking your father could be capable ... where's your *faith*, Francesca? You need to back off this whole thing with PAAUL, it's crazy.'

I left soon after, reeling from Sheila's vehemence – and more confused than ever.

Lucy called mid-afternoon to ask if we wanted to go to St Cecilia's for a concert of sacred music that evening. I braced myself for her to start crying again, but she sounded much less emotional than she had earlier and didn't mention Harry once. I was used to her mood swings but even so I was surprised. She sounded almost chipper, though of course – I reflected – she might just be putting a brave face on her emotions.

'I'm meeting Dad and Jacqueline for an early supper first,' she said. 'They'd love it if you came along.'

She often asked me and the kids along to events like this. Maybe she was just being nice – she certainly never pushed her Catholicism at us – but it still felt like a subtle pressure to get more involved with the religion I'd rejected years before. Sometimes I went, mostly to be polite, though Ruby always grumbled and Rufus had started, in the past few months, to point-blank refuse to engage in any kind of church-based family get-together.

Today I'd cried off citing the fact that both Ruby and Rufus had school in the morning and we all needed an early night. Truth was I didn't really want to see Lucy. More, I couldn't face Dad with all the unanswered questions about his relationship with PAAUL still bouncing around my head.

Harry himself tried me again, twice – though he left no message when I didn't answer. And then, fifteen minutes before four, with Rufus grumpily holed up in his room and Ruby helping me bake some football-themed fairy cakes, my phone trilled with a text.

'I'll get it.' Ruby picked up my phone. A moment later she looked up from the text with a frown. 'I don't get it.'

Wiping my floury hands I took the mobile and read:

REPENT AND DESIST. 1 Corinthians 3:17

I stared at the screen in shock.

'What does "dess-est" mean?' Ruby asked, looking up at me with wide, curious eyes. 'And what's Cor ... corint ... ans?'

My heart thudded, loud in my ears.

'It's a bible verse,' I said, a dread rising in my throat. I checked the sender: *number with held*. 'Just religious fruitcakes sending out junk texts.'

'But what does it mean?' Ruby persisted, her little face screwed into a worried frown.

'Nothing,' I said, deleting the message. 'Look, it's gone. It's a mistake. Get the eggs out of the fridge.'

I left Ruby carefully cracking and beating the eggs and hurried next door to look up the Corinthians verse on my phone. My fingers trembled as I read:

If anyone destroys God's temple, God will destroy that person; for God's temple is sacred and you together are that temple.

I'd seen this verse before. It was one of the main bible quotes featured on the PAAUL forums Harry had led me to.

It was used by PAAUL followers to explain their certainty of the bible's – and therefore God's – justification of the use of violence against abortionists.

Panic swirled in my chest.

This was a threat. A threat to me from PAAUL.

HARRY

Harry waited for Fran to call but she didn't. He tried her himself several times but she didn't answer. He would have left a message, but he had already said and done everything he could think of to persuade her to talk to him. The afternoon wore on. His phone rang twice. Both times Harry rushed to answer, hoping it was her and, both times, wished he hadn't.

The first call was from his sister Kayleigh. As he'd told Fran, Kayleigh – a single mother with three kids by three different fathers – was depressed. Indeed, since their mum had been taken ill last year she'd occasionally seemed suicidal. Harry was worried about her. Though he was more worried about his mother, who bore the brunt of Kayleigh's 'bad days' and wore herself out looking after the kids.

Despite the fact that he'd only just left Manchester, Kayleigh wanted to know how soon he'd be able to come back. Apparently little Aaron, her middle child, kept asking when he would see Harry again. Aaron was a sweet kid but what he really needed was a dad. And with Harry based in London there was no way he could properly substitute for one of those. Kayleigh sounded down again and Harry felt guiltily relieved when she said she had to go after a few minutes.

Alexandra Spencer called almost immediately afterwards. Harry's heart sank as soon as he heard the clipped tones of the *Record*'s news editor.

'What the fuck, Harry? I've only had the bloody police on the phone. *Arrested*? For *harassment*? You're supposed to be investigating a story, not sexually assaulting your contacts.'

With a sigh, Harry explained how his cover story had been exposed.

'It was when you called me on Friday, actually,' he said, hoping she might soften when she understood it was her call that had, inadvertently, revealed his true identity.

But Alexandra didn't take the bait. 'So your cover is blown and you're no closer to any proof about Jayson Carr being a terrorist than you were before I approved you starting down this path?'

Harry frowned. Anything he said was likely to aggravate her. The woman was hard as nails, completely ruthless – especially when it came to celebrity exposés – and had a voice that oozed contempt, whatever she was saying and whoever she was talking to.

He needed to close the investigation down. If Alexandra Spencer thought there was a chance of a story she was perfectly capable of turning him off the case and putting another reporter onto it.

'I don't think the evidence against Carr stacks up to anything,' he said.

'Really?' Alexandra sounded sceptical. 'The fact that Carr's gone bonkers, chucking injunctions and whatever threats out of his pram says he's guilty to me.'

'Or maybe it just says he's very protective of his daughters,' Harry suggested.

'Ah, yes, the daughters,' Alexandra sneered. 'I understand from the extremely unpleasant police officer who called me, you've been attempting to shag one of them.' She sniffed. 'Nice, by the way.'

'Whatever Carr is doing, I'm certain there isn't a story,' Harry said, ignoring this.

'Useless fucking incompetent.' There was a click as Alexandra rang off.

Harry sighed. Life as a freelancer was hard enough without senior news editors thinking you were a liability. He knew Alexandra Spencer well enough to be sure she was unlikely to be discreet about his failings.

Was he going to end up without either his reputation *or* his girl?

Another hour later and it was starting to look like it. Fran still hadn't returned any of his calls. Had she even looked at the evidence on her father he'd given her? Would it change her mind about him?

Harry thought back to their evening at Revelations. Before Dex had turned up, all posh-boy charm and effortless good looks, Fran's sister Lucy had hung on Harry's every word. He'd sensed she liked him. Even if he'd misread her interest as sexual, at the very least he was sure she'd approved of him as a potential boyfriend for her sister. Which meant that maybe, if he chose his words carefully, there was a chance he could get her to intercede with Fran on his behalf.

He knew from his conversations with Fran that the rest of her family worshipped at St Cecilia's church, just around the corner from their house in Kensington. Lucy was devout – her attitude to the 'blasphemous' icons at Revelations reinforced what Fran had already told him about the daily mass Lucy attended and the church work with which she filled her time. What had she said? Something about a Guild of something or other and another group with 'Mary' in the title on Sundays ...

Harry quickly checked the St Cecilia website. The Legion of Mary meeting was due to finish in the next hour or so. Harry had just enough time to get there and, hopefully, speak to Lucy as she left.

People were milling in the church forecourt, ignoring the soft drizzle that had been falling all day, when Harry arrived. He saw Lucy, dressed in a long white dress and saggy cream cardigan, straight away. She was chatting outside the church with two older women. Harry loitered across the road, waiting for her to leave. The sun came out briefly from behind the cloud as Lucy crossed the road. She walked, as she stood, with a slight stoop. Harry guessed she was self-conscious about her height. She must be at least five foot eleven, far taller than her sister. She hadn't noticed him. Harry walked up to her, his eye caught by the dark outline of her skinny legs through the front of her dress.

'Oh, Harry.' Lucy blushed, clearly thrown at his appearance. She glanced quickly up and down the road, shielding her eyes from the glare.

Harry held out his hands. 'I am so, so sorry for everything I've put you and your family through.'

Lucy tilted her head to one side and appraised him.

'Daddy and Jacqueline are livid,' she said. 'Francesca too.'

'I'm sure.' Harry hesitated. Was the fact that she'd left herself out of that last statement in any way a hint of her sympathy? Or did she just want to avoid a personal confrontation? 'Look, I just came over to apologise and ... that is, please tell Fran I'm really sorry.'

Lucy met his gaze. Back at Revelations she'd seemed nervy and shy but right now there was a distinctly confident directness in her eyes. And was that a smile curling around her lips?

'You're a bit of a mess, aren't you?' she said, sounding suddenly very like her sister.

Harry, taken aback, couldn't help but grin.

'Would you like to come back to ours?' Lucy asked. Catching the wary look on his face, she gave a rueful smile. 'Don't worry, I'm the only one there, Dad and Jacqueline are out all afternoon. I'm meeting them later for an early supper at Canovanni's then there's a concert at the church this evening.'

'Okay, er, thanks.' Feeling slightly off balance, Harry

followed her along the few short streets that led back to the Carr home.

The sun was setting by the time they arrived. Lucy led him across the hall then stopped at the foot of the stairs.

'I guess you'd better come up,' she said, a faint flush creeping over her cheeks.

Feeling a little bewildered, Harry followed her up to the first floor, where Lucy led him into a large bedroom that overlooked the back of the house. It was obviously hers. For a start the whole room was white: from the lacy coverlet on the bed to the thick embroidered curtains. There was even a white rug on the wooden floor. Harry frowned. Why had she brought him in here?

He glanced at the wall above the bed where a wooden figure, presumably supposed to be Christ, hung from a cross. A chain of rosary beads dangled from the foot. It was the only sign of decoration in the room. The rest of the house was neat and minimal in a designer kind of a way, but this was positively ascetic. A wooden wardrobe stood in the corner and a dressing table – empty apart from a leather-bound bible – under the window. The dim light that filtered through the glass cast a thick stripe over the black leather.

Feeling awkward, Harry leaned against the dressing table. He peered up at the crucifix above the bed. Imagine sleeping with that hanging over you every night. He had never had any kind of religious faith himself. What was it like to believe as devoutly as Lucy did?

'Why did you really come to see me?' Lucy asked.

'Are you still trying to write a story on Daddy? Because I should tell you there's no way he's done anything wrong.'

'No, I've dropped that,' Harry said. 'I'm not doing anything further – not even *talking* about it unless Fran is okay with it.'

'So you really like her?' Lucy fixed him with a penetrating gaze. Her eyes, so like her sister's in shape and colour, looked almost gold in the shadowy light. 'That wasn't an act? You're in love with Francesca?'

An uneasy feeling crept over Harry. He fixed his gaze on the chipped black paint of Christ's sandal.

'She's in love with you too,' Lucy went on, just the tiniest shake in her voice. 'I mean, she's really angry at the moment so she won't admit it, even to herself. But the fact that she's so furious is a sign of how much she cares.'

Harry's pulse pounded against his skull, partly from embarrassment – this bizarre encounter was absolutely not what he'd expected – but also from the hope that was now charging through him.

'Right.' His voice sounded foreign ... hollow ... to his ears.

'I think you two would be great together,' Lucy went on. 'I know you did a stupid thing but it was hardly a mortal sin. Anyway St John Vianney says our sins are nothing but a grain of sand alongside the great mountain of the mercy of God. Francesca will see that in time.' She paused, taking in Harry's bewildered gaze. 'You should tell her how you feel. Women can't just switch off their feelings, you know. Don't give up.'

Harry stood up. He was, for one of the few times in his life, completely speechless. 'Er, thank you, I . . . I . . .'

'. . . need to leave?' Lucy smiled sadly. 'Course you do. I'll see you out.' She hesitated. 'Just one more thing, it's not about Francesca. Just . . . please take care. Your digging around in the dark web and . . . and murder and extremism . . . it's such a dangerous job . . .'

'It's hardly bomb disposal or lion taming,' Harry said with a grin.

'Just . . . be careful.' Lucy crossed herself.

Ten minutes later Harry was sitting in a café on Kensington Church Street, trying to process the conversation that had just taken place. All thoughts of his story on Carr had flown out of his head. He couldn't think of anything else but seeing Fran again.

The waitress set down his coffee and Harry settled back in his chair, a smile spreading across his face.

Maybe, after all, there really was a way back.

FRAN

I had deleted the actual text message, but its contents were seared across my mind's eye:

REPENT AND DESIST. 1 Corinthians 3:17

Well, the first part was clear enough. Whoever sent it must be aware of my involvement in Harry's investigation – and wanted me to stop looking.

Which meant what? That I was being watched? That they knew where I lived? That they'd seen Harry come round earlier and give me his laptop? They'd certainly been careful to block their caller ID.

A shiver snaked down my spine as I studied the Corinthians verse:

If anyone destroys God's temple, God will destroy that person; for God's temple is sacred and you are that temple.

Also clear. With such biblical references, I knew, PAAUL justified 'eye for an eye' vengeance. And though it seemed to me contradictory to say simultaneously that it was okay to kill certain people *and* that all life was sacred, I knew that to anti-abortion extremists such thinking made perfect sense.

I let the new reality settle: Harry had been right about PAAUL.

He had been horribly wrong in the way he'd gone about getting proof, but there was no doubt in my mind now: PAAUL was behind Caspian's murder. It hurt to imagine: my poor husband, his only crime a desire to serve the women who needed his help.

It was evil.

I put my head in my hands.

My thoughts turned to Dad. So many things pointed to his involvement: his name was all over the PAAUL supporter forums, his move away from the pro-life limelight coincided with the start of the abortion doctor assassination campaign – and he'd denied any knowledge of PAAUL when I first asked him about it. Knowing how open and honest he usually was, this last point weighed heavily on my mind.

Dad would *never* personally send – or sanction the sending of – such a menacing message to me, his daughter. But that didn't mean someone else at PAAUL hadn't done so. Or maybe someone close to Dad who knew of my suspicions and wanted to protect him?

I sat up. What about Auntie Sheila? She was certainly rigid in her pro-life beliefs, and look at the way she'd jumped down my throat when I'd asked her about Dad this morning.

I thought it through. Since the truth had come out about Harry, I'd expressed nothing but anger at his lies to everyone I met. Everyone, that is, except Sheila. She was the only person to whom I'd hinted my continuing suspicions about Dad and PAAUL. And she had been *furious* with me. The kind of defensive anger that someone might feel if a person they loved very much and knew to be guilty was being accused of a crime. Indeed, Sheila had gone so far as to order me to stop asking questions, not just about Dad, but to back off the whole idea of associating Caspian's murder with PAAUL.

Could *she* have sent the threatening text to me in order to protect Dad?

My phone rang: *Dex calling.*

I snatched up the mobile.

'Dex?'

'Hey, Dumpy, you okay? Mum told me you're in a bit of a state over Harry. I can't believe it. What a wanker, seemed a nice guy too.'

'He did,' I said, barely taking in what he was saying. 'Dex, listen. I'm fine, but I'm . . . I'm just wondering. I know this is going to sound mad but do you think your mum might be covering up for my dad?'

There was silence on the other end of the line.

'Dex?'

'What on earth . . .? Has this got something to do with Harry's lies?' Dex sounded concerned. 'Has he fed you more bullshit?'

'No.' I closed my eyes. The living room seemed to spin around me. 'I'm probably just going mad.'

'Don't sweat it.' Dex gave a sympathetic sigh. 'And

to answer your question, I can't believe Mum would ever go outside mainstream Catholic teaching and cover up murder, even to protect your dad. You know how authority-pleasing she is, always delighted when the priests take notice, looking up to my arsehole of a father even after he'd abandoned her. Even now, believing he's changed, when he's clearly still spending most of his day getting wasted in the Three Crowns.'

Dex was right. I sank back in my chair, defeated. I was getting completely paranoid. PAAUL was responsible for Caspian's death – of that I was now sure – but there was no way any member of my family was involved. It was hysterical to think so.

'Honestly, Franny.' Dex's voice sounded strained now. 'If you'd seen the way Dad treated her when they were together you'd never think Mum capable of endorsing *any* kind of violence.'

Was that true? I'd done a paper on the cycle of violence at university. Statistically, victims of abuse often became desensitised to it, even accepting violence as normal behaviour.

My mind flitted back to a memory from childhood. Dex, though never beaten himself, had used to call my parents when his parents fought. He was a mess at the time: desperate to protect his mum but neither physically nor mentally strong enough to stand up to his dad. Once I remember hearing my own dad on the phone calming Dex then pleading with Sheila to 'take responsibility, for your son's sake as well as your own'. Of course I had no idea at the time what was going on,

I just knew that Dex was sometimes moody and that my dad worried about him.

'I'm sorry,' I said. 'It was thoughtless of me to ask.'

I rang off and fell back to thinking. Could Sheila be protecting Dad? It hurt me to imagine any scenario in which Dad was guilty of conspiracy to murder. But it was impossible, now, to shake myself out of the terrifying possibility, with PAAUL's warning text running through my brain on repeat.

Who could I turn to in order to find out the truth? There was clearly no point trying to talk to either Dad or Sheila about it again, but maybe I should confront Uncle Graham. Even if he didn't want to expose Sheila's involvement ... even if he didn't know about it ... he was obviously in close contact with her and might have inadvertently picked up information. Either way, it would be better than sitting here doing nothing.

A few minutes later I'd called Ayesha and discovered that Lori was, thankfully, free to come over and babysit. As soon as she arrived I set off for Graham's first-floor flat in Ladbroke Grove. I hadn't been there before, though Dad had given me the address so I could send a card at Christmas. Not that I'd bothered to do that – after all, Graham made absolutely no effort to send cards himself, even on the kids' birthdays.

There was no reply from the buzzer by the wooden front door. I looked up at Graham's flat. It was late afternoon and the streetlamps had already come on, though the light still clung to the gloomy day. A pair of grubby curtains with a distinctive criss-cross pattern were drawn across the windows. No lights were on inside.

My heart sank. Graham wasn't here.

Spending most of his day getting wasted in the Three Crowns.

Dex's words about his father sounded in my head. I glanced across the street. The Three Crowns was a few doors down, its windows smudged with dirt. I scurried over the road and inside. It smelled – the sour smell of stale beer engrained in the grungy brown carpet.

Uncle Graham was sitting alone in the far corner. Unlike the smiling, chatting people around him, he cut a morose figure, hunched over a newspaper with what looked like two fingers of Scotch set in front of him. He didn't see me until I was standing right in front of him.

'Hi,' I said awkwardly.

Graham looked up, bleary-eyed. Jesus, was he already pissed? It was barely 5 p.m. He took a moment to focus, then scowled.

'What the fuck are you doing here?'

I swallowed, wondering how to make him open up.

'Can I get you another drink?' I offered.

'Fuck off,' Graham snorted. I frowned. If the man didn't want alcohol the situation was, surely, hopeless. 'Wait.' He scowled at me. 'I guess I could handle another. Better make it a large one, okay?'

I bought a double whisky for him and a lemonade for me and headed back to Graham's table. He indicated the chair opposite. I sat and the chair rocked unevenly.

'What do you want?' he asked.

'I wondered what you know about an organisation called PAAUL. It's pro-life, extreme, violent.'

A nasty smile curled around Graham's mouth. He fixed me with a glazed stare. 'My bonkers ex-wife told me you'd got it into your head this group killed hubby dearest,' he sneered.

'That's right,' I said.

Graham blinked rapidly, presumably with surprise at my openness. 'Sheila also said that some hack told you St Jayson himself was responsible.'

I focused on his face, trying to read every twitch of muscle. 'What do you think?'

'Me?' Graham gave a sardonic laugh. 'Jesus wept, Francesca. I've been a confirmed atheist for years, I don't make a habit of following the group activities of religious nutters.'

'That's not what I asked.'

There was a pause. Loud chatter rose up at the bar across the room. Graham kept his glazed eyes fixed on my face.

'This is killing you, isn't it?' he said, sounding suddenly sober.

I looked down at my lap. 'I just want to know the truth,' I said.

Graham laid his hand on the rough wooden table next to my lemonade glass. His fingernails were stained and chipped. Condensation ran down the outside of the glass. I was seized with the desire to hold it against my forehead. I felt hot and dirty. I shouldn't have come. Graham tapped his hand twice, slowly, on the table.

I looked up.

'The truth that you're looking for is that my brothers are hypocrites,' Graham said slowly. 'Jayson and Perry are both up to their necks in evil.'

My breath caught in my throat. 'What do you mean?'

'This group PAAUL,' Graham went on, lowering his voice. 'You're on to something ... the murders. Sheila knows it too, but she'll never admit it. Too loyal to St Jayson.'

'Really?' I drew back, sceptical. Was he sincere or just trying to wind me up?

'I know things ... *serious* things ...' Graham went on, lowering his voice and leaning closer. 'Jayson and Perry use Lanagh as an HQ. They pretend all they've ever done is investigate PAAUL but they never wanted to stop the extremism. Quite the bloody opposite. All that moderate tolerance is a smokescreen. They've had a secret plan for years to get a load of abortion doctors bumped off, especially ones that do late abortions.' He lowered his voice. 'I reckon they even had your husband topped.'

I gasped. 'Why ...? How do you know all this?'

Graham shrugged. 'I'm still in touch with a lot of people from when we were all younger. It's common knowledge among certain circles. Nobody has any proof of course ...' He finished his whisky and took a gulp of the fresh glass I'd just bought him. 'But there must be evidence about it somewhere. *Has* to be. Jayson's such a neat freak, he'll have some file on it all.'

'I looked in Lanagh,' I said, unable to stop myself.

'There's nothing but reports, stuff that backs up Dad and Uncle Perry investigating PAAUL, not being a part of—'

'It'll be in Jayson's house,' Graham insisted. 'Something incriminating, I'd bet on it.'

'No.' I drew back. Graham was drunk. And vengeful. He didn't know Dad like I did. I folded my arms, trying to convince myself that he was wrong. 'It's impossible.'

'Not to me,' Graham growled. 'Clearly you're as blind and arrogant as Sheila ... and the rest of them.' He waved his hand vaguely.

'Graham, can you—?' I started.

'Enough,' he interrupted. 'Because I'm really not fucking interested in *anything* you have to say or in talking about this any longer.'

I hesitated. 'Please,' I said. 'Calm down.'

'Please,' he said, mimicking me in a high-pitched voice. 'Fuck off.'

There was no point trying to talk to him any longer. I stumbled out of the pub. It was dark and the temperature had dropped. I made my way to my car and slumped into the driver's seat.

Yet another allegation against Dad. I couldn't bear any more of this. I had to find out if he really was involved with PAAUL once and for all.

I started the engine. Graham had seemed convinced there was evidence connecting Dad with PAAUL actually in his home. Tonight was the sacred music concert at St Cecilia's Lucy had invited us to. She, Dad and

Jacqueline were having an early supper at a local Italian restaurant beforehand, which meant they would be out between 6.30 and 10 p.m. or so.

I could go over there, let myself in and see if I could find something. It felt like clutching at straws, but Graham's accusations reverberated around my head. I had to do something. Sitting at home and worrying about it all was no longer an option.

As I drove away from Ladbroke Grove I called Ayesha on the hands free and asked if Lori would mind babysitting a little longer.

'Tell her to order in pizza, I'll pay when I get back,' I offered.

Ayesha said she'd go over herself. Relieved, I gritted my teeth and headed to Kensington, planning my search of the house as I drove.

HARRY

It grew dark outside the café and Harry could wait no longer. Fran still hadn't answered any of his calls and he needed to know whether the information on his laptop had convinced her he'd been right to investigate her father. Most of all he wanted to find out if she believed he truly wanted to make amends. He had to get past her fury that he'd lied to her, but at least maybe he'd opened the door to a future conversation.

It was raining hard as he strode to Notting Hill tube station and still drizzling as he emerged at Southfields. Fran's house was a couple of streets away. Harry's pulse thundered at his temples as he stood on her doorstep, remembering the look of hurt and betrayal in those caramel-coloured eyes of hers as he'd given her the computer. It seemed strange that had happened just last night; it felt like years ago. Harry steeled himself as the door opened. He was expecting Francesca – or possibly one of her children. But instead Ayesha stood there, tall and fierce in a long orange tunic and pink leggings.

'You,' she said, rather theatrically. 'What the hell do you want?'

Harry drew himself up. 'I'm looking for Francesca.'

'She's out,' Ayesha spat. 'And she won't want to see you.'

'It's important,' Harry insisted.

'You tosser.' Ayesha advanced towards the door, nostrils flaring. She was far shorter than Harry yet filled his entire field of vision. 'Go away.'

She slammed the front door in his face. Stunned, Harry stood, staring at the chrome knocker. What did he do now? Ayesha was clearly not going to tell him where Fran was. He glanced up at the first-floor window. Fran herself was quite possibly in the house, letting Ayesha act as her guard dog. He took a step back so he could see to the second floor as well. All the rooms were in darkness. If Fran was inside she was staying well hidden.

A rap on the window to the left of the front door floated over the distant hum of traffic. Harry looked across. A small, pale face wreathed in smiles peered through the glass. It was Fran's daughter, Ruby. She had the same dark hair and elfin face as her mother, though her eyes were paler and rounder. She waved and Harry motioned for her to open the window. A little hand reached up to the latch and a second later they were face to face.

'Hey, Arsenal,' Harry whispered.

'Hey, Man City.' The little girl giggled.

'I was looking for your mum,' Harry said. 'Is she in?'

Ruby shook her head. 'She's at Granddad's,' she hissed. She glanced behind her. 'Gotta go.' She disappeared from the window.

Yes. Fran had gone to her father's house at a time when he knew, from what Lucy had told him earlier, the family would be out. Which could only mean one thing. She was looking for information on Jayson Carr's connection with PAAUL.

Harry turned and trotted down the rain-spattered steps, his mood lifting.

FRAN

An hour passed as I searched Dad's study. Memories of exploring Perry's basement haunted me, especially the gay porn I'd unearthed. I braced myself every time I opened a file marked *private*.

But there was nothing remotely scandalous buried in Dad's paperwork. I yawned as I scanned file after file, taking in random lines of reports and spreadsheet figures. Most of the information stored here related to Dad's business interests – he was on the board of at least six companies – and his property portfolio. The only personal items were to do with tax and accounting. I lingered briefly over Dad's will which, I already knew, left everything equally to Jacqueline, Lucy and myself – then flicked past a series of insurance documents going back ten or so years.

I turned to Dad's computer. He had a small laptop which he carried with him and which I knew was password protected, but his desk PC was easy to open. I did a couple of searches using the keywords 'PAAUL' and 'abortion'.

Nothing.

I checked the time. It was almost 7 p.m. Lucy, Dad and Jacqueline would be out for another three hours at least and I was determined to carry on searching. Trouble was, I had no idea where to look next.

The doorbell rang. I ignored it. Then my mobile trilled. I glanced at the text, bracing myself for another warning.

I'm outside @ your dad's. I need to speak to you. Please open the door. Harry.

How the hell did he know I was here? And what on earth did he want?

The doorbell sounded again.

Exasperated, I scuttled across the polished parquet floor – Jacqueline had insisted on it being relaid last year – and opened the front door. Harry stood outside, his jacket crumpled and his hair dishevelled from the wind that whipped up the street. He stared at me, an expression of consternation on his face.

'Are you alone?' he asked.

'Why?' I snapped. 'Worried my dad will beat you up?'

'Your sister told me she and Jayson and Jacqueline were going to a concert this evening, but I . . .'

'You spoke to Lucy?' Why on earth hadn't my sister mentioned that?

Harry nodded. 'I came to see her to . . . to tell her . . . to talk about you,' he said.

'Oh,' I said. My heart hammered. Harry moved closer. His presence was overwhelming. I gazed up into his intense eyes. I should just slam the door on him. I should feel angry.

But instead, I felt excited. Attracted.

Hopeful.

'I'm guessing you've come here because you've read the files I gave you and you're trying to find out the truth ... looking for links between your father and PAAUL.'

I stared at him, knowing my face was giving away the fact that he was right.

'That's what I thought.' Harry smiled. A thrill of desire shot through me. How could I feel so connected to someone who'd deceived me so badly? 'I want to help,' he went on. 'Please let me help.'

'You're just trying to get your stupid story.' Fury rose inside me. After everything he'd said. All that bullshit about liking me. I pushed at the door, trying to shut it.

'Wait.' Harry wedged his foot in the gap.

I glared at him. 'Go away.'

'I promise I've *dropped* my story,' he said, pushing back against the door, keeping it open. 'I'm only offering to help because I can see *you* need to know.'

'You have to be kidding.' Surely he couldn't think I'd be so gullible as to trust him again?

'You can decide what we do with whatever we find,' Harry persisted. 'I've already given you all my notes. My entire bloody laptop in fact. There are no copies. No back-ups.'

I wrestled with the door. Harry was still forcing it open.

'Please,' he said. 'I just want to help. I'll do whatever you—'

'You're a liar. A fraud. I don't believe anything you say.'

'Believe this then.' Harry chucked something through the gap between the door and frame. I glanced down. It was a black leather wallet. Two sets of keys followed, then a tablet. 'That's all my cards, the keys to my flat. My iPad. Take them. Keep them. Give them back when I've proved I mean it.'

I hesitated, still pressing the door against his foot. Harry let it go, until only the tip of his toe was preventing me shutting it entirely.

'I know I screwed up,' he went on, his voice low and suffused with shame. 'But I've told you before, I never meant to upset you. I . . . I didn't know how much I'd like you.'

Shit. My head fought with my heart. Of course I shouldn't trust him; once bitten, twice shy was exactly how I should feel. And yet every instinct told me he was sincere, that he did like me and that he genuinely wanted to make up for lying to me before.

'I *said* back in that bar that I needed to tell you something. I was going to confess everything, the whole undercover thing, the lies I'd told . . . Then you asked me back to your house and I was so . . . so over the moon you liked me it went out of my head.'

'Right,' I snorted, trying to force some steel into my voice. 'You're a lovesick puppy. Give me a break.'

'Please, Fran,' he went on. 'Even if you don't ever

want to see me again, this is a massive house. I can *help* you—'

'I don't need your help.' But even as I said the words I knew they weren't true. It *was* a massive house and there was no way I could manage to ferret my way solo through all the main storage spaces before the others returned home. I looked down at the worn leather wallet and the house keys glinting on the parquet floor.

'What about your car?'

Harry fished in his pocket and handed me a Vauxhall key. 'The car itself is at home, but I'll drive it over with the spare key if—'

'I don't want your stupid car.'

Harry fell silent. I couldn't see him on the other side of the door, but I could hear the rain falling, heavy on the front path. Further back, in the road, something zoomed past at high speed. Mum used to complain about the traffic when Lucy was little. 'It's all very well being so central,' she'd grumble to Dad. 'But the road is a rat run, cars race down here, all the faster because they've been stuck in jams for hours.'

I felt like one of those cars now. I'd been stuck in a state of indecision, swinging this way and that over Dad's involvement with PAAUL. And now here I was actually acting on my fears, trying to get to the bottom of it. The prospect of going to bed tonight still without any answers was unthinkable. Perhaps I should let Harry help. Whatever we found would be useless to him unless he kept the proof and I could make sure he didn't do that.

I opened the door a fraction so that I could see Harry's face. His brown eyes met mine. I still couldn't trust him. But maybe I could make use of him. I let the door swing fully open as I stepped back to pick up his wallet and tablet and keys. I put them all in my hand-bag, which was where I'd left it, on the hall table, then beckoned him inside.

'You can help,' I said. 'But you don't leave my sight and I keep all your stuff for as long as I want.'

Harry nodded and came in. He shucked off his jacket and rolled the sleeves of his jumper up his arms. His forearms looked muscular – strong and brown. I tore my gaze away.

'Follow me,' I said.

I led Harry into Dad's study and showed him the files on the top shelf which I hadn't had time to explore yet. According to the labels they contained data on Dad's old property portfolio, but maybe there was something incriminating inside. I made sure Harry was posi-tioned examining the files where I could see him, then resumed my search of Dad's PC.

We worked in silence. I was only half-concentrat-ing on Dad's files now. My mind ran over what Uncle Graham had told me. I wouldn't pass on any of that to Harry. Nor would I let him talk about his feelings any more. What had he said to Lucy? She would be in the middle of that concert right now, but I was going to ask her as soon as she got home.

After twenty or so minutes Harry cleared his throat. 'I don't think there's anything here,' he said. 'You say you've examined most of these files. There's nothing remotely connected to religion here, I just don't see your dad storing PAAUL info with all this legit business stuff.'

I sighed. Annoyingly, he was probably right.

'So where do you think the PAAUL stuff might be?' I asked.

Harry shrugged. 'Somewhere more personal, like a bedroom?'

I made a face. Jacqueline kept their bedroom pretty tidy; I couldn't imagine Dad creating a hiding place for secret papers there.

'Is there a safe?'

I shook my head. 'Just a locked box for Jacqueline's diamonds. But it's too small for anything but jewellery.'

'Does your dad have a dressing room? Somewhere he relaxes on his own?'

'He uses the spare room next to Lucy's to keep old suits . . .'

'Let's take a look.' We went upstairs and searched the spare room, then checked all the cupboards in Dad and Jacqueline's bedroom.

Nothing.

It was now past 8 p.m. and I was tired and hungry. I sat on the bed with a sigh. Harry looked up from the wardrobe he was investigating. It was empty apart from three of Jacqueline's hat boxes.

'Do you want to stop?' he asked, sensing my frustration.

I shook my head.

A beat passed. 'Is there anywhere else?' Harry asked. 'Somewhere people don't go very much? A place which is a bit of a dumping ground for your dad's things? Maybe a bit of a mess?'

'No,' I said. 'Jacqueline keeps the house shipshape, as she would say. Even the attic only has a few bits of furniture and a box of silverware and that's all my mum's.'

'What about the garden?' Harry asked.

I shrugged. 'There's a summer house,' I said. 'That *is* full of junk. More of Mum's old stuff mostly, but Dad stores things there too. Jacqueline never uses the place. No one does any more.'

Harry nodded. 'Let's take a look.'

I led Harry across the lawn and through the copse of trees to where the summer house stood. I hardly ever came out here any more, in fact I hadn't been any further than the patio for years. Growing up, the house had seemed very normal to me, but I was aware now that this was a massive garden by London standards: wide as well as long, with the trees almost masking the main house – and its neighbours – from view.

The summer house was about six feet by eight and made of painted white pine with green gloss – now chipped and peeling – at the windows. Surrounded by a rockery made of smooth white stones, it had once seemed an almost magical place in the middle of the trees. When we first moved here I told Lucy in a fit of big-sisterly meanness that it was the house that the witch in Hansel and Gretel lived in and that if she went inside she would be captured and eaten.

I could still remember the look of panic on her little face as I'd spoken. I'd got in big trouble for that and rightly so. I can't imagine Ruby ever doing anything half so cruel.

I found the spare key under the third stone from the door. Inside the air was stale and cold. Even using my phone as a torch we couldn't see much, but it was obvious that the place was crammed with Mum's old bits and pieces, long since replaced in the main house by Jacqueline's more streamlined designer tastes: an old coffee table, two small stools, upholstered in wide cream-and-pink stripes, an ornate wooden bookcase. There was also junk from the garden: folded, faded canvas loungers from when we were kids, a pile of moth-eaten blankets, an old boules set in a tin box. Everything was covered with dust. Clearly nobody had been in here for years. I felt a sudden pang of loss for the free, easy childhood I'd enjoyed out here, the long summer days playing with Dex, Lucy tagging after us, when the sun beat fiercely on our heads and the air was clotted with heat. At least that's how I remembered those summers. One thing I knew from my psychology degree is how faulty memory can be, how easy it is to idealise the past.

Harry found a battery-operated garden lantern with a set of batteries still in their plastic wrapping taped to the outside. He set the lantern up and shone its light into the corners of the room. 'I'm going to pull stuff away from the walls, see if there's anything interesting hidden behind.'

While he worked, I examined the pile of blankets, checking nothing was concealed in or under them. I didn't hold out much hope.

'I can't imagine Dad ever comes in here.' I glanced around. 'No one does from the look of it.'

'Someone's been here recently.' Harry pointed to a dust-free path I hadn't noticed before. It ran between two sets of lounger cushions and led to another suspiciously dust-free wooden box. The box stood on a faded red rug, wedged between more cushions.

I pulled the cushions out of the way. One had a rust-coloured stain in the middle.

'God, is that blood?' I said, peering at the stain as Harry fumbled with the lid of the box.

'Looks like it,' he said. 'Old blood.'

I looked up.

'Empty.' He dragged the box towards me so I could see. As he did so the rug shifted, revealing the jagged edge of a floorboard.

I stared at the dark space to the side of the board. There was just enough room to slip a hand around it. Harry followed my gaze.

'Go on,' he said.

I crouched down beside him and slid my fingers past the rough, cold wood. I gripped the board. Lifted it. It gave easily. Harry let out a long, slow whistle. He leaned over my shoulder, peering into the space beneath.

'Do you think it's a hiding place?' I asked, pulse quickening.

'What's in there?'

I felt into the darkness. My hand lit on a slim, flat piece of plastic, the size and shape of a credit card.

I drew the card out and shone a light on the front of it.

It was yellow, with a logo made up of intersecting cubes and the words *Ed Evans Storage* written across it in blocky caps.

Harry took the card from me and flipped it over. A magnetic strip ran down the back. 'It's a key card,' he said, 'to a storage room or ... or a locker.'

I took the key card back. 'Ed Evans Storage,' I read out loud. 'I've never heard of them.'

'Me neither. Shall I check them out?' Harry pulled up the browser on his phone. A moment later he showed me the screen.

'Their website says they have two storage facilities, one in Birmingham and one in an industrial estate in Walthamstow.'

'Walthamstow is only an hour or so away,' I said.

'I know,' Harry said, peering at the phone again. 'According to this, the storage place there will be closed right now, but there's got to be a way in.' He stood up. 'Let's go and check it out.'

'Wait,' I said, jumping to my feet. 'There'll be millions of lockers, you'll have no idea which one this opens.'

'I know.' Harry pushed his way past a folded lounger, heading for the door. 'We'll just have to try all of them until we find the right one.'

'But it might not contain anything to do with PAAUL,' I protested, feeling into the gap under the floorboard again. It was empty. 'There might be PAAUL stuff somewhere else.'

Harry stopped. His expressive face registered impatience and confusion. 'You're right,' he conceded, 'we don't know if this card will give us anything to do with PAAUL, but we need to find out, don't we? I thought that's what all this investigating was about?'

I let out a frustrated sigh. It was 8.35 p.m. If I left with Harry now to go on some wild goose chase to Walthamstow I'd have to give up my exploration of Dad's house for this evening.

'I can go on my own,' Harry said, reading my concerns. 'You stay here, carry on looking.'

I shook my head. No way could I trust Harry to be alone with the storage card.

Harry gave an exasperated sigh. 'Look,' he said. 'You've got all my stuff. Keep my wallet and keys and tablet and computer. Let me take my phone and a bit of cash. I'll call you when I get to the storage place. Deal?'

'Call me as soon as you've taken a look,' I said. 'The very next minute.'

'Okay,' he said.

'I'm serious. *As soon as* you've seen what's in the storage place?'

'I promise.'

'And whatever you find you have to bring straight back to me,' I said. 'I'll go to the police and say you stole the card if you don't.'

'Agreed.'

We hurried back into the house. As we passed through the kitchen I took a small knife from the block. The metal blade felt cold as I touched it.

'You might need this to force a lock to get inside the storage place,' I said, handing it over. 'And don't forget to call me. I want to know what you find as soon as you find it.'

'I promise that the very first thing I do will be to send you a picture.' Harry grinned, then raced off.

I fetched a proper torch from the house and went back to the summer house. With the better light I could see a row of boxes tucked in the corner of the room. The more I thought about it, the more likely it seemed that the storage card was probably old and disused – a dead end. Maybe it had even slipped under the floorboards. The boxes in front of me were a much better bet for finding a connection between Dad and PAAUL. I shoved the tiny wrought-iron table in the corner out of the way and resumed my search. I tried not to think about Harry as I worked but it was impossible.

Did he mean what he said about helping me?

I couldn't trust him, obviously, but suppose he really did like me? Suppose he had decided to let me choose what we did with what we found? Could I seriously turn Dad over to the police?

What would Auntie Sheila, who idolised him, say? Or Uncle Graham, who hated him? And how could I tell Lucy any of this?

My thoughts in turmoil, I ransacked box after box, searching carefully past old swimming togs and loops of discarded electrical wiring and memories that threatened to rip my heart open if I stopped and let them.

Harry

It took Harry just over an hour to get to Walthamstow, then another fifteen minutes to find the industrial estate containing Ed Evans Storage. Fran filled his head – the way she'd looked, furious and vulnerable in her sweater and jeans – and the way she'd listened to him ... against her own will, he'd sensed. But she *had* listened and she'd let him help her and if he could just find out what was in the storage locker and bring it back to her, surely he would have *proved* he meant what he was saying.

He forced himself to stop thinking about her when he reached the industrial estate. He had to focus now. Do whatever it took to get what he'd come for.

It was almost 10 p.m. and a Sunday evening so he wasn't surprised that the place was deserted. Trees and a muddy ditch half full of water marked the western boundary of the estate and the gloomy lighting and the silence gave the row of industrial sheds a spooky feel. According to the diagram at the entrance, Ed Evans Storage was at the furthest, darkest end of the estate.

Harry bent down, feeling for the small kitchen knife Francesca had given him earlier and which he had tucked inside the top of his boot. It felt strange not to have his keys and his wallet, but the knife did at least make him feel slightly more confident. It was small but sturdy – and the blade was sharp. Lucy's earlier warning to be careful flashed into his head as he hurried towards the storage facility.

Harry kept to the cover of the trees. A row of terraced houses was just visible through the branches. Lights were on in some of the homes. They seemed to belong to another world, far removed from the still darkness of the industrial estate. A minute or two later and Harry reached Ed Evans Storage. He stood, peering through the trees at the building. It was a square-fronted shed with a bright-blue front door, just like all the others in the row. He scouted around the outside. There was no window, no other entry point he could see, but it didn't matter. If Harry could just force his way past the front door, he'd be inside, no problem.

He was about to take a step out of the trees, towards the shed, when a uniformed security guard emerged.

Harry shrank back, heart racing.

The guard lit a cigarette and puffed away, blowing smoke rings into the night air. He was older than Harry, late forties at least, and not as tall. But he looked bulky and muscular. If it came to a fist fight, Harry wasn't at all sure he could beat him. Anyway, it couldn't come to that. Harry's priority was to get in and out of the storage facility without anyone seeing. He couldn't risk the guard raising an alarm.

After a few minutes the guard stubbed out his fag and went back inside. Harry waited a moment, his heart still thumping, then crept over to the front door. He peered in through the small wire-mesh window. The guard sat with his feet up at a desk a few feet away. He was sideways on to Harry, his fingers tapping on the landline phone in front of him and totally absorbed in whatever was on his computer screen.

Beyond him was a door marked *storage*. That must be where the key card in Harry's pocket would find its home. That was where Harry needed to be. He just had to get past the guard.

He checked the time again then ducked into the shadows and took out his phone to text Fran that he'd arrived. If everything went tits up in the next two minutes, he wanted her to know that he was here, doing his best to keep his promise to her.

There was no signal.

Great. Harry sighed. He'd have to try again later. If he waited any longer, he might lose his nerve.

Making sure the phone was on silent, he shoved it in his pocket and hurried around the corner. His throat felt dry as he took the watch off his wrist. Checking the time, he set the alarm to sound on repeat in one minute then laid it on the ground and hurried away, to the shadows at the side of the building.

He stood in the silence, waiting. If this went wrong, he could well be arrested. He gritted his teeth. He wouldn't let it go wrong. Trying to count down in his head, the alarm still surprised him, blasting into the night air on full volume.

Harry held his breath. It wasn't the first time he'd used a watch in this way but he couldn't remember a time when the consequences had mattered more. After several long seconds, the security guard appeared, grumbling to himself. Harry grinned with relief as the guard hurried towards the sound of the alarm, letting the front door swing shut behind him.

Swiftly, silently, Harry sped out of the shadows, catching the door before it shut. As the guard disappeared around the corner, Harry slipped inside. He raced past the desk and straight through the door at the far end.

He was in.

FRAN

I worked my way through the summer house, checking in every possible receptacle and behind every scrap of furniture to make sure nothing else was hidden. I tapped against the walls and the floor, dragging the junk that had been dumped here out of the way each time. After an hour I was covered in dust and grime and I had found nothing.

I tried calling Harry but his phone went straight to voice mail. Was he still on the tube? Or out of range? Had he actually gone to the storage place in Walthamstow? Or had he run off to write his story about Dad after all?

No. He wouldn't have done that – apart from the fact that he'd sworn to me he wouldn't do *anything* without my go-ahead, there *wasn't* a story yet. Perhaps I'd been stupid to let him take that key card. Still, I had all his belongings, including the keys to his flat. I could do what I liked with them. And there had been something so genuine about the way he'd looked at me earlier ... Surely I could trust him?

Exhausted and frustrated, I wandered over to the gap under the floorboards where we'd found the key card. Had we missed something? I carefully patted the whole way round, as far as my hand could reach. It was definitely empty. I gave the wooden plank below the removed floorboard a frustrated shove. To my surprise it shifted in my hand. Just a fraction, but enough to suggest it had been laid on top of another board. I reached further, struggling to find its edge. *There*. I lifted the top board as far as I could, feeling underneath it. Nothing met my grasping fingers. There wasn't room for anything much, anyway, certainly nothing with any bulk. And then my hand touched the edge of a small, flat plastic bag. Holding my breath, I pulled it out.

HARRY

Harry shut the door softly behind him. He couldn't be seen from the entrance lobby in here, but he must make as little sound as possible once the security guard came back from his expedition to find the source of the alarm. Harry could still hear it, a muffled distant peal.

Ignoring the sound, he focused on what was in front of him. He was standing at the head of a long corridor. Two doors on either side stretched ahead. Which meant four rooms, each potentially containing the storage locker that the key card in his pocket would open.

Outside, the alarm on his watch stopped trilling. *Already?*

Shit. The security guard would be coming back inside at any second. There was no time to lose. He tiptoed along the corridor, opening every door in turn. As he'd feared, each one led to a room full of containers. These varied from big metal boxes the size of large cupboards to smaller boxes that resembled squat gym lockers. Every container was labelled with an ID number and the letter A, B or C. A quick scan confirmed that the letters were allocated according to size, with the bigger containers marked as 'A's and the smaller ones as 'C's.

Harry studied the key card from the summer house. A 'C' was printed in the corner. Harry darted from room to room. The 'C' containers were no more than a metre square. There were lots of lockers in each room and Harry had no idea which one his key card would open.

He could hear the security guard stomping back inside, slamming shut the front door. Harry refocused his efforts, trying to be as quick and as quiet as possible. Creeping to the start of the first room, he held the magnetic strip of the key card to the plate on the locker just above the number. It didn't open. He tried the next. And the next. Working systematically he covered the entire room. No joy. He moved next door to the second room and began again, checking each locker in turn. He was halfway along his first row when footsteps sounded in the corridor outside. Harry froze, the key card clutched in his hand.

He whipped around, his eyes fixed on the door.

With a soft creak, it started to open.

FRAN

My heart lurched into my mouth as I peered down at the transparent plastic bag I'd taken from under the floorboards.

It was the size of the bags they make you put your toiletries in at airports and it contained a small white envelope with typed print on the front:

Jeremiah 1:5–6

What did that mean? Was this a reference to another bible verse, like the one I'd been sent from Corinthians? The envelope wasn't sealed, the flap simply folded over. I felt inside and drew out six scraps of paper, clearly torn from different sheets. Each scrap was torn at the edges and creased, as if it had been folded and refolded several times. I studied them in turn. Each one contained two typed words ... except that they weren't words at all, just a jumble of letters. I frowned. What did they mean? Was each scrambled word a separate code? Or did the six separate bits of paper add up to a message of some kind?

They must mean *something*, or else why would

whoever had hidden them here have gone to so much trouble?

Perhaps the clue was in the bible reference. I looked it up on my phone. Dad, Jacqueline and Lucy always used the New International Version of the bible, so that was the version I picked:

Before I formed you in the womb I knew you, before you were born I set you apart; I appointed you as a prophet to the nations.

'Alas, Sovereign Lord,' I said. 'I do not know how to speak: I am too young.'

I frowned. I'd come across the first part of this quote several times before. It had cropped up in several of the anti-abortion posts Harry had led me to. If I'd had any doubts before, they vanished now; this was definitely something to do with PAAUL.

And, as I was in Dad's house, this meant yet another connection between Dad and PAAUL.

I leaned against the lounger cushion with the red-brown bloodstain, forgetting how earlier I'd recoiled. I shone a light on the scrambled letters on the top piece of paper, frowning as I tried to make sense of them:

uwdh bBprsawh

My head spun, filling with memories of spy films and codebreaking methodologies involving machines and number sequences and references to specific lines on specific pages of specific books.

I glanced back at the bible quote. Could this be a book cipher? It beggared belief. After all, this was Dad whose jumbled words I'd found, not some code-cracking genius from Bletchley Park. Still, maybe PAAUL insisted on using encryption for security reasons.

I stared back at the two words on the top scrap of paper. I knew how book ciphers worked, they were easy to crack once you had the relevant line from the book and almost impossible if you didn't.

I grabbed a pen from my bag and jotted down the exact words from the bible quote. With a basic cipher you just had to allocate each letter in the given line its own letter of the alphabet. In this case the first letter was 'B' so, presumably that was really an 'a' while the second letter 'e' was actually a 'b'.

I worked my way to the end of the bible quote but ran out of letters after I reached 'u'. Hoping against hope I tried to fit the letters I'd found to the words on the first scrap of paper. They made no more sense than they had before.

Frustrated, I studied the other scrambled words. The capital 'B' appeared several times, as did capitals for 'A' and 'I'. I looked back at the line from Jeremiah. There were capital 'B's, 'A's and 'I's in that too.

I sat up. Suppose the five capital letters in the bible quote each corresponded to a letter of the alphabet too?

I started on a fresh piece of paper, writing out the quote and allocating letters as I had before but this time with the capital 'B' from 'Before' given an 'a' and the lower case 'b' from 'womb' allocated a 'p'.

I went back to the first scrap and its jumbled words. According to my reworked cipher the 'u' was a 'j', the 'w' an 'o', the 'd' an 'h' and the 'h' an 'n'.

john

The first word unscrambled itself in front of my eyes. Holding my breath I worked on the second word: *bBpr-sawh*. It took a few minutes to tease it out, my heart drumming against my ribs as my eyes searched frantically for the alphabet match, but soon I had it: *paterson*

John Paterson

I blew out my breath, my fingers tightening around the six pieces of paper. This was one of the names from Harry's research ... one of the abortion doctors he was convinced had been killed by PAAUL.

HARRY

Harry darted behind the end of the row of lockers. The security guard was just a few feet away. And getting closer. Harry held his breath as the man chatted away on his phone. Light danced over the metal tops of the lockers opposite. *Shit*. The guard must be shining his torch up and down each row. Harry flattened himself against the lockers, hoping the man wouldn't come any closer.

'Yeah, weird, like I say,' the guard was saying. 'Alarm going like the clappers, someone must have dropped the watch earlier. Scared the bejeesus outta me.'

Footsteps sounded. Harry tensed. This was it. And then the light flickered away as the guard padded out to the corridor, still muttering into his phone. As he shut the door again Harry let out a silent sigh of relief. His palms sweated as he resumed his search of the lockers. Surely one *had* to open for him soon?

FRAN

I tried to recall what Harry's files had said about *John Paterson*. The doctor had been killed in 2012 in Glasgow. In his late fifties, with a wife and three grown-up children, he was beaten – most likely with a baseball bat – close to a nightclub where he was seen drinking and dancing with two unidentified women. The implication in the news reports Harry had gathered was that the beating was meted out by an angry boyfriend: a pre-planned murder dressed up to look like a spontaneous attack.

I turned to the next scrap of paper.

sBadyo Bny

Was this another name? I compared the letters with those from the cipher.

It took a few minutes before I had it: Rashid Ali. I remembered him too: just twenty-five and stabbed to death in Bradford in September 2013.

I stared at the third name:

fBabyBh dwIItBh

The capital letters and the length of the words told

me who this was, even as my brain refused to process the information. I forced myself to work through the cipher, heart thudding against my ribs.

The name, decoded, stared back at me.

My murdered husband: *Caspian Hoffman.*

HARRY

Harry entered the third room, a sense of futility creeping over him. Perhaps he'd got the whole thing wrong. For all he knew he and Fran could have found an ancient, unused key card – or one that belonged to a storage box at the Ed Evans Storage in Birmingham.

He set off down the next row of C-marked containers, holding the key card to each metal lock in turn. The movement was mechanical now, done with virtually no hope of success. Harry's thoughts drifted to Fran. He had promised he would let her decide what to do with whatever they found. But suppose it was concrete evidence of Jayson Carr's complicity in the abortion doctor murders? If he let Fran bury it then he would be guilty of covering up a crime.

He would do what she wanted, he had promised her that. But, for the first time since she'd kicked him out of her house on Friday night, Harry wondered if the truth might not destroy their relationship, before it had even begun.

With a faint pop the locker in front of him opened.

Harry stared at the door in surprise. It had worked, just as he'd stopped expecting it to. The key card had found its home.

Forgetting the moral dilemma he'd been grappling with just moments before, Harry pulled the locker door fully open and peered inside. A small transparent bag met his eye. He drew the bag towards him and stared at its contents, clearly visible through the plastic.

FRAN

Here, hidden away in my father's house, was a kill list. And third on that list was my husband's name. I stared at the scrambled letters that made up Caspian Hoffman. Slowly I put the piece of paper down. I felt sick. The dark of the summer house pressed down on me; outside the wind whistled through the trees. Dad's house was only fifty feet away, on the other side of the little copse outside, but it felt as if I was in the middle of nowhere, cast adrift from everyone and everything I knew.

Numbly I turned to the next name:

fdsyapwbdrs fBsawh

It took me just over a minute to work out that this was Christopher Carson, close to retirement and killed with a single blow to the head just outside Torquay in Devon in September of last year, 2015.

I had picked up by now that 'a' signified 's' and that 'h' meant 'n', which gave me the next name as soon as I peered at it:

aytwh byhhrs

Simon Pinner

I sat back, nausea roiling in my stomach, and forced my brain to face the truth: these names formed a list of the men my father had ordered to be killed in the name of PAAUL. He was a liar and a hypocrite. A terrorist. He was responsible for murdering all these men. Good men. Doctors.

Above all, he had killed my Caspian. His own son-in-law, the father of his grandchildren.

It was beyond belief. The pain of it deeper than losing Mum.

Just one scrap of paper was left. One name on the kill list.

I hesitated. Was this another victim? Another doctor recently murdered?

I put it down, unwilling to look. I felt dirty, almost complicit. Tears bubbled into my eyes. I wiped them angrily away. This was no time to get upset. I needed to work out what I was going to do with what I'd found. Should I confront Dad? Or just go straight to the police?

The thought of calling DS Smart again was intimidating. After all, what did this collection of scrambled names prove? At face value it was simply a list of murdered men, yet surely the code used to hide the names and the fact that they'd been hidden under the summerhouse floorboards, made the list's existence peculiar, if not downright suspicious?

Why had Dad put them here? I knew from my studies on psychopathy and compulsive behaviour that killers often kept trophies or used signatures to mark their crimes. Was that what he was doing here? It didn't really make sense.

But what other explanation was there?

With a shudder I stared down at the final set of jumbled letters:

dBssg rnnywp

I stared stupidly at the words, trying to force my brain to unscramble them. It felt like a dream. Dad had killed Caspian. All these others. Which meant Uncle Perry was surely up to his neck in the murders too – he and Dad were thick as thieves. What on earth was I going to do? I felt sick. I would have to tell Harry. Perhaps he knew already. If he'd made it to the storage locker.

If he hadn't betrayed me too.

Harry.

As I thought his name, the letters of the first word rearranged themselves in my mind's eye. I clutched the paper, adrenaline racing through me as I stared at the second.

It was him. His real name. The last name on the kill list:

Harry Elliot

HARRY

Holding his breath, Harry studied the contents of the bag he had found. He could make no sense of what was inside. It looked valuable but damaged and, though he needed to take a closer look in better light, not obviously incriminating. So why had it been secreted away in a storage locker? And how on earth was it connected to Jayson Carr and the deaths ordered by PAAUL? Perhaps Francesca would know. As soon as he was outside and had a signal he would call her, as he'd promised. Right now his priority was getting out of here.

He shoved the bag in his pocket and crept into the corridor, ears pricked for any sounds from the security guard on the other side of the door. There was no way he could get out through the front of the building without the guard seeing him.

He *had* to find another way out. He shone his torch app onto the skirting board. Two thin white wires ran discreetly above the wood. Harry glanced towards the door that led to the guard. It was firmly shut. He tiptoed in the opposite direction, following the wires. They led over each individual room's doorframe and back down to the skirting boards. Harry knew, from his late teens and early twenties spent working on building sites, that this meant they were part of a system most likely added after the storage facility had been built. As the building was modern it would have been built with an alarm system as standard, so these wires meant an extra level of security. Something that could be operated from the inside, switched on and off to allow the building as a whole to remain secure while bringing items – probably large items – through a separate door.

Which made sense. Harry hadn't noticed an exit when he'd looked outside, but if it was operated only from the inside, there wouldn't be any obvious handles or knobs out there. Harry's heart beat fast as he followed the wires into the only room he hadn't yet explored fully. He crept up and down the rows of lockers. *There.* A double fire door he hadn't noticed on his initial and cursory sweep of the room was visible in the corner. It should take him out onto the estate just beside the trees and the ditch. Perfect.

Harry examined the wires carefully. They were attached to a small box to the side of the fire door, presumably an alarm. Even though it was clearly designed to protect the facility from external intruders, Harry was pretty sure the alarm would sound if the door was opened from the inside too, unless it was switched off first. But he could see no way of doing that here – there was no switch on the wall or on the box. He shone his light all over the door. Nothing.

Swearing under his breath, he took the small kitchen knife out of his boot and sliced through the two wires. Every muscle in his body tensed as he waited for an alarm to blast out. Nothing happened. He pressed down on the bar handle, then pushed. The door swung open, its base scraping across the concrete ground. The noise filled the night air. Harry slipped outside, sweat beading on his forehead. Had the guard heard? He closed the door behind him and raced to the cover of the trees. He stood in the silence for a few seconds.

Yes. No sign of the guard. Harry shoved the little knife securely back into his boot and reached for the plastic bag in his jacket pocket. Elation swept over him. He had done it.

He couldn't wait to tell Fran.

Pulling out his phone, he walked as fast as the rough ground would allow, still hidden by the trees, the half-filled ditch just to his right. Its stagnant stench crept into his nostrils but he barely noticed. All he could think about was calling Fran, then meeting her and giving her what he'd found.

He hurried on, his impatience building, until the storage facility was out of sight. He was almost at the edge of the industrial estate. Safety and the train back to Fran were just a few minutes away. He took out his phone. Still no signal. At least he could email her a picture of what he'd found, even if he couldn't make a call. He'd promised to do that. He bent over, snapping a photo, then attaching a brief message.

Rustling sounded behind him. Harry looked over his shoulder, shivers running up and down his spine.

He couldn't see anyone. A twig snapped to his left. Then another.

Harry broke into a run.

FRAN

I stared at Harry's name, the summer house around me and the cold, dark night outside forgotten.

Harry was on the kill list. He was the next victim.

My heart in my mouth, I grabbed my phone and dialled his number. Out of range.

I had to warn him. I dialled again. And again. Still no connection.

I checked the bars on my phone. The signal here was strong. It must be a problem where he was. Unless he'd done something to his phone in order to avoid my call.

No. I didn't believe that. I just needed to give him a couple of minutes to move into range.

Absently I bundled the list of names and little envelope into my handbag. I replaced the floorboard and the rug and repositioned the wooden box and the cushions that had stood on top of them. I stood up. My breath was coming in sharp jags. Could Dad have really organised all this?

I didn't understand any of it: not just the sheer impossibility of imagining Dad ordering Caspian's death, but why he would store the victims' names here. It didn't make any sense. Neither did the presence of the key card. Were the contents of the storage locker it opened somehow related to Caspian? Or the other men who'd been murdered?

These questions ran on a loop in my head.

Nowhere near a couple of minutes had passed, but I couldn't wait. Surely Harry's phone had a signal by now? I dialled again. Still no connection.

I locked the summer house and stood outside, the chill wind against my face.

I dialled again. Nothing.

I put the key back under the third white stone from the door.

I reached for my phone. Again, nothing.

I couldn't stop dialling and redialling.

Please be okay. Please.

Harry's phone rang. *At last.* I held my breath, waiting, as it rang a second time.

Answer. Come on.

The line went dead.

'Harry?' I shrieked into the phone. '*Harry?*'

But there was no reply.

HARRY

Another twig snapped, this time directly behind him. Harry spun around, fists clenched.

'Who's there?' he called out.

Was it the security guard? Had he been followed?

Fear coursed through him. Harry turned and pelted towards the industrial estate's iron gate. His breath was harsh and rasping, the ground squelched under foot, moonlight glistening off the water in the ditch just beneath him. Only a few metres and he'd be through the trees. A few more and he'd reach the exit and be close to the lights and bustle of the nearby high street. The phone in his hand vibrated. His heart leaped. He was nearly out, almost safe.

He stumbled over a large stone, almost falling. He slowed, regaining his balance, as his phone vibrated a second time. Was that Fran?

A hand grabbed him, yanking his arm almost out of its socket and twisting it high behind his back. Before he could even yell a sharp prick pierced his neck. Then something cold seeping into his flesh. A numbing sensation radiated across his head and down into his back. His legs buckled underneath him.

Fran. He thought he was calling her name, but no sound came from his mouth. All he could feel was his tongue. The metal taste of blood. He had bitten his tongue as he fell. He couldn't move. A dark figure loomed over him as the mud met his face. Wet, cold earth. He was pushed, rolled, his legs useless, down, into the ditch.

Face down in the mud, a foot on his neck. He could feel nothing. Could move nothing. He tried to reach for the knife hidden in his boot, but his arm was numb. Pain ebbed away even as wet dirt filled his nose, his mouth. He couldn't breathe.

A terrible fear gripped him. A silent scream. Lights exploding behind his eyes. And then the world turned black.

HIDDEN

Sunday 17 January 2016–
Monday 18 January 2016

FRAN

1

I stand outside the summer house, shivering in the cold night air.

Where is Harry? Why has his phone gone dead? Is he all right?

Or has PAAUL already got to him? Has my father's assassin already taken his life?

The list of victims is stuffed in my handbag but the scrambled names on their scraps of paper are burned into my retinas. If I can just reach Harry in time and warn him ...

I've lost complete track of time. It feels like the middle of the night but I know it can't be much after 10 p.m. Are Dad, Jacqueline and Lucy home from their concert yet? I peer through the trees. Lights are on in the house. I lean against the nearest tree, my stomach in knots. From here I can see into the kitchen. Jacqueline is pottering about, fetching a mug, easing off her heels.

Does she know what Dad has done? I'm certain now that Sheila does. Could they all be in on it? Sheila and Jacqueline aren't close, but they both adore Dad.

Oh, Mum. My heart hurts. Mum loved Dad very deeply, but she was courageous where Sheila is meek and strong where Jacqueline is shallow. If she were here none of this would have happened. I swallow down my misery, watching as Jacqueline leaves the kitchen, plunging it back into darkness. She hasn't checked the back door, hasn't realised that it is unlocked, that I am out here.

There's no way I can face any of them. Not right now. My head is spinning, I need to think through everything I've found out. Most of all I need to make sure that nothing terrible has happened to Harry. Still hiding in the trees I try his mobile again. No connection. Which means what?

I try to tamp down the fear that burns through me, but it's overwhelming. All Harry's suspicions are confirmed. Everything I've seen and read and been told by him and Simon Pinner and Uncle Graham and all those people writing on internet forums ...

It's all true: my father is a killer.

The back of the house is still in darkness. I creep across the lawn, then tiptoe over the patio and in through the kitchen door. I lock it softly behind me, then hurry across the kitchen, into the hall.

I can hear Dad laughing as I tiptoe along the hall and ease the front door open. He is in the living room next door, warm and cosy with his wife and younger daughter. I can just picture him smiling at Jacqueline, sharing a joke with Lucy, everything as normal as can be and all the while he knows he has ordered the deaths of six people, including his own son-in-law.

Rage flares inside me. White hot. Impotent.

Caspian was my husband, my life partner, the father of my children. How could Dad justify taking him away from me? From the kids? How can he justify any of it? Even if you are against abortions, it's still obscene to kill the doctors who carry them out.

And Harry. There's no reason other than cowardice for killing him.

Harry. Whatever his faults, whatever our future, I can't bear the thought of losing him.

Should I call the police? Tell them he's missing?

No. It's too soon. His phone might simply be out of range.

My mind runs rapidly as I race along the pavement, going over everything. Bitter tears trickle down my cheeks. Dad's crimes feel so personal, so targeted against me. Perhaps they are. Perhaps his killing of Caspian is the ultimate expression of his control over me? Payback for all my years of teenage rebellion? The assertion of his fatherly power.

I don't risk a look back at the house until I reach my car. It's okay. No one is watching from the window. They don't know I've been there.

My hands are shaking, sobs rack my body as I start the engine. Somehow I negotiate the central London traffic, and make it home. I call Harry's mobile several times along the way. No reply. I realise I'm no longer expecting him to answer. In my heart I'm sure something terrible has happened to him.

Ayesha sees I'm upset as soon as I walk in. She and Lori are watching TV, my kids sound asleep upstairs. I thank God for Lori's presence, which is all that prevents Ayesha from pushing me to tell her what is wrong. I promise we'll speak in the morning, thank them for the last-minute babysitting then send them home.

I try Harry's phone again, this time with a feeling of hopelessness. I clean my teeth and put on a sweatshirt.

Perhaps I should tell someone he's not answering ... but who?

I don't have any contact details for his mum or sister. There's DS Smart, of course. His number is logged in my mobile. But what would I tell him? My heart sinks. That a man who has previously lied to me about his name, his job and his intentions is not answering his phone?

I would have to tell DS Smart about the kill list in Dad's summer house. Should I tell him about that?

I know I should. But right now, as I sit shivering, looking out of the window, it seems impossible.

The night passes agonisingly slowly. I'm too strung out to sleep for more than a few snatched minutes at a time. At least today is one of my non-working days. Ruby is up at seven thirty as usual, bounding in to demand I plait her hair. I have to drag Rufus out of bed at seven forty-five and force breakfast down him. He grumbles, oblivious to my pale face and strained eyes, as he heads out of the door to catch his bus. Ruby chats about her art project as I walk with her to school but I'm barely listening. I've already tried Harry's number twice since I woke from my last fitful doze. As before, there's no reply. Maybe he's choosing not to answer me and in no danger at all. In the cold light of day it seems more likely that he has run off and simply blocked my number.

Which means that he must have found something significant in that storage locker and is planning to write a story about it after all.

Another betrayal.

Another mark of Dad's guilt.

As I return home from dropping Ruby and make myself a cup of coffee I try Harry's mobile yet again. This time the number goes to a continuous tone, as if the phone no longer exists. As if he has taken out the SIM and stamped it to smithereens.

I sink into a chair, my head in my hands.

My mind careers about: on the one hand, Harry's grand gesture in leaving me his stuff could, now I think about it, easily be a clever bluff; he could have backed up everything on his laptop and given me a fake bunch of keys. He might even be prepared to ditch the backpack, the computer, the tablet, the wallet and all their contents for a good enough story.

And yet, on the other hand, I can't quite believe it. My instincts told me Harry genuinely wanted to make up with me. And surely it's too much of a coincidence that he vanishes just at the moment when I know for a fact that his life is under threat?

I sit at the kitchen table until my coffee turns cold. What do I do now?

At two minutes past ten my phone rings. It's Ayesha. I ignore the call and a few minutes later she's here, knocking on my front door.

'I've called in sick at work. What the hell is going on?' she demands, shucking off her pink coat and tossing it over the bannister. 'You looked last night like you did when ... like you'd just been whacked around the head.' She steps back, appraising me. 'And you look the same now. Did you sleep?'

I shake my head.

Ayesha takes my hand. 'I'm not going until you tell me what's wrong. Is it Harry? Being lied to like that, just after you'd opened up after Caspian?'

I take a deep breath. I can't possibly tell her about Dad. I can't tell anyone. Not yet.

'It *is* Harry, partly,' I say. 'But not like you think.'

'Like how, then?'

Squirming, I attempt a partial version of the truth.

'I'm worried about him. He came to see me – well, you saw him, he called here first, didn't he? Asking where I was?'

Ayesha nods, a frown creeping across her forehead.

'Well, he tracked me down and said that ... that he was very sorry about tricking me over who he was.'

'Only very sorry because he got caught,' Ayesha said with a snort.

'Maybe, but he said he was dropping the whole story and that he wanted to make up with me ... and at the time I believed he meant it.' The words burble out of me, a superficially truthful version of events. 'I met him yesterday evening, just briefly, then later he promised he'd call but he didn't and I tried him over and over but it was like his phone had gone dead … and still this morning, nothing. I can't reach him and I've got this feeling he's had … er, been in an accident or something.'

Ayesha studies me, a sceptical expression on her face. 'I don't know why you'd be worried about that douchebag,' she sighs. 'I'm sure he's fine.'

I meet her gaze. 'I'm sure he's not. He knows some … some dodgy people.'

Ayesha sighs again. 'Okay, well, if it will put your mind at rest let's call some hospitals, see if he's been brought in?'

We get on our mobiles and make call after call. At least it's something to do. As I wait on the line for yet another hospital switchboard to put me through to the right department, my thoughts turn to Dad again. He's always had a forceful personality, a fiery one even, but I've never known him be violent and I've never seen him approach an argument without logic.

I simply cannot imagine a world in which Dad could order Caspian's death. Family is every bit as important to him as his faith, and Caspian was his son-in-law. Not a blood relative, of course – but to Dad marriage *made* Caspian part of his close family. Anyway, for all Dad's passion he's a deeply rational man.

Unless that rationality is actually a manifestation of

a cold detachment he keeps hidden most of the time, covering up his lack of feeling with a show of intensity.

I see a vision of Dad's face, crumpled with misery as he realised I suspected him. Was all that grief and concern really an act?

The little I know about violent psychopaths tells me that they are likely to come across as charming and intelligent and acutely able to manipulate others; definitely capable of faking emotions to get what they want.

Could Dad be a psychopath, keeping the kill list papers and the locker card as mementoes of his triumphs?

It's surely unthinkable.

My mind whirls with fear and doubt as Ayesha and I stay on our phones. It takes us two hours to call every A&E in the South East of England. I have Harry's ID of course, so we're asking about John Does as well as both Harry Dunbar and Harry Elliot. Nobody has been brought in who bears any resemblance to him. What does this mean? It could mean anything. I veer from fear that he's been murdered like the other men on the kill list to conviction that he has done a bunk and is hiding from me. How stupid was I to trust him? I should never have let him take the key card. I should have stopped him from going to that industrial estate.

'Franny?' Ayesha squats down in front of me, her feet flat on the floor. I remember the first time I saw her do this and exclaimed at how flexible her hips were and she told me how she had sat like this as a child with her grandmother, who spoke no English, mixing powders for dyeing cloth. 'Franny?'

I meet her gaze.

'Is there something else? Something you're not telling me? Because I know you and Harry had a thing, but you seem ... I don't know, not just sad that he's gone but troubled, *really* troubled.' She hesitates. 'Is it bringing back Caspian being mugged before *he* was ...' She trails off and I stare at her blankly.

I still can't tell her what I've found out, that I believe my father killed my husband and other doctors, and has now ordered Harry's death on the grounds that he is close to uncovering the truth about these murders.

'I guess it does make me think about Caspian,' I say, which is true, if not the whole truth.

'Oh, sweetheart.' Ayesha leans in and pulls me into a big hug. I stare over her shoulder into the corner of the room. Harry's backpack stares back at me, his laptop poking out of the top.

At some point soon I will have to tell the police about the key card and the kill list. It has to be done, whatever the cost to Dad. I owe that much to Caspian. Not to mention the other doctors who have died.

And though I'm sure the police will insist Harry has gone to ground on his own initiative, after using me to get a story, maybe I can persuade them to look for him and warn him.

I remember Harry's face as he apologised last night: his expression of shame and misery, then the intense look of sincerity as he promised to contact me the second he managed to access the storage locker that the key card opened. Well, that was a lie. He didn't text and he didn't call. The very last thing he said was that he promised to send me a picture of whatever he found. And I've received nothing. I've checked my phone a million times. I disentangle myself from Ayesha who sits back with a sigh.

The backpack and edge of Harry's laptop is still in my line of sight. Would he really have left that and all the other things behind just for the sake of his story? What if Dad ordered his henchmen to follow Harry before he even reached Ed Evans Storage? Or what if they caught up with him as he left? What if they killed Harry and took whatever he found in the storage locker? It's surely possible that Harry's body just hasn't been found yet.

The thought sends a shiver down my spine.

I imagine the industrial estate as a deserted landscape, a wasteland, with Harry's lifeless body lying behind a dilapidated shed. Maybe he did try to call me and there wasn't a signal. Surely that's just as likely as him not bothering to try and contact me at all.

A new thought threads its way through my brain and I stare at the laptop again, my heart racing.

I turn to Ayesha. 'Thanks so much,' I say, 'but I'm feeling better now, you don't need to stay.'

It takes a few minutes but Ayesha leaves at last, insisting that she will pop round later to check on me and offering to look after Ruby and Rufus after school if I need 'a bit of time to myself'.

As soon as she's gone I hurry over to Harry's laptop. Using the password he gave me earlier I log on to the

Gmail account saved on his browser bookmark bar.

There's nothing in the sent emails.

Nothing in the outbox.

I sit back, doubting myself – and him – all over again. For a moment there I'd clung to the memory of the promise he made to send a picture of whatever he found at the industrial estate, hoping against hope that he would have tried to keep that promise, *especially* if he couldn't make a call. My instincts shriek at me that he sincerely intended to contact me.

But, I reflect with a grimace, I can trust my instincts about as far as I can trust Harry himself.

I'm about to put the laptop away when I notice there's an email in the draft folder.

Suppose he wrote something but didn't have time to send it? My heartbeat quickens as I open the message. It *is* for me. My email address is at the top and it's dated last night.

Found this in storage locker. Don't know what to make of it. Any ideas?

Found what? My fingers tremble as I open the attachment. What on earth was Dad hiding? A weapon? Or maybe a recording of some kind? Possibly even a written confession?

I stare at the picture that pops onto the screen. It's of a watch ... broken and stained ... inside a small plastic bag. The lighting in the photo isn't great, it was obviously taken on Harry's phone in the dark. I peer closer. It's a man's watch: a Breitling Navitimer. The glass on the front is cracked, which is where the stain has seeped in. I can see it clearly against the white rim, though I can't tell what colour it is: brown or dark red.

My mind flashes back to the tiny stain I saw earlier on the lounger cushion in the summer house.

Blood.

The stain is blood.

A memory stirs inside me. I've seen this watch before, or one very like it. I close my eyes, grasping at the fleeting pictures that race through my head. And then my eyes snap open.

I'm sure this is Dad's watch.

I frown, struggling to remember when I last saw it. I can't recall. I certainly remember him wearing it when I was at uni. We fought constantly then – had done since my early teens – and I have a strong memory of him thumping his fist on our dining table, emphasising each point against my wayward liberal values as he made it. Once he even slammed the wall. That was when I was in my mid-twenties during our worst row ever, after he found out about Lucy's abortion.

I can't recall seeing the watch in the recent past, but I didn't spend much time at home in my late twenties so that doesn't help much. It's so frustrating not being able to see the actual watch ... just this badly taken picture of it through a plastic bag. I peer at the edges of the bag. It's the same sort as the one that contained the kill list of names. Why would Dad have saved the names and the watch that way? In fact, I sigh, coming back to my earlier question, why on earth would he have saved them at all?

I close my eyes and lie back and think and think, trying to work out a way of answering all these questions and making sense of what I've found.

Frustrated, I turn back to the names. I study each piece of paper and then the envelope. There's nothing on either the front or the back except the typed Jeremiah reference. Idly, I lift the flap.

There's a logo on the inside of it: a cross with a halo and pair of angel wings in the centre. I didn't notice it earlier because I didn't pull the flap open before.

I stare at the logo, my heart hammering. I know this logo, it was part of a pack ordered online. I'd laughed, made some crack about how gauche and sentimental it was while still 'shoving your religion down everyone's throats'.

But it wasn't Dad who'd ordered the envelopes.

It wasn't Dad I'd been mocking.

And suddenly I see who has saved the names and the watch. It never really made sense that Dad would have done so. After all, why would anyone keep incriminating evidence against themselves? But someone else might well have a reason; someone who knows we have the summer house . . . someone who has gathered proof against Dad but who hasn't had the courage to use it.

Someone, in short, who knows what he's done, but can't bring herself to denounce him.

It's Lucy.

2

I pace around the house working it through: The names are a link to a series of murders that Dad has sanctioned. If the broken watch is his, perhaps the bloodstain is his too. Or maybe I was wrong about that. Maybe the watch isn't Dad's after all. Maybe it belonged to one of his victims.

Whatever, Lucy would only be keeping the watch and the papers if she knows what Dad has done. She was using two hiding places that I know of – the floorboard and the storage locker. Maybe there are other places . . . more pieces of potential evidence.

I have to speak to her and find out. I ask Ayesha to look after the kids again and head straight over to Dad's house to confront Lucy.

I let myself in super-quietly. I don't want to see Dad until I'm ready. I can hear him and Jacqueline in the kitchen talking about their upcoming refit.

'What on earth is a proving drawer?' Dad is asking.

'Oh, Jayson.' Jacqueline sounds like she's rolling her eyes. 'What do *you* think, Angie? I loved the one you put in for Stella Marbury.'

Jesus, they've got their interior designer with them. How bizarre. How can my father be a murderer and yet discuss remodelling his kitchen in that matter-of-fact way?

I hurry up to Lucy's room. She answers the door with damp hair. Her unmade-up skin is pink from the shower. I grip her elbow. 'Inside,' I hiss, pushing her back into the room and shutting the door behind me.

Lucy sucks in her breath. 'Francesca?' She sounds fearful, wary. 'What's the matter?'

I hold out the plastic bag with the typed names.

'I found these where you hid them. In the summer house.'

Lucy's eyes widen. She retreats to her bed, grabbing her rosary from the bedside table. She sits against the pillows, hunched over her knees. The gigantic wooden crucifix looms over her. I remember the horror I'd felt when I first saw it in here, the feeling that my sister was a person I didn't ... couldn't ... know any more. She told me the figure made her feel Jesus was taking care of her. To me it seemed she had finally and willingly let herself be subsumed by her faith, that she had given up taking responsibility for herself, that if God was watching over her, it was not in any tender, helpful way, but like a prison guard might keep a beady eye on a brainwashed prisoner.

Light from the window bounces off the paint on Christ's feet and the wisps of stray hair that have escaped from Lucy's ponytail. Her face is clouded with anxiety.

Downstairs I can hear two sets of heels – Jacqueline's and the interior designer's – tapping across the entrance hall. Their voices rise up the stairs.

'Come up to the second floor,' I urge. 'I need to talk to you where we won't be overheard.'

Lucy gulps, but follows me upstairs without a word.

There are just three rooms on the second floor: a spare bedroom, a bathroom and Mum's old study, which Jacqueline now uses as an office. I head into the office. I haven't been in here in years and the room is unrecognisable from the cluttered, cosy, paper-strewn space I remember. The only sheets of paper are neatly contained within a rack of black mesh in-trays while the photographs of Lucy and me that once festooned the walls and the bookshelves groaning with fiction have been replaced with a series of tasteful, abstract black-and-white prints.

The only item in the room that predates Jacqueline is the large oak desk. Mum had it specially made for her when she embarked on her failed attempt at novel-writing.

I run my hand over the polished wood as Lucy clears her throat. It's a beautiful piece of furniture. I'm not surprised Jacqueline has adopted it, in spite of the fact it belonged to the first Mrs Carr. Dad once told me the thing had cost almost £20,000 and its value is reflected in the simplicity of the design. Which, in turn, fits well with Jacqueline's own minimalist aesthetic.

'Francesca?' my sister ventures.

'I worked out the cipher,' I say, watching her intently. 'I know what these names mean.'

'Oh.' She gasps.

'I also found a key card to a storage locker. Harry went there last night.'

Lucy's eyes widen.

'Harry sent me a picture of the watch he found in the locker – it was cracked and bloodstained,' I carry on, 'but he isn't answering my calls. I'm worried something has happened to him, but ... but ...' My voice trembles as I realise that Lucy must have known Harry was under threat for days. 'But you know his life's in danger already, don't you? Like you knew all about Caspian and Simon Pinner and the other doctors.'

Lucy stares at me, her expression unreadable.

'Say something,' I press her. 'Because what I really want to know is why you haven't told anyone about all this. Why you've just hidden the evidence and not—'

'It's not evidence,' Lucy whispers at last. 'The names and the watch ... they're not enough.'

Silence falls. Downstairs Jacqueline's voice is joined by Dad's low rumble. They're too far away for me to hear what they're saying but presumably they're showing out the interior designer. Something inside me dies as I realise that Lucy is admitting to what she's done, which means she's acknowledging Dad's guilt. I sink back against the edge of the desk.

Lucy's mouth wobbles and two fat tears roll down her face. I have a sudden flashback to the day I discovered she was pregnant. My emotions then whirled through anger and bewilderment to a fierce desire to protect my fifteen-year-old little sister.

In some ways, in spite of everything that has happened to us, nothing has really changed since then. I take her hand, my earlier irritation fading.

'We'll get through this,' I say. 'We'll find a way but ... but we have to do something.'

Lucy meets my gaze. 'You mean the police?' She looks horrified. 'But that would break Dad's heart.'

'Break his heart?' I frown, confused. It seems a strange phrase to use, given the circumstances.

'Yes,' Lucy goes on. 'You know how loyal he is. And, oh goodness, the shame of it coming out would destroy him.'

'What are you talking about?' My head spins as I hold out the plastic bag with the scraps of paper again. 'I've seen these names, the doctors that Dad ordered to be killed, including ...' A shudder ripples through me. 'Including Caspian and now ... now maybe Harry.'

'What?' A frown creases Lucy's forehead. 'No, Francesca, *no*. I told you Dad would *never* order people killed.'

A beat passes. 'Then who?' I shake my head, bewildered. 'I don't under—'

'It's *Uncle Perry*. He's the head of PAAUL. He's the one who had everybody killed.'

A fresh wave of shock breaks over me. '*Uncle Perry?*' I shake my head. My oldest uncle might be pompous – and he's certainly capable of keeping secrets – but surely he's no murderer. 'No way,' I say. 'It can't be him.'

'But it can be *Dad*?' Lucy's eyebrows shoot up.

'Uncle Perry's always been more extreme than Dad. Don't you remember him giving Dad a hard time over resigning from *Shield*?'

'Not really,' I say.

'Well I do and ... and you told me yourself that all the rumours on the internet forums were about Lanagh, which is Uncle Perry's home.'

'*Some* of the rumours,' I protest. 'And I've looked in Lanagh.' An image of the cover of *Black Inches* flashes across my mind's eye as I speak. 'There's nothing in that house about PAAUL except the old reports Perry and Dad did, no direct connection between Perry and—'

'*That*'s the connection.' Lucy points to the bag of coded names in my hand. 'I found those in Lanagh. I was helping Perry sort out some files and ... and I came across them in his safe.'

'He has a safe?' I think back to my exploration of Lanagh with Harry. 'Where?'

'It's in his study, behind the print of St Francis.'

I frown, remembering the picture. 'What were you doing opening his safe?'

'I told you, I was helping him file stuff and one day I saw the code he used for the safe. I didn't do it on purpose, but you know how technophobic Perry is, he was huffing and puffing, complaining it was stuck or something. It was hard *not* to look. Anyway, a few days later he had to leave before I was done and I just thought I'd be helpful and put the legal documents we were working on in the safe. And that's when I saw the bag with the jumbled words.'

I stare at my sister, my heart racing. Uncle Graham's words from yesterday ring in my ears. Now I thought about it, his accusation against Dad had included Uncle Perry too. What had he said?

Jayson and Perry are both up to their necks in evil ... They've had a secret plan for about three years to get a load of abortion doctors bumped off.

Could Dad be involved in this *with* Perry? No. As soon as I had the thought, I dismissed it. The fact that Lucy had found the kill list and the broken watch in his safe pointed to Perry and to Lanagh. If Dad had been more prominently accused than his brother on the internet forums it was only because he was better known and because they shared the same surname. It had to be Perry. And yet ... it was still hard to imagine my uncle as a murderer.

'Do you really think Perry is capable of killing people? Of ordering Caspian's death?'

Lucy chews her lip. 'Honestly, Francesca, I'm not sure how much Uncle Perry cares about anyone except himself. But I do know Daddy could never have hurt Caspian.'

I close my eyes. In my heart I want her to be right. I want to believe Dad is innocent, even if it makes his brother a killer.

'You really found the coded names in Uncle Perry's safe?' I ask. 'When?'

'I found the first three just before Caspian died. I had no idea what they meant, just gobbledegook, but—'

'What about the bible quote?'

262

'That was in there too. But like I'm saying, I didn't know what any of it meant. I copied down the Jeremiah reference and the words but when I couldn't make sense of them I ... I, well, basically I forgot about them.'

Downstairs the front door shuts. The interior designer must have left. Footsteps echo along the hall: Jacqueline's light tap and the soft thud of Dad's brogues.

'So when did you find the rest of the names? And the watch?'

'Just a few days ago. I don't know what made me ... it was some kind of intuition. Uncle Perry was behaving so oddly, jittery and more snappy than usual. I went to Lanagh with Daddy and while he and Perry were talking I slipped away and opened the safe and ... and I found three more jumbled-up names and ... and the watch.'

'I'm sure I remember Dad wearing that watch,' I say.

'Perry had one too. They were gifts from their father. I reckon that's why he kept it, even though it was broken.'

I stare at her. I have only vague memories of our grandfather, but I knew his end was a long and painful battle with colon cancer that took my own father away from home a lot during my years at uni.

'I didn't know Granddad gave Dad and Uncle Perry a watch.'

'He handed them out just before he died, I think he was trying to avoid inheritance tax or something.'

'How come I didn't know?'

Lucy offers me a nervous smile. 'You weren't around much at the time. It was after ... after that *Catholic London* reporter found out about my "episode". You and Mummy and Daddy were barely speaking.'

I nod. She's right. I hardly went home for almost a year.

'Did you see the back of the watch?' Lucy asks.

'No,' I say.

'Well, it has an inscription, "from a loving father". I think Dad's did too. He lost his on holiday the year before Mum died.'

'So what made you take the watch and the names out of the safe in Uncle Perry's house and hide them here?'

'Well, I could see, like you, that the watch was cracked with a bloodstain which made the whole thing suddenly sinister instead of just mysterious. So I took the watch and the bag of names and hoped Perry wouldn't notice, which I don't think he has, because he's been here in London for most of the time since I took them, and I went back to the bible quote and I started working out what the mixed-up letters meant. It took me ages, two whole days to crack it, but once I'd realised you could use the quote to decipher the words I ... I realised they were a list of names of people who had been killed. Doctors ... including poor Caspian and Simon Pinner who had just died.'

'And Harry.' A new anger is rising inside me. 'You saw Harry's name there, which meant he was a target, and you still did nothing.'

'I didn't realise it was him then,' Lucy insists. 'I knew about Caspian and Simon and the other doctors ... which is why I hid the names and the watch away. But I didn't know about Harry until yesterday. He told us his name was Harry Dunbar, remember? It was only when you called Daddy on Saturday morning that I found out he was Harry Elliot, the same name as on the list.'

I stare at her. What she says is true. And it explains something else. '*That*'s why you were so upset?'

'Yes, because I didn't know what to do. I realised Harry was in danger but I thought that if he dropped his story, which he said he would, he'd be safe. He's not an abortion doctor like the others. At the very least I thought I had a bit of time. And I warned him ... when he came round looking for you. I couldn't tell him exactly why, but I told him to be careful ... but now ... I don't know ... especially if he's missing ... Oh, dear Lord ...' Lucy's face crumples. 'I'm scared. The thought of talking to the police ...' she trails off, her cheeks red with shame. 'I'm so sorry, Francesca.'

I turn away, looking out of the window. The pavement below is empty but cars zoom past, one after the other. I remember Mum saying how she loved working up here, how much she enjoyed looking out on the busy streets of Kensington, knowing life was right there, just outside the house. She was always so open, kind, so generous, especially about people. She made endless efforts with both of Dad's brothers. Uncle Perry was her doctor, he helped her with her diabetes and was devastated when she died. I've always tried to see him through her eyes, overlooking how pompous and mean-spirited he often was. But now people have been murdered. And poor Harry is in danger. Perhaps he's already dead. And Lucy is sure Perry is responsible. It's beyond belief. And yet the evidence is right here. I stare down at the pieces of paper in my hand.

'Why do you think Perry kept these?' I ask.

'I assume because they give him some sort of hold over the actual killer he's using.' Lucy clutches my wrist. Her face is white and strained. 'I'm sorry, Francesca. Tell me what we should do now and ... and I'll do it, whatever you think is best.'

I turn away from the window, take out my phone and scroll to DS Smart's number. I get his voice mail, his laconic tones requesting I leave a message.

'Please call me,' I say. 'I need to talk to you about Caspian's murder. I've got new evidence.'

I ring off. Lucy crosses herself. She's leaning against the desk and whispering under her breath: a silent prayer.

I point in the direction of the stairs. 'I think we should go down and talk to Dad and Jacqueline. Let's show them these names. Maybe we can all confront Perry together.'

Lucy jumps up, a look of horror on her face. 'No,' she says. 'I can't do that. I'm sorry ...'

I stare at her. 'Think of Harry,' I urge. 'He's out there, missing. He could be *dead*. We have to try and help him.'

Lucy hesitates. 'I just can't . . .' She turns and stumbles out of the room.

I listen to the sound of her light footsteps flying down the stairs to the first floor and, presumably, her bedroom where she can shut the door and crawl under that stupid crucifix and carry on blocking out the truth.

I'm alone. A wave of sickness rolls up from my guts. For a moment I think I might actually vomit. I hurry over to the window, flick the latch and ease the sash open. I lean out, resting my hands for a moment on the deep ledge where Mum used to keep a window box of blue flowers a million years ago. The air streams in, cool on my face. London traffic noises drift up, a man shouting, a woman screeching with laughter. Normal life. I take a deep breath then lower the window.

'Come on,' I say to myself.

I leave the room and head down the stairs. I march straight into the kitchen where Dad sits at the table, bent over his phone, and Jacqueline stands in front of the whiteboard, busy writing an instruction to her housekeeper about picking up some dry cleaning. To my surprise, Lucy is here too, visibly nervous and lurking in the corner. Dad looks up as I walk in and gives me a warm smile.

'Hello, sweetheart.'

My whole body trembles as I walk over to the table. Lucy edges closer. Perhaps in her terrified way she is trying to support me after all. The thought gives me some strength.

'Dad?' My voice falters.

'What's the matter?' Dad stands up. Across the room, Jacqueline turns from the whiteboard, eyebrows raised.

I hold up the plastic bag of names. 'It's this.'

'What's that?' Jacqueline flicks a dismissive glance at the scraps of paper in the bag.

Dad holds out his hand for the bag and I pass it over.

'It's a kill list,' I say, voice shaking. 'Uncle Perry's kill list.'

3

Jacqueline's eyes fill with surprise. 'A *kill* list? What on earth are you talking about?'

'Francesca?' Dad sounds genuinely horrified.

'It's a list of all the abortion doctors PAAUL murdered. Uncle Perry is behind it. He ordered their deaths.' A sob rises in my throat, choking me. 'Including Caspian.'

'*What?*' Jacqueline splutters.

Dad looks at Lucy, who hangs her head. He turns back to me.

'Francesca ... darling,' he says, his voice low and soothing. 'You're obviously very upset and—'

'Stop it,' I hiss. I know that voice. It's the one he uses with Lucy when she's getting hysterical. 'It's the truth. I've even been threatened over it.'

'Francesca, please calm down.' Dad lays one of his large, strong hands on my arm. 'This is ridiculous.'

Furious, I shake him off. 'I *am* calm. And it's not just me.' I glance at my sister. She gives me a tiny nod. 'Lucy found the names. They were in Uncle Perry's safe. Along with the watch your dad gave him – all cracked and—'

'In his safe?' Jacqueline shakes her head. Her nude Manolos tap smartly on the kitchen tiles as she walks over to the table. 'You mean that ancient box behind his St Francis print? Please, this sounds like something out of an overblown TV drama.'

'Indeed.' Dad ventures a supercilious chuckle. 'A list of names and a broken watch hardly amounts to a murder confession.'

I shoot a glance at Lucy. She's shrinking against the door that leads out to the garden. Tears leak from her eyes. For a second I feel irritated at her weakness. Then I pull myself together. It's not her fault.

'I've called the police,' I say. 'You can listen to them if you won't listen to me.'

'You did *what*?' Jacqueline shrieks. She turns to Dad. 'Do something, Jayson. We can't have the police here again, especially after that journalist, Harry whatever. We'll be a laughing stock.'

'Perry's ordered Harry to be killed as well,' I go on. 'He disappeared last night. He's missing.'

'Harry Elliot, the reporter?' Dad looks increasingly bewildered. 'How is it that you're even still in touch with him?'

'He was here last night, helping me look for more evidence about the PAAUL murders.'

'Here?' Jacqueline clutches Dad's arm. She glares at me. 'You let him into this house to … to snoop around?'

Dad clenches his jaw. I can see the anger in his eyes. 'That was not smart, Francesca.'

'And after the way he treated you ... after everything we did to help you ...' Jacqueline's eyes narrow in fury.

Dad sucks in his breath. 'First me, now my brother. I imagine Harry Elliot's having a field day at our expense.'

'I told you, Harry's missing,' I persist. 'Uncle Perry's targeting him too, because he's getting too close to the truth.'

'Or else Harry's just run off with whatever information he managed to steal from this house and is planning his next news story.' Dad's voice rises.

'I think you should leave, Francesca,' Jacqueline says icily.

My jaw drops.

'Oh, no, please,' Lucy weeps softly, shrinking back against the door.

Jacqueline turns to Dad. 'Perry will be here any minute. I don't want Francesca upsetting him with this nonsense.'

Dad nods. A dull weight sinks in my stomach. Why doesn't he step in and stand up for me? Why won't Lucy back up what I'm saying? I reach for my phone to show them the threatening text from yesterday then remember I deleted it. All I have is the picture of the broken watch – and I'm guessing that, as it came from Harry, it won't count for much in Dad's eyes.

Perhaps I *should* leave. It strikes me I don't have to wait for DS Smart to call back. I can just walk into any police station and say I want to make a statement. There's no need to wait any longer. Dad and

Jacqueline aren't going to listen and Lucy isn't going to help.

'I'm going to the police right now.' I walk away.

'Wait. Francesca, *stop*!' Dad's fist lands with a thump on the kitchen table.

I halt in my tracks and face him. He is standing between Lucy, whose eyes are wide with alarm, and his wife, her face bright red with fury.

'This has gone far enough,' Dad snaps.

'No, Dad,' I say. 'It hasn't.' I turn and hurry away. I'm across the hall and yanking open the front door in seconds. I hurtle down the steps to the front path. And run smack into Uncle Perry.

Horrified, I jump back.

'Francesca, for Pete's sake,' he snaps. 'Watch where you're going.'

Heart hammering, I disentangle myself as my uncle adjusts his coat, giving the lapel a fastidious brush with his hand.

'Where are you running off to in such a hurry?' Uncle Perry asks, a sneer playing around his lips. 'Got another date with your conman journalist?'

My stomach lurches into my throat. I grab his arm. 'Where's Harry? What have you done with him?'

'Get off me.' Uncle Perry shakes my hand away, his face clouded with irritation.

'I know you're behind PAAUL. I know you had Caspian killed. I know you ordered all the abortion doctor murders.' I watch him closely, trying to catch any hint of acknowledgement in his eyes.

'What are you talking about?' Perry snaps. 'You silly hysterical girl. What are you getting yourself in a lather over now?'

He doesn't wait for an answer, just pushes past me and strides inside. I make my way, more slowly, to my car. I switch on the engine, still reeling. How could Perry lie to my face like that?

I grit my teeth and drive off. There's a police station at Notting Hill. It's a little further away than the one in Kensington but I know it's open twenty-four hours a day. Perry might have refused to engage with me, but let's see how well his defences hold up in the face of some serious police questioning.

I'm two streets away when a text pings on my phone. I stare at the screen. It takes a few seconds for the words to sink in.

involve the police and your children die

I stare and I stare, numb with shock. The car and the world outside whirl around me. The sender has blocked their number. But Uncle Perry *has* to be behind it. The bastard. Blind rage fills me. I swing the car half-round, gripping the steering wheel so tightly my knuckles whiten. I will go back to him and knock his stupid head off its neck. I yank at the car, trying to force the wheel to turn further. A lorry skims past, horn blaring, missing me by inches. Cars behind me join in the honking. I'm about to yell. To scream.

And then I remember that though Perry is behind all the murders, he cannot possibly be the actual killer. He must use someone else – possibly several people – to carry out his violent orders. Another connection suddenly fires in my mind. What did Harry say in his USB-stick video? That Dad's prison rehabilitation charity would be a great way to meet violent criminals?

Perry goes with Dad to lots of those charity functions. He could find and use ex-convicts easily. My breath catches in my throat. I can't take the risk. Whoever the killer is, Perry will easily be able to contact them. Which means that if I go back and confront him again, he just has to make a single phone call and Rufus and Ruby will die.

I gulp. Should I try calling Dad? No, he'll only point out I have no proof this horrible, threatening message comes from Perry. And he'll undoubtedly insist – with Perry right there in the house – that I call the police in spite of what the message says. In fact, he's quite capable of calling them himself.

Which mustn't happen until I have the kids safely with me.

Yes. I blow out my breath, trying to calm myself. Before I do anything, I have to get the kids.

I reverse the half-turn I'd made, ignoring the catcalls and car horns all around me. I grit my teeth and drive on. I try to focus, to make a plan: once I've picked up the kids we will all go to the police. I will show the officer at the station the threatening text, get him to call DS Smart and tell him everything. Maybe he can use tracker software to trace the blocked number of the phone that sent this latest text.

Hopefully, once the police realise my children have been threatened, they'll believe Harry is in danger too. I have to trust that they will find him. I have to believe that the police will protect us all.

I grab my phone and call Ayesha.

'Do you have the kids?' I ask as soon as she answers. 'Is Rufus back from school yet?'

'Er, no. Rufus is on his way, he should be here any minute. And Lori took Ruby for ice cream at Mariner's.'

My heart pounds. Mariner's is a public place and she's there with only Lori – a fifteen-year-old innocent.

'Shit.'

'What's the matter?'

'Listen.' I think fast. 'I'm going straight to Mariner's. As soon as Rufus arrives, bring him round there. Call me if there's any problem. *Any* problem.'

'Okay but …' Ayesha hesitates. 'Franny, what is going on?'

My entire world has been turned on its head: my uncle ordered the deaths of my husband and five other men, my sister knows and will do nothing and my father and stepmother won't believe it's true.

'I'll tell you when I see you,' I say.

'Franny, you're scaring me. I'm not getting off the phone until you explain what the matter is.' Typical Ayesha, persistent as ever.

I frown. Perhaps I *should* tell my best friend how serious this is. I need her calling Rufus to hurry home, then watching out for danger as she drives him to Mariner's.

'It's to do with ... it's my family. I need to go to the police.'

'Jesus Christ. Why? Who? Has something happened to Lucy? To your dad?'

'No, no one's hurt. It's *other* people who've been hurt.'

'You mean hurt by someone *in* your family?'

I hesitate. It's not that I mind confiding in Ayesha, but I don't want to have to go through all the sordid details again – and, anyway, my priority right now is Rufus.

'Is it Dex's dad?' Ayesha persists. 'He was violent to your Auntie Sheila once, wasn't he?'

'Ayesha, please, just get Rufus to hurry back and—' My voice breaks.

'Franny?' Ayesha suddenly sounds uncertain. 'Are you okay?'

I mean to say 'yes', but what comes out of my mouth is, 'Oh, Ayesha, I'm scared.' As I say the words I realise that I'm actually shaking. 'Please just bring Rufus to Mariner's. I'll explain everything there.'

'Okay, you know I'll help in any way I can,' she says, her tone changing again: now brisk and determined. 'See you soon.'

'Thank you.' I ring off and speed all the way to the ice cream parlour.

Ayesha sends a text to say that she's got Rufus and they're on their way to Mariner's. She's already outside the ice cream parlour when I arrive, leaning against the wall by the door, a plum-coloured scarf slung over her

276

pink coat. Her expression is grim as I get out of my car and hurry over.

'Is Ruby here? Where's Rufus?' I demand.

'They're fine. They're inside.'

I follow her finger pointing through the far window. To my huge relief both kids are sitting with Lori at a booth in the corner. Ruby is smiling, pointing at the menu. Rufus is staring sullenly at his phone. They're safe. I relax slightly.

'So before ...' Ayesha starts hesitantly. 'You said about going to the police ... I'm just wondering and I'm sorry to ask again, but ... *is* this something to do with your uncle?'

I spin around to face her. 'Uncle Perry?' I exclaim. 'Why are you asking about him?'

'I'm not. Like I said before, this is about your other uncle ... Graham ... Dex's dad.' She frowns, wrapping her scarf around her neck more snugly.

'What?' I stare at her. 'What are you talking about?'

'Jesus, this is hard. It's just ... okay, there was this one night at one of your parents' parties ... the one just a week or two before your mum died ...'

'That's nearly five years ago,' I say, impatient with her. 'What does—?'

'Listen.' Ayesha's eyes flash with urgency. 'So your mum was coming out of the bathroom as I was going in and she'd been crying and we were both drunk. I asked if she was all right and she mumbled something ... well, basically, she said she was scared.'

'*Mum* said that?' I gaze at Ayesha, utterly bewildered.

'Yes, so I asked her: "Scared of what?" And she says, "Not what, who," so I wonder if she's talking about your dad and I'm shocked because your parents always seemed to have like this ridiculously happy marriage so I blurt out: "You're frightened of *Jayson*?" And your mum looked back at me and said, "Of course not. It's not him who's got the power over me," which was kind of an odd thing to say so, like the heathen I am and being pissed myself and thinking how your family are all these mad Catholics, *I* said: "Who are you talking about then, *God*?" And your mum, she was *really* drunk, she said, "No, but he acts like God." And then she laughed, and told me to forget it, but I kept asking who she was afraid of and in the end she said it was your Uncle Graham, that he's well known for his violent streak, and then she hurried away. But I didn't believe she really meant Graham. There was something in her eyes that … I don't know … I sensed she was just giving me a name to make me back off.'

'Do you think she might have meant Uncle Perry?' My mind catapults across this latest possibility. Could Uncle Perry's history of violence go further back than the first abortion doctor's death? It would be logical if it did. People rarely turn into cold-blooded killers overnight. I shiver, then fix my gaze on the kids through Mariner's window. Ruby is still chatting with Lori, Rufus still poring over his phone. They are safe. I need to cling to that. In a moment I will gather them up and take them to the police and pass on everything I know.

'I didn't get any sense of who your mum really

meant, just that she'd given me Graham's name to stop me asking any more questions. Why are you asking about Perry?'

'Did Mum say anything else?'

'No. I was going to ask the next time I saw her but before I did she ... well, she ... had passed away.'

I meet Ayesha's anxious gaze. 'Why didn't you tell me this before?' A worm of resentful misery coils itself around my heart. Yet more secrets kept from me.

'It wasn't any of my business,' Ayesha says. 'Like I say, your mum was really drunk at the time and it wasn't like she'd mentioned any specific incidents or threats. I did wonder after it came out that Perry found her ... you know, when she fainted and fell down the cellar steps ... I thought maybe he was covering up for Graham ...'

'You thought one of my uncles might have killed my mum and the other one covered it up and you didn't say anything?' I stare at her, appalled.

'What could I say? It was just a stupid bit of drunken conversation. And like I keep telling you, I didn't really believe at the time she was scared of Graham. But I never forgot how she'd said she was scared of *someone*; that bit seemed genuine.' Ayesha fixes me with those fierce brown eyes of hers. 'After what you told me earlier I thought you should know, in case it's relevant now.'

I stand in the wind and gaze inside Mariner's again. Rufus and Ruby are still in their corner booth, doing exactly what they were doing when I peered through the window a few seconds ago. And yet somehow the whole world has shifted again. I feel dazed. I have no idea how this latest revelation fits into what I already know. I'm already reeling because my family are not who I thought they were – and now here is my best friend revealing suspicions about my uncle and a confidence about my mother that she has kept from me for years.

'Are you all right?' I've never heard Ayesha sound so uncertain. She moves closer and her scent fills the air: herby and musky.

'No.' I turn away. The air is cold on my face as I pace across to Mariner's front door. Ayesha hurries after me. 'I need to get the kids. We have to go to the police.'

'What *has* happened?' she asks. 'Is there some threat to the children? I thought maybe it was that, that was why you wanted to come here and get them so urgently.'

'Later.' I hurry into the warmth of the ice cream parlour.

Truth is, I can't bring myself to talk to her: not about the threatening text I've just received nor about any of the discoveries that lie behind it. I can't trust her. I can't trust anyone, including myself. Not when my judgements about people have been so wrong. Even Ayesha has concealed things from me, and I thought we shared all the important stuff.

Lori and Ruby are now chatting with the waitress; Rufus sits beside Lori, still staring glumly at his phone. I sit down next to Ruby, pulling her into a hug.

'Thank God you're all right,' I sigh, breathing in

deep lungfuls of her hair, burying my face.

'Oof, Mum, get off.' Ruby disentangles herself, cheeks pinking. She rolls her eyes at me in a highly Ayesha-like fashion.

I reach across the table and grasp Rufus's arm. He pulls it away.

'We have to go,' I say.

Ruby's face falls. 'But we ordered milkshakes,' she protests. 'Lori plaited my hair, look.' She turns her head to show me the thick, dark plait snaking onto her neck. Two hairgrips with little footballs on the end hold stray wisps of hair in place.

I smile at Lori. 'Looks great.' Then turn back to Ruby. 'We'll take the milkshakes to go.' I sit back. At least the children are okay. As soon as their drinks arrive we will all go to the police station together and I'll get them to contact DS Smart for me. I'll call Lucy once we're on our way and tell her to meet us at the police station. She might not be prepared to talk to Dad and Jacqueline, but she won't be able to refuse the police.

Rufus mumbles something but I'm not listening.

In some ways it will be good for Lucy to have to give a statement. She's been under Dad's wing too long. At some point I'll have to tell her what Ayesha's just told me about Mum being scared before she died. I should speak to Auntie Sheila about that too, find out if Mum said anything to her. Another horrific thought strikes me, my imagination in freefall. It was Uncle Perry who found Mum's body, after her supposedly accidental trip down the cellar steps. But what if Mum had just discovered Perry was a murderer? What if she'd threatened to expose him? What if he'd murdered her – and made it look like an accident – in order to keep her quiet?

I put my head in my hands. It's too much. I can't think about poor Mum and her death right now.

'Mum? For God's sake! Where are we going?' Rufus's shout shocks me out of my musings.

'Don't yell at me.' I frown.

Rufus glares at me. 'Are we going home?' he asks. 'Because I want to go home.' He flashes a venomous glance at Lori and Ayesha. 'I'm fed up with being dragged about to people's houses.'

'I'm afraid we can't go straight home,' I say. I meet Ayesha's gaze. How on earth am I going to explain a visit to the police to the children?

'What?' Rufus's voice rises in fury. 'Where the fuck are we going then?'

Beside him, Lori gasps. Ruby shrinks back in her seat.

'Rufus!' I hiss. 'Apologise! Right now.'

The café is only a quarter full and every single person in here is now looking at my son, red-faced and gimlet-eyed. He suddenly reminds me of Dad during one of our many rows when I was a teenager.

Ayesha raises her eyebrows. 'Maybe I should take all the kids home with me?'

'No fucking way!' Rufus stands up, shoving the jug of tap water in front of him so hard half of it slops onto the table. He storms out of the café, slamming the door behind him.

In an instant he's out of sight.

I jump up. 'Ruby, stay with Ayesha and Lori.' I turn to Ayesha. 'Don't let her go anywhere.'

I run outside. It's completely dark here now, only ten or so cars in the car park behind the café. No sign of Rufus. My heart thuds as I race round to the front of the building. I scan the street in both directions. I can't see Rufus anywhere.

Panic erupts inside me. Has Perry's hired killer seized him leaving the café?

'Rufus!' I yell. 'Rufus!'

I cross the road, heart pounding. Turn 360 degrees. Relief courses through me. He's there, hunched over at the bus stop: skinny and gangly and unbearably vulnerable, his hoodie pulled low over his face.

I race over. 'Rufus?'

He looks up. His dark eyes are still angry, but I can see the misery in them too.

I hesitate. The revelation that Uncle Perry is a murderer will be devastating for the kids. Since Caspian died Rufus has spent a lot of time with my side of the family. What I'm about to tell the police will be hard on him . . . and only just over a year after he was destroyed by his father's death.

'Oh, Rufus.' Tears well in my eyes. 'I'm so sorry things are so difficult.'

He stares at me, uncertain.

'They're difficult for me too,' I say. 'I miss Dad so much. I can only imagine you miss him too.'

Rufus bites his lip.

'Something very bad has happened,' I say, choosing my words carefully. 'I need to talk to the police. That's where you and me and Ruby have to go now.'

'What's happened?' he asks.

'I can't explain right now,' I say. 'I'm asking you to be really grown-up and come back into the café and we'll get Ruby and we'll go. And if it means spending more time with Lori and Ayesha, at their house or . . . or just with them while I have to do difficult stuff, then I'm asking you to help me. Can you do that?'

He shrugs and gazes across the road.

I want to say more, but I hold back, letting him work it through in his own time.

The skies are dark, the air cold. I shiver. I rushed out so fast I left my coat behind. At least it's not raining any more.

Rufus turns to face me. Our eyes meet.

'Okay?' I ask.

He nods. Then walks beside me back to the café.

As we get closer I peer in through the window. I can just make out our booth. Ayesha's back is to the glass, blocking my view of the seat opposite. I take a few more steps. There's no sign of either Ruby or Lori. Feeling anxious again, I hurry inside, Rufus right behind. The warmth of the café steams up, enveloping us. I feel trapped, like I'm living a nightmare from which I can't wake.

I reach the table. The milkshakes the girls ordered are here in their clear plastic containers. But Ayesha is definitely alone.

'Where are the girls?' I ask. 'Where's Ruby?'

'In the loo.' As Ayesha points to the door at the end of the counter Lori emerges from it. She saunters over to the table and picks up her milkshake. She gazes warily at Rufus, who takes a gulp from his own drink.

'Sorry 'bout earlier,' he mutters.

'Lori?' My heart races. 'Where's Ruby?'

'Still in the ladies, I guess.' Lori smiles.

'She'll be fine,' Ayesha says, indicating the other people in the café – mostly after-school mums, au pairs and kids – with a wave of her hand. She lowers her voice. 'It's just *us* here.'

She means 'us' as in 'not the person that I'm scared of'. But it's not Uncle Perry himself who terrifies me right now. It's whoever he is using to carry out the PAAUL killings – whoever he has lined up to carry out his threat to murder my children. My phone beeps as I rush across the café. I glance down, distracted. It's just Lucy asking if I'm okay, if the kids are all right. I open the door and hurry along the corridor to the toilets. The ladies is on the left. I open the door. There are three stalls. Two have open doors. Empty.

I stare at the third door. 'Rubes?' I call. I push at the door.

It swings open. Also empty.

My phone forgotten in my hand, I rush back into the corridor. Blood pumps violently at my temples. There's a fire door a few feet away. I race over. *Shit*. It's ajar.

Panic rising, I pull the door open. Outside is an alley-way full of bins and bits of plywood studded with nails.

The wind picks up, whipping at a couple of plastic bags and bringing with it the smell of fried onions from the café next door. I run into the alley.

'Ruby!' I yell. *'Ruby!'*

But my daughter is gone.

TAKEN

Monday 18 January 2016

LUCY

Poor Francesca, in a state of total confusion and misery over events she still doesn't know the half of.

She's worked out some things, for sure, but there are other, secret, things I'm going to make certain she never finds out – especially about you. I'm not protecting you for your sake. Those days are long gone. It's all for her. Because, well, frankly it would kill her to know.

You know all about the first secret: that started when I was a child and you blasted away my innocence, corroding me to my very soul.

No. I've promised myself I won't dwell on that right now. For now I just want to focus on poor Francesca. She thinks she has the full story. Her children's lives are in danger and, like any mother, she's prepared to do what it takes to keep them safe.

What she hasn't taken into account is *you*.

She doesn't know you. That is, of course she knows you. But she doesn't *see* you. Not like I do.

I sent her a text a few minutes ago, asking if she's all right, if she's with the children yet. She hasn't replied.

Which is par for the course. I'm not making a thing of it, I know she's frantic and panicking about everything she's found out, especially that the kids are under threat. But all our lives it's been me letting Francesca call the shots, never making a fuss if she forgets to take me into account. Well, you know that as well as anyone. Not that Francesca has ever been anything but loving and caring towards me. We weren't close when we were younger, the age gap between us is too big for that, but when I was pregnant all those years ago she really tried to help. At least that's what she *thought* she was doing.

Wait. I'm getting ahead of myself. I can't just throw in the abortion without explaining the context. And that, as ever, brings me back to you and what happened when I was that lonely, misfit teenager whose vulnerability you exploited for your own sinful ends.

Everything changed because of you and what you did. I won't go into the details now. It's enough to say that, afterwards, I kept my promise to say nothing. The shame of what had happened was far worse than the physical soreness between my legs, which faded within a couple of days. Mummy found the place where I'd been sick in the garden and expressed irritation that 'Francesca's friends had been out of control'. She never suspected for a minute that the pile of vomit was mine.

After three days where I'd hardly left my bedroom she took me to see the doctor who said 'hello there, young lady' with his usual kindly twinkle, as if I was still eight years old instead of fifteen. I liked our paediatrican, I really did, but at the time he seemed like a creature from a distant planet, an old man (though I guess he was only in his mid-forties) and among the very last people in the world to whom I could have confided any aspect of what had happened to me. He listened to my chest and prodded my abdomen, when I said I had 'a sort of stomach ache', then whispered to Mummy that it was probably just 'growing pains' and that a combination of a decent diet and moderate exercise would set me straight.

I did my best to eat the food put in front of me, but it all felt like cardboard in my mouth. I put on enough of a show after a few more days to stop Mummy from fretting – luckily she had a series of pre-Christmas lunches with various friends which distracted her – and gradually I developed a hard enough shell to fool the most perceptive observer into thinking I was fine. By the time I went back to school after Christmas I appeared outwardly normal. But inside the hurt was as bad as ever.

I started self-harming, just little slices with a razor blade on my thighs and stomach. If I'd had the guts I would have gone further, but it fitted with the narrative I had of myself to hold back: I was too weak and pathetic even to properly hurt myself, just as I had been too weak and pathetic to make you love me in the right way before.

Every time I thought about what we'd done it broke my heart all over again, sending me straight to the razor and the miserable darkness of my self-loathing.

What it came down to was pain – a cycle of fear, anger and loneliness that had me hooked as hard as any drug. The many secret times that I reached for my razor and sliced at my own skin gave me some release from that pain. The whole winter which followed was a terrible time and it left my thighs covered in tiny scars. I look at them often, even now, and remember how utterly lost I was.

Francesca came home at the end of March for the Easter holiday. She was at her most rebellious at that time, revelling in uni life away from home and delighting in taunting us all for our 'uptight' and 'repressive' ways. She stayed out all night on the Saturday between Good Friday and Easter Sunday, causing Mummy no end of anxiety. There was a big row when she finally loped in, make-up smeared down her cheek and clearly still drunk – or even possibly high.

I crept up to my room and got stuck into my holiday homework, trying to ignore both the nausea that constantly plagued me and the black cloud that pressed on my head, threatening to smother me with a sense of utter hopelessness. As I attempted to revise a list of dates for my upcoming history exam, trying to block out the sound of Francesca yelling that Mummy was a Nazi, it occurred to me I hadn't had a period in a while. When I counted back, I was shocked to discover my last period had been just before my birthday at the end of November. I stood in front of the mirror and studied my body. My breasts seemed bigger than ever, despite my ongoing attempts to keep them in check by watching my weight. I frowned at my stomach. Was that the start of an outward curve?

With shaking hands I bought and carried out a test, but in my heart I knew the result before the blue line showed on the stick.

I was pregnant.

With your child.

I often think about that child. He or she would be a teenager now. Older than Rufus. I would have been a mother first, before Francesca.

Which is funny. For years I envied Francesca being a mother. But not any longer.

Not now the children are in danger. Not now Francesca is so terrified for their safety. Not now, as I sit here remembering what you are capable of.

What you once did to me you would surely do to another child.

FRAN

My feet take me back inside the busy, bustling café before my head registers what has happened. The scent of coffee and the sound of children's chatter whirl around me. Ruby has been taken. I'm numb with the shock of it. It can't be real. An image of her little face slams in front of me and my breath catches in my throat.

I have to get her back. It's all I can think. Adrenaline surges through me as I reach for my phone to dial 999. But as I take it out of my bag it pings with a text. A blocked number.

You were warned. Harry is dead.

What? My legs give way. *No.* A stab of pain sears through my panic. Up until now I'd clung to the hope that Harry was still out there but here is proof he is gone.

Before I can even begin to process this there's another text:

You were warned. Ruby will be next.

Terror fills me.

Uncle Perry has used his killer to murder Harry. And to kidnap Ruby. The reality of it slams home: my daughter's life depends entirely on what I choose to do now.

Barely able to breathe, I stumble over to the table where Ayesha and the kids are sitting. I clutch at the back of the nearest chair, panic hammering like tiny fists at the inside of my skull. Ayesha is smiling, but the smile drops as she clocks my expression.

'Franny?' She stands up. 'What's the matter?'

Another text. I stare down at it.

Get rid of everyone at the table. Talk to ANYONE and Ruby dies.

'It's nothing,' I say, covering the screen with my palm. Rufus is staring moodily at the game he's playing on his phone. At least he is all right. I must cling to that. Keep him safe.

'Nothing?' Ayesha frowns. 'Where's Ruby?'

'She's ... er, she's not well.' I think fast. 'She's been sick. I think it might be a bug. I, er, I just came out to ask if you'd take Rufus back to yours for a couple of hours so I can focus on her, get her home without infecting everyone else.'

'I thought you wanted us all to stay together?' Ayesha frowns, drawing me aside. Around us the café is full of steam and chatter. 'What the hell is going on? You look as white as the menu card. Is this something to do with going to the police?'

I press my lips together, determined not to cry. I nod, not trusting myself to speak without breaking down.

295

'What about Ruby?' Ayesha goes on. 'Should I call an ambulance?'

'No,' I whisper. '*Please* just take Rufus home, keep him safe till I get there. I promise I'll tell you everything as soon as I can.'

'Okay.' Ayesha reluctantly turns back to the table. 'Come on, kids, let's go.'

Rufus looks up. 'We're going home?' he asks hopefully.

'No,' Ayesha says. 'You're coming with me and Lori back to ours. Mum'll pick you up later.'

'What?' Rufus stands, facing me down. He's only a little bit shorter than me now. 'No way. What about what you said before, Mum?'

He means about going to the police.

'Please don't argue.' Tears prick at my eyes. 'We'll do … what I said, later. Right now Ruby's not well … please, Rufus …'

Rufus lets out an exasperated sigh but doesn't resist any further. He walks away. Ayesha hurries after him. Lori gulps down the last of her milkshake. She looks across at Ruby's unfinished drink.

'Take it,' I urge.

'That's okay,' Lori says with a gentle smile. 'I'm full. Tell Rubes I hope she feels better.' She follows her mother and Rufus out of the café.

I watch as they head to Ayesha's car. I sink down into my seat at the booth and place my phone on the table beside Ruby's milkshake. I touch the cool plastic with trembling fingers.

Fifteen long minutes pass. I check each message again – there's no way of responding to any of them. Another text arrives:

Well done. First test passed. Now call the police and tell them you have nothing to say after all.

I stare at the message. Is the sender watching me? He or she *must* be. How else do they know the others have gone? Are they close enough to hear what I'm saying? I stand up and look around the café. No sign of anyone behaving suspiciously. It strikes me that the person who has taken Ruby is most likely not the same person who is watching me and sending texts. It's a bigger operation than just Uncle Perry and a single hired killer. I'm up against the entire might of PAAUL.

I sink back into my chair, sick with panic. Another ten minutes tick by. What should I do? Call the police and retract what I said before, just as PAAUL has ordered? Or dial 999 and take the risk that Ruby will be killed before the police find her? Oh, God, how can I be sure Ruby is alive now?

As if in answer to my question, another text comes through.

Do as we say and Ruby will be returned early tomorrow.

There's a link to a video beside the text. I click on it and suddenly Ruby's there on film, eyes closed, murmuring. She's clearly been sedated. God, she will be confused and scared and ... I grit my teeth, fury and fear both building inside me. I study the video: she's on a couch that's been covered with a white sheet. Nothing else is in view except the edge of a piece of purple-and-white fabric, just above the couch.

I play the snippet over and over, losing myself in my daughter's face. She looks hot, her hair has come out of her plait and sticks to the side of her face.

Please let her be okay. *Please.*

The café is more crowded than ever. It's heaving with a mix of after-school teens and old ladies who seem to have just tipped noisily out of some bingo hall. There's no way I can keep track of who is coming and going and who has been here all along. But I'm certain I'm still being watched.

It seems wrong not to involve the police. Wrong and stupid. I don't want to retract my earlier call to DS Smart. If anything I want to call him again and urge him to get the whole of the Met looking for Ruby. Is there any other way to get her back? A direct appeal won't work. I think of Uncle Perry's contemptuous face earlier – and Dad and Jacqueline's refusal to believe in his guilt.

Who can I turn to?

Lucy. She at least believes Uncle Perry is behind Caspian's death and all the other PAAUL murders. And poor Harry.

Fingers trembling, I make the call, but as soon as I hear my sister's timid voice on the line I know I can't burden her with the truth. It's too horrific. I pretend I just wanted to have another go at convincing Dad that Uncle Perry is a murderer. Lucy tells me Dad and Jacqueline have gone out for the night – she doesn't know where they are or when they'll be back. She says she can hear something awful has happened from my strained voice, but I refuse to talk about it.

Instead I ring off and dial DS Smart's number. Even as the phone rings I don't know what I'm going to say.

'Hello?' The police officer's tone is brisk and efficient.

I hesitate, still battling with myself. Recant and go without police support? Or talk – and risk losing Ruby forever?

One thing I know for sure is that PAAUL is capable of cold-blooded murder. And whoever is watching me is almost certainly still here, waiting for me to carry out PAAUL's instructions.

'It's Francesca, Jayson Carr's daughter,' I say. 'I left the message for you earl—'

'Yes, I was going to call you back,' DS Smart says. 'You've got new information? Something you've remembered about Simon Pinner? I'm afraid we don't have any new leads, so anything you can tell me ...'

I hesitate, the image of Ruby's face filling my head. I should tell the detective that she has been kidnapped, that Harry is dead, that my Uncle Perry is a monster, a murderer.

'It's not about Simon Pinner ...'

'I see. Er, is it to do with your husband's death?' DS Smart presses.

I look around the café again. Whoever Perry sent must still be looking at me, listening to me. I don't have any choice. I have to do what Perry ... what PAAUL has ordered. I can't take the risk of speaking out, not with Ruby's life at stake. Once she is safe I will tell the police everything.

'No, in fact I made a mistake before, I was wrong about what ... what I said.' My voice sounds hollow. 'I'm sorry I bothered you.'

'That's all right.' I can tell from DS Smart's tone that he doesn't know whether to believe me. 'Are you sure you don't want to tell me what it is? Sometimes it's the little things that are the most important.'

'No, I was wrong,' I repeat. 'Thanks for your understanding.'

I ring off and stare outside. A soft drizzle is settling on the tarmac outside the ice cream parlour, glistening in the lamplight above. I feel like it's almost midnight but it's still only five thirty in the afternoon.

Another text comes through.

Well done. Ruby is fine. You'll see her tomorrow.

So I am still being watched. I glance around the ice cream parlour, a shiver snaking down my spine, then stare helplessly at the text again. *Tomorrow?* I want her back *now*. Is she really okay? How on earth am I going to last until tomorrow?

Another half hour passes. I'm in a daze, numb with fear.

'Francesca?'

I look up. My sister is standing beside me, her eyes full of concern. 'You sounded so upset earlier that I called Ayesha. She told me she was worried about you, that you were taking Ruby home 'cos she got sick at Mariner's. But I went to your house and you weren't there, so I thought I'd try here and ...' Lucy looks around. 'You're sitting here on your own, even though you were supposed to leave an hour ago. And ... and where's Ruby?' She frowns. 'What's going on?'

'Oh, Lucy,' I sob, the tears that I've been holding back now sliding down my cheeks.

My sister slithers into the seat beside me and puts her arms around me. It's the most tactile she's been with me in years. I lean against her.

'Tell me,' she urges. 'Let me help you.'

I shake my head. The texts were clear and I daren't go against them ... except Lucy already knows about the kill list; she already thinks Uncle Perry is behind the PAAUL murders. It won't make any difference if I tell her Ruby has been kidnapped. And I don't think I can cope without confiding in someone.

'Talk to me,' Lucy insists. 'You've always been there for me, helping me. Let me look after you for once.'

I sit up, wiping my eyes, then beckon Lucy close. If I talk quietly then hopefully whoever is watching me won't be able to hear what I'm saying.

'It's Ruby,' I whisper, fresh tears rising as I say her name. 'She's been taken. From there.' I glance at the door to the ladies. 'Uncle Perry will get PAAUL to kill her if I talk to the police.'

Lucy's eyes widen with horror.

'No,' she gasps. 'No, he *wouldn't*.'

A fresh wave of misery washes over me. 'One of the texts they sent said ... oh, Lucy, it said that Harry's dead too.'

'No.' Lucy slumps back in her seat, her pale face now ashen.

A few moments pass. I sit, swamped with desolation, my head in my hands.

Lucy shakes my arm gently and I look up at her. There are tears in her soft brown eyes.

'What ... what did the texts say about Ruby? How can you ... how can we get her back? Do you have any idea where she is?'

I shake my head. 'This is all I have.' I show her the video on my phone. Lucy watches, appalled.

'You have to tell the police now, don't you?' she asks.

'Didn't you hear what I said? I *can't*.' My voice cracks. 'Someone's watching me. Someone from PAAUL. They're making sure I do what they've ordered. They knew when I called the police and retracted my earlier statement. They know *everything*.'

'Oh, Francesca.' Lucy shrinks back as she looks anxiously around the ice cream parlour. I gaze down at the video of Ruby sedated. A memory flickers in my head, just out of reach. I frown, straining to place it, but it's gone.

'Well ... well, if you've done what Uncle Perry ... what PAAUL asked, then Ruby will be all right.' Lucy's terrified voice brings me back to the booth.

'Maybe, but the texts said I'd get her back tomorrow and I don't think I can bear it ... not knowing if she's all right until then.' My chest heaves with a dry, agonising sob.

'Sweet Lord.' Lucy crosses herself then pulls me into a hug. 'It's going to be okay, Francesca,' she whispers, fierce and hot in my ear. 'We're not going to let *anything* bad happen to Ruby. She's going to be all right, you *have* to believe it.'

LUCY

All my life Francesca has been there, watching over me, helping me. And now I want to help her. The truth is I owe Francesca a lot ... in a strange kind of way she's responsible for my faith, certainly for the direction my life has taken.

I want to help her get Ruby back. And I want to protect her from knowing about you. I'm not sure if I can do both those things, but I plan to try.

I owe her that much.

Back when I was fifteen and secretly pregnant it was Francesca who guessed something was wrong. Though even she didn't work it out until a couple of weeks after I found out myself. The truth was that for most of those first two weeks I put the knowledge I was carrying a baby in a room in my head and shut the door on it. This seems crazy to me now, but I have to remember I was only fifteen and a few months at the time – and had led a particularly sheltered life by twenty-first-century standards.

I did make a few efforts to see if I could somehow

lose the baby through natural means, though it was hard to find reliable data on the subject. I had got my first mobile phone for my birthday but of course back then all it did was make calls and texts. I had access to the internet on our home computer, but I didn't dare do a search for fear of it being stored on the PC's history.

So, in the end, I had to make do with our public library. Not a great source of information, sending me firstly to a health food store in search of parsley tea and angelica – neither of which worked – and then to our liquor cabinet for a bottle of gin.

The gin terrified me. Apart from the vodka-laced orange juice you gave me, I'd only ever had tiny amounts of alcohol before. A few sips of cider at the parties of my school friends and half a glass of champagne at Mum's fiftieth. By my age Francesca had been going to raves and pubs for a couple of years and I could still remember the trouble she'd get into when she stumbled home late at night, having ignored all attempts to contact her earlier.

I ran a scalding hot bath and took a huge mug of gin into the bathroom. I forced myself to drink over half of it before I vomited into the toilet and took myself, sobbing, off to bed.

It had now been over a fortnight since I'd found out I was pregnant. I had no idea how to measure a gestation period but I knew I'd conceived in the middle of December. Which meant right now I must be around four months pregnant. I also had no idea about abortion law – how the twenty-eight-week limit imposed by the 1967 Act had been reduced to twenty-four weeks in 1990. Again, it seems crazy to me that I didn't take any of these factors into consideration but the truth is that officially terminating my pregnancy never occurred to me. Not just because I'd been brought up to believe abortion was a terrible sin, but also because taking steps to get rid of the baby would have meant acknowledging the poor creature was inside me in the first place.

The weather in the middle of April was beautiful: sunny and warm. Francesca was still at home before going back to uni. That Saturday, she announced she was going to a nightclub and wouldn't be home until dawn. Mummy ordered her not to go which led, as usual, to a big row and me creeping off to my room.

Of course, Francesca arrived home very much the worse for wear the following morning and Mummy shouted at her that she was setting a bad example for me, with a face like Jesus when he's angry with the money lenders.

I felt some of her resentment myself. It seemed ... still does seem ... terribly unfair that Francesca should have lived such an immoral existence for so many years, while I had transgressed just once and was being punished so profoundly for it.

After the row, Mummy and I went to mass. I'd been dreading going to St Cecilia's that morning – I'd managed to get out of it the previous two Sundays, certain that my pregnancy shame must be written all over my face, but now I had run out of excuses. Mummy was so busy chatting with her friends that she didn't notice how quiet and unhappy I was.

The service – one of Father Gabriel's more barnstorming performances – left me feeling worse than ever, the mental door that I'd shut on my pregnancy not only now open but banging loudly against the walls.

'Mortification is of the body, where we repress the indulgence of our sinful sensual desires, and it is of the soul, where we feel our deepest, darkest shame.'

As Father Gabriel spoke of sacrifice and damnation in deep, reverberating tones I rubbed my fingers hard against the rough edge of the pew. I had always liked the feel of the coarse wood but now when a splinter came away in my hand I didn't hesitate to press it deep into the centre of my palm, enjoying the elevated, almost spiritual, sense of suffering it caused. Of course I could only tolerate the pain so long and as soon as I stopped my head filled up instead with a deep and horrible awareness of my shame again. My anguished thoughts had little form to them, mostly just dark waves of self-loathing: I'd been an idiot, careless, stupid ... God was punishing me for my fornication ... I had to have the baby, to redeem my sins ... I couldn't have the baby, it would shame me and mortify my family, publicising my transgressions and providing a constant reminder of an incident I was desperate to leave behind.

I almost talked to Father Gabriel. I wish now that I had, but that evening Francesca drifted into my room, rested and freshly showered.

'Dad's just got home from his conference and he's

taken Mum to dinner and I said I'd do your tea,' she said in a tone of smug self-sacrifice, slumping into the small chair where I read my bible every morning. 'D'you fancy takeout ... pizza?'

'Sure.' I gave Francesca the same fixed smile I'd been using all day on everyone from Mummy and Father Gabriel to the church mission committee ladies.

'What's up?' she asked, seeing through my mask immediately.

'Nothing,' I said. I kept on saying it, but within five minutes Francesca announced she wasn't leaving the room until I told her what was wrong and within ten she got the truth out of me.

'I'm pregnant,' I finally admitted.

Francesca stared at me, genuine shock in her eyes. 'I didn't think ...' She frowned. 'I guess I assumed you hadn't even ...'

I looked away. My virginity seemed a long-ago prize, like the sports day trophy I'd won aged thirteen for a running race. That victory had come easily, my legs being longer than any of my classmates'. I was happy and popular at the time and didn't think twice about how I looked until, a few months later, I grew – as I saw it – freakishly tall and felt awkward and clumsy in my lanky ways. My friends withdrew and I learned to look back on the popularity I'd basked in on sports day with nostalgia and envy, just as now, my virginity seemed to belong to an unfathomable Eden to which I longed to return and from which I knew, in my heart, I would always be barred.

'How ... Luce, sweetie, how did it happen?' Francesca, her abrasive, self-satisfied patina now completely gone, slid her arm around my shoulders.

I wriggled away, not wanting her pity. 'The usual way.' I shrugged.

'Lucy, for God's sake, talk to me.'

I stood at my bedroom window and cast my eyes down to the garden. From here I could see the edge of the trees that led to the summer house where you hurt me so badly in my soul as well as my body. I didn't see what happened then like I do now. Back then I saw your brutality as a seduction for which I was to blame. I blanked out the pain and the fear of it, reframing the experience as a dash of danger without ugliness. Exactly what the silky, slippery word 'seduction' suggests. To me, at the time, it was a choice I made; a sin on both sides. Now I see that you were the bigger sinner, that I was a child. That though I must take some responsibility for putting myself in a compromising situation, I was in no way to blame for the violence that followed.

'It was a man I met in a bar,' I lied.

'What were you doing in a bar?' Francesca looked appalled. Which really was very hypocritical of her, considering how she behaved when she was my age.

I shrugged again. 'I just went in for a drink of water. I was on my way home from school and I was thirsty but as I was drinking I noticed this man. He kept staring at me and I felt really uncomfortable.' I bit my lip, amazed at how easily lies were tripping off my tongue.

Francesca leaned forward, her face wreathed in concern. 'What happened next?'

I gulped, wondering if I could sustain my story to the end. 'So he came over and started chatting and he was really nice and he asked where I went to school and what my name was and I wanted to impress him so I lied and said I was almost eighteen and made a show of putting my mobile on silent. And then he bought me a couple of cocktails which he said were non-alcoholic but I think that was a lie.'

'I bet it was.' Francesca clenched her fists. 'What a fucking creep.'

'So I got a bit woozy,' I said, remembering how it had felt when you gave me the vodka. 'And he saw me yawn and he asked if I wanted to go up to his hotel room to lie down.'

'Lucy, you didn't . . .' Francesca's mouth gaped. 'How could you be so naïve?'

I gritted my teeth, irritated that I was failing to come over well even in my own invented story. 'I felt a bit sick by then,' I stressed, warming to my tale. 'And he was really nice.'

'How old was he?' Francesca asked.

I shrugged, wandering over to the bed. 'Daddy's age, maybe a bit younger.'

Francesca curled her lip. 'What a bastard.'

'So we got up to his hotel room and he opened a bottle of something and I didn't really want it but I didn't want to be rude so—'

'Jesus fucking Christ.'

'Anyway the next thing I was letting him kiss me and then ... then it happened and afterwards I ... I was really sore ... er, down there and I realised Mummy had been ringing for two hours wondering where I was.' I paused, imagining what would have happened next.

'Where was this bastard at that point?'

'In the shower,' I said quickly. 'So I got my clothes and left and I had a terrible headache and I was still sore but I carried on walking home and called Mummy and said I'd been at a school concert rehearsal and wasn't feeling well. And when I got in I had a bath and went to bed and in the morning I still felt sore but the headache was gone so I just went to school like a normal day.'

There was much truth in my story, I realised as I finished, though of course it barely scratched the surface of what had really happened.

Francesca was reaching for her phone. 'We need to call the police. The man's a fucking paedophile rapist.' She fixed me with a stern gaze. 'Where was this bar? What was his name? Which hotel was it?'

I shook my head. 'I don't know,' I said, anxious to put a lid on any attempt to investigate my lies. 'I was in such a state I don't remember. Seriously, Francesca, I wouldn't recognise him if I saw him again.'

'Oh, Lucy.' Francesca put down her phone. To my surprise tears bubbled up in her eyes. She gazed at my belly. 'Okay, well, even if you don't remember much we should still tell the police and we'll have to tell Mum too so that—'

'No.' I sat up straight. 'No, there's no point going to the police. I agreed to go up to the man's room. I know I'm underage, but ... but he didn't know that. And it's all so hazy ... plus I don't still have ...' I'd been going to say 'the bruises' but I stopped, guessing this wouldn't help my case.

'What about Mum and Dad?' Francesca asked, reaching for my hand.

'No,' I said, letting her squeeze my fingers. Not squeezing back. 'No, I don't want them to know. Not about the man.' I put my hand on my stomach. 'And definitely not about this.'

Francesca fell silent. Outside the wind rattled the blossom-heavy branches in the back garden. The lawn was strewn with fallen petals: another metaphor for my fallen state. I closed my eyes.

'Okay, I get that you don't want Mum and Dad to know,' Francesca began, her voice hesitant. 'But what exactly *do* you want?'

I hung my head, eyes still shut.

'When did all this happen?' she asked.

'December,' I said without thinking. 'Before Christmas.'

'What!' Francesca sprang up from her chair and stormed over. She lifted my top before I could stop her and stared at the tiny swell of my belly under my T-shirt. She looked up at me. 'Lucy, you've got to be ... *four months* at least ... Jesus *fuck*!'

I looked away, pulling down my top.

'You can't wait any longer.' Francesca's voice was

tense. 'If you want to get rid of it you have to act now.'

Nausea rose inside me. I should never have told her.

'Please, Lucy. It will decide *for* you if you don't do something.' She walked over and knelt in front of me, her tone becoming more gentle. 'It's very simple. Do you want this baby?'

I pressed my lips together.

'It's up to you, but a baby would change your whole life,' Francesca went on. 'And most of those changes will be really hard.'

For everyone else, I thought, as well as for me.

'So do you want it?' Francesca asked again. 'Bearing in mind right now it isn't even a baby, just a collection of cells. And the father is a rapist paedophile bastard who deserves to be shot?'

A long moment passed, then I gave a tiny shake of the head.

Francesca stood up. 'I'll sort it all out,' she said. 'You don't need to worry about a thing.'

To be fair, she was as good as her word. She kept my secret and she organised the termination – as the pro-choicers like to call it – at a local private hospital. I went through the next few days in a daze, in limbo, just waiting for it to be over. Since confiding in Francesca I had felt strangely numb about both being pregnant and the planned abortion. I knew somewhere inside me that it was profoundly wrong, against all the values we'd been brought up with, but Francesca's words rang loudly in my ears:

313

A baby would change your whole life ... And most of those changes will be really hard.

The morning of the abortion I felt jittery. Francesca had picked a day when everyone else at home would be away so, as she put it, I could 'get over the procedure' privately. She didn't have a car at the time, so took me to the hospital in a taxi. She sat with me while the nurse fussed around, checking me over and asking questions. It was an easier interview than with the doctor who'd sanctioned the abortion in the first place. With her I had been forced to go over the story I'd given Francesca and deal with a similar reaction: I should make a statement to the police, I should tell my parents. Plus: I should see a counsellor.

I refused to do any of these things, maintaining that there was no point as my memory was so hazy. At last the doctor backed off, though I sensed her disapproval.

Or maybe the disapproval was mine and I just projected it onto her.

At last it was time for the anaesthetic.

'I'll be here when you come round,' Francesca promised. And the last thing I remember before I went under was her kissing my forehead. When I came round I felt very groggy. She was holding my hand, telling me it was all over.

I didn't open my eyes.

An hour later I woke again. This time it hurt. I registered the dull ache of it and then it hit me.

I was a murderer. I had allowed them to kill my baby. How could I have been so cruel, so full of sin? God, in

His infinite wisdom, had created new life inside me and I had thrown it away. I had shamed myself, my family and my religion. I was worse than sinful – I was evil. Among the worst of the worst.

The numbness lifted and I cried. Bawled, in fact. For hours. Francesca was beside herself, alternately remonstrating, rationalising and weeping alongside me. I said nothing. There was nothing to say. If only my tears could wash away the stain on my soul. But I knew in my heart that I would carry the scars of my crime with me for the rest of my life.

As, indeed, I do.

It starts to rain outside the café, drips trickling down the window by our table.

'Can you think where Perry might have had Ruby taken?' The urgency in Francesca's voice brings me back to the bustle and steamy heat of the café. 'Do you think she could be in Lanagh? Or would he try and keep her away from anywhere he's connected with?'

I shake my head, feeling helpless in the face of her anxiety. 'I don't know.'

Francesca's face crumples. 'What about who he's using. The actual kidnapper. Can you think who that might be?'

I look away, unable to meet her eyes. *You.*

'I don't know what to do, Lucy.'

I look back at her. For the first time ever I feel like the big sister. It's not a role I have any idea how to play. Francesca is usually so sorted and capable. Even after

Caspian died she kept it together. But right now I can see she's on the verge of disintegrating. What is it about having a child that does that? What is it that Francesca feels for Ruby that, for all my shame and sense of loss, is a world apart from my own feelings for my own lost baby?

'I think,' I venture timidly, 'I think we need help.'

'But we can't go to the police, I already told you. If I go to the police PAAUL will kill Ruby.' Francesca raises her hands in desperation. The gesture reminds me of Mummy.

'I didn't mean the police,' I explain. 'But what about Daddy? We could ask him to talk to Uncle Perry for us. I know he didn't believe you earlier, but that was because I was too scared to speak up . . . and before he knew about Ruby.'

'I don't know.' Francesca groans. 'You said yourself you don't even know where he is. Oh, Christ, maybe I'm wrong. Maybe we should go to the police after all.'

I nod, trying to show support, but fear swirls in my chest. What on earth will you do if Francesca goes to the police?

'Maybe we should think about it,' I say. 'Um, I'd like to say a prayer. Will you pray too?'

Francesca shakes her head.

Which is fair enough, I guess. There's no reason she should suddenly find a long-lost faith just because she's *in extremis*. Maybe that will come later, once Ruby's safe. I haven't given up hope. The café is so stuffy and I tell Francesca I need some air. I go outside, and lean against the cold brick wall. I close my eyes. Prayer is harder here, outside an ugly café with traffic roaring past instead of in my bedroom or on the plushly cushioned pews at St Cecilia's. But I need to pray: for strength, for Francesca, for Ruby, for my faith.

My phone rings, breaking the fragile peace inside my head. My hand shakes as I look to see who is calling. Because I know before I see the name on the screen – it's you.

FRAN

Thank goodness Lucy is with me. I don't think I could handle this alone. I stare through the café window. She's out there now huddled over, sheltering from the rain against the café wall. Her head is bowed. Is she praying?

She's probably praying.

If I can't call on the police for help I'm almost ready to try praying myself. I put my head in my hands, trying to take in what has happened, but my mind reels, too traumatised and overwhelmed to process anything except my fears for Ruby.

Lucy's suggestion to call Dad penetrates my panic. Maybe it's worth a shot. I try his number but there's no reply. Rain drips slowly down the windowpane. I rock backwards and forwards in my chair, trying to contain the helpless fear inside me. I sense the waitress, the other customers watching me with wary, curious faces and I'm suddenly claustrophobic. The texts, I suddenly realise, didn't say anything about staying in the café, just that I mustn't talk to anyone.

I jump up and hurry outside to where Lucy is leaning against the wall, trying to shelter from the drizzle. Her face is paler than usual, the strain showing in her eyes. Raindrops have settled on her hair and her lashes.

'Have you heard anything?' she asks. 'About when you get Ruby back?'

'No, they're still making me wait.' Anger rises alongside the nausea and the fear. 'It's not fair. I've done what they asked.'

'What do you want to do?' Lucy clasps her hands together and twists the fingers anxiously. 'Is there anything we *can* do?'

'I don't know,' I snap.

'We could try praying again?' Lucy suggests.

I stare at her. For Pete's sake. She shrinks away and closes her eyes.

Ignoring her, I huddle against the wall and look at the video of Ruby on my phone again. My poor girl. I'm filled with misery and sickness and terror and fury. The car park spins around me. I focus on the film, playing and replaying it. And then, all of a sudden, the vague sense of memory I felt before coalesces around the tiny bit of fabric just above the sofa. It's only in shot for a couple of seconds but that white-and-purple criss-cross pattern is definitely familiar.

'I know this material.' I frown. 'It's got to be a wall hanging or ... or a curtain. I'm sure I've seen it somewhere. Look.' I pass the phone discreetly to Lucy, in case I'm still being watched.

319

Lucy peers intently at the fabric. 'I don't recognise it,' she says. 'I'm sorry.'

'Maybe I should tell the police after all, tell them I recognise the material,' I mutter, though of course I know I can't. That if Perry knows I've gone back on my promise to keep quiet, Ruby will be killed.

'How will the police be able to help if you don't know where you saw it?'

She's right. But if I can remember . . . I keep looking at the video. Surely if I stare at the fabric hard enough, often enough, I'll be able to work out where and when I saw it.

'Er, Francesca, I had an idea . . .' Lucy suggests timidly. 'Maybe we should talk to Auntie Sheila?'

I look up. 'Why?'

'Well, for one thing she might know where Daddy and Jacqueline are. Maybe we could even get her to talk to Daddy with us.'

'Auntie Sheila won't listen to *anything* I have to say.' I grimace, thinking of our heated exchange earlier.

'She might if we *both* talk to her,' Lucy suggests.

I visualise mild-mannered Auntie Sheila, her normally gentle presence, her adoration of my father. 'She was just so adamant that Dad couldn't be behind anything violent or criminal. She got really angry with me, to the point where I thought she might be covering up for him.'

'She's just very loyal. And after all, she *was* right to stick up for him.' Lucy wrinkles her nose. 'It's worth a try, isn't it? Sheila would *want* to help us if she could, she's a good person.'

320

Typical Lucy, always seeing the best in people. In spite of everything, I smile.

'Apart from anything else, Auntie Sheila really cares about Daddy,' Lucy goes on. 'He's like a brother to her. They've been close forever. I think he'd listen to her more than to us on our own.'

I hesitate. Maybe enrolling Sheila is a good idea after all. And at least it means we're doing something *and* getting away from whoever is watching me. After all, they haven't told me to stay put. And if I stand here much longer just staring at this video I will go insane.

Sheila lives in Fulham, on the way from Mariner's in Putney to Dad's house in Kensington. It's not a long journey, but the traffic is gnarly. At least that hopefully means I've lost whoever was watching me at the café. My mind flickers constantly to Ruby. Will whoever Perry has got to kidnap her think to feed her? Give her a drink? I can't bear to imagine her like she is in that video: barely conscious. She'll be scared and disoriented.

'Francesca?' I realise Lucy is speaking and glance across.

'I was just asking if you've told Ayesha about Ruby being taken?'

'No, though she knows something awful is happening, that I'm scared.'

I see Ayesha's face, confiding her long-kept secret about Mum being frightened of someone just before she died. I wasn't at home much at that time, but Lucy was living there. Could she have picked up on Mum's fears?

'Just before Mum passed away . . .' I venture, '. . . did she ever seem scared of anyone?'

'No.' Lucy stares at me. 'Where on earth did that come from?'

'Nothing. It doesn't matter.' All that matters is getting Ruby back. Once I have my daughter in my arms I can start working out everything else.

Lucy gazes out of the window. We're nearly at Sheila's now. 'If anything, Mum seemed angry before she died, rather than scared,' she muses.

'*Angry?*'

'With Daddy. They weren't very happy, not in the last few months.' She looks at me, a small crease between her eyebrows. 'They used to argue *all* the time just before Mummy died.'

I drive on, letting this unexpected admission settle. 'What did they argue about?'

'Mostly me,' Lucy says with a sigh. 'The rows were connected to my . . . my *episode*. It was my fault.'

Irritation rises inside me. Trust Lucy to make it all about her. 'You mean your abortion?' I ask. She winces. She doesn't like the word. Well she's just going to have to deal with my plain speaking for once. 'Because I don't see how you having a termination at fifteen that they find out about when you're nineteen explains them being at each other's throats years and years after that.'

'I'm not saying they were *only* angry about my episode, but that was the beginning of it. That was the beginning of the end.'

LUCY

Don't think I'm being heartless, telling Francesca the truth about the past when she's so upset about Ruby. But it's important she knows there's more to our family and the relationships between us than her own version.

I watch her face, the emotions rampaging across it, as I talk. She knows some of what I'm saying already, of course. For instance, she knows that I became withdrawn and depressed after my abortion. At the time every adult in my life knew that, though no one apart from my sister knew the reason why. I was discussed and dissected both at home and at school, where the range of possible reasons and solutions for my worryingly lacklustre attitude were many and varied. My teachers – and this was an old-fashioned Catholic school, remember – thought that I was mostly bored and possibly hormonal. The headmistress got all strict with me and urged me to reconnect with my studies and to put in greater effort to fulfil my potential.

Francesca, who, of course, knew that it was my abortion which had prompted this change in me, told me, in her typically forthright way, that I needed to see a therapist.

'I've been seeing one at uni, Luce,' she told me earnestly. 'It's been so good to talk over all the ways Mum and Dad oppressed us. I think you'd find it really helpful to do the same thing, away from their brainwashing.'

She meant that she imagined talking to a therapist would help me reframe my response to my abortion. The fact that I didn't feel in the slightest bit oppressed or brainwashed or in need of reframing anything didn't seem to register with her.

Mummy also reached out for help for me, though of course she turned to the church rather than a therapist. Naturally, this deference to our religion riled Francesca no end, but Mummy was in charge and I was hauled off for an excruciating half hour with a visiting priest at St Cecilia's: Father James. To the rest of the family he was young (about thirty) and hip (in that he wore jeans and designer shirts). Plus he'd been open about his own battle with homosexual yearnings, not that I was aware of that at the time. He would, they were all certain, find a way of communicating with me that might get to the bottom of whatever was causing my two-month-long slump.

To me, Father James seemed phony as well as intimidatingly handsome, in an older-man sort of way. I stared at his chiselled cheekbones and bright white smile and it just reinforced my view that he was the very last person in whom I could confide what you did to me, or the abortion that followed.

Instead I resolved to try harder to hoist a happy, engaged mask on my face whenever I was at school or around my family. It was, in all honesty, a strain. I sought refuge in self-harm for a while but the cuts on my thighs no longer gave me the same level of release I'd once experienced.

I ached for that sense of liberation. I hurt, all the time, without it. And I soon found something that at least dulled my pain. We had a party at home where June and I sneaked several sips of Mummy's pink cocktail while she was chatting with guests.

It was sweet and delicious. The first alcohol I'd ever tasted that I'd properly enjoyed. Which wasn't saying much. As you well know, I was a dutiful child who rarely broke any rule. But late one night – I think it was after a horrible evening where you didn't seem to notice me because, at least in my imagination, you felt so terrible about what had happened between us – I snuck down to the kitchen, emptied a small water bottle from the fridge, and filled it up with a little bit from every alcoholic drink in the house. It tasted disgusting, of course, but suffused with bitter shame as I was, that only made me more determined to drain the bottle to the bottom. I remember almost revelling in my gluttony: it made me feel special, that whatever I did I would take to an extreme. I did the same thing the following night – though with a smaller selection of drinks: just the white ones, then just the brown. And again. And again, experimenting with tastes until I worked out that I really didn't like the dark liquors at all, that I'd drink gin and vodka if they were all that was available, but the purest drink, the one that seemed to fit me best, was tequila. Of course after a week or so the diminishing levels of liquid in the drinks cabinet were noticed. Poor Francesca – who was visiting for a few days – got the blame, which led to her being lectured on the evils of drinking and exploding in another furious row.

After that I decided I would buy my own booze. The next day everyone was out. I'd found a little off-licence a few streets away where the staff were young and male then I 'borrowed' Francesca's tightest top and squeezed my feet into a pair of her highest heels. I unbuttoned the top so that my (to my eyes hideously large) cleavage was on display, then I applied a dusky smudge of eyeliner and some of Francesca's lip gloss. I tottered out of the house, desperately hoping no one I knew would see me. A house along the road was having building work done and the workmen stopped what they were doing to call after me as I passed. Embarrassed to the core, I almost turned back, but I knew that when night fell I would want that drink, so I gritted my teeth and kept going.

My heart was beating like a drum as I walked into the off-licence. I had no fake ID, and no idea what I would say if I was challenged about my age. I needn't have worried. That was the one question the spotty-necked youth behind the counter didn't ask, though he wasted no time in demanding to know my name (Ilsa, I said, attempting to channel the elegance of the Ingrid Bergman character in *Casablanca*, which I'd watched with Mummy a few evenings before) and if I'd like to go for a drink with him that evening. Flustered, I politely said 'no' and scurried home, clutching my two bottles of tequila in their plastic bag.

I hid the bottles at the back of my wardrobe, under an old ski suit. I washed off my make-up and returned Francesca's shoes and top – though not before Francesca noticed they were missing and accused me of stealing them. I denied it of course, in tears, then secretly returned them as soon as Francesca's back was turned. Mummy took my side, entirely convinced Francesca had simply mislaid the items. My sister insisted I'd taken the clothes out of spite. I'm sure she never guessed why and how I had actually used them.

My success at deceiving her and Mummy reinforced my excitement that I'd actually carried out my plan and got away with it. The tequila was mine! On top of which the guy in the off-licence had wanted me. And I'd been brave and resourceful to achieve my goal.

I felt, for a few moments at least, special again.

Of course the bottles I'd bought soon ran out but I saved my allowance, which just about managed to cover the amount of alcohol I was now drinking. When Francesca came home again for the summer holidays I wondered if she'd be able to tell I was secretly necking down tequila almost every night when I went to bed. After all, she'd sensed when I was in trouble before.

But Francesca was preoccupied with herself and her uni life and still rebelling against everything we'd been brought up to believe in. She spent August and early

September in a whirl of arguments, loud music blaring out of her bedroom at all hours of the day and night. Meanwhile I sank further and further into misery, while trying harder and harder to appear the normal, hard-working, biddable schoolgirl that I also essentially was.

My agony reached its peak on the nine-month anniversary of your terrible sin against me which was, of course, nine months on from the date I'd got pregnant. I wasn't aware at the time that nine calendar months from conception do not give a precise due date; in my head this was the day my baby would have been born.

Alcohol blotted out the pain I felt but, as I said, had never brought me release. I turned back to self-harming again for a while, cutting tiny slices on my thighs after bad days that brought a small and temporary relief from my shame. But it wasn't enough. I developed a horror of my own body, a deep desire to rid myself of the flesh that had proved so evilly tempting for you. It was my developing body, I reasoned, that had caused all my problems and I resolved to punish it.

After learning about St Agatha on her saint day the following February, I bound my breasts with bandages in an attempt to contain them. Later I took a solemn vow not to eat between breakfast and dinner, a neat way of denying my body the fuel that made it grow while avoiding Mummy's stern gaze at mealtimes.

At school I attracted the nickname of Bin, thanks to my habit of throwing my packed lunch in the trash as soon as I arrived at school. While this was clearly not meant in a nice way, I wasn't singled out for bullying in the way that some girls were. The nickname simply confirmed my position as a loner and an outsider. Which suited me fine. I had no real friends, though at school I hung around with a small group of other quiet, studious girls. We would sit together at break times, reading or working, ignoring the raucous behaviour of the more extrovert girls around us.

I was ignored. Virtually invisible.

Looking back it is clear to me that I simply wanted to disappear. It beggars belief that nobody either at home or at school realised how unhappy I was, but I had learned to be bright-eyed and superficially engaged at home and made sure I paid just enough attention at school and that I always did my homework on time. Things improved a little during my last term in the sixth form: prompted to socialise by Mummy, I started hanging out with a couple of girls from church. We didn't do much more than read and chat at each other's homes – the height of our vanity and camaraderie was encouraging each other to try out new hairstyles and admiring a new nail polish. But it helped a little. I had worked hard and done well at school and when I was accepted at London University (I had insisted on staying at home for my degree) to study history that autumn my confidence increased still further.

Of course in mid-September the terrible anniversary came around again. As I had in previous years, I sobbed into my pillow, imagining my unborn child on their birthday – this time wreathed in cherubic smiles and all excited to blow out their candles. But all in all, I was starting to recover. I began my history degree and though I steered well clear of the heavy drinking and socialising in which most of my peers indulged, I found for the first time in a long while that my life had structure and meaning.

And then, the following April, almost exactly four years to the day since my abortion, when I had managed to build a fortress of sorts around the sin I had committed, came some devastating news which laid siege to all my hard-won defences and threatened to expose my shame to the world. I realised then that my sin was not gone, merely temporarily buried – an unexploded bomb that could still destroy my family.

All I have left is my faith. It sustains me but, as I sit here in this airless car, beside my sister in her agony, I realise how deeply I have failed her. If only Francesca had faith, maybe she would be able to get through this. Without it, I can't see all of us surviving.

FRAN

I'm hunched over the steering wheel, trying to keep my focus on the traffic ahead. For goodness' sake, what is Lucy's problem? She keeps going on about faith and the power of prayer ... doesn't she understand that I'm in agony here?

Ruby is gone. I can't bear to think of how utterly terrified she must be feeling, that's if she's still ... no, I can't let myself think that ...

Meanwhile Lucy is still banging on about her termination from a million years ago. 'It fractured everything,' she muses, an expression on her face that makes me want to slap her. 'It started the rot between Mummy and Daddy.'

'How?' I demand, wrenching the steering wheel to speed around the next corner. Only another few minutes and we'll be at Auntie Sheila's. 'As I remember Mum and Dad were furious at *me*, not each other.'

'Yes, maybe at first. But even then they were furious differently. Mummy was angry because she was jealous that I'd gone to you, not her. Daddy thought the whole thing was as much Mummy's fault as yours. More, actually.'

I say nothing. Who cares about the ancient history of our parents' relationship? All marriages have their ups and downs. Which Lucy would know if she hadn't led such a bloody sheltered life. I gaze at the soft light from the streetlamps as it glimmers on the wet road ahead. If only I could somehow let Ruby know I was thinking about her, trying to find a way to get her back.

When we were younger Dex and I made up a game called Telepathy Cousins. It was basically a trick on Lucy, a way of paying her back for dripping round after us, being annoying. We would pretend to be able to mind-read what word the other person was thinking. We fooled Lucy many times before we got bored. But there was one time when it actually worked. I'd imagined the word 'red' and much to both his and my astonishment, Dex guessed it.

Maybe, if I concentrated hard enough, I could perform the same trick now with Ruby. I imagine her face.

Ruby. I'm thinking about you, Ruby. I'm here, baby girl. I'm going to find you. Everything's going to be all right.

Lucy is still babbling in my ear, but I'm barely listening.

'So you see my ... my *episode* really did drive them apart,' she explains. 'Mummy got more and more depressed, she couldn't settle to anything, she got bitter and sad. And ... and I think in the end she might have looked for comfort elsewhere.'

Her words suddenly penetrate my silent communion. 'What?' I glance round.

Lucy looks up at me through long eyelashes.

'You're saying Mum had an affair?' She cannot be serious. I turn off the main road onto Auntie Sheila's street. 'What makes you think that?'

'Just stuff I picked up at the time,' Lucy says vaguely.

I'm seriously doubtful – and really not in the mood to think about my parents' marriage right now. I pull up outside Sheila's manicured front garden. A pair of chintzy curtains, closed, hang at the kitchen window. Lights are on both upstairs and downstairs. The fabric in that video flashes into my mind's eye again. Why can't I place it? Why can't I picture anything else in the room where I saw the fabric? It makes no sense. Curtains and wall hangings don't exist in isolation.

'To be honest, Lucy,' I say with a sigh, 'all I care about is getting Ruby back.'

'Of course.' Lucy nods. 'Let's go in.'

As we hurry up the path to Sheila's front door, the frosty air biting at my cheeks, I fight the panicky sick feeling in my stomach. I press the bell. One of Ruby's old drawings is visible through the glass panel of the door, pinned to Sheila's noticeboard. It breaks my heart.

My darling girl, I'm doing my best to find you.

Is she okay? I glance at my phone. It's barely an hour and a half since Ruby was taken and only 6.30 p.m. – though the dark sky above and my strung-out nerves make it feel much later. There's no way I can make it through to morning. Sheila *has* to help us talk to Dad. And Dad has got to help us confront Perry.

It's stopped raining but the air is damp and heavy as well as cold. Lucy's blonde hair glints gold under the porch lights. Auntie Sheila welcomes us in with a look of surprise.

'Francesca, three times in one week? Is everything all right? Oh, Lucy. Hello, come in.'

I stride into the kitchen. How do I begin? A man's coat hangs over one of the chairs.

'Is Uncle Graham here?' I ask, too stressed to be subtle.

'Yes, well, not like *that* ...' Sheila blushes. 'He's upstairs taking a shower. But it's not what you think, I—'

'I don't care,' I say, relieved that at least if he's upstairs I won't have to deal with him on top of everything else. 'Sheila, I need your help.'

'Of course, dear.' Sheila frowns. 'What is it?'

'Do you know where Daddy is?' I ask.

'No, I'm afraid I don't,' Sheila says. 'Why? Is something wrong?'

'It's Uncle Perry,' I say. 'We ... we're fairly certain he's involved with PAAUL the, er, the extreme anti-abortion organisation.'

Sheila stands, blinking at me. Beside me Lucy shuffles from foot to foot, her fingers anxiously entwined.

I take a deep breath. 'He's had Ruby taken. Whoever he's got to kidnap her is threatening to kill her.'

Sheila's mouth falls open.

'It's all because of PAAUL's campaign to kill off abortion doctors in the UK. We think ... we're sure Uncle Perry is behind the campaign.' My guts twist into a knot. It's almost impossible to say the whole truth out loud. 'Perry had Caspian killed and ... and I just found out Harry Elliot too ... and now Ruby's been kidnapped to stop me speaking out.'

'No, that can't be true,' Sheila gasps. 'None of this.'

I turn to Lucy. She bites her lip. *Come on*, I urge her silently. *Step up for once.*

'It is true, Auntie Sheila,' Lucy stammers at last. 'And we need you to help us talk to Dad ...'

'... so we can get Ruby back,' I finish.

'Oh dear Lord,' Sheila breathes.

I lean against the kitchen counter, feeling faint. There's the soft pad of footsteps down the stairs. I brace myself as Uncle Graham walks in. He looks far better than when I saw him yesterday in the pub: sober and in clean clothes, with his damp, pink skin glowing from his shower. He's a big man – taller even than Dad – with a strong, storm-cloud sort of presence. Right now he exudes an air of barely repressed anger. It's not hard to imagine Mum being scared of him. Perhaps she wasn't making up what she told Ayesha after all.

He raises his eyebrows. 'What's all this then?'

I glance at Lucy. She's always been intimidated by Uncle Graham. True to form, she's shrinking back against the fridge as if she's trying to make herself invisible.

'I'm hoping Auntie Sheila will come with us to speak to Dad,' I say. 'It's important.'

'Course it is,' Graham sneers. 'Always is where bloody St Jayson's concerned.'

'Please don't start, dear,' Sheila says wearily. She turns to me. 'Francesca, all these things you've said ... I can't believe they're true ... I'm sure there's been a misunderstanding. Perhaps Perry took Ruby out somewhere and forgot to leave his phone on. I'm always doing it myself and you know how absent-minded he can be.'

Has she not heard a word we've said?

I stare at her, aware of Graham grinning nastily by the kitchen door. For a moment I hesitate, not wanting to speak in front of him. Then I remember it was Graham who told me my father and uncle were 'up to their necks in evil', which was what prompted me to search Dad's house in the first place.

'Uncle Perry is a murderer.' I say the words slowly, for emphasis. 'Dad doesn't know but we need to make him see it's true.'

Sheila's cheeks flush a deep red. 'I'm sorry, dear, but I don't want to listen to any more of this. If you're really intent on badmouthing your family, I'm going to have to ask you to leave.'

She simply doesn't want to face the truth. The thought hits me like a brick. Surely there's no other explanation for this refusal to help. Which effectively means that, like the rest of my family, she is closing ranks – with me and my children on the outside: the black sheep to the end.

An image of poor Ruby on that video sent to my phone sears through my head. I see her on the sofa, that still somehow familiar fabric behind. The pain of it coruscates me.

I can't stay here any longer.

Without speaking, I turn and hurry out of the house. No one will help. I'm all alone. I can't breathe. How on earth am I going to make it through the rest of the evening, the whole of the night, knowing how scared Ruby must be? Panic fills me. I should never have come here. I hurry inside the car and roar the engine. I drive fast along the back streets, eager to get away. I have to go to the police. Don't I? Whatever the risks. Oh, God. If Harry were here he would know what to do.

But he's dead. Gone, like Caspian. A tear trickles down my cheek. I wipe it angrily away. Me feeling sorry for myself is the last thing that will help Ruby. As I stop at the next set of lights I look at the video again. I'm hoping that the sight of my little girl's sweet face will give me courage and strength. I'm not even thinking about that criss-cross patterned fabric – but, this time, as it flutters into view I know what it is.

I know where I've seen it before.

Lucy

Francesca's driven off. Goodness knows where. And I'm stuck here. Abandoned without a word. Left to find my own way home. As I leave Auntie Sheila's, I pray for poor Ruby. And for you. Even though I hate you, I must pray for you also. It's the right thing to do.

Though there was a time not so long ago when I could not have brought myself to do that. Certainly not on that grim April morning, as clouds gathered outside in a steely grey sky, and Mummy came into my bedroom with a face to match.

At the time – the Easter holiday at the end of my second term at uni – my faith was still only a nominal outer coat I wore as and when I thought of it, while my taste in décor hadn't moved on much from when I was fourteen. I had a pink duvet, soft toys on the bookshelves and a row of prints from Mummy's ballet dancing collection along my rose-wallpapered walls.

Mummy walked straight in – she never knocked – and said: 'Lucy, I need to talk to you.' There was a terrible uncharacteristic solemnity in her voice.

Mummy was the lightest, sparkliest of people. I knew at once something awful had happened.

Mummy shut the door, muffling the sound of the dance music blaring out of Francesca's room along the corridor. It was a total coincidence Francesca happened to be visiting at the time – and on her own. She was going out soon with some friends, which was why Mummy hadn't made a fuss about the volume.

I put down my book. 'What's the matter, Mummy?'

'Is it true, darling?' she asked.

I gawped at her, genuinely having no idea what she was talking about.

'Lucy?' Mummy's voice cracked. 'Please, for goodness' sake, tell me.'

'Tell you what?' I sat bolt upright and made the sign of the cross – a theatrical gesture really. At the time crossing myself was a habit put on to impress.

Mummy perched on the end of my bed. 'I've just spoken to your father. He's had a phone call from a reporter with *Catholic London*.' She cleared her throat. 'The man claims to have evidence from a clinic that four years ago, when you were fifteen, you had a … an abortion.'

My chest tightened.

'Your father told him to get lost of course, that there was no way our daughter … you … that it wasn't even possible … Daddy was threatening injunctions and libel suits but the reporter just laughed and said none of that would hold up because he can prove the story is true and that Daddy is a hypocrite for speaking out against abortions while allowing his underage daughter to have one ... that it calls into question Daddy's integrity.' She sighed. 'Daddy's furious ... says it's the new editor, that he's always been resentful of your father's success and that he must be making things up, but ...' Mummy leaned forward. The fear in her eyes was unbearable to see. I looked away.

'We need to know the truth, Lucy.' Her voice shook. A long, terrible silence filled the room.

'It's true,' I whispered, staring down at my duvet. Shame filled me, worse than ever. 'I'm so sorry.' I clutched at the edge of the pink cotton. 'I sinned. I sinned and I know God hates me and now you'll both hate me and ... and I hate myself ...' I dissolved into tears and, though I didn't realise it at the time, they were partly tears of relief. It had been harder than I'd known to keep my terrible secret.

Mummy's face went ghost-white.

'How ...?' she gasped. 'Who ...? I didn't even ... oh, my darling, why didn't you tell us?'

I bit my lip and hung my head. Another long stretch of silence until I finally murmured, 'I didn't want you to be ashamed of me.'

'Oh, sweetheart.' Mummy took my hand. 'Who ... how did it happen? How did you meet the ... the boy?'

It wasn't a boy. It was a man.

It was you.

There was no way I could say that of course so instead I just mumbled: 'It was a one-off thing, an accident ... not someone I knew ...'

341

'I see.' Mummy's voice grew colder. 'And what did this boy say when you told him about . . . that you were pregnant?'

'I never saw him again . . . I didn't tell him . . .'

'Who did you tell?' Mummy demanded. 'Lucy? Who did you tell?'

'Just Francesca.' I regretted giving her name as soon as it was out of my mouth.

'Francesca knew?' Mummy crossed herself – the customary action dramatic and exaggerated in much the same way, I realise all these years later, as I used to do it myself. 'Did Francesca arrange the abortion?'

I hung my head.

Mummy stormed to the door. Every muscle in her body seemed tense with fury. I thought at the time she was angry that I'd taken an innocent life but now I know better. She was actually just furious that I'd confided in Francesca.

As with everything with Mummy, it was all about her.

'Francesca!' she yelled. I could hear her thumping on Francesca's bedroom door which was, presumably, locked. 'Get out here!'

A second later Mummy appeared in my doorway again. Her cheeks were flushed with fury, her long dark hair wild around her face.

'Francesca helped me, please don't be cross with her.' I clasped my hands together.

'Was the abortion Francesca's idea?' Mummy asked, her voice like ice as she walked over to me.

'I don't know.' My own voice was barely a whisper. 'I just know I've regretted it ever since. It was a terrible—'

'Was it Francesca's idea?' Mummy repeated.

'Was what my idea?' Francesca was leaning against the doorframe, grinning. She was dressed in denim shorts and ripped tights with heavy eye make-up, the very antithesis of Mummy's flowery shirtdress.

'Lucy's . . . baby and what happened to it,' Mummy said, her voice shaking. 'You knew?'

A terrible silence fell.

Francesca nodded.

'You pushed her into an abortion?' Mummy gasped.

'What?' Francesca frowned. 'No, I just—'

'That's not fair.' I scrambled off the bed. 'You can't blame Francesca.'

'She was a *child*.' Mummy glared at Francesca. 'You know our beliefs . . . Lucy's beliefs . . . and you flew in the face of them, encouraging her to do what *you* wanted.'

'I didn't,' Francesca protested. 'I was trying to help her.'

'Support me whatever, that's what she did,' I sobbed, beside myself.

'Lucy was a *child*, only fifteen. You had a responsibility to tell us, to follow *our* ethical principles, not selfishly push her into your own immoral—'

'I was doing what Lucy wanted,' Francesca spat, eyes blazing. 'It was her body. Her choice. Not mine. Not yours.'

'Please,' I said. But no one was listening to me.

'I need to speak to your father,' Mummy said, her voice harder than I'd ever heard it. 'He will be bitterly disappointed in you.'

I sucked in my breath, horrified.

A terrible silence fell across the room. 'Please, please don't be angry with Francesca.' Tears poured down my face. 'It was my sin, my shame.'

'For goodness' sake, don't let her talk like that,' Francesca said. 'There's no sin or shame. Some arsehole took advantage of her. It was just a mistake to be taken care of.'

Mummy curled her lip. 'Stop that disgusting talk.' She stormed out. Francesca turned and fled in the opposite direction.

I collapsed in floods of tears. Great sobs racked my body. It felt like my very soul was splitting in two.

The next day was awful. The story was published in *Catholic London*, a weekly publication that didn't have a huge circulation, but whose subscription base included Daddy and Mummy's entire social circle. That evening the family got together for a powwow ... which simply led to everyone shouting at everyone else. I was made to have a long talk with Father Gabriel, who made me see it was God's forgiveness I needed before anything else.

'But I need to make things better for Mummy and Daddy,' I told him earnestly. 'They're arguing because Mummy blames Francesca and Daddy blames Mummy for not keeping a better eye on me when ... when it happened,' I sobbed.

'I know, my child,' Father Gabriel said sonorously. 'And your concern for your family does you great credit but it is your soul we must focus on. And the soul of the baby that died.'

'Oh.' I didn't know what to say. 'I am truly sorry. I pray every day for the baby's soul. Each year in September, on the day when it would have been born, I say a long, long prayer.' I bit my lip, unwilling to share the other mortifications of the flesh that I had inflicted on myself.

'I am concerned, especially about excommunication,' Father Gabriel went on.

My eyes widened. This was a body blow I hadn't expected. I might not have a strong faith any more, but being chucked out of the church was about the most shameful thing I could imagine.

'I don't want that. And it will make things even worse for Mummy and Daddy, they'd be terribly upset,' I stammered.

A look of intense pain crossed Father Gabriel's face. I knew that Mummy had filled him in with the story I had given her – a rehash of the one I'd told Francesca four years before.

'I hope it will not happen,' Father Gabriel said slowly. 'And right now I think we should focus on your penance. It is important that whatever penance you undertake should quiet the disorders of your soul, not inflame them.'

'I don't understand.'

He sighed. 'Let's look at the twin temptations that

345

led you to the sins you committed: firstly you were tempted by the attention that the stranger offered. He plied you with drink and flattery. Your sin there was one of vanity, of pride.'

I nodded. Of course you were no stranger, but I *was* flattered when you seemed to want me that way – as if it made me special.

'For this I would recommend a daily prayer,' Father Gabriel continued. 'I will give you guidance on the form and on a very practical level I feel strongly that you should renounce alcohol and excessive use of cosmetic products and undue interest in clothes.' He waved his hand vaguely. 'Anything that might lead to behaviour likely to encourage the wrong sort of attention.'

I nodded again. This didn't sound too difficult – I had almost stopped drinking except on my occasional nights out at uni. And I already liked my clothes to be modest and my make-up minimal, so that I could avoid male attention.

'That's how Daddy likes us anyway,' I said.

Father Gabriel nodded. 'Of course, and the solid grounding in Christian values you have received is a core part of your armoury.' He cleared his throat. 'Now the second temptation arose because you failed to confide in your parents and instead allowed yourself to be swayed and persuaded into a mortal sin by your older sister. This was a sin of weakness.'

I lowered my eyes. It wasn't fair to blame Francesca. I was certain – still am – that if I'd told her I wanted to keep my baby she would have supported me in that choice. But I didn't protest to Father Gabriel. Indeed I'm ashamed to remember the way I allowed him to think of me as a cowardly, easily led child.

He talked on and subtly, slowly, I weaselled my way out of most of the responsibility for my actions. The truth was that, beyond everything else, I was greedy for mercy. Indeed all these years later, it is the selfishness of my avarice that appals me most.

'Your soul is in a fragile state,' Father Gabriel went on. 'I know this will be a big sacrifice for you but I think it vital that you leave university, for the time being at least.'

'Oh.' This came as a shock. At first I felt profoundly disappointed. It wasn't as if I had moved away from home or undergone any big upheaval, but being at university gave my life purpose. 'What should I do instead?'

'I suggest some voluntary work with one or two of our church groups,' Father Gabriel suggested. 'That way we can keep an eye on you and help you find your way back to God.'

'I see.' I looked up at him. A thick white hair was growing out of his left nostril. 'Do you think that will help Mummy and Daddy feel better?'

He smiled sorrowfully at me. 'I will speak to them too, explain the sacrament of your penance to them. You are a good, loving child, Lucy. I don't want you to hate yourself for any of this.'

'No?' I wondered if he would say the same if he knew how ugly my soul felt to me.

'Remember the words of St John Vianney: our sins are nothing but a grain of sand alongside the great mountain of the mercy of God,' Father Gabriel intoned.

Father Gabriel was as good as his word. Not that his steady support stopped Francesca being furious. Ironically, just as the church believed I was an innocent with a one-time stain on my character, easily swayed by the sins of others, so Francesca totally bought into the liberal and – to my mind – patronising line that insisted I was being brainwashed by my religion.

As far as I'm concerned, I made my own decision. In the end leaving uni wasn't as hard as I'd anticipated. I actually found I enjoyed my church work more than I had my studies. Father Gabriel and others at St Cecilia carried on counselling me to make good works my path to righteousness and God's mercy. And, increasingly, the idea of going back to pick up my history degree seemed pointless and irrelevant. My main concern was that my actions had splintered my family and divorced me from their love. Francesca rarely visited now and Mummy, though still angry with her, was also cold and stiff with me. This particularly brought me great pain. And of course you stayed away a lot and when you did see me, you barely looked me in the eye. To make matters worse, I was faking my faith. I had dutifully stopped drinking, though I still allowed myself bouts of fasting and even self-harmed when things got tough. But spiritually I felt empty. I kept busy with my church work, but though I went through the motions of daily prayer my heart wasn't really in it. It was as if I was living in a kind of limbo, waiting for something to come along to shake me up and show me my path.

Which, thanks to you, it did.

In this way several years passed. And then came the earthquake that shattered my entire universe. The second of your killings, following on from the murder of my innocence: the assassination of my hope.

It was a little while after Mummy's birthday party – the one where she told Ayesha she was scared of you – and there was a terrorist scare in central London. I was in Brompton meeting a friend from church for coffee and we both freaked out when the police started closing off roads.

I hurried home, hours earlier than I'd intended, feeling shaken. I knew Mummy would be in, she'd been away for the weekend and had told me she was planning to sleep late then potter about at home. Thinking she might be resting was the only reason why I didn't call out when I let myself in. Instead I went through to the kitchen and opened the drinks cupboard. I stared at the bottle of tequila. I hadn't felt tempted to drink for ages but right then I badly wanted a shot. Shutting the door on the cupboard and feeling decidedly disgruntled, I wandered upstairs to my room. As I reached the door I heard a low moan coming from the spare room at the far end of the corridor. It was an animal sound. Guttural. Sexual. I stopped in my tracks, my heart beating fast. Who on earth was in the house? Surely not Mummy? She was in her room asleep. Even if she wasn't, I could imagine no reason why she would be in our spare room making such noises.

I crept along the corridor. The spare room door was pulled to, but not properly shut. Another moan, then whispered voices. There were two people in there. One of them definitely male. I held my breath as I peered through the crack. It took several long seconds before my brain accepted what my eyes were seeing: Mummy's face all intense like I'd never seen, eyes shut, her expression lost in lust and adoration. A man standing behind, bending over her, his face hidden as he buried his lips on her neck, one hand inside her open dress, the lace detail of her bra.

The man moved.

I saw his face.

The face of my abuser.

From the heart of my family.

You.

FRAN

How did I not see it before? I lean closer, watching the video again. The fabric in view for a few seconds at the start is the edge of the curtains in a first-floor flat I stood outside only yesterday.

Uncle Graham's flat.

The cars behind honk at me and I hurry into gear. As I glance in the mirror to check the vehicles behind my own strained eyes stare back at me.

How is this possible? What does it mean? That Uncle Graham has kidnapped Ruby? That he is involved with PAAUL? That *he* is Uncle Perry's hired killer?

I drive, confusion and indecision whirling in my mind. If Graham is caught up in Uncle Perry's murderous campaign, why would he have been so open with me when we spoke about it?

There's a big roundabout up ahead. Do I keep going or turn back? I'm closer to Sheila's house than I am to Graham's flat. And Graham himself is in Sheila's house. Part of me wants to go back there and demand he releases her.

Except there's every chance he'll refuse. Worse, he may attack me, leaving me unable to do anything for Ruby. And Auntie Sheila will get caught in the crossfire. That's if she isn't up to her neck in the whole thing already.

The traffic slows as I get close to the roundabout. What should I do? Clearly Ruby is in Graham's flat. At least she was earlier. And if she is still there, Graham must have left her, sedated, while he went to visit Sheila. He didn't look like he was about to leave Sheila's house any time soon. Does that mean Ruby is in his flat alone? Or is some other PAAUL operative standing guard over her?

I reach for my phone. Never mind turning up at the station, it's time to dial 999.

Except . . . my fingers hesitate over the screen. Calling the police is exactly what PAAUL has ordered me not to do. If I call, they will kill Ruby before I can get to her.

My phone rings in my hand. It's Lucy.

I can't talk to my sister right now. I cancel her call and set down the mobile. I will go to Graham's flat myself. The worst that can happen is that I don't find Ruby and that PAAUL realises I've been looking for her. But even if that happens, they'll quickly realise I'm alone and that I haven't called the police. They can't kill Ruby for that.

I circle the roundabout, taking the turning for Ladbroke Grove. I should be there in twenty minutes or so. There's no way Graham could get there before me, even if he left Auntie Sheila's now. My stomach clenches with fear as I press down on the accelerator.

Thoughts tumble through my head: how on earth has Uncle Graham got involved with PAAUL? It doesn't make sense. He's not remotely religious and he hates Uncle Perry almost as much as he hates Dad.

Money. That has to be it. Graham has been broke since his attempt at setting up an antiques business spun him into bankruptcy for the second time. Maybe Uncle Perry is paying him to kill – and now kidnap. I zoom through a just-turned red light, desperate to get to the flat.

The car in front of me slows and I'm forced to brake yet again. I try to focus on how on earth I will get Ruby out of Uncle Graham's flat. The first step will be to get into it myself. I am quite prepared to break the door down if I have to, but I remember from yesterday's visit that the building's front door is made of solid wood. I don't have any tools with me and there's no way I'm strong enough to shoulder it down. Even if I can get past that I have to negotiate the front door of the apartment itself, up on the first floor.

I tap my hands on the steering wheel. Of *course*. I know exactly who to ask for help: someone I trust, who understands my family ... and who knows what Graham is capable of.

Without thinking about it any further I call Dex.

He answers immediately. I can hear the clink of crockery in the background.

'Are you busy?' I say.

'As a whore in a garrison,' Dex says in his usual cheery way. 'I've got the kids. It's a madhouse here.'

'Oh, Dex.' My voice cracks.

'What's up, Dumpy?'

It's hard to say all that I know and fear out loud.

'Franny?' The cheeriness fades from Dex's voice. 'Is something the matter?'

'I think your dad might have done something really, really awful,' I stammer.

'Oh, right,' Dex chuckles, back to cheery. 'Worse than his usual really awful?'

'It's not funny. I'm going to his place now. But if I can't get in I'm going to have to call the police.'

'Whoa.' Dex is suddenly serious. 'Jesus, what the hell? What are you talking about?'

My heart sinks. I can't tell him. I should have realised. Even if Dex is prepared to turn on his own father, he'll want to protect his mum. Anyway even he, who knows that his dad can be violent and cruel, will find it hard to accept straight out that he is capable of kidnapping a little girl, his own niece . . .

'Don't worry, I—'

'Don't tell me not to worry.' Dex sounds concerned. He must have gone into another room, the background noise has disappeared. 'You can't start talking about calling the police and not expect me to . . . Look, what is it you want to do?'

'I . . . I want to have a look round your dad's flat, but I need your help to get inside.'

'How do you know he isn't there to let you in?'

'He's at your mum's. I was just round there.' I leave out the fact that Graham had been in the shower when

I arrived, suspecting this will be the last detail Dex wants to hear.

There's silence on the other end of the phone.

'Shit,' Dex says with feeling. 'I should come over and be with you.' He hesitates. 'It's just Marla's dumped the boys on me last minute and ... can it wait until later?'

'No,' I said, indicating as I see a signpost for Ladbroke Grove. I'm not far away now. 'I need to get inside. *Now*. Otherwise I'll have to dial 999 and—'

'Whoa. Wait. Before you start calling the cops ... there's a spare key to his flat under the doormat outside the apartment front door.'

'Seriously?'

'Yeah, I know, really secure. Not. But that's what happens when you're a pisshead who lives alone and loses his keys every five minutes when he's drunk.' Dex blows his breath out. 'Jesus, this is ... Look, you should be able to get one of the other flats to let you in at street level, then the key under the mat will get you inside Dad's flat.'

'Thanks, Dex.'

'Are you sure you're all right? What's all this about?'

I hesitate. There's no traffic suddenly and I reckon I'm only two or three streets away from Graham's apartment. I need to get off the phone. Apart from anything else, the last thing I need is to get pulled over for failing to use a hands-free device.

'I'll call you later,' I say.

'Okay, are you sure—?'

But before he can finish I ring off and put my foot down. Two minutes later I'm outside Graham's building. Lights are on in the ground-floor flat so I ring that bell. I'm psyched up to give a reason for needing to come in, but the young male voice on the intercom just presses the buzzer and I'm through in a flash.

I hurry up the stairs to Graham's front door.

Ruby is just the other side of this door. I'm sure of it. My palms sweat as I fumble under the mat. The key is exactly where Dex said it would be. I'm shaking as I turn the lock and open the door.

Inside the flat is silent and dark. All the curtains are closed, the lights off. There's a smell of stale air and damp, sour clothes. The heating has been on recently. The radiator in the hall, a shirt laid across it, is still warm. It creaks as it contracts and the sound echoes against the bare walls. I creep towards the open door of what looks like the living room. I can see the curtains and the edge of a sofa, a white sheet lying tossed and crumpled over the seat.

Definitely the curtains and sofa from the video.

My pulse thunders at my temples. I tiptoe closer. Is someone in the room, ready to jump out at me? Or will I just find my daughter, still sedated? Or worse?

I reach the door, every cell in my body tensed with anticipation.

The room is empty.

The sofa is bare.

I peer down and see a small hairgrip with a football

on the end peeking out from a creased fold of sheet. Ruby was wearing this earlier.

She was here and she has been taken away.

I hurry to tug back the curtains, letting in light from the streetlamps outside, then I storm around the flat, turning on lights, peering into the big cupboard in Graham's grubby kitchen and tossing aside the dishevelled duvet on his bed.

There is nothing that suggests where Ruby might be now. A terrible desolation fills me. If only Harry were with me. He would have known what to do. I am completely lost.

Why isn't Ruby still here? How on earth did Graham know to move her? Christ, perhaps he took her away as soon as he made the video – or told someone else to. There's certainly no way he could have got here before me from Sheila's house. I should have known. This is PAAUL, an organised body with links and resources. What was I doing to think I could outwit them? They killed Harry yesterday. A grown man. What chance does my poor Ruby stand against them?

I sink onto the sofa, devastated, the little football hairgrip in my hand. Is Ruby even still alive? Perhaps Graham killed her straight after filming her. The thought roots itself around my heart, squeezing the life out of me.

No. That's not logical. If PAAUL kill Ruby, they have no leverage over me. And, so far, I have done exactly what they asked. They have no reason to murder her. I stare at the spot next to me, where I saw Ruby on the video, then up to the purple-and-white curtain behind the sofa. A framed photograph propped up on the table next to the window catches my eye. It shows a puffy-faced Graham from about ten years ago, some sort of silver trophy in his hand. The resemblance to both his brothers is striking: Graham looks very like Perry around the eyes and nose, though his face is rounder. And he resembles Dad even more strongly: the same chiselled jaw and slightly arrogant tilt of the head.

My eyes settle on Graham's wrist, in the foreground along with the trophy he's clutching.

I gasp. He's wearing the same watch that Harry found . . . that Harry was killed for. I peer more closely. Definitely the same watch.

As I snatch up the photo my phone rings. Lucy again. I answer, feeling dazed.

'Francesca, where are you?' She sounds close to tears. 'I've been ringing and ringing. You tore out of Auntie Sheila's like a demon. I've been so worried.'

'I thought I knew where Ruby was,' I say, my head still whirling. 'But she isn't here.'

'*Where?* Where are you?'

'Lucy, is there any way Uncle Graham could somehow be involved in PAAUL, maybe even carrying out the murders for Uncle Perry?'

'What? No, I mean I know he was violent to Auntie Sheila when they were together, but he's the last person who'd do anything for any religious—'

'What about for money?'

358

'I don't know ... I guess, maybe ... why are you asking this?'

'There's a picture of him here wearing a watch just like the one you put in the storage locker, the one Harry was ... attacked for and—'

'Francesca, where are you?' Lucy interrupts. 'How come you're looking at a picture of Uncle Graham?'

'I'm in his flat.'

'What?' she shrieks. 'How? *Why?*'

'I found the spare key and let myself in. Lucy, the curtains in the video of Ruby are the same ones here in Graham's living—'

'Please, Francesca, I'm begging you. Whatever the truth, Graham will *kill* you if he finds you snooping about. Get out of there now.'

'Okay, but I'm taking all this straight to the police.' I put the photo of Graham into my bag.

'Hurry,' Lucy urges. 'Francesca, I know you're in a state about Ruby but you can't take risks like this. Please, come home, to ours. I've just got back and – I should have said this first – there's a note I didn't see before, it's from Daddy and according to that he will be back soon in the next half hour or so. I know Sheila won't help but we can talk to him, you and me. Get Dad on board before we go to the police. Maybe even get him to confront Perry about where Ruby is, like you wanted.'

I hesitate. An hour ago I'd have said yes but I'm past the point of being able to think straight, let alone talk. Unless I'm talking to someone who can get Ruby back.

And I no longer believe Dad will be able to make that happen. Whatever is going on with PAAUL, with Perry, with Graham ... it's far bigger than Dad can control.

'I'm going to the police,' I said. 'I should have done it hours ago.'

'Wait, Fran—'

I end the call and walk over to the lamp by the window. As I switch off the light a key turns in the front door. I spin round, heart hammering again. Is that Graham come home?

Footsteps pad across the hall. My breath catches in my throat as the living room door opens and a dark shadow falls across the threadbare carpet.

LUCY

For Pete's sake. Francesca hung up on me! This is all going *totally* wrong. Once again she's getting scarily close to working out the truth. I mean, she's off by a measure as well, but she's getting close. Too close.

I know you will deal with it. I just hope you know what you're doing. You've certainly messed things up so far. How careless to leave clues like that curtain. Things should never have come to this. My poor darling niece should not be in this position. And I can't bear seeing Francesca so frantic. Not that she hasn't asked for this, she's part of the reason it all started in the first place.

But this is mostly about you. Your weakness. Your uselessness.

Your crimes.

When I saw you with Mummy that afternoon something died inside me. Neither of you noticed me, you were so intent on each other. I stumbled away, back to my bedroom. I could barely breathe. I felt dirty. Ashamed. Utterly betrayed.

I sat on the bed for a few minutes, unable to get the vision of the two of you out of my head. Then I stood up. I had to get out of the house. I hurried downstairs, covering my ears so I wouldn't hear any more sounds from the spare room. I rushed outside and ran across the road, not looking before I stepped out, not caring in that moment if I lived or died. I kept going until I reached Holland Park. It was emptier than usual considering it was a hot summer's day, though at the time I didn't notice. I'd completely forgotten about the terror scare earlier.

I tore through a patch of undergrowth and found a dense group of bushes where I sank down. The earth was cold and hard under me, the bushes scratched at my bare arms. I didn't care.

I didn't care about anything any more.

I lay down, my face pressed against the damp ground. The air grew more and more humid, the sky overcast. Soon it started to rain. I lay still, raindrops pattering through the bush and onto my head. I lay there for hours, absorbing what I'd seen.

Thoughts flew like furies around my head:

How dare Mummy do this – she was married with two children?

How dare she do it with *you*? It was disgusting.

How *did* she do it with you – she was old and had wrinkles and a saggy stomach, how on earth had she got you to look at her with such desire?

Why wasn't it *me* you wanted?

Why hadn't I told her what you did to me? That

would have taken the bright, adoring look out of her eyes.

The rain grew heavier and the sky grew dark. Hours must have passed. If I'd stopped to think at all I would have realised that by now I'd be missed at home, but all I could focus on was the hot, hard, resentful anger that swelled inside me, frightening me with its power. I wanted to expose you. I wanted to stop you.

I wanted to kill you.

And I knew, even as I fantasised about the shock-waves I would send through our entire family and the knife I would plunge, butter soft, into your heart, that I would do none of those things.

And my cowardice led me to despair and my anger turned inwards and as night fell around me I started to plan my own suicide.

This would show them. This would make them stop.

I would sacrifice my life to end the pain of your betrayal.

It had stopped raining but the humidity still lingered and the air was thick with heat. I wasn't cold but my whole body was stiff and sore. I had no idea what time it was. Late. The park was closed.

I was free to die.

I closed my eyes and, as hours more passed, I must have fallen asleep. I dreamed of darkness, an unending night. And then, as I dreamed on, a light appeared. Distant at first, it drew closer and closer and instead of the shapeless energy I realised the light was emanating from a woman dressed in a long blue cloak, her pale face shrouded in a hood.

'Mary.' I don't know whether I spoke aloud or not. But I knew it was the Virgin.

The light shimmered, somehow over me and beside me and inside me all at once. Mary smiled as she raised her hand, a gesture of infinite gentleness. 'Lucy ... Lucy ... listen to me, for your name means "light".'

Wide-eyed, awestruck, I stared at her. A great warmth filled me. And even then I wasn't scared because I recognised the warmth as love.

'Your life, all life, is precious,' Mary whispered, her words and the light she made manifest ebbing and flowing inside me. 'Your life, all life, has purpose. Your purpose is to find a way to bring light out of the darkness of your sins.'

I nodded, shame suffusing me. Of course. Mary could see everything. Know everything. She knew I had committed an abortion. She knew I was a murderer, a taker of innocent life.

'It will take courage. It will mean sacrifice. But if you succeed yours will be a life lived in love. For God and His goodness is in all of us.'

The shimmering vision flickered and faded. Suddenly I was aware of the hard, cold ground beneath me. Was I still dreaming? I opened my eyes. Above me, through the bushes, the moon was vanishing behind a cloud.

'Please, don't leave me,' I whispered.

'Remember.' Mary's voice echoed in my head. 'Seek

to protect those who sin against you, for they know not what they do ...'

She was gone. The moon disappeared. I sat up, wide awake.

Courage ... Sacrifice ... A life lived in love.

Mary had come to me. I had experienced an actual vision in my dreams.

The Virgin had spoken to me, given me a message, offered me guidance. I clasped my hands together, kneeling to give thanks in prayer. Despite my cold, stiff body I was brim full with joy and hope. The world was a huge place, a glorious place and my own private hurts and dramas only a tiny part of the whole. I would rededicate my life to the good works Father Gabriel had spoken of in that first week after my abortion was revealed. Only now I would be carrying them out in the sure and certain knowledge I was bathed in God's eternal love.

I left the park and hurried home to find that it was almost 11 p.m. and Mummy was frantic with worry and on the verge of calling the police. I told her I had gone for a walk in the park this afternoon, stopped to rest in the heat and somehow fallen asleep. The lie jarred as I told it, but I reminded myself that Mary had told me to protect those who sinned against me. And in lying I was protecting Mummy from the terrible consequences of her affair with you becoming public knowledge. What you and she were doing was a terrible sin against me, but I armed myself with God's love and felt His grace help lift me above any need for vengeance.

Driven by my yearning for inner purity I cleared my room of childhood toys and books and had the walls painted white. I decided to wear white myself from now on and to live as simple a life as possible. I bought the crucifix that still hangs above my bed and which caused Francesca to have a conniption when she saw it. As usual, she misunderstood. Because the crucifix was not so much a way of giving myself up to God as a way of providing me with a constant reminder of Him after so many years of worshipping *you*.

Even now, after so many years since the scales fell from my eyes, it still helps. Even now I spend too much time reflecting on the past and how I once adored and idolised you. At least I'm not the only one. Even now many people are still under your spell.

And I am still protecting you, bringing light out of the darkness of my sins, living a life of love.

FRAN

I hold my breath, heart beating wild and hard, as the dark figure turns to the light.

My cousin stands in front of me, brows furrowed with concern.

'Dex?' I put my hand on my chest, almost giddy with relief. 'Oh, thank goodness it's you. But ... but I thought you had the boys?'

'I asked the neighbour to babysit.' Dex shoots me a typically sardonic glance. 'What the hell is going on, Dumpy? You sounded mad earlier, ranting on about Dad and the police. I'm worried about you.'

I stare at him, not knowing how to begin to tell him everything I've found out.

'So what is it?' he goes on. 'I called Lucy on the way over, who wouldn't tell me anything. Then Ayesha, who wouldn't shut up but clearly has no clue what's really going on. She kept saying it was something about Ruby, the kids ... but didn't seem to know what exactly. So tell me. What is happening? Why are you here?'

'I ... I can't ... I ... don't ...' I stop, unsure what

to say. I was told to say nothing to anyone and have already crossed that line both with Lucy and in a futile attempt to get Auntie Sheila on my side. There's no way Dex will be able to help me, like Sheila potentially could have done, but the urge to confide in my cousin, my oldest friend, is huge.

Too huge to resist.

'It's Ruby,' I blurt out. 'They've ... oh, Dex, she's been taken.'

'*Taken?*' Dex says, clearly shocked. 'What do you mean? Like, *kidnapped?*'

'Yes. It's this organisation called PAAUL. Religious. Terrorist, basically. Like Harry said. Except it's not Dad who's behind it, it's Uncle Perry and ... and I think your dad's helping him.'

Dex laughs. 'Yeah, right.'

'I'm serious. They've killed abortion doctors. Including, oh God, including my Caspian and ... and yesterday they murdered Harry Elliot, that journalist, because he was investigating them.'

Dex stares blankly at me. He's not smiling any more. 'I thought Harry lied about all that PAAUL stuff? Are you sure he's dead?'

I moan with impatience.

'Yes, they killed him to stop him ... and as a warning to me. Look, it's too complicated to go into right now, but Harry's dead and Ruby's been taken. Look.' I fumble with my phone, scrolling to the video of poor Ruby.

Dex takes the mobile and stares at the screen.

'Oh, Christ,' he says.

'You can see she was held in *this* room.' I point to the curtains. 'Which means your dad must have brought her here. But now he's had her taken somewhere else and I don't know where.'

Dex frowns. 'Franny, there's no way Uncle Perry or my dad could be behind this . . . That's not our family. I don't know how but it *must* be someone else.'

'It's *them*. You don't know what they're capable of,' I say, voice rising. 'Seriously, Dex. They are *monsters*.'

'Hey.' Dex opens his arms, still holding my phone. 'Hey, come here.'

I let him hold me for a few seconds, his hands stroking my back. But I'm in no mood to be soothed or comforted. I pull away, taking my phone back and staring down at Ruby again. Where on earth is she? Fear seizes my insides, twisting like an ice rope. Is it possible Graham has already killed her?

'You do believe me, don't you?'

'I guess.' Dex frowns. 'Though I still don't understand why my dad—'

'For money?' I say.

'Oh.' Dex nods slowly. 'Fuck.'

'I know.' I take a breath. 'Do you see now? I have to go to the police.'

Dex nods. 'Look, there's a station about five minutes away. I had to pick Dad up from there once after a caution. I'll take you, come in with you.' He squeezes my shoulder. 'Whatever our family has done, it's still you and me, Dumpy. Always has been, always will be.'

I gratefully agree. As we leave the flat I show the photo of Uncle Graham to Dex. 'Do you know anything about this watch?' I ask. 'Like when or how your dad got it?'

'Sure,' Dex says as we go outside. The air is cold on my face. 'It's from Granddad. He gave one to each son: your dad, my dad and Uncle Perry.'

I nod. This ties in with what Lucy has already told me. And it explains why Perry kept his brother's watch in his safe. Graham must have been wearing it when he carried out one of the killings. The bloodstain presumably came from a victim and therefore ties Graham himself to the murder.

'It's leverage,' I mutter. 'A way for Perry to control Graham.'

Dex doesn't hear me. He's striding along the pavement towards his car, which is parked snugly behind my own.

He reaches the BMW and opens the front passenger-side door.

'In you get, Dumpy.'

I glance over at my own car.

'Don't even think about it.' Dex wags his finger at me. 'No way are you driving in this state. Just get it into your head that I'm here and I'm looking after you.' He grins. 'Wouldn't be seen dead in that rust bucket of yours anyway, you can come back later and pick it up if you must.'

I smile, in spite of myself. Dex has always had the ability to find light in the midst of darkness. It's a quality that Caspian, with his earnest views and solid presence, never had. Harry did though. As I slide into the comfort of Dex's leather upholstery my guts wrench at the thought I will never see him again.

I gulp down the sob that rises inside me as Dex starts the engine. I need to pull myself together so that I can talk to the police. I glance around the car. Considering Dex must have had the kids in here earlier the car is remarkably clean and tidy. Dex passes me a half-empty water bottle from the holder between us. 'When did you last eat?' he asks.

I shrug. 'I'm not hungry.'

'Well, drink something at least,' he says.

I glug a few gulps of water. It glides down my throat, smooth and silky. I hadn't realised how thirsty I was.

For the first time in hours I feel a glimmer of hope. Dex is with me. He will help me get through what now needs to be done: I must tell the police everything. Let them find and demand answers from Perry and Graham.

It's the only way.

I offer Dex the bottle of water.

'I'm good,' he says.

I take another few sips. 'Where's this station then?'

'Two streets away,' Dex says. 'Don't worry, I know the way.'

I settle back in the seat. Dex has put the heating on and I'm suddenly overwhelmed with tiredness. It must be the stress and, now, suddenly the knowledge that I can let other people help me.

I close my eyes and offer up a silent pledge.

I'm coming Ruby, I'm getting help.

The tiredness is all-consuming. I try to open my eyes but I can't. The effort makes me feel sick. *Dex.* I'm trying to speak, but my mouth won't make the words.

What is happening to me? An alarm sounds, deep inside my brain. Something is wrong. Very wrong. I can't sleep. I need to talk to the police. Ruby needs me to stay awake.

'Franny?' Dex is calling me. He's in the driver's seat, right next to me, but it sounds like he's at the other end of a vast, echoey hall. The heat is overpowering, my muscles immovable. I try to answer but I can't. I'm slipping down a dark hole, away from everything and everyone. Deep inside me fear coils itself around my heart. What is happening?

And then I hear Dex's voice. He's speaking to someone else. Not to me. *About* me.

'Yeah, I'm telling you, Franny's out of it. No ... no, it's fine. I don't really have the kids, that's just what I told her. Nobody knows where ...' A pause. 'Stop being so hysterical, will you?' Another pause. 'I'll see you then.'

Silence. A flicker of light passes across my eyes. I fight to hold on to consciousness. To make sense of what is happening. He has drugged me. Dex, my cousin, my friend, has knocked me out. He is taking me somewhere that is definitely not the police station.

Thoughts whirl around my head, images of Dex and Harry and Caspian and my dad. I've been tricked and lied to and I don't understand. Where is Ruby?

I need to get to Ruby.

I have to save Ruby.

I make a final, enormous effort to open my eyes. But the darkness presses down. Too big, too heavy.

My last thought before I lose consciousness altogether is that Ruby needs me.

And that I have let her down.

LUCY

You call me to tell me you have Francesca.

And despite my frustration and my loathing my heart still skips a beat when I hear your voice.

Dex.

It's you.

It was always you. You've been here from my beginning. And I mean my very beginning: I have a photo of you holding me in your arms a few hours after I was born. You were five and a half, just a couple of months younger than Francesca, and extremely cute with your dark hair and green eyes and long black lashes. In the photo you're sitting back in a big hospital armchair and beaming at the camera: half shy, half proud, totally sweet. It's the same utterly charming smile you still have. I, on the other hand, look revolting – all red and ugly and scrunched up in your arms. Of course Francesca is in the picture too. You always preferred her, the best of friends growing up and close even now.

Anyway. When I say I've known you my whole life it is literally true. This fact notwithstanding, it is also true that during the long summer at the end of your A-level retakes, just before you went off on your travels around Australia and Thailand when I was thirteen and a half, you were round at our house practically every day and you barely noticed I existed. Devastated, I pined, tortured and alone, hugging my misery around me like the security blanket I still (in a secret known only to my mother) sometimes used. Eighteen months passed when we didn't see each other at all and you faded to the back of my mind as my friends and my school life took centre stage. Until the December just after I was fifteen.

Mummy and Daddy's pre-Christmas party was underway. The first guests had arrived downstairs but I was still in my bedroom, fretting over what to wear. Nothing fitted. After two years or so of feeling like a lumpy sack of potatoes in everything the weight had suddenly dropped off me, leaving me with long skinny legs and – to my horror – large breasts that stuck out in front of me like party balloons. I'd finally got rid of the braces on my teeth, which was good, obviously, though I hadn't yet stopped covering my mouth every time I opened it. The acne that had plagued my skin for ages had disappeared too, except from my forehead, which I kept hidden behind a thick fringe. Looking back I can see that I was prettier than I realised – my face fuller and fresher than it is now and my hair a mass of natural blonde highlights – but also gut-wrenchingly timid. In all the photos from that time I look perma-nently startled, as if I'd had a glimpse of adult life and found it terrifying. I don't remember if that's exactly how I felt, though I do know I was intimidated by my parents' friends and in awe of my outgoing sister and her uni mates.

I also know that I was obsessed with the fact that you were going to be at Mummy and Daddy's party that particular Christmas. Francesca had arrived home from uni for the holidays and several of her friends, including you, were coming over for part of the evening. You'd all be going off clubbing later, which Mummy and Daddy would hate, of course. So there'd probably be a row, though if anyone could diffuse the tension it would be you. Mr Charisma. Francesca just wound our parents up back then, but you were always charming. At least you had been in the past.

Nobody knew how I felt about you, how I'd always felt for as long as I could remember. I still had that picture of you holding me in your arms the day I was born. I hadn't looked at it much for the past few months but that evening, knowing I would see you soon, I got it out along with a load of other photos from our shared past. I pored over these alone in my room, until Mummy barged in, wine glass in one hand, pearls wound around the other, telling me that the guests were 'flooding through the front door, darling' and urging me to 'get downstairs, now!'

Francesca was already there, in a black mini-dress that I knew Daddy would think was far too short. He'd always been very strict with us about clothes. I never minded, but Francesca was forever rebelling against his orders. Now she was away at uni he couldn't control what she wore any more and he knew it. I was sure that's why she did it. I, on the other hand, followed my parents' dress code as I followed pretty much everything else they laid down the law on – including their religion. Francesca, naturally, had refused to be confirmed but I had dutifully gone through the motions just a few months before.

I stood in the hall with the rest of my family, politely greeting guests and taking coats while Mummy sparkled and Daddy charmed and Francesca entertained all their middle-aged friends with her confident smile and her far-too-short skirt.

Well, she managed about fifteen minutes of that and then her own friends started turning up and Francesca vanished into another room. I clung to Mummy, feeling shy as one guest after another commented on how much I'd grown. Quite a few of the men glanced at my chest. Even Uncle Perry clocked it – not in a lecherous way. But I saw him notice and it filled me with embarrassment. It wasn't really their fault. My hideous balloon boobs swelled out, tight against the navy wool of the dress, even though Mummy and I had bought it only a month earlier. The dress had a long, pleated skirt that stuck out from my waist. It was kind of old-fashioned and middle-aged and – apart from the inadvertent tightness across the bust – actually very modest. Still, it was also too old for me and though inside I was all adolescent excitement at the prospect of seeing you the dress must have added to the impression I was obviously giving of being more mature than I was.

Or maybe I'm making excuses for you. Even now.

An hour or so passed and the party was in full swing. I had slunk into the shadows of the kitchen, ostensibly to help the caterers but really in order to snack on the canapés and sip at my Coca-Cola. I could have tried to sneak a glass of wine I suppose, but it honestly didn't occur to me. At school there were girls who were out every weekend drinking and smoking but I was scared of such things. I was scared of everything, pretty much. I was definitely scared of upsetting my parents, especially Daddy, who I idolised at the time.

I heard Francesca shrieking with laughter out in the hall.

'Dex!' she cried. 'That's so cool!'

So you were here at last. Mouth dry, heart pounding, I peered into the hall. I didn't see you at first. Francesca and her uni friends were huddled together looking at something. Then one of the girls moved and I saw they were looking at a man's forearm, holding it between them, examining a swirly tattoo which I later discovered was the yin/yang symbol from Taoist philosophy – or heathen flim-flam, as Daddy would have said.

'What does it actually mean?' someone squealed.

'Balance, opposites attracting, stuff like that.' It was you, your voice as familiar to me as my own. 'I got it done in Thailand, couldn't understand a word the guy said, so it probably means something rude too.'

'Yeah,' Francesca laughed. 'Like "I am a pretentious arse".'

More laughter, including yours. I moved closer, eager to see you. As I did, two of the girls drifted away and you came into view. I melted on the spot, you were even more gorgeous than I remembered. I soaked up your face: your dark hair curling over your collar, the dimple in your chin, the rash of stubble over your cheeks. As I stared, you looked up and met my gaze. You blinked. Did a double take, then waved me over. You said something I couldn't hear to Francesca. She shrugged, then turned to Uncle Perry who was behind her and suddenly, out of nowhere, you and I were face to face in the middle of the busy hall and there was music in the background and chatter and the sound of glasses clinking but all I could see or hear or think was that you were still looking at me with those wonderful sea-green eyes of yours as if you were just now noticing me for the first time in your life.

'Lucy?' you said, and the world's most beautiful smile curled around your lips. 'You look amazing.'

'Oh.' A soft sigh escaped from my mouth. I must have looked as frightened as Daniel when the Angel Gabriel appeared to him. I certainly felt it: my heart pounding, my throat too dry to speak.

And still you gazed at me. 'Hey,' you said, lowering your voice slightly. 'You know what you look old enough for?'

I shook my head.

Your smile widened and I swear I almost fainted.

'You look old enough for a drink,' you said. 'And I'm going to find you one and take you somewhere you can drink it where your parents won't see. How does that sound? Like a plan?'

'Plan.' I gasped out the word.

'Follow me.' And with a wink, you turned and threaded your way through the hall. For a second I stood, too stunned to move. Then I hurried after you, through the kitchen – where you picked up a carton of orange juice from the stocks on the counter – and out into the back garden. Uncle Perry and one of Daddy's friends were on the patio, whisky tumblers in their hands, deep in conversation about the right tactics to use in the pro-life debate.

'Logic and humour, dear boy,' Perry was saying as we passed. 'Give them a bit of Reagan's "I've noticed everyone who is for abortion has already been born" reasoning. It's impossible to contradict, but it keeps the lines of communication open.'

Neither man glanced at you as you strode past and on, across the lawn and into the trees. You were heading in the direction of the summer house. Was that where you were planning to take me to have a drink? And were we really just going to have orange juice? Unsure whether I was relieved or disappointed by this I slunk around to the side path, then crept along past the bushes where you had disappeared and through the trees.

You were waiting for me in the clearing by the summer house, emptying some of the juice onto the ground. Mystified I watched you crouch down in the moonlight, your shadow like a beckoning finger across the grass. It started to rain, a light drizzle pattering onto the dark leaves. I glanced back through the trees at the lights that glowed inside the house.

'Hey, beautiful.'

I turned towards you as you straightened up. You were smiling and my stomach somersaulted. I was so nervous I almost felt sick.

You held out the carton. 'Would you take this for a sec?'

I crossed the grass – my legs trembling – and took the carton as you fished a flat glass bottle from your jacket pocket. 'Hold it steady,' you ordered.

My hands were shaking so I gripped the carton tightly, hoping you wouldn't notice.

'God, but Uncle Perry's a smug old queen,' you said, unscrewing the top of the glass bottle.

'He's gay?' My mouth fell open. 'Are you serious?'

'For sure.' You gave a world-weary sigh. 'Made a pass at one of my friends last week. Perry was round for dinner with Mum and apparently there was a "moment" outside the upstairs bathroom.'

'No.' I was genuinely shocked. And not fully convinced.

'Anyway I don't care whether he's gay or straight or whatever, I just wish he'd stop being so pompous. I mean, did you hear him back there? I know you guys have a soft spot for him, but really ...'

I didn't know what to say to that. I'd always been

fond of Uncle Perry. He was kind when I was ill and tried hard to be jolly whenever he came over. He was, like Mummy and Daddy, a devout Catholic. I knew he had never married, but the idea he might actually be homosexual was beyond shocking.

I privately decided your friend must have got the wrong end of the stick and pointed to the bottle in your hand.

'What's that?' I whispered. The rain was growing stronger, drops trickling from my hair onto my face and shoulders.

'Vodka.' You held the top of the glass bottle over the spout of the carton, then put your other hand over mine. Gently you tipped the vodka into the juice. 'God, you're freezing,' you said.

I glanced behind you at the summer house. 'We could go in there,' I suggested, amazed at my extraordinary daring.

'Good idea,' you said, righting the vodka bottle and screwing the top back on. 'Key still in the usual place?'

I nodded, my mind going back to the year we moved here. Back then the garden had seemed massive to me. The day we moved in Francesca whispered in my ear that the summer house in the middle of the forest (in reality a small copse of trees) was the house where Hansel and Gretel's witch had once lived. For a week I refused to set foot in the garden until Mummy unearthed what was troubling me, a revelation that led to Francesca being sent to her room and Mummy patiently accompanying me as I examined every inch of the summer house and the clearing in which it stood. When the warmer weather arrived, she decked out the summer house and surrounding area with fairy lights and that part of the garden quickly became my favourite place in the entire world. Francesca, you and I played out here all that summer. Mummy sat on a lounger just a few feet from where we were now, watching as I splashed about in the paddling pool. You spent a lot of time here then. Your parents had just split up and you wore a slightly haunted look, smiling less than you did before. Sometimes you and Francesca – though of course she professed herself far too old for 'playing in baby pools' – would join me in the water. Francesca often got annoyed with me and would kick water in my face but you would always stop her. 'Lucy's just a little kid,' you'd say.

My mouth felt dry as I followed you over to the rockery surrounding the summer house. You went straight to the white-painted stone where Mummy kept the spare key. All my life you had seen me as that 'little kid'. But now, here I was, just fifteen and about to drink vodka and orange juice with you.

You passed me the carton as you reached for the key. It was wet from the rain. 'Give it a good shake,' you instructed.

I did as I was told while you opened the summer-house door. Tiptoeing inside it smelled musty from all the garden furniture stacked away for the winter.

'Guess we better not turn on the light,' you said with a chuckle. 'Don't want your dad finding you boozing.'

The thought of Daddy knowing what I was doing right now made me shiver.

'Yeah, it's still cold, isn't it?' You slid off your jacket and placed it carefully around my shoulders. The damp of my dress pressed onto my skin. 'Now let's have a drink.'

You took the carton from my hands, released the cap and tipped it back. I watched, enthralled, as you glugged what seemed like a huge amount.

'Your turn.' You handed me the carton.

Hoping in the dark that you wouldn't see I was still trembling, I tried to copy your tipping action. Liquid streamed out, sweet but with a harsh edge that burned my throat. I managed to get down some of it, but I'd taken too much and the excess dribbled out of the sides of my mouth. Mortified and choking, I backed away, wiping my lips.

'Whoa, steady.' You laughed.

I coughed, my face hot with humiliation. 'Sorry,' I said, taking another, more modest sip. This time, though the harshness was still there, it didn't hurt. The scent of the drink filled my nostrils. 'It tastes like Mummy's hairspray,' I said, then blushed again, fearing I'd sounded stupid.

'You know, I've always thought that's exactly how it tastes,' you said, taking the carton and having another expert swig. 'Is this the first time you've ever had vodka?'

I looked away, torn between my desire not to lie to you and my embarrassment at being fifteen and such an alcohol virgin. 'It's my parents,' I said. 'They're so anti-drinking.'

'God, I wish mine were.' You handed me the carton and leaned against the closed door. 'That is, Mum doesn't drink much but Dad ... well, you know ...' You grimaced.

I nodded, trying to look like I understood exactly what you weren't saying. I hadn't been told anything directly about Uncle Graham and Auntie Sheila, but I'd picked up enough to know that your dad was a drunk who'd wasted all his money and treated your mother very badly.

I sipped at the carton. I was genuinely enjoying it now and, much to my surprise, I didn't feel anywhere near so anxious any more. At the time I put this down to you being so lovely. Now, of course, I'm very aware the vodka had a lot to do with it. A warm, fuzzy feeling was creeping through me, emboldening me to the point where suddenly I felt able to ask you a question I would never have imagined voicing even minutes before.

'Them getting divorced, Auntie Sheila and Uncle Graham ... was that really hard for you?' I took another sip.

You met my gaze. Even in the shadowy moonlight through the window I could see the intensity of your eyes, the strong cut of your cheek and chin. You were so gorgeous, I could hardly believe I was really here with you.

'No, it was far worse before ... when they were together.' You swallowed the distance between us in a single step. You stood, close, looking down at my face. 'That was really hard. You won't remember, you were too little, but ... but there were times when they were arguing, before Dad left ...'

I gazed up at you, my throat dry, the carton clutched in my damp hand.

'Dad did things ...' You carried on, your voice low and husky. 'It happened when he'd been drinking. He ... he hit Mum. Like there was this one time, I was watching from the stairs. He was trying to leave – I guess to go and see his latest squeeze, though I didn't know that at the time – and Mum was upset and shouting. Horrible things she was saying. At the time I felt angry with her.' He paused again. 'Then before I even realised what was happening Dad grabbed her face and pushed her and she stumbled back and he ... made a fist and said, "Shut it, you cunt," and she leaped forward, right into his face and said, "You're the cunt, you bastard."'

'Oh, Dex,' I breathed, unable to imagine meek, uptight Auntie Sheila either shouting or cursing. I'd never heard either of my parents swear and, thanks to our internet lock and Daddy being as strict about film certificates as he was about alcohol, I'd not come across swearing all that much online or in movies, either, though of course there were plenty of girls at school who seemed to think it made them look more grown-up to use bad language.

You closed your eyes, your face screwed up with pain. 'Then Dad just lost it. He let out this roar and ... and he punched her.'

386

I gasped. 'No.'

'She flew across the room and landed on her side and yelled from the pain. And Dad turned around and walked out and slammed the door.'

There was a pause. 'That's awful,' I said.

You opened your eyes. 'It was.' You cleared your throat. 'It wasn't the only time either. Anyway, sorry, Lucy, I didn't mean to say all that.'

'It's the drink,' I said, remembering a phrase we'd learned in Latin a few weeks before. '*In vino veritas.* It means drinking makes you tell the truth.'

'Does it, indeed?' You took the carton from my hand and set it by the summer-house door. Tiny thrills ran up and down my body as you walked back to me. 'Want to know another truth?'

'Yes,' I whispered, my heart beating so loud I was sure you would hear it.

You tilted your head closer to mine. 'You're very, very beautiful, Lucy Carr.' Your lips hovered over my mouth. I held my breath. 'In fact,' you went on, your lips brushing mine, 'I'd say you are the most beautiful girl in the whole of London.'

My breath came out ragged as you kissed me, soft, then stronger, your tongue pushing into my mouth, your hands running down my arms, over my back. I could taste something sweet on your breath, and every part of me was on fire, my legs threatening to give way.

And then you drew back. I stared up at you, my whole body trembling. Your breath was almost as uneven as mine now, your eyes hungry. You took the jacket off my shoulders and let your hands slide down my arms again, then across my breasts. You groaned with pleasure as you touched me and I swelled with pride.

'Oh, Lucy.' You kissed me again, more roughly than before, pressing me back against the only spare bit of summer-house wall. Your hands ran down my front again, then further down. Suddenly your hands were under my dress, on my thighs. Your fingers found my underpants.

I froze, shrinking back.

Instantly you stopped. Took a step away from me. 'This isn't what you want?'

I couldn't speak, couldn't look at you. Humiliation filled me.

'You're a good girl, Lucy,' you said, and maybe I imagined it, but I thought there was an edge to your voice. 'Your daddy's good little girl.'

Tears filled my eyes. My cheeks were burning. I darted to the summer-house door, knocking over the carton as I did so. Liquid splashed out. Automatically I picked up the carton and fumbled with the door.

'I'm sorry,' you said, the harsh edge gone. 'It's just you're so desirable and you don't even realise. I mean I've never, literally never, wanted anyone more.'

I stood in the open doorway. Most of me wanted to dart away into the darkness to dry my eyes then go back to the safety of the house. But a voice in my head pierced through those fears.

This is what you wanted ... all your life ... Dex

saying these things ... wanting you ... and you want him back, you know you do, and it isn't wrong if you love someone and maybe you'll stay together because you want each other so much and even though you're cousins maybe the bishop will still let us get married and then it will be okay anyway ...

I took a long drink from the carton, draining it to the bottom, then I threw the carton out onto the grass. Tomorrow Daddy would just think it was one of the party-goers. He would never know it was me.

Nobody needed to know.

Moonlight streamed through the summer-house window, lighting up your beautiful face. I had no idea what I was going to say until I opened my mouth. And then, suddenly, out came the truth:

'I'm scared I don't know what to do,' I whispered. 'And ... and it won't be any good ... I won't be any good ...'

You smiled and held out your hand. 'D'you have any idea what a precious thing your virginity is to me? There is no way that it couldn't be anything other than the most amazing experience of my life.'

I walked towards you. The vodka was really kicking in now and I stumbled. Deftly, you caught me and held me tightly against your body.

This is what you want, I told myself again. Never mind Daddy and school and Sister Teresa's morality lectures on how fornication was a second-rate choice: 'Do not be deceived, girls, fornicators and adulterers will never inherit the kingdom of God.'

It was you. It had always been you.

'Let's lie down,' you said. Without waiting for me to respond, you turned and dragged a lounger cushion away from the wall. You placed it carefully in the middle of the summer house then took your jacket and folded it into a pillow. You stretched out and beckoned me over. 'Why don't we just take off our clothes,' you said. 'I promise we don't need to go further than you want.'

'It'll be cold,' I said, perching on the edge of the cushion. Practical girl that I was.

You chuckled. 'I'll warm you up.' You were already reaching for the zip on my dress. You drew it down and peeled it off my arms. I was wearing a plain white bra. A second later you had undone the strap at the back and the bra fell. I tensed with the shock of exposure, my breasts being hideously large and ugly in my eyes. You didn't notice my discomfort, just stared at my chest, smiling. Suddenly I felt a rush of power. Confidence filled me. I could do this. You pulled me towards you and kissed me. Gently at first, then harder. Your stubble was rough on my face. Your hands roamed over my chest, then down again. My dress bunched at my waist, the top half was down, the bottom half pulled up. I braced myself as you tugged at my underpants.

'Lucy, you are so beautiful,' you murmured. 'This part of you is so beautiful.'

I closed my eyes, letting you touch me. I was starting to feel light-headed, I didn't mind your hands now. The sensations from your fingers were waves of pleasure rippling through me. And then you stopped. I opened my eyes. You were fumbling with your belt, your zip, pulling down your trousers. I stared at your jockey shorts, suddenly anxious again. I knew about sex, of course. We'd covered the basics in biology, but my school was very much against any kind of sex education unless you counted Sister Teresa's lectures and Mummy and Daddy hadn't exactly filled in any of the gaps so I only had a bit of anatomy knowledge and a bunch of second-hand stories from girls at school to go on. Still, I knew what was inside your shorts.

'Have you ever …?' you asked, following my gaze.

I shook my head. You took my hand and placed it over the front of your shorts. It was harder than I was expecting. I gulped. Your breathing grew uneven again. You pulled down the front of the shorts and I stared, fascinated and horrified all at once. It was neither ugly nor beautiful, but it was surprisingly large.

'That goes inside me?' Again, the words were out of me before I could stop them.

I blushed, but to my relief you gave a low chuckle. 'If I turn out to be the luckiest man on the planet.'

You drew me to you again, your fingers working away at me. I lay back and stared up at the ceiling. The summer house spun around me. Out of the corner of my eye the edge of the metal tin containing the boules set we used to play with when we were younger glinted in the moonlight. I don't know how much time passed before you rolled on top of me. Still murmuring how beautiful I was, how amazing it was to be with me, you pushed yourself inside me.

'Relax,' you crooned in my ear. 'You're everything, everything.'

I closed my eyes, willing myself to make it work. Down there it hurt a little, but not more than I could bear, and anyway what did a tiny bit of pain matter if I got to hear you say such things.

You grunted, moving on top of me. And then with a sudden thrust you pushed harder. A searing pain shot through me.

'Aagh.' I caught my breath, embarrassed. I didn't want you to think I was pathetic.

You lay still. The pain lessened to a dull throb.

Maybe you were nearly done. I summoned all my courage and looked up at you.

'Almost halfway in,' you whispered, eyes twinkling.

Only almost halfway? My stomach contracted.

'It hurts.' The words almost squeaked out of me. I turned my face away, ashamed I was being such a child.

'Just relax,' you grunted.

I bit my lip, willing myself to do so. But it was impossible. The pain was building. I couldn't see your face but you sounded like you were concentrating as you moved in small thrusts, each one leaving me in agony.

'Please.' A tear trickled out of the corner of my eye. 'Please.'

I meant 'please stop'. But I said it so quietly it's possible you didn't hear. Your mind was on what you were doing. With another thrust that seemed to tear me in two you let out a low, triumphant roar.

'Yes,' he murmured. 'Oh, fuck, yes.'

I squeezed my eyes tight shut. 'Please stop.' Shame flooded through me as I whispered the words. I had failed to do this properly.

Again, you didn't seem to hear.

You pumped into me. Each thrust more violent than the last. My head spun. I felt sick. My voice seemed lost deep inside me but somehow I found it.

'Stop,' I said, louder than before. 'Stop.'

You thrust again.

'Stop!' I said, even louder.

This time you definitely did hear.

'Soon,' you crooned. 'Soon, beautiful.'

'Please.' I was sobbing now, suffused with pain and shame. I couldn't even get it right when it came to asking you to stop. 'Please, Dex, it hurts.'

You ignored me and deep inside me something broke. I could feel myself withdrawing into myself. Silence consumed the summer house, the world. You were right inside me but the distance between us filled oceans. I was only the pain between my legs, radiating through my whole body. I willed myself not to be sick, counting the thrusts. One. Two. Three.

Soon, surely, it would be over.

On the ninth thrust you gave a loud groan. You stopped moving, held yourself above me, eyes closed and panting for a few seconds, then you rolled over. I lay still, locked inside myself. The pain was harsh and burned through me. But worse than the pain, even through my vodka-induced nausea and fuggy-head-edness, was the deep, dark shame roiling through me like a wave.

There was dampness between my legs and under me. I knew from the textbooks that was the ejaculation, the semen. It felt like the dirtiest thing in the world. I pulled my bunched-up dress down, over the shame.

You sat up, tugging your trousers back over your hips. You stood up, adjusting the belt.

'Dex?' You must have been able to hear the miserable shake in my voice but you didn't look at me. Just ran your fingers through your hair, brushed down your shirt and picked up your jacket.

I watched you, stunned. Where had the loving, crooning Dex of just a few seconds before gone?

'Er, guess we better keep this under our hats,' you said, looking at me at last. You sounded uncharacter-istically awkward.

I nodded, covering my chest with my arms.

'Promise?' you asked.

'I promise.'

You turned and left without another word. I got up, feeling numb. I could barely walk, partly from the sore-ness between my legs, partly from the drink. The rest of the night is a blur. I just about managed to get my clothes back on. The lounger cushion was stained with blood – I had a vague memory of wide-eyed whispers in the school playground that this was normal when you lost your virginity but it still frightened me, particularly the idea that my parents might see. I shoved the cushion behind all the others and folded up the chair. I locked the summer house, replaced the key under the stone, staggered over to a tree and was violently sick. I might have even blacked out for a few minutes, I'm not sure. But the next thing I remember is being back in the house and creeping up to bed and Mummy coming to find me about ten minutes later and exclaiming that I looked very pale. I said I had stomach ache – which was true. By this point I ached all over, and was desperate to wash but didn't dare risk the questions that I'd generate if I ran a bath in a house full of party guests.

Mummy drew the covers around my neck and kissed my forehead. I expected her to smell the alcohol on my breath but what I didn't know then – though you presumably did – was that vodka leaves no tangible scent. Then she left and I lay alone, still numb, still drunk, still hurting down there like I'd been ripped into pieces.

I closed my eyes but the darkness scared me, so I stared out of the window at the moon. I would like to say that I was planning to get up in the morning and tell my parents exactly what had happened, but it wouldn't be true. I already knew that, whatever the future held, I would keep my promise to you. I've thought a great deal about why I kept quiet. Mostly, I think, it was pride. Two sorts of pride . . .

I couldn't bear to admit to anyone, especially my parents, what I'd let you do. I was ashamed of how far I'd fallen from the standards that Daddy, in particular, had set for me and knew that it would doubly hurt him because he had already so spectacularly, in his own eyes, failed to get Francesca to live by those standards.

And I still, at that point, thought you might call me or want to see me the next day or soon after. I still hoped that you loved me. Which is a different kind of pride, but sinful nevertheless.

Of course now I'm aware that what I thought of as my failing, my ineptitude in your seduction of me, was in reality a rape.

Child rape.

A crime.

The murder of my innocence.

And the first time you killed. Though not the last.

HOME

Tuesday 19 January 2016

FRAN

I wake, groggily, aware only of my thick head and the dull ache around my wrists and ankles. It's hard to force my eyes open. I have no idea where I am or what has happened, just that it's dark and cold. I'm indoors, on the floor. Bare boards. Dust in my nose. Shadowy shapes rear up all around me. I kick out; my feet are bound together, the rope straining as I try to push them apart. There's rope around my wrists too: tighter, cutting into my skin. It takes a huge effort to sit upright. Blinking away the sleep from my eyes I look around. What the hell?

Jesus. I'm in the summer house in Dad's back garden.

How on earth did I get here?

A footstep in front of me. It's Dex, a scarf in his hand.

And in an instant it all floods back:

Ruby taken. Harry dead. Uncle Graham's flat. And Dex, so helpful, so supportive, urging me into his car, insisting on taking me to the police, offering me a drink ...

'The bottle of water?' I gasp.

Dex gives a curt nod.

'*You?*' I gulp. Tears prick at my eyes. Dex is my cousin, my best friend from childhood. Why on earth would he want to hurt me or Harry or ... oh, no ... Ruby? I struggle to sit up, fighting the dizziness.

'Where's Ruby? Do you have her? Is she all right?' I strain against the ropes that bind me.

Dex says nothing, just crouches in front of me, the scarf open in his hand. For a single, horrible second I think he's going to strangle me with it. Then I realise he is trying to wind it around my mouth, to gag me.

I wriggle back, away from him. 'I don't understand.' My voice rises as I picture my daughter, semi-conscious in Uncle Graham's flat. 'Where's Ruby?' I repeat. 'What have you done to her?'

'She's had the same drug as you,' Dex says. He is frowning, clearly agitated. Is he high? His green eyes gleam like cats' eyes in the moonlight. Dust motes float in the beam around his head. 'She'll be fine. You'll both be fine.'

'Why are you doing this?' I fight against my bindings again. 'Are you working for PAAUL? Helping your father? I don't under—'

'Dad has nothing to do with it. He lets me use his flat from time to time, that's all,' Dex says.

'What about Uncle Perry?' My words are cut off as Dex thrusts the scarf against my face, winding it around my mouth.

He pulls it tight against the back of my head. I yell

out but he just yanks on the scarf, knotting and reknotting it. I'm screaming now, but the sound can't get out. I'm impotent. Panic courses through me.

What are you doing? Where's Ruby? Let me go!

It's all muffled. A second later, Dex is gone. The summer-house door bangs behind him.

'Help!' I yell. 'Help!'

A terrible silence falls.

I sit, terrifying thoughts rampaging through my head. What is happening to Ruby? Is Rufus still okay? What is Dex going to do with us?

I have no idea how much time has passed since I got in his car. It was early evening then. I wriggle back so I can see properly through the window. The moon is high in the night sky now. How many hours have passed? I look around. There's no sign of my handbag, which contains my phone. Everything's gone.

I strain against my bindings again, wincing at the sharp nip of the rope around my wrists. And then, with a slow creak, the summer-house door opens. My sister stands, trembling, in the doorway.

'Thank God.' It comes out as an incoherent mumble. I twist around and hold up my wrists to indicate how they're tied behind my back. 'Lucy, get these off. *Lucy!*' My words are inaudible but it must be obvious what I'm asking her to do. Still she doesn't move, just stands looking at me with big eyes that gleam with fear in the moonlight.

'Lucy!' I don't have time to be patient with her. I stamp my feet on the dusty summer-house floor. More tiny particles rise up into the moonbeams. 'Get over here!'

She scuttles over and crouches down beside me. She picks at the knots in the scarf around my mouth. I listen out for signs of Dex coming back. Impatient. Terrified. Adrenaline surging through me.

It takes over a minute but at last the scarf around my mouth is loosened. My head feels clearer. 'Dex has Ruby,' I say, as soon as I can speak. I hold up my wrists for my sister to try and untie. 'We have to find her, we have to go to the police.'

Lucy steps away from me and stands up. She edges back to the doorway, fidgeting from side to side, murmuring something under her breath.

'What are you saying?' Fear and irritation rise inside me. 'Come on! We have to get out of here.'

'I can't.' Her bottom lip wobbles. 'Francesca, I'm sorry but ... I'm scared.'

'Of what? *Who?*' My breath catches in my throat. 'Of *Dex?*'

She nods, tears gleaming in her eyes. I kneel up, the floor hard under my knees. 'Lucy, listen to me. I get that Dex has ... has whatever he's done ... threatened you. He drugged me and tied me up. So I get that it's shocking and ... and terrifying, but—'

'It's not new,' Lucy whispers.

'What?' I lean forward, trying to catch what she's saying.

'Dex ... he's been violent before ... he raped me when I was fifteen.'

'He *raped* you?' My stomach falls away. 'But ... but ...' I shake my head. 'That doesn't make sense ... Dex couldn't ...'

I stop. Of course he could. If he could drug and kidnap and threaten, of course he could rape.

I fall silent as two fat tears slide down Lucy's cheeks.

'Sorry,' I say. The worst response you can give a rape victim is to express disbelief that the crime took place. 'I didn't mean to doubt what you said.'

'Dex did it. He raped me.' She hesitates. 'He made me pregnant.'

I gasp. 'That was *his* baby?'

Lucy nods. 'He didn't ... doesn't ... know it was his ... I never told him at the time and when the abortion came out years later I don't think he connected it ... with ...' She pauses. 'What he did ... the rape ... he acts like it never happened.'

I stare at her, struggling to reframe the whole of the past fifteen years. 'Jesus, I don't ... I can't ...'

Lucy sniffs back her tears. 'It's not just what he did to me. Dex has killed people too. I swear I didn't know until just now but he's the person Uncle Perry used.'

'*Dex* is the killer?' My head spins. 'The PAAUL killer?'

Lucy nods again.

I slump down, sitting back on my heels. My arms ache from being tied together. I don't understand how any of this is possible. How can charming, irresponsible, light-hearted Dex have raped his child cousin? Or carried out assassinations for PAAUL? 'But he isn't even religious ...' I bleat.

'I know.' Lucy gulps. 'Uncle Perry's paying him. I heard them talking on the phone just now.'

'Oh, Christ. What about Graham? Is he involved too?'

'No. Dex was just using his flat. He often borrows it.' She makes a face. 'I think he takes women there.'

Oh, Christ, my poor Ruby.

'And I think Uncle Graham owes him,' Lucy muses. 'Whatever, it's not like the two of them are close. When you think about it, Dex isn't really close to anyone.'

He's close to me, I think. *He was close to Caspian.* A memory of Dex and Caspian watching Six Nations rugby over a beer in our living room sears through me. Caspian was laughing at something Dex said. Dex could always make him laugh. He has always made me laugh too. The three of us were friends.

'Dex needed money that badly?' My voice is hollow. The ropes around my wrists and ankles bite harder. This is surreal. A nightmare from which I will surely soon wake up. I suddenly feel desperately alone. If only Harry were here. But he is gone and Ruby is taken and the people I love are ruthless or weak.

'He's in a lot of debt,' Lucy goes on. 'He likes expensive stuff. You know that. And his dad spent everything and Dex's job doesn't pay that much and you know how he feels about his divorce and all the maintenance payments ...'

'Okay.' I hold out my wrists again, shoving all the confusion to the back of my mind. 'All that doesn't matter right now. You need to untie me and let's get out of here and go to the police and tell them everything so they can find Ruby.'

Lucy looks away.

'Lucy, please, you *have* to be brave. Dex has Ruby.' The thought turns my stomach. If he's really capable of rape and murder what might he do to my sweet little girl? 'Think how scared Ruby will be? Come on, Luce, you can do this.'

'Ruby's okay,' she says, meeting my gaze. 'She's fine. Dex put her indoors, up in my bedroom. She's fast asleep, doesn't know anything about what's happened.'

'You're certain?' A thread of relief weaves through my shock and fear.

'Dex would never hurt her,' Lucy goes on, sounding more emphatic. 'He just wanted to stop you going to the police.'

'I need to get to her.' I hold up my hands again, twisting round to show her the way they're tied. The rope cuts into me, fiercer than ever. 'Lucy, *please*. Ruby's all alone.'

Lucy fidgets, fingers twisting nervously around each other. 'I daren't. I'm so scared. Dex is ... he'll hurt us ...' She dissolves into tears.

'Okay.' My mind reels, searching for a way to persuade her. I *have* to get to Ruby. *Think*. 'I'll do whatever Dex wants,' I plead. 'Let me go into the house and talk to him. I'll be fine if I know Ruby's okay. But it's been hours and—'

'It's not that late,' Lucy interrupts. 'Only just past midnight.'

'Where's Dad?' I ask, fresh hope sprouting. My

father might be prepared to cover up for his brother, but not if it means threatening the lives of his daughter and granddaughter. 'Earlier you said Dad would be home soon, is he back yet?'

'He never arrived. Jacqueline called him away again. They're out all night now,' Lucy says. 'He left a message on the house phone. It's somewhere with no phone signal. They won't be back till tomorrow morning.'

'Right.' I grimace. 'Come on, Lucy, we need to find Ruby and—'

'I told you, Ruby's okay,' Lucy says.

'Lucy, for God's sake, you don't know *how* she is,' I erupt. 'She's been given a drug and ... and Dex isn't a doctor, he might have given her too much of whatever it—'

'He won't have. He told me when I found out what he's been doing. He's used to using drugs like that. It's how he overpowers people before ... before killing them ...' Lucy leans against the doorframe. 'He did it to you.'

I gulp, my heart hammering. All I can think about is getting Ruby away from Dex. Ruby is far younger than Lucy was when she says he raped her ... but how can I be sure that Dex won't ... I can't let myself think it. A dead, sick feeling fills my gut. What else can I say to Lucy?

What will make her listen?

'What about God?' I plead. 'Think about what God would want you to do. You've said yourself Dex is violent and dangerous. God would want you to do something about that. If you won't untie me, then go and call the police.'

'I can't.'

'You *can*. Where's your mobile?'

'Dex has it,' she says, in a voice so utterly helpless that I swear if my hands were free I might just slap her face in frustration.

'So go into the house and find the nearest phone, the one in the hall, and dial 999. That's all you have to—'

'I *can't*.' Her voice rises.

'Okay, okay.' I think fast. 'Look at it this way: we know Dex is a killer and if you and me and Ruby are in his way, he'll kill us too, won't he?'

She gives an imperceptible nod.

'So it's just a matter of time. Now ... tell me, did Dex send you to talk to me?'

'No, he doesn't know I'm here.'

'So you were brave enough to come and find me. You can be brave enough to call the police. *Please*, Lucy.'

She meets my gaze. 'I can't,' she says. 'Dex is a psychopath. He'll kill me.'

My heart sinks. She's not going to budge. Or maybe she needs more time to build up her nerve.

'Will you at least go and check on Ruby again?' I ask, trying to make my tone more conciliatory. If I can just get Lucy to take baby steps towards action, perhaps I can increase her confidence to the point where she's prepared to take a bigger risk.

'Okay,' she says, turning.

'If Ruby's awake,' I call after her, 'tell her I love her and that I'm coming for her.'

But Lucy has already slipped away.

I turn my attention to the rope that binds my hands and feet. It's tightly wound and there's no way I can reach the knot, but maybe I can cut through the rope on something sharp. Lucy hasn't replaced the scarf that Dex used to gag my mouth, but I don't want to alert him to the fact by yelling for help. Anyway, I know from my childhood that the trees surrounding the summer house deaden most noises.

I shuffle across the floor in search of anything that might cut through my bindings. I'm certain there are no knives or tools in here. Nothing useful. It's mostly just old games and bits of garden furniture – but maybe I can find a piece of broken metal or splintered wood.

I manage to yank one of the loungers a few inches away from the wall where it's stashed. I turn my back to the spring and rub the rope against its rough edge.

It's no way near sharp enough. Swearing under my breath I haul myself over to the tin box that contains the boules set. The edge of that is sharper – I remember Mum warning us about it when we were little – but still not remotely capable of cutting through rope.

I squint out of the window. It's an almost full moon, thank goodness, and my eyes have adjusted to the gloom inside the summer house. I look around, still determined. *I'm coming, Ruby.* And that's when I see Mum's old sewing kit on a shelf above the pile of loungers. She was very taken with the hobby when I was in my teens, when Lucy was still at primary school. I think it came after her life-drawing phase and before she tried to write a novel. For a few months she sat at a recently purchased top-end sewing machine, surrounded by silks and soft jersey fabrics, trying to make me and Lucy dresses. As so often with Mum, she'd bitten off more than she could chew and after several frustrating weeks all she'd managed to finish was a sky blue pinafore dress for Lucy with a crooked hem. The sewing kit ended up in here, along with so many of her other things. I'm certain it will contain a pair of scissors. Strong scissors, hopefully sharp enough to penetrate the rope around my wrists and ankles.

I force myself to my feet. I can't reach the sewing box with my hands but I head-butt the shelf. Once. Twice. I'm panting with the effort. At last the box falls with a smash. Its contents scatter across the floor: skeins of thread and folds of green silk and blue jersey and long needles still in their packets. A thimble rolls across the floor, glinting in the moonlight.

I peer at the thread and the fabric and the needles, desperately sifting them with my bound feet. My heart bangs against my ribs as I look for the scissors. I keep this up for five minutes, my ears pricked for the sound of anyone approaching. The night is silent, my ragged breathing the only sound I can hear.

At last I stop, utterly defeated.

There are no scissors.

I sink down onto the floor, tears leaking from my eyes.

All I want is to get to Ruby, to save her, to make sure she and Rufus are all right, but I'm trapped here at Dex's mercy, trussed up like an animal. Powerless to save myself or my children.

If only Harry was here. Because he was right, all along, about PAAUL – he just got it wrong about who exactly was behind the crusade to kill the abortion doctors. And for all his lies, he was always on my side. But he is gone and I'm powerless, alone with my fear and my misery.

Several long minutes pass. Is it really only just past midnight, as Lucy said? It feels like the middle of the night at the end of the world. I stare out at the moon, light filtering in through the trees. I'm freezing cold, my arms and legs are stiff, my back is sore and I can't feel my hands and feet.

A million thoughts go through my head: fury that Uncle Perry is prepared to hurt Ruby, bewilderment that Dex is unimaginably far from the charming cousin who I've known all my life. Lucy says Dex is a psychopath. True psychopaths lack conscience and empathy. Is that really Dex, who has always been so loving?

Or has he? When I think back to the really tough times – Mum's death and Caspian's – Dex was hardly around. It was Ayesha I leaned on most, plus Dad and Lucy for practical things.

But still ... that doesn't account for rape, does it? For murder?

God, why does Lucy have to be so bloody weak? Did Dex even really rape her? Lucy is so odd ... so infuriatingly passive ... could she have misunderstood in some way? No. I feel guilty for even thinking it. Rape is rape.

And maybe being raped and telling no one are part of what has *made* Lucy so different from other people. Right now she's clearly suffering from ... what's it called? Ongoing Traumatic Relationship Syndrome or something. I did it on my degree. It's where the victim is so locked into the abusive dynamic, like with battered wives, that she can't break free.

I shudder. If Dex is capable of rape and kidnapping and murder, I can see no reason why he will let Ruby or me go. Jacqueline and Dad are away all night. Dex can take his time dealing with us. There's no one to help us.

I miss Harry more than I would have imagined possible. It still feels surreal that Dex killed him. Fear grips me, a physical pain in my chest. Why doesn't Lucy come back? What has Dex done to her and Ruby? What will he do to me?

The key in the summer-house door turns. I scrabble away, towards the wall. Oh my God. Every nerve in my body is shrieking. It's Dex, he's come to kill me. I know it.

The door opens slowly, casting a streak of light from the moon outside along the dusty wooden floor. I hold my breath as the toe of a brown leather boot appears around the edge of the door.

The last person I expect to see steps into the moonlight.

HARRY

Harry peers into the gloom. Someone is definitely there, crouched in the dark corner of the summer house. His throat constricts. Is it Fran?

'Harry!' Her breath escapes in a gasp as her pale, terrified face turns towards the moonlight. And to him.

He rushes over, taking in all at once the strain in her eyes and the ropes around her wrists and ankles and the hope and relief that jump and bump in his chest.

'Are you all right?' He hugs her, fierce and hard, fumbling for the ropes.

'I . . . I thought you were dead.' She leans against him; she's trembling.

'Not so far.' He rubs his neck. 'I got injected with something, knocked me out for hours. I came round in a garage with Dex standing over me. I thought he was going to kill me but he gave me food and drink then left me in there tied up for hours.'

Harry brandishes the small knife Fran gave him when he last saw her, then starts sawing through the rope around her wrists.

'My hands were tied tight to a pipe so I couldn't get hold of this,' he explains. 'Dex got me out a few hours ago, brought me here in the boot of his car, then forced me into the utility room by the kitchen. I was tied up again of course, but this time I could reach my knife so—'

'Did he hurt you?' Fran's eyes widen.

'No.' Harry concentrates on the rope. He's about halfway through. 'I saw you from the utility room, Dex carrying you out here. He wouldn't say if you were okay, I've been going out of my—'

'What about Ruby? Did you see Ruby? Is she okay?' There's a terrible urgency in Fran's voice.

'Ruby's here?'

'She's upstairs, in Lucy's bedroom. At least that's where Lucy thinks she is. Lucy's here too.'

'I know about Lucy. When I got free just now I wanted to call the police, but Dex had taken my mobile and I could hear him and your sister in the hall. She sounded distraught.' Harry can still feel his heart thudding at the sound of their voices. It had been too big a risk to try and get past them so instead he had headed into the garden where he was sure he'd find Fran at least.

'It was Lucy who put the watch in that storage locker,' Fran gabbles. 'She found it in Perry's safe last week. He's the one behind PAAUL, not Dad.'

'Your Uncle Perry?' Harry frowns. 'Whose house we went to? Lanagh?'

'Yes, there was a safe in the study I didn't know about. Lucy found the watch and the names of all the murder victims in there. All the doctors who've been killed. And you. Though she didn't know until Saturday it *was* your name.'

'Jesus, why didn't she *say* something?' Harry asks grimly.

'She said she did warn you. When you spoke to her that afternoon.'

Harry snorts, still sawing through Fran's ropes. 'She told me to "be careful". But what I mean is: why didn't she tell your dad? Or the police?'

'You can't blame her,' Fran insists. 'She's always been ... not weak exactly but really fragile. And our family is her whole life.' I stop, wondering why I'm defending Lucy so strongly. She's no longer a child, and no matter how devastated she was to find out that Perry was responsible for multiple murders, she should still have spoken up. 'Anyway,' I go on. 'Now she's found out Dex is involved and he's totally terrorised her – there's history between them, she's too scared to stand up to him. I'm terrified he'll kill her when he's done with us.' She gazes at him, her eyes huge with sorrow. 'We have to rescue them both. Lucy as well as Ruby.'

Harry's heart plummets. Finding Fran has been risky enough. But he can hardly leave her to rescue her daughter and sister alone. He tugs at the rope. It's looser but still holding fast.

'I'll get them,' he says, redoubling his efforts. 'I want you to go over the fence to the neighbours, you can break in if you have to. Raise the alarm. The police will—'

'Won't work,' Fran says, her voice rising with anxiety. 'The fence on both sides is too high.'

'Okay then, we'll yell for help.' Harry slices through the final bit of rope. Fran's hands are free. 'There.'

She hugs him tightly. He smells of oil and dust and fresh sweat. It's a strange mix; oddly reassuring.

'Thank you,' she breathes, rubbing her wrists, as he moves on to the binding around her ankles. 'But we can't yell for help. If Dex hears us he'll kill Ruby. Harry, he's killed *everyone*. For Perry. He's the head of PAAUL, you were right about the whole thing, except it's him and not my dad.'

'Right.' Harry grunts his frustration as he carves through the thickest part of the rope. 'Damn it. Do you know where Dex put our mobiles?'

'No,' she says.

'Done.' The rope comes away in his hands.

'There's a house phone in the hall.' Fran struggles to her feet. 'We can call the police on the way up to Ruby.' She flexes her ankles. 'Come on.'

Outside the wind is sharp and cold. Fran stumbles as they hurry through the copse of trees, her feet still numb. Harry can only imagine how she feels: betrayed by her uncle, attacked by her cousin, desperate to get to her daughter. Her breath comes in pitiful jags. He takes her hand as they reach the edge of the trees.

The lights are off in the kitchen, across the whole back of the house. Which means anyone looking out will see them crossing the lawn in the moonlight.

'Fast as possible,' he whispers.

Still holding hands they race over the grass and the patio and into the kitchen. Harry puts his finger to his lips as they stand inside, listening for sounds. The house is silent. Spooky.

'D'you think Dex has gone?' Fran whispers.

They creep across the tiled kitchen floor and into the hall. An old-fashioned house phone stands on the table next to the living room door. Sweat gathers at the nape of Harry's neck as he gently lifts the receiver off its base.

'Thanks, but I'm very tired. Shall we pray now?' Someone is speaking on an extension. It's Lucy. She sounds upset. Harry opens his mouth to speak, then remembers what Fran said. Lucy may scream if she knows they are free.

He glances at Fran and shakes his head. She points up the stairs, eager to get to Ruby. Harry hesitates. If he puts the phone back down Lucy and whoever she is speaking to will surely hear the click. Instead he lays the receiver quietly on the hall table.

They tiptoe to the stairs. As Fran hurries up to Ruby, Harry glances at the front door just a few feet away. He could leave. Right now. Run for help. He looks up to the first floor. Lucy is clearly still in the house, either up there or on the second floor above. Dex is most probably up there too. Fran is heading straight into danger. Even if he runs up now and tries to drag Fran away, he knows it won't work.

Fran will never leave Ruby.

And he can't leave Fran.

He hurries after her up the stairs and across the first-floor landing, catching up with her as she reaches Lucy's bedroom.

Fran glances at him, her elegant features riven with fear.

'Ready?' she mouths.

Harry nods, holding his breath as Fran turns the handle and pushes open the door. Moonlight streaks across the coverlet pulled smooth and neat. The rosary dangling from Christ's foot gleams.

But underneath the bed is empty.

FRAN

Ruby isn't here.

I look around the room, desperate, is she hiding somewhere? Is there anywhere she could have been shut away? No. Lucy's closet and cupboards aren't big enough.

After the adrenaline rush of our escape, of finding out Harry is alive, the misery and terror of not finding Ruby crushes me. Harry's strong hand touches my shoulder. I sink back against him, all hope sucked out of my lungs along with my breath. 'Oh.' The noise I make is a strangled moan.

Harry grips my elbow. His voice is fierce in my ear. 'We'll find her.'

'Francesca! Harry!' Lucy's hushed whisper makes us spin around. My sister is in the doorway, her eyes wide with shock. 'What are you doing? How did you—?'

'We've come for Ruby.' I keep my voice low. 'Where is she? You said she was in your room?'

'Dex moved her. Oh, dear Lord.' Lucy hurries into

the room. She clasps her hands together so tightly the knuckles are white. 'What are you doing? He'll be so mad, he'll—'

'He's going to kill us anyway.' Harry's impatient voice cuts across hers, quiet but firm. 'Is Ruby still in the house?'

Lucy hops from foot to foot. 'I think so, I don't know, I don't know.'

I stare at her. How can she be so useless? Ruby is her niece. My baby. I know Lucy adores her, so why won't she act?

'Come on!' Harry pulls me round. But before we can take a step, Dex rushes into view. He stands, panting for breath, in the doorway. There's a gun in his hand.

I stare at the gun, my mouth open in shock.

'Feeling okay, coz?' Dex asks, a frown creasing his forehead. He sounds totally sincere.

'You bastard!' I snarl. 'Where's Ruby?'

'What did you use to get free?' Dex demands.

Beside me Harry ducks down, pulls the knife out of his boot and rushes at Dex. 'This,' he says.

Dex sidesteps him neatly, backing away and pointing the gun at Harry, who shrinks back.

'Drop the knife,' he orders.

Shocked numb, I look up from the weapon and into my cousin's eyes. I've known him since we were babies. How is this happening? Is it drugs? Or a totally hidden side of his personality?

Harry growls with fury. He is still holding the knife.

'Who are you, Dex?' The words sputter out of me

like the dying flicker of a light. I don't think I've ever felt more lost in my life.

'He's psychotic,' Harry says.

Dex gives a small, impatient shake of the head. He glances at Harry. 'Last chance to drop the knife.' He turns the gun to point at me.

Harry lets the little kitchen knife fall to the carpet.

Lucy darts forward and picks it up.

'Here.' Dex holds out his hand.

For a second Lucy hesitates. I will her to stand up to him but instead she scurries over and puts the knife in his palm. She retreats across the bedroom. A black wave of despair washes over me.

'Where's Ruby?' I ask again. 'Is she all right?'

'She's here, she's fine.'

Thank God. I take a step towards the door. Dex bars my way, the gun still in his hand. I jolt to a stop.

'Let me see her.'

'Soon. She's still unconscious.' Dex looks me in the eye. 'I'm not going to hurt her, Franny. I was never going to do that. I didn't kill Harry either. I couldn't do that to you.'

'How can I believe anything you say?' My throat swells with emotion. 'I know what you've done, all the people you've killed.' My voice breaks, my body shudders. 'You murdered Caspian, Dex, who I loved *so* ... you took away my children's father ...' I'm too choked to speak.

'It wasn't my fault,' Dex says. 'I didn't have a choice.'

'What about Lucy?' I snap. 'You *raped* her. She was barely fifteen and—'

420

'It wasn't rape.' Dex glares at Lucy, who shrinks against the wall.

Panic engulfs me. If he thinks he can justify sex with his fifteen-year-old cousin, God knows what he's capable of.

'Please, let me have Ruby, plea—'

'I told you, you'll see her soon. Now shut up for God's sake.' As Dex speaks, Harry shifts so that more of his body is in front of mine. It's a small gesture but a deeply protective one.

And it gives me strength. 'So what's the plan, Dex?' I ask, more steel in my voice than before. 'I'm guessing you're not going to let that gun off in the house.'

'Yeah, apart from anything else, Jayson and Jacqueline won't be happy if you make a mess on their landing,' Harry snaps.

'I told you to shut up,' Dex barks, sweeping his gun to take in the three of us. 'We're only here because this third-rate reporter wanted a crappy story on Jayson Carr. And because you . . .' He glares at me. 'Because *you* recognised that stupid curtain in Dad's flat. This is your fault, all of you.'

I glance at Lucy, remembering what she said about Dex being a psychopath. Here he is blaming others, refusing to take responsibility for his actions. Just as he did with his marriage. How did I never notice before? Lucy's head is bowed; her shoulders shake with fear. If Dex is a classic psychopath then Lucy is a stereotypical victim: trusting, insecure, sensitive. I should have seen that before too.

'*Our* fault?' Harry snorts. 'We're not the ones killing off abortion doctors and kidnapping children.'

'Enough.' Dex turns to Lucy. 'Where's my phone?'

Lucy's mouth opens and shuts wordlessly. Then she scurries off, presumably to fetch Dex's mobile. How can she be so submissive?

'What are you going to do with us, Dex?' I ask.

'There's no way out of this,' Harry adds. 'You should put the gun down and turn yourself in.'

'Thanks for the advice.' Dex strides out of the room, slams the door on us and turns the key. A moment later his footsteps sound, stomping down the stairs.

Harry hurls himself at the door. I join him. But the door holds fast.

'Lucy?' My heart thuds. 'Lucy, are you there?'

'We *have* to get her to let us out.' Harry paces up and down.

'Lucy?' I call more loudly.

'I'm here.' She sounds out of breath, as if she's been running. 'I don't have long, he's on the phone.'

'Let us out!' I insist.

'I can't, he has the key.' There's a sound of paper rustling on the other side of the door.

'Lucy, did you see Ruby, is she all right?' I ask.

'Go and dial 999,' Harry orders. 'Tell them all our lives are in danger.'

'Listen, Francesca, I wasn't lying about Dex and what happened when I was fifteen.'

Harry and I exchange a frustrated glance.

'That doesn't matter now, Lucy,' I say sharply.

422

'Nothing matters right now except saving Ruby and calling the police. Nothing matters right now except doing the right thing.'

There's silence on the other side of the door. *Shit*. Ruby is here somewhere, terrified and alone. I need to get to her. *Now*. But it was stupid to snap at Lucy. She needs to be heard. Perhaps if I can make her feel supported, she'll be able to stand up to Dex.

'Luce?'

She gives a loud sniff. 'I know you think I'm pathetic, but it's so hard to talk about it all. I've been carrying everything for ... for so long.'

'I don't think you're pathetic, Lucy, I promise I don't. And I do believe you ... about what Dex did. It's just we really need to get out of here.'

'I need to explain,' she whimpers.

'For God's sake,' Harry mutters under his breath.

'Explain what?' I force myself to sound patient.

The sound of paper rustling again, a couple of pages clearly torn from a pad or notebook appear under the door.

Harry grabs them; holds them up.

'What's this?' I ask.

'Mum's diary,' Lucy says with another sniff. 'It wasn't just me. Dex used her too. You have to believe me.'

I take the pages. They are written in Mum's distinctive handwriting: forward slanting and rounded with dots over the 'i's and 'j's.

'We don't have time to read an effing journal, *Jesus*,' Harry hisses.

I bite my lip, calculating how long I need to pretend to read in order to win Lucy over.

'Okay, Lucy, I'll read this,' I say. 'But you need to dial 999. Tell them about Ruby and that ... that Dex has threatened to kill us, that you're scared, that we're locked in. Will you do that, please?'

'I'll try.' Lucy's voice sounds small and terrified. I hear her padding away.

'For Christ's sake, this is ridiculous.' Harry heads to the window and tries the latch. It's locked. 'Maybe I can smash through.' He looks around for something to use.

'Okay.' I don't hold out much hope. Like all the windows in the house this one is not only double-glazed but toughened and tempered to resist break-ins.

I force myself to focus on the pages torn from Mum's notebook. I'm not at all sure Lucy will really call the police. Maybe if I demonstrate I've kept my word and read some of this diary she'll gain confidence. I try to focus on the line at the top of the page. The date given is a week or two before Mum died, around the time of that party where she told Ayesha she was frightened. How does what Mum is writing here connect with Dex? The word 'miracle' catches my eye. I brace myself for a religious outpouring and read on ...

A miracle. I'd been dreading the whole event so much and then I saw him. My Apollo. He was across the room. All tall and muscular, his sleeves rolled up. I spilt a splash of champagne on my blouse, which was sheer, and I caught him staring. Weird, seeing him look at me in that way. Weirder to feel the tug of desire thrilling through me in response. He came over and I could feel how much he wanted me. It was in his eyes. Such hunger. 'How is this possible?' That was what he said. Not then, of course. Then he just told me how he was planning to visit Tate Modern the next day, what a shame it was to see beautiful things and have no one to share them with. I volunteered to go immediately. I didn't hesitate. And when he touched my arm we both felt the electricity. Honestly I couldn't have stopped if I'd wanted to. And I didn't want to stop. I knew then. We met. We looked at art. We laughed. We told each other how much was missing in our lives. Then he took me away from the crowds and leaned me against a wall and kissed my face and touched my breasts under my dress and told me he'd been wanting to do that since the party. I thought my body would dissolve with pleasure. I shook all over and he took me to a hotel and – oh, I have never felt anything like I did when he touched me. And now I'm at his mercy, terrified of his power over me. He acts like God, omnipotent. Oh, Dex, my Dex, bringer of wave upon wave of delirious ...

I can't read any more. Feeling sick, I put the paper down.

So this is what Lucy wanted me to know ... that Dex not only abused her, but seduced our mother.

He acts like God.

Those were the very words Ayesha reported Mum had said in that moment of drunken indiscretion at the party. My heart thuds. Mum claimed she was talking about Uncle Graham, but I'm guessing she really meant Dex. Having given her feelings away in an unguarded moment, she must have pretended she'd meant Graham in order to stop persistent Ayesha asking questions.

I put my ear to the door. Where the hell is Lucy? More than ever, I just want to get to Ruby, to save her, to hold her and never let go.

Across the room Harry slams the base of Lucy's bedside lamp against the window. The glass holds firm. As I guessed it would.

'Francesca?' At last Lucy's back, on the other side of the door.

'Did you make the call?' I lean in close.

'Yes.' Lucy's voice is a faint, trembling whisper. 'Police and an ambulance for Ruby.'

Oh, thank goodness. 'Well done, Lucy.' I let out a shaky sigh of relief. Across the room Harry raises his eyebrows. I give him a nod.

'I'm so scared though,' Lucy goes on. 'When Dex finds out . . .'

'You need to hide from him,' I say. 'Then the police can deal with him before he can get to you.'

'We won't let him hurt you, Lucy,' Harry adds, walking over to me. 'Promise.'

'Thank you,' Lucy whimpers. 'Did you read the diary?'

'Most of it,' I say. 'It's a shock. But ... Lucy, you should go and hide. We can talk about this lat—'

'I was devastated when I found out,' she whispers.

'I know,' I say. 'I really thought all that time that Mum and Dad were so happy.'

'I knew they weren't,' Lucy says, her voice even smaller than before. 'I knew they weren't before Mummy died. I knew she was having an affair. I mean, I didn't just suspect, like I said earlier. I actually knew it for sure.'

'Oh.' More secrets. The pain of it a dull weight in my chest.

'Daddy doesn't know about Dex,' Lucy says. 'I don't think he even knows Mummy was seeing someone else.'

'Right.' It's too much to take in. 'Okay, Lucy, you need to hide. Now.'

'I will,' she says. 'I just need to tell you one more thing. About Mummy and ... and how she died. It ... it wasn't an accident.'

My heart constricts as I guess what's coming.

'There's no time,' I say, not wanting to hear it.

'I need to tell you this first,' Lucy insists.

'Okay,' I sigh, bracing myself. 'I'm listening.'

'Mummy was murdered. Dex did it. I was there, I saw the whole thing.'

Even though I was half-expecting her to say it, the brutal words are still a shock. Lucy's bedroom spins around me. I put my hand on the doorframe to steady myself.

'Bloody hell,' Harry says.

I close my eyes. On top of everything else, Dex killed Mum. And Lucy saw. Except ... how on earth does that fit?

Harry squeezes my shoulder and I open my eyes.

'Lucy, are you sure?' I protest. 'Because Mum's death was an accident. You know that as well as I do. Uncle Perry found her at the bottom of the cellar steps and said she must have fainted due to her diabetes. You weren't even there.'

'I was there. And Uncle Perry lied,' Lucy says. 'He faked the blood tests ... said he'd talked to her about the faints, as her doctor, loads of times including earlier that week. It was all made up in order to avoid a post-mortem.'

I frown. Perry is clearly evil, but I can't imagine a reason he'd want to cover up the murder of his sister-in-law, a devout Catholic who he liked, for the sake of his dissolute nephew.

'Why would Uncle Perry—?'

'Dex blackmailed him about being gay.'

'Oh.' I remember the porn I found in Perry's basement and suddenly it makes sense. Clearly Perry and Dex have had some kind of toxic contract for years: Dex using blackmail to coerce his uncle, then Perry offering hard cash to get Dex to carry out the PAAUL murders.

Harry lets out a low whistle.

'It's true,' Lucy goes on. 'Dex got angry and pushed Mummy down the stairs. I was there. I saw him do it.'

A shiver runs down my spine. Lucy isn't safe out

there. The police could still be minutes away. I have to find a way to protect her and Ruby until they get here.

'Okay, Lucy, I listened, just like you wanted. And it's good you've told me . . . we'll make sure the police know about Mum. We will. But now you really have to hide.'

'Look in my bedside drawer if you don't believe me.' She lowers her voice. 'It's proof. That's Mummy's blood on Dex's watch. *The* watch. It used to belong to Uncle Graham. I'm sorry I lied about it before. I knew it wasn't anything to do with the PAAUL murders. I remember it smashing when Dex killed Mummy. Uncle Perry must have kept it to have a hold over Dex. You know, because of the DNA on it from Dex and Mummy. I stole it off Dex earlier.'

I exchange an appalled glance with Harry. He turns and heads over to the bedside cupboard.

'Lucy, I hear you. Now go.' There's a short silence, then I hear her pad softly away. I lean against the door as Harry reaches into the drawer and holds up the cracked, bloodied watch, still in its plastic bag.

'It's definitely the one I found at the storage locker,' he says.

I grab the bag and stare at the dark stain on the watch face. I feel sick. Mum's blood.

The thought of Mum sends a claw of fresh panic tearing at my insides. Where is Ruby? I need to be with her, to hold her, to make sure she really is all right.

Hands shaking, I flip the watch over to read the inscription.

from a loving father

'Shit,' I mutter, remembering Lucy's words and how I saw this same watch on Graham's wrist in the photo in his flat. 'Graham got this from his father, and passed it on to his son.'

'Lucy must have known what Dex is capable of all along,' Harry says.

I nod. 'God, I can't imagine how terrified she must be of him, to have to lie all this time.'

Harry grits his teeth. 'Bastard, he's really done a number on her.'

I press my ear to the door. I can hear nothing. I lean against the wood, trying to calm the panic that roils again in my mind.

Hold on, Ruby, I whisper under my breath. *I'm coming.*

Footsteps sound across the landing. Heavier than Lucy's. I step back, bracing myself. Harry puts a protective arm across me. The door swings open. It's Dex. The gun still in his hand.

He beckons us out of the room.

'Up there.' He points the gun towards the stairs. 'All the way up to the attic.'

Harry and I head across the landing. There's no sign of Lucy. Hopefully she's found a hiding place. Surely the police can't be too much longer.

'Where's Ruby? Is she really okay?' I demand. 'Dex, I need to see her.'

'She's fine,' Dex snaps. 'As I already told you.'

We climb the stairs to the second floor. Dex directs

us past Mum's old office and up the next short flight of steps in the far corner to the attic.

The attic door creaks open. It was originally used to store Mum's phenomenal overspill of rare books. Most of these are sold now but a large number are still here lining the whole of the back wall. Mum's old Turkish rug is up here too, rolled up in front of a couple of chests of drawers I vaguely remember Jacqueline trying to sell. All of this stuff has monetary value of some sort; that's why Jacqueline has kept it. There's a box in the shadows which I'm pretty certain is full of ancient silverware. Other than these things, the huge attic is empty.

Harry walks in ahead of me. He can only stand up fully in the centre of the room. Dex waits on the stairs below, still gripping his gun, while I pass. As I join Harry on the thin brown carpet, Dex follows us inside.

'Why are we up here?' Harry demands.

'I want to see Ruby. Please, Dex?' I wring my hands. '*Please?*'

'She's over there.' Dex points towards the rug.

My heart lurches into my mouth. I race over.

Yes. Ruby is on the other side of the rug, hemmed in between it and a chest of drawers. She's lying very still on the ground, her hair across her face. I drop to my knees, rolling the rug out of the way, and feel her skin. She's warm, her breathing soft and shallow. As I touch her she murmurs.

'Ruby?' I pat her cheek lightly. 'Ruby?'

She grunts and makes a face.

'What did you give her?' I demand.

'Rohypnol,' Dex says. 'It'll wear off soon.'

I glare at him. The date rape drug. Dex stares back at me, reading the accusation in my eyes. 'I *told* you, Franny. I'd never hurt her. Or you. And I couldn't bring myself to kill Harry either, not once I had the watch back. I didn't think there was any need. And you'd already lost Caspian ...'

'Because *you* killed him,' I shake my head. 'How could you do that, Dex? He was my husband, your friend.'

Dex's expressive, handsome face registers a deep misery.

'I told you that too,' he says. 'I didn't have a choice.'

'You mean Perry?'

Dex says nothing. I turn back to Ruby, too disgusted to speak. She's dressed in the same jeans and jumper she wore in the ice cream parlour. Her little blue boots are still laced right up. She doesn't look like her clothes have been moved or messed with.

Across the attic Harry is peering into the box of old silverware. What is he looking for? And where is Lucy? Has she found a hiding place? Is she safe?

'Come here.' Dex orders Harry to the centre of the room. 'Kneel.'

With a glance at me, Harry does as he's told. I stiffen. For a horrific moment I think Dex is going to shoot Harry in the head. Then he shoves Harry to his knees and takes out a coil of thin rope.

'What's the plan now, Dex?' There is fear as well as sarcasm in Harry's voice.

'Shut up.' Dex winds the rope around Harry's wrists.

Harry winces.

I stroke Ruby's face again. She makes a soft, snuffling noise. For the first time since I received the text threatening the kids' lives I relax slightly. I'm with her. She's alive and Rufus is safe with Ayesha.

'What are you going to do with us?' I look up at Dex.

He ignores me. He gives the rope a hard yank. I watch him, my heart in my mouth. 'Are you going to kill us?'

Dex says nothing.

'Is that the plan? To murder us like you murdered Caspian? We're your *family*, Dex. You've known Ruby since she was a few hours old.'

Dex still says nothing, just tightens the rope around Harry's wrists.

'What about Mum?' I persist. 'I saw her notebook. You had an affair with her before she died. Lucy says you killed her.'

Dex finishes knotting Harry's rope. He glares at me. 'Get over here.'

'No.' I put my arms around Ruby's stirring body. No way am I leaving her, even to cross the room. 'No, you keep saying you won't hurt Ruby and nothing was your fault and you're not a bad person. So if you mean that you won't hurt us either.'

'Shut up.' Dex strides over to me, grabs my arm and spins me around. 'I'm not going to ask again.'

The gun metal is cold on my cheek. I drop to my knees beside Harry, fury coursing through me. The rope is rough on my skin. 'You did it all, just like Lucy said.' The words spit out of me. 'You killed Mum and Caspian. And all those other—'

I gasp as Dex gives the rope a sharp tug.

'Your mother was an accident,' Dex mutters.

My heart seems to stop in my chest. Is he actually owning up to killing her?

'How?' I demand.

Silence. Dex knots the rope. Gives it another tug. My wrists burn.

'Yeah, right,' I sneer. 'So Mum was an accident. You know what I'm hearing? *Everything*'s an accident; *nothing*'s your fault.'

'Your mum was unhappy with Jayson, that's the truth. If it hadn't been me it would have been someone else.'

'And that justifies you killing her, Dex?' I ask, ignoring the pain that shoots through my wrists as he tugs a third time on the rope. Surely the police will be here any second. I try to focus on that: the police will be here and Ruby will be okay and soon this nightmare will end.

'She wanted to leave Jayson for me and I told her that wasn't going to happen,' Dex explains. 'She got hysterical and . . . and fell, that's the whole story.'

Footsteps on the stairs. We both look up. It's Lucy. Eyes wide with anxiety, twisting her hands over each other, she stands in the attic doorway.

My heart constricts. Are the police here already? I can't hear anyone in the house.

So why isn't Lucy hiding?

LUCY

I didn't call the police like I told Francesca. I couldn't. I know lying is a sin but I just couldn't do it.

I look at you and it takes all the courage I have to meet your cool gaze, to look into your ice-green eyes, so full of contempt. 'Please don't be angry, Dex, but I want Francesca to know the truth,' I say.

I can see from my sister's face that she doesn't care about the truth. She just wants to take Ruby and get out of here. But it's important she knows exactly what you've done. What I've sacrificed to protect you.

'What truth?' you snap. The disdain on your face crucifies me. It's so unfair.

'Lucy?' Francesca is staring at me, like she's trying to read my mind. She's on the floor, kneeling. Harry's next to her. They look like communicants. You stand in front of them, the gun outstretched in your hand, like a priest with wine and wafers.

'The day Mummy died I was up in my bedroom,' I explain. 'I heard Mummy open the front door, she didn't know I was in. I tiptoed out onto the landing and peered over the bannisters. *He ...*' I point my finger at you. '*He was in the hallway, kissing Mummy.* They were practically eating each other. It was disgusting.'

'Oh, *shut up.*' There is more loathing in your snarl than I can bear, but I need Francesca to understand the depth of your depravity, how your third murder changed both our lives forever.

'So they went into the kitchen,' I continue. 'And I crept down the stairs and the kitchen door was open a crack so I peered into the room. Mummy was crying, Dex was cross.'

'She was hysterical.' You wave your gun. 'I was trying to reason with her,' you say, clearly furious. Fear crosses Francesca's face.

But I'm not scared. Because I know the truth.

'Mummy was begging Dex not to end it,' I explain to Francesca. 'She was telling him how she loved him more than anything, more than her life.' I close my eyes, reliving the pure hurt of the words Mum had used. 'More than us. More than her own children.' I meet Francesca's unhappy gaze. Now she can share in the truth with me. 'Dex was saying mean stuff, that Mummy was too old, that it had just been a bit of fun, that he didn't want a relationship. Mummy was crying worse and worse. It happened fast. Mummy slapped him. Then he punched her. She stumbled backwards. And ... and he hit her again. Harder. And she flew back ... through the open door and fell all the way down the steps to the cellar.'

'I lost it, just for a second,' you mutter.

I cross myself. 'I'll never forget the sound of her body banging against the steps or that last moment when ... when her head hit the stone flags at the bottom.'

I keep my gaze on Francesca's face. She's listening, transfixed.

'Then afterwards there was this moment of silence, a ... a stillness. Dex raced down the steps to the basement. I stood there, I couldn't take it in. Dex was calling Mummy's name and it was like I was hearing him through a mist. And then his voice grew more urgent and I had to see what happened though in my heart I knew. So I went down the steps. I didn't look at Mummy until I was right there, then I forced myself. At first I just looked at her foot ... her left foot, half out of its strappy sandal.' I glance at you, but you don't meet my gaze. 'And then Dex noticed me and he said: "Lucy, she's not breathing." Then the F-word over and over again. He was hyperventilating. I turned my head slowly and let my eyes travel up Mummy's body. Her blue dress, the strap hanging off one shoulder, the black lace edge of her bra, the line of her make-up. I remember thinking how much make-up she was wearing. A dark pink lipstick. Her eyes were open. She looked like ... like she had just seen something that surprised her. There was blood coming from under her head. Dex had blood on him from fumbling about, feeling her neck and her wrist. "There's no pulse, she's dead." He said that, then more F-words, then he looked up at me and he said: "What have I done? Lucy? What have I done?"'

I pause, hands clasped, reliving that moment when

you needed me, the fulcrum of our co-existence, the point where my own life truly began.

'That's enough.' You storm over, your eyes dark like thunder.

I'm shocked back into the present. Across the dusty attic Francesca's mouth hangs open. Harry stares. And suddenly you are looming over me, shaking me. Furious.

I scream. I run. Down the stairs to the second floor. I hear you follow. You stop for a second to slam the bolts across the attic door, locking the others in. Then you're pounding down the steps behind me.

Coming for me.

FRAN

The bolts slam on the other side of the door.

'Hey!' I yell, pushing Lucy's terrible story out of my mind.

'Let us out!' Harry shouts.

But they're gone. The rope around my wrists bites deep as I shuffle over to Ruby. She's still asleep but her breathing is regular and even.

'Fran, come here!' Harry whispers, his voice hoarse.

I spin around. He's pulling a shard of broken mirror from out of his sleeve. 'It was in there,' he explains, pointing to the box of old silverware he was examining earlier.

I hurry over. I turn my back so Harry can reach the rope around my wrists. He saws away at the binding and for a second I experience a dizzying *déjà vu*. He cut me free less than an hour ago in the summer house. It feels like years ago.

'Are you all right?' I ask.

'I'm fine,' he says. 'Do you think Lucy called the police?'

'No,' I say. 'I'm certain she didn't. God, I hope she's all right.'

Harry mutters something under his breath, slicing through the final bit of my rope. I rub my wrists then take the shard. I pull the sleeve of my jumper over one end of its sharp edge and position myself to deal with his binding.

Harry's hands are wet. I lean closer, trying to see why and catch the scent of something metallic. 'Is that blood?' I ask. 'Shit, did you cut yourself when you were doing my rope?'

He nods. 'I had to hold it tight to get a proper grip. It's fine.'

I work away at Harry's rope, keeping my jumper double-folded over the end of the mirror to protect my own hand. The edge is blunted after cutting through my own rope. My breath is coming in heaves thanks to the effort. My hands are slick with Harry's blood. He says nothing, though it must be hurting like hell.

At last I'm through. Harry struggles to his feet, wincing.

'Let me see.' I examine his hands, wiping away the blood with my sleeve. There's a deep cut between the thumb and forefinger of his right hand. 'Shit.' I reach under my jumper and rip a strip of cotton from my T-shirt. I bind it around Harry's hand then race over to Ruby. She's stirring, her eyes still closed.

Please be okay.

'Come on,' Harry urges. 'Let's get her out of here.'

I join him at the door. The two of us square up to it. 'On my count,' Harry orders.

'Three. Two.'

I brace myself.

'One.'

I put everything I've got into my body blow. Beside me Harry rams the door with his shoulder. It doesn't budge.

We try again. Twice. Still nothing.

'Damn it.' Harry stomps across the attic floor, exuding frustration.

'Mummy?' Ruby's voice is thick and blurry. 'Mummy?'

My stomach gives a lurch. I rush over and kneel beside her. Ruby's eyes are open at last. Fearful, dazed, she blinks at me.

'Where am I?' she says.

'Granddad's house,' I say, leaning closer. 'Are you all right, Rubes? Does anything hurt?'

Her lips are dry. She opens and closes her mouth. 'But ... but ...'

I stroke her hair. 'Just rest a moment.'

Harry is still pacing around the attic, but I'm soaking up my Ruby, touching her face, her arms. She feels warm, unbroken. I pull her towards me.

'What happened?' she asks, tears moistening her eyes. 'I was in the ... we ordered milkshakes ...'

'I know, I know.' I stroke her hair. 'Some bad people put us up here but we're going to get out.' I hesitate. 'Does it hurt anywhere, Ruby?' I can't help but glance down at her jeans. Dex was adamant he hadn't hurt her, but ...

441

'No, just my head aches,' Ruby says thickly.

I nod, relieved.

'Over here.' Harry's voice breaks through: strong and urgent. 'I think I've got something.'

'What is it?' I ask, standing up.

'Mummy?'

'I'll be right here.' I go over to Harry. Ruby sits up, following me with her eyes. She looks pale and frightened but she seems okay, thank God.

'We're going to break out,' Harry says grimly.

'How?' I demand, looking wildly around. 'We can't shift the door and there aren't any windows.'

'We're not going through the door or the windows,' Harry says. 'We're going through the ceiling.'

My jaw drops. '*What?*'

'It's easier than it sounds.' Harry indicates a patch of roof in the corner where the sloping ceiling is at its lowest. 'Follow me.'

Baffled, I follow him to the corner. 'Now tap the slope. All the way across.'

I knock on the ceiling with my knuckles. Harry listens carefully.

'What are we looking for?' I ask.

'A place between the struts.' He taps at the ceiling just an inch above my own hands. The sound is hollow. 'There.'

Ruby staggers to her feet. 'Mummy, why are ...? What's going on?'

'Don't worry about anything,' I urge. 'Harry and I are going to get us out of here.'

Harry drags the box of old silverware towards me. He's using the hand that isn't cut. The other hangs by his side in its makeshift bandage. He deposits the box at my feet. It's full of silver: picture frames, a bud vase, a pair of matching goblets and of course the mirror with its broken shards hanging half out of the frame. The tips of two tarnished candlesticks peek out, just visible above a large, heavily scratched bonbonnière. Harry grabs one of the candlesticks in his good hand.

'Take the other,' he orders. 'Grip it hard.'

I do as he says.

'Now ram it against the slope like this.' He bangs at the ceiling just above our heads with his unbandaged fist.

I stare at him.

'It's just plasterboard, it'll give.' He turns to Ruby and gives her a huge wink. 'We'll be okay, won't we, Arsenal?'

She nods, her eyes like huge saucers.

'Ruby, stand back a bit.' She obediently shuffles away across the floor. I clutch the candlestick and give the sloping ceiling a thwack. The board cracks. I turn to Harry with a triumphant grin.

Taking it in turns we hit at the plasterboard. Within seconds a small hole appears, then a series of splintering cracks spreading out from the hole.

'Yay!' Ruby's voice rises in a squeal.

'Ssh!' I say, though if Dex and Lucy are still on the second floor, just below us, they are bound to hear us pounding the plasterboard anyway.

'It's going to work,' Harry says with a smile. 'Keep going.'

I take aim and drive the candlestick at the centre of the cracks. Again. Again. Again.

'What about what's on the other side?' I ask, stopping to catch my breath for a second. 'How will we get through that?'

'The plasterboard is nailed onto beams about forty centimetres wide,' Harry explains. 'All we have to do is push out the struts and the tiles that go between them. Then I'll crawl out onto the roof.'

'The roof?'

Our eyes meet.

'To call for help,' Harry says.

Suddenly I'm not sure. I glance down at Harry's hand. A dark spot is spreading across the strip of cotton tied around the skin.

'I can do it,' he insists. 'Come on, keep going.'

We carry on hammering against the plasterboard. Another few thwacks and we've made a big enough hole to see the insulation on the other side.

Harry reaches in and grabs a handful with his good hand. 'Now we just have to pull that out.'

I follow his lead. The insulation is dark yellow: thick and rough and scratchy. It sticks to my fingers as I hurl it to the attic floor. 'How do you know about roofs?' I ask.

'Worked on a building site when I was a student.' Harry grins at me. 'Remember? Instead of a poncey gap year in Thailand?'

'Right.' I nod, coughing as dust from the insulation rises into the air.

Behind me Ruby coughs too. I swing around. 'Are you all right?'

She nods, her little face tense.

'Move back, Arsenal, yeah?' Harry winks at her.

Obediently she scuttles backwards.

I yank out another chunk of insulation and throw it to the floor. The struts that run between the beams come into view, the tiles slanting down on top.

I point to the tiles. 'What about those?'

'We just push them out.' Harry is already knocking at the nearest one with his candlestick. It shifts slightly. I take aim and strike hard. My tile doesn't budge.

'More,' Harry commands. 'Harder.'

I put my whole bodyweight behind the punch. I land a clean blow. *Yes.* The tile slides sideways, letting in a blast of cold air.

'That's it.' Using his good hand, Harry pushes my tile clean out. Then three more. One by one they clatter softly down the roof. I hold my breath, hoping the noise won't have travelled through the house to wherever Dex is.

Harry, clearly having the same thought, looks towards the door. We wait, listening hard. There's no sound of voices, no footsteps. I grin at him and push out the last tile in the row. We've done it. We've made a hole big enough to crawl through. Across the room Ruby is smiling too, though her eyes are still wide with fear.

Harry reaches through the gap, a hand on either side of the hole. As he clutches the edge of the tiles with his bandaged hand his face contorts with pain. He tries to haul himself up, but it's clearly agony.

'Shit,' he gasps.

'I'll go.' My heart thuds. I'm not afraid of going out there, but I don't want to leave Ruby without me. Not now I've just found her.

Harry grimaces.

'It's fine,' I insist. 'Just . . .' I look around at Ruby.

Harry leans in so only I can hear his whisper.

'I won't let anything happen to her.'

I hesitate. If I'm out on the roof yelling for help and Dex hears me he will come for Ruby to stop me. And how will Harry be able to prevent that?

'It's our only shot,' Harry hisses.

He's right about that. Unless . . . I look around the room, trying to work out where the hole in the sloping roof is located in relation to the house below. We're at the front of the building, and on the right-hand side. Which means the room immediately beneath is Mum's old office on the second floor. I was in there earlier when Lucy told me about Uncle Perry being the head of PAAUL. I felt sick and opened the window. I remember leaning on the deep ledge outside. But did I push the sash down again? Did I lock it?

I rack my brains. I'm certain I lowered the window, but not all the way. I definitely didn't lock it.

I turn to Harry and whisper my plan. His eyes widen as he moves closer, his breath hot on my ear. 'That sounds suicidal,' he hisses.

'I can do it.' I hurry over to Ruby. 'I'll be back in

a minute.' I give her a hug and a kiss, shoot Harry a final glance, then I haul myself out, clambering onto the cold, damp tiles. The wind whips around me, searing through my thin jumper. The moon, so bright in the sky just an hour earlier, is covered with thick grey clouds. It's about to chuck it down; already spits of moisture are landing on my face.

'Mummy!' Ruby's plaintive cry follows me as the cold air sweeps across my face. I can hear Harry reassuring her as I hoist myself properly onto the tiles. The roof slopes at about forty-five degrees. I'm halfway down with my feet just above the gutter. I look up into the night sky: navy and steel. For a second I feel a strange sense of peace. And then I look down.

The roof falls away to the street. It seems to spin around me, empty, far away. Wind dashes my hair in my face. I shake it off.

A man with a dog is walking by, right underneath. Forgetting my fears about Dex hearing I cry out instinctively. 'Help! Help!' My words are whipped away, into the wind. A crack of thunder sounds in the distance. The spits of rain become pellets. *Shit*. I needn't have worried about anyone inside the house hearing me ... I can barely hear myself.

I turn back to the roof, heart pounding, and claw at the tiles beneath me. My jeans and trainers are already damp, my hair plastered to my forehead.

'Are you okay?' Harry asks from inside.

'Mummy!' Ruby wails again.

'I'm fine,' I yell, though I have no idea if they can

447

hear me. Back to plan A. I am going to lower myself down off the roof, clamber back into the house through Mum's old office window and get Harry and Ruby out of the attic so we can all escape. I run through the layout of the building again: the second-floor office window is just below the gutter. It has a wide window ledge. There will be room for my feet on that. It's doable. I just have to trust that I won't fall.

I inch down, slowly, my body pressed as close to the roof as possible. It's a savage drop to the ground below. I don't look down.

Furious thoughts whirl in my head. This is all Dex's fault. And Perry's. And that of everyone who belongs to or believes in PAAUL. What cowards. What selfish bastards they are. My legs dangle over the gutter. I feel for the wall beneath. Crawl sideways like a crab till I feel the brick turn to the glass of the office window. I have to lower myself now, give up my body. Slowly, slowly, I let myself down until only my chest and head and arms are still on the roof.

My feet flail, looking for purchase. Where is the window ledge? I visualise the box with the blue flowers Mum used to keep there. I *know* the ledge is there. I know it is deep enough for me to stand on. I just have to trust those things.

I lower myself further.

Further.

My body slides down. Down. My arms stretch and strain. *Oh, God*. I grip the gutter, it's taking my whole weight, cutting into my hands.

Where's the ledge?

Blood pumps furiously at my temples. The pain sears through my armpits, along my arms and up into my wrists. I can last maybe five more seconds like this. Four. Panic rises. Three. I'm kicking. Reaching for the ledge. Two. Where is it?

I can't hold my whole weight through my arms any longer. I *have* to find the ledge.

I brace myself, panic clutching my throat, too terrified to scream.

And then my hands slip.

HARRY

Harry peers through the hole in the sloping ceiling. All he can see are wet tiles and dark sky. His cut hand throbs painfully but he barely notices.

Where is she?

'Fran!' he yells. The sound is sucked away by the storm. The rain drives against his face. He reaches out to the tiles, pressing down, testing his cut hand. It hurts to the touch. Any weight and the hurt turns to agony. He grimaces to himself, the worry building. There's no way he can clamber out there.

'Is Mummy all right?' Ruby's voice is plaintive and wavering.

'She's fine,' he says, hoping it's true. Blinking away the raindrops he turns to the little girl at his feet. 'Hey, Arsenal,' he says, attempting a smile in order to win one from her.

She stares up at him with trembling lips.

Harry tries to swallow his own fears but he can't stop himself picturing Fran out there in the wind and rain. He imagines her hanging by her fingertips from the gutter, trying to get into the room below. She's over two floors up. She'll fall to her death. Christ, he should never have let her go out there.

'So how often d'you play football?' he asks.

'Every week on Saturdays.' Ruby's eyes follow him as he walks over to the attic door and presses his ear against the wood. There are no sounds. At least that hopefully means Dex isn't directly underneath them on the second floor.

'Attacking or defending?' he asks. 'Which d'you like best?'

Ruby purses her mouth, considering. 'Attacking, scoring goals.' Her voice is small and shaky.

'Me too,' Harry says with a grin. 'At least I used to, when I played.' He gulps. If Fran has fallen, then it's up to him to save her daughter.

He goes back to Ruby and crouches down in front of her.

'I know you're scared,' he says. 'And it's okay to be scared. But there's nothing to worry about. I'm going to look after you until your mum gets back. I won't let anything or anyone hurt you. Okay?'

She nods and her huge, solemn, trusting eyes break his heart.

FRAN

My hands slip. Only the tips of my fingers on the absolute edge of the gutter. I'm stretched to my limit, agony through my arms, my shoulders.

There. At last I feel the broad concrete of the window ledge beneath me.

I ease myself down and stand, panting for breath for a few seconds. Then I gingerly feel for the gap at the bottom of the window. Thank God the opening is still there. I hook my right foot under the window and lift the sash. It slides up and I ease my way down the glass and into the room beneath.

There's no time to catch my breath. I have to get to Ruby and Harry. I creep across Mum's old office to the door. I'm now on the second floor. The narrow steps up to the attic room are just a few feet away, on the other side of the square landing. I pause, listening for sounds from the rest of the house. The murmur of low voices rises up the stairs. Heart racing, I tiptoe across the landing. The floor creaks as I reach the base of the steps up to the attic. I put my foot on the bottom step as a familiar, crotchety voice drifts up from the floor below.

'I'm telling you, Lucy, I could go to jail.' It's Uncle Perry. I freeze. What is Perry doing here? Has he come to oversee Dex killing us?

My sister says something I can't catch.

'It just *can't* come out. I'd be ruined. I *need* it, Lucy.' Perry's querulous tone gets louder. He's directly beneath me, at the bottom of the stairs that lead up here. I glance towards the attic door. The bolts are firmly in place. I won't be able to slide them back without making at least some noise. Perry will see me as soon as he reaches the top of the stairs anyway.

'Where is it? In the office?' Perry goes on.

Does he mean the office up here? My uncle's heavy footstep on the stairs tells me he does. There's no time for me to hide. I hold my breath, flattening myself against the wall, praying he will somehow walk past and not notice me.

'No. Wait.' That's Lucy. She sounds out of breath. 'Stop.'

Perry pauses halfway up the stairs. He's looking down at Lucy, as I am looking down at him. His thinning grey hair is a neat line above the pinstripe of his suit jacket collar, there's a sharp crease at the top of the sleeves.

Make him go back down.

'It's all gone too far. I need to—' Perry turns and takes another step up the stairs. Our eyes meet.

Shit.

453

'Francesca!' His eyes almost pop out of his head as he stomps up the rest of the way to the landing. 'What are—?' More footsteps pattering up the stairs. Lucy flies up next to him, breathless. The two of them face me, then Uncle Perry turns accusingly to my sister. 'What is *she* doing here?'

Lucy gapes, clearly at a loss for words.

'How could you?' Fury fills me to my fingertips. 'Your own great-niece. And Caspian. All the other doctors. How *could* you?'

I'm half-expecting some grandly pompous justification but instead Uncle Perry's eyes fill with confusion. 'What on earth are you talking about?'

'You're the most evil person I've ever met. And you can hide all you like behind your stupid religion but you're a coward. You and all the people in PAAUL.'

Perry is slack-jawed. He genuinely looks completely bewildered. 'Have you gone *mad*, Francesca?'

Jesus, he can't even admit to what he's done, even after getting Dex to kidnap Ruby and me and Harry. He's beneath my contempt.

'Where's Dex?' I ask Lucy. 'Has he gone?' I need to know if my uncle is the only one holding us here, because he doesn't seem to have a gun or a knife and whereas Dex is muscular and armed, I reckon Harry and I could easily take Perry between us.

'Dex was *here*?' Perry turns to Lucy too. 'Dex was here *as well*? Dear Lord. Why didn't you sell tickets?'

Confusion floods through me. Surely Perry knows Dex was here.

'He said he was going abroad tonight,' Lucy says. 'Leaving the country forever. A fresh start.'

Perry snorts. 'Like father, like son. Sodding fantasist.'

Still confused, I take a step away from them.

'I'm going to get Ruby and Harry,' I say. My best chance now is to bluff my way out. 'You need to let us go before the police get here. They're on their way, they'll be here any second.'

'The police?' Perry clutches wildly at his forehead. He doesn't sound like the head of anything, let alone a bunch of religious terrorists. 'The *police*?'

'No, er, actually I didn't call them,' Lucy says softly.

I glare at her. What is wrong with her? Can't she see I'm trying to trick Perry? Lucy's lips tremble as she clocks my expression. In the midst of my frustration I feel a surge of guilt. I must remember that Dex has terrorised her, that she's a victim here too. Dex might not have taken her life, but he has ruined it.

'Of course Lucy didn't call the police. And you can't either.' Uncle Perry grabs my arm. I try to shake him off but he's stronger than I expect.

'Get off me!' I growl.

'Please, Francesca.' Lucy's voice wavers. 'We'll get in so much trouble if we talk to the police.'

'I'm not having my reputation shot down in flames over this,' Perry snaps. He tightens his hold on my arm. 'Have you told anyone about ... about what you found in my basement?'

Does he mean the porn? Is he talking about the fact

455

that he's gay? I can't believe it. In fact it would be funny if it wasn't so horrific.

'Are you seriously still worried about people knowing you're gay after all the terrible, terrible things you've done?' I demand. 'Don't you think them finding out you're a murdering terrorist might slightly overshadow your sexual preferences? Anyway, nobody these days *cares* about people being gay.'

I twist and turn, desperate to get out of Perry's grasp, but he holds me fast, that look of confusion back on his face. I glance towards the attic again. Ruby and Harry will be worried sick by now, wondering where I am. I need to let them out and get away and go to the police.

'I don't know what you mean by terrible things or ... or murder and terrorism.' Perry sounds positively injured. 'I'm a victim in all this.'

Unbelievable. Is that really how he sees himself?

'Okay, let's start at the beginning,' I snap. 'When Mum died, instead of covering it up, you should have stood up to Dex. You should have protected Lucy. You were stronger than her, you should have led the way, not done what Dex said.'

'What *Dex* said?' Uncle Perry shakes his head, still gripping my arm. He seems genuinely bewildered. For the first time I hesitate. Have I misunderstood what Lucy told me about Mum's death?

What about PAAUL? Is Perry really behind all the murders?

Suspicion creeps through my mind.

Could Lucy have got that wrong?

Might she even have lied?

'Francesca, please, calm down,' Lucy pleads. She's on my other side now, hands clasped, eyes glistening with emotion.

At the sight of her tears I glare at Perry. Rage overwhelms my suspicions. Of course Lucy hasn't lied. Perry might call himself a victim, but Lucy truly is one.

'See what you've done by letting Dex blackmail you all those years ago? You've allowed him to carry on intimidating Lucy. You've—'

'My dear Francesca,' Perry cuts in, as scathing as I've ever heard him. 'I think you've got the wrong end of the stick.'

'Uncle Perry!' Lucy's voice is like ice. Her head is high, the tears gone from her eyes.

My suspicions rear up again. I doubt everything.

And in that instant I know what Perry is going to say. He lets go of my arm with an exasperated shake of the head.

'It wasn't Dex who blackmailed me,' Uncle Perry snaps. 'It was your sister.'

LUCY

I cross myself. Too often I do this on auto pilot but now I am calling on the saints to protect me; and to Mary, who blessed me with my mission, to give me the words that will show my sister my motives are – and have always been – pure. She's staring at me now as if she's never seen me before.

'You blackmailed Uncle Perry?' Francesca's eyes are wide. '*You*, Lucy? About Mum's death?'

'Indeed she did,' Uncle Perry blusters. 'Called me at my club in hysterics, forced me to do the fake blood test and make up conversations about diabetic faints and lie about the cause of death to you and Jayson and the police so that we could avoid a post mortem. It was a nightmare.'

'*Why?*' Francesca asks me. 'Why would you do that?'

I say nothing. How can I explain? My heart feels like lead. How can I possibly expect my faithless sister to understand?

'I was trying to find a way to bring light out of the darkness of my sins,' I venture at last. 'To make a life lived in love.'

'*What?*' Francesca's forehead is screwed into a series of frown lines. 'What the fuck does that mean? Dex abused you, killed our mother ... and for some warped reason you feel you have to protect him?'

'It's not a warped reason,' I protest. Oh, Dex, how I wish I could explain about you in words Francesca will understand: what you have meant to me, the Godliness of turning the singular evil of your lust-fuelled sin into the greatest of humane and merciful loves.

'Never mind this nonsense,' Uncle Perry snaps. 'I want the film.'

'What film?' Francesca demands.

'That day when I saw Dex and Mummy through the kitchen door I had my phone in my hand ... and I started filming them,' I explain, blushing to remember it. 'I thought ... I know it was naïve, but I thought maybe I could use it to show Mummy later, to make her see how pathetic she was being, how morally confused she was. But then Dex pushed her and she fell down the stairs. And of course I put my phone away at the time, but afterwards I realised I had a record of her actual murder and it felt like God had engineered the whole thing to give me a way of persuading Dex to carry out my mission.'

'Unbelievable,' Francesca breathes.

'Whatever,' Uncle Perry snaps. 'If that film comes out then I'll face a lot of very awkward questions about why I pretended your mother died from a diabetic faint when Dex quite clearly killed her.' He turns to me, glaring. 'I *want* the film. *Now.*'

Francesca is wide-eyed. She glances towards the attic and I know she is thinking of Ruby.

'What about Dex?' she asks. 'You're saying he really had nothing to do with blackmailing Uncle Perry?'

'Oh, yes, Dex was long gone when I arrived,' Perry says with a contemptuous sniff. 'He left it all up to Lucy here.'

'I didn't mind,' I tell them, eager to explain. 'I told Dex to go straight home, that I'd look after him.' I pause, remembering your beautiful face on that day: wild with terror as you clutched at your hair, panic radiating from every pore. 'His watch that he'd just got from Uncle Graham broke when he hit Mummy, then he got blood on it when he touched her head. He was freaking out about it so I told him I'd get rid of it but I didn't. I just called Uncle Perry and while I waited for him I said the Hail Mary over Mummy's body. And I pledged that I'd make something good come out of all the bad, a sacrifice for all our sins.' I close my eyes. I'd been calm then. Serene. Knowing, in the epiphany of that moment, that I had found my purpose ... a way to bring light from all the darkness. 'And I did.' I open my eyes. 'I made everything right.'

'How?' Francesca asks. Her voice is hollow. 'How did you make everything right? Please tell me, because I'm imagining ... just, please, tell me what you did.'

I shake my head. She looks so appalled, has she forgotten where all this started?

'Dex raped me when I was fifteen,' I remind her.

'I know.' A look of deep sorrow passes across my sister's face. 'But—'

460

'*Rape?*' Perry looks appalled. 'Dex *raped* you?'

I sigh, wishing Uncle Perry wasn't here. It's Francesca whose understanding I need.

'And when he raped me he made me pregnant,' I go on, my eyes on hers.

'Okay, but—' Francesca starts.

'That was *Dex*'s baby you aborted?' Uncle Perry's eyes widen.

'Yes.' I draw myself up. 'It was his fault I got pregnant and his fault I got pushed into that abortion and his responsibility to make amends.' I hesitate, thinking how I've carried the pain of your sin ever since ... your first murder, the slaughter of my innocence in that rape, then your second: the killing of my baby. 'Do you understand? When I saw him kill Mum it was the third murder, the third denial of life and hope. But as I stood there I ... I realised how I could get him to make up for what he'd done to me, how together we could bring light out of the darkness of our sins.'

Francesca stares at me, still clearly confused. I wait to see the soft glow of understanding dawn on her face. Our future depends on it. Surely, even without a faith, knowing everything as she now does, she will at least see the logic and the beauty of my mission.

But instead, her eyes fill with horror.

FRAN

'That year's ...' I remember what she said just now about organising the murders to coincide with the September anniversary of when her baby would have been born.

I face Lucy, feeling like my legs are about to buckle. The silence between us is the blackest of my life.

'It was *you*,' I gasp, the terrible truth finally settling inside me. '*You* were behind Caspian's death ... and all the other doctors'. Not PAAUL. Not Perry. *You*.'

The second-floor landing, the most humdrum place on earth, spins like a vision of hell around me.

'You got Dex to carry out all those murders.' Bile rises into my throat. All along I've been seeing conspiracies and organised campaigns. The whole time Harry and I were searching for links with PAAUL and, in the end, PAAUL had nothing to do with it.

It was just Lucy.

I glance up at the attic. For the first time since she went missing I am glad Ruby isn't by my side. I never want her to know any of this.

'I was twenty-two weeks pregnant when I had the abortion. Dex and I ... we murdered my baby.' Lucy's voice is high and anxious, her fingers twist around each other just like earlier, but I'm no longer buying her victim act. She is a monster, as bad in her way as Dex. Worse, maybe. 'But I was barely more than a baby myself. If the doctors had refused ... if the law had been different.' She looks at me, her eyes sorrowful. 'If I'd had a sister who knew right from wrong.'

'Oh, Lucy.' A tight band is around my heart: fear and pain, squeezing, constricting me.

Out of the corner of my eye I can see Perry leaning against the doorframe of the office. The look of shock on his face tells me he didn't know any of this.

'So it was revenge?' I ask, my voice shaking with emotion.

'Justice, not revenge. Every September since Mummy passed, on the anniversary of when the baby should have been born.'

'What?' I can't believe what she's saying. 'That's ... Caspian was my husband and ... and you love me, you adore my children. How could you take away their father like that?'

'Caspian's influence prevented you from seeing that you'd made a terrible mistake over my abortion,' Lucy snaps. 'It was hard for me to take him out of our lives, but it was a necessary sacrifice, better for you in the long run.'

'No.' I'm lost, unable to take in what she's saying. 'You really believe that?'

'I originally chose a different doctor, but Caspian's

name kept coming up in my prayers, so it was God's choice in the end. Caspian had to be that year's sacrifice.'

'That year's . . .' I remember what she said just now about organising the murders to coincide with the September anniversary of when her baby would have been born.

'What about Simon Pinner? He was killed *this* month. And Harry isn't even a doctor.'

'Simon put himself in the picture by turning up at Caspian's memorial,' Lucy says coolly. 'And Harry got too involved, too curious. As soon as I realised who he really was, I knew he would have to go. I got Dex to follow him, waiting for the right moment, but once we realised he was heading for the storage locker that was it. I ordered Dex to kill him and retrieve the watch. Don't you see, Fran? It's a just war. And killing is justified in a just war.'

'What I see is an insanely twisted belief that you are entitled to murder any doctor who carries out an abortion and any journalist who tries to investigate their death – and all because *you* had a termination fifteen years ago.' My voice sounds flat to my ears.

'I was abused into murdering my own baby,' Lucy says, her voice rising. 'Abused by everyone involved.'

Including you are the words she leaves unspoken.

We stare at each other. 'You said the termination was what you wanted.' My breath hitches in my throat. 'I would have supported *whatever* you chose.'

Lucy shakes her head. 'There shouldn't have been a choice.'

Uncle Perry crosses himself. I have no idea why. And

I'm filled with a new fury. This is Catholicism's fault. If it wasn't for the stupid religion ...

Except ... I think of Dad and all his work for the prison rehabilitation charity and Jacqueline and all the positive causes she supports and meek Auntie Sheila with her devotion to mass and her own charity work. Even weak, vain Uncle Perry has surely done good things through his faith.

'So Perry didn't have anything to do with killing Caspian?' I breathe. 'You made all that stuff up about him running PAAUL? Killing the abortion doctors?'

'Lucy?' Perry finally releases his grip on my arm. 'What is Fran talking about?'

Ignoring him, my sister nods. 'I made it up,' she says. 'I had to.'

'And ... and ... those cipher papers with the names, that you claimed you found in Perry's safe? They were *yours*?' I ask.

'Yes, they were how I told Dex who was next ... who needed to be sacrificed,' Lucy says. She sounds unbelievably matter-of-fact. 'I put the names in code so Dex would have to physically handle the papers. I wanted his fingerprints all over them, that's why I kept them. Of course they're ruined now. All smudged with *your* fingerprints.'

My jaw drops. It's all so ... so calculated.

'You did all this? You *killed* people?' Perry asks, looking as shocked as I feel. 'And you pinned it all on me?'

'And on PAAUL,' Lucy explains. 'Everyone seemed to think that if the deaths of the abortion doctors were connected to each other, then some sort of organisation must be behind it. I just played along. I did everything I could to make my mission a success.'

'This is all really just *you*?' I still can't believe it. 'What about the internet rumours about Dad and Uncle Perry and Lanagh?'

'They were just rumours,' Lucy explains, as if it's obvious. 'They started because Dad got Uncle Perry to organise those reports on PAAUL and when he sent undercover investigators into PAAUL some people thought he was infiltrating it, intending to take over, using Lanagh as a base. The rumours built from there. It's ironic really. I helped Uncle Perry file all the paper-work at Lanagh, which is how I got to read the reports he and Dad made on how PAAUL operated in the US.'

She glances at our uncle. Ashen-faced, he gives a nod.

'Reading those reports,' Lucy goes on, 'made me realise that if I didn't want to be caught I needed to operate in a completely different way: a variety of weapons, of locations ...'

I gawp at her. She sounds so calm and collected, like she's talking about how she organised a success-ful church fete rather than a series of cold-blooded murders.

'Did Uncle Graham know any of this?' I asked. 'He was so insistent Dad was involved.'

'I'm sure he was,' Uncle Perry says bitterly. 'Any chance to stick the knife in.'

'Or Auntie Sheila?' I go on. 'She was so very adamant that Dad *wasn't* involved.'

'All Uncle Graham knew was what you'd told Auntie Sheila,' Lucy explains. 'Sheila confided in him like she always does, because she was upset. Daddy inspires strong feelings in people. Sheila adores him. Graham hates him. That's why he wanted you to think all those lies about Daddy on the internet were true. Honestly, Francesca. None of them knew anything about my mission. Not Daddy or Jacqueline or Graham or Sheila.'

'Or me,' Perry adds.

'Just you.' The words are almost too brutal to say but I say them anyway. 'You and Dex.'

Lucy makes a disdainful face. 'Dex is *such* an idiot. He made a terrible fuss about working for me, in spite of everything he'd done to me and to poor Mummy.'

'You mean he didn't want to kill all those doctors? He didn't want to kill Caspian?' I ask. Somehow this makes the whole thing even worse.

'Of course not. And he was freaking out over killing Harry too, so soon after Simon Pinner . . . he said it was too much; he was delaying, prevaricating.' She curls her lip. 'Dex is *so* weak. He's never understood what I was trying to do at all,' Lucy says. 'But I told him today, like I've told him many times before, that if he didn't carry out my mission, I'd show everyone the proof that he killed Mummy. Sometimes you have to be tough with people, like when I sent you those texts . . . I needed you to believe Ruby and Rufus were in danger, to stop you running to the police and ruining everything.'

'It was *you* texting?'

'Yes,' Lucy admits proudly. 'And I put a bug in your

467

phone as well. That's how I could hear everything you were saying in the café.'

I shake my head. I can't believe how conniving, how manipulative she is. My supposedly fragile sister ... quick-thinking and ruthless as a shark.

'Talking of the proof,' Perry snaps, 'it's time to hand it over. I've waited long enough. I want the film *and* the watch. Both of them link Dex to your mother's murder, which incriminates me.'

I stare at him, appalled by his self-interest.

'You don't need to worry about the watch, Dex has it,' Lucy explains. 'I took it off him earlier when he was distracted, so I could show Francesca. But Dex took it back before he left. There's no way he'll want anyone else to know about it. I imagine he's destroyed it already.'

'What about the film?' Perry asks, his face screwed up with anxiety. 'I really need that film.'

My scorn for him deepens. He has just heard, like I have, a litany of blackmail and betrayal and murder committed by his niece and facilitated by his own cowardice. And all he cares about is covering his own back.

'You can take the film so long as you promise to destroy it too,' Lucy says. 'I don't want Daddy to see how Mummy really died.'

'I can promise you that is the last thing I want either,' Perry says, grim-faced.

'So where is it?'

Lucy bows her head. 'It's in my bedroom.' She sighs. 'Until yesterday I stored all three bits of evidence against Dex – the film, the watch and the papers with the names – in separate places. For security. I told Dex I'd left instructions with people to release them if anything happened to me. Of course I hadn't, but Dex believed it. He still thinks that the film is safe somewhere and will come out if he kills me. Like I said, he's an idiot. Gorgeous, I guess, but still an idiot.'

Unbelievable.

It's like Lucy is a different person. I shiver. I can't think about what my sister has done any longer. 'I'm going to get Ruby and Harry,' I say.

'No,' Lucy says.

'It's over,' I tell her. 'We know the truth now. It's over.'

Lucy draws Dex's gun from her pocket. I stare in disbelief. Fear creeps through me. I'm afraid to my bones.

Afraid of a person I never dreamed would hurt me.

'I'm getting the film for you,' she says to Uncle Perry. 'Whatever you do, don't let Francesca make a phone call.' She hands him the gun and scurries away, flying down the stairs to the first floor.

Perry looks as shocked as I am, but he holds the gun firmly. He's still blocking the doorway to the office and the only phone on this floor.

'I'm going to let Ruby and Harry out,' I say, turning towards the attic door.

'No,' Perry says. But he doesn't stop me as I go up the steps. 'I didn't know about . . . what Lucy's done,' he babbles after me. 'Whatever happens next, Francesca, it can't come out that I covered up your mother's true cause of death. It just can't. I'd go to jail.'

'Right.' All these people dead and he's still only

thinking about himself. What a mean-minded, selfish coward. I don't believe he will shoot me. The thought gives me courage. I hurry up to the attic door and lift my hand to draw back the bolts.

'No!' Perry shouts.

I spin around, suddenly terrified that he's about to pull the trigger after all. But he's not looking at me. He's staring down the stairs. I follow his gaze. A line of flames flickers across the bottom step. I freeze as my brain catches up with my eyes.

Lucy has set the stairs on fire.

As the realisation hits me, a high-pitched smoke alarm screams. I turn to the attic door, fumbling with the top bolt. On the other side I hear Harry calling Ruby's name, telling her to stand back.

'Oh, dear Lord, she's trying to kill us,' Perry gasps. There's a thud as he drops the gun. I don't turn around. All my focus is on the door. I wrench back the top bolt and crouch down to deal with the one at the bottom. My hand slides off the metal, I can't get a grip. The smoke alarm screeches. My heart races. I force the bolt back at last and fling open the door.

Harry is right there, a candlestick in his raised arm. He sees me and drops the weapon, a look of relief on his face. I peer into the gloom. Where is Ruby?

And she's running towards me, hurling herself into my arms. I cling to her, clutching her tight. Lucy was once this little, this innocent. I give myself a second to hold her, then put her down. 'Come on.' I reach for her hand and she slips it into mine.

'What kept you?' Harry's tone is carefully light but his face is wreathed with worry. 'I heard some of your conversation but—'

'Lucy.' My voice cracks. 'It was Lucy, the whole thing . . . Come on, we need to hurry.'

There's no sign of Perry on the landing though the gun is still on the floor. Hope flickers inside me. With a bit of luck we should be able to get past the small fire on the stairs and get out of the house.

'Fran!' The urgency in Harry's voice spins me round.

My jaw drops. Because the line of flames on the bottom step is now hidden by wreaths of thick grey smoke that pour up the stairs towards us. Ruby coughs.

We are trapped up here.

'Mummy?' Ruby's wavering voice rises in fear, barely audible above the alarm.

'It's going to be all right,' I reassure her. But in reality I don't see how it can possibly be all right. There's no way Harry and Ruby would be able to climb out onto the roof like I did and, anyway, we wouldn't necessarily be safe from the fire out there. No. Our only way out is down the stairs and it's completely blocked.

'Okay.' Harry clutches his forehead. 'Where's the nearest phone?'

Of course. I turn and dart into the office. I snatch up the landline on the desk. No dialling tone. I press the '9' button. Again. Nothing. Smoke swirls around my feet. The alarm screeches.

Ruby and Harry stand on either side of me as I try the phone a third time.

'There's no dial tone,' I shriek. 'Why doesn't it work?'

'That was me,' Harry groans, clapping his hand over his forehead. 'I tried to call the police when we were coming through the hall, remember? But Lucy was talking on the line so I put the receiver on the table instead of the base.'

'Oh my God.' We look at each other. The landing outside the office is already swirling with trails of smoke. We surely only have minutes before we suffocate in the fumes. 'What are we going to do?' I ask.

Harry storms over to the window, still open from where I crawled in earlier. He peers out, then slumps as he sees what I already know is there – a sheer drop down to the pavement below.

'Help!' he yells out of the window.

'Help!' I hurry over and join him. 'Help! Fire!'

A couple passing on the street below stop and look up at us.

'Fire!' I yell again.

'Call the fire brigade!' Harry shouts.

'We're trapped,' I yell.

The couple both nod. The woman takes out a phone. Harry pulls his head back inside. More smoke snakes into the room as the alarm stops. Ruby clings to my waist, trembling. I pull her over to the window.

'Mummy, what's going to happen?'

'We're going to be fine,' I insist. 'Those people will call for the fire service and they will get us out.'

I meet Harry's gaze. Even if the fire brigade gets here within the next few minutes, we could still suffocate from the toxic fumes now trailing across the office. Especially Ruby. She's only nine. Her lungs are smaller. She's already coughing. I draw her closer to me.

Harry nods, understanding. 'What about the other rooms on this floor?' he asks. 'Could we get out through those?'

I shake my head. 'No, it's all sheer drops, except . . . wait!' I suck in my breath, heart pounding with sudden hope. 'The bathroom opposite! There's a balcony on the floor below directly underneath.'

Harry is already tearing out of the door. Gripping Ruby's hand, I follow him across the landing. The smoke is unbelievably thick out here. How on earth has the fire spread so fast? Ruby's coughs sound like they'll tear her lungs in two. My own throat is sandpaper-sore even though I'm trying to keep my breaths shallow. We race into the bathroom. I slam the door shut on the smoke while Harry wrestles with the window.

'It's locked.' He turns, eyes wild. 'Where's the key?'

'No idea.' I gasp, an idea jumping into my head. 'What about the gun? The glass is reinforced, but we could shoot the window lock.'

Clenching his jaw, Harry rushes outside to the landing. Ruby is bent double, still coughing. 'My head hurts,' she whimpers. 'It's burning in my chest.'

Panic rises inside me. After everything that's happened tonight I won't . . . I *can't* lose Ruby just as I've got her back.

'Come here.' I grab the hand towel from the rail,

run some water over it and tie it around Ruby's face. 'Breathe in as little as possible, okay?'

She nods as Harry races back in, shutting the door behind him again. He motions Ruby and I away from the window, then takes aim at the window lock. I cover Ruby's ears as he pulls the trigger.

But I can barely hear the empty click of the gun.

'What the . . .?' Harry examines the weapon, then turns to me in terror and frustration. 'It's not real. It's a replica.'

Shit. Shit. Shit.

What on earth are we going to do now? Harry and I stare at each other. Smoke wisps around us, acrid and grey.

'Those people outside saw us,' I say. 'They'll have called the fire brigade. It's probably on its way right now.'

'How long d'you think it'll take?' Harry asks. He's coughing almost as badly as Ruby now.

'Maybe ten minutes?' I say, the smoke tightening my throat. It feels hoarse to speak. The smoke alarm is still blaring.

Harry shakes his head. He looks down at Ruby. And I know exactly what he is thinking.

Ruby doesn't have ten minutes. Inhaling the poisonous clouds that swirl around us will kill her long before that.

'We have to go down,' he says.

'But the fire?' I gulp.

'We have to try and get past it,' he says. 'Maybe it

hasn't spread past the stairs yet.' He indicates Ruby, who clings to me with one hand as she clutches the damp towel to her mouth with the other. She's making horrible wheezing sounds, her face a terrifying shade of grey. 'Put her on my back,' he says. 'And stay right behind us.'

There's no time to discuss it. He turns and I hoist Ruby onto his back. She starts to pull the towel away, to try and speak, but I fasten it and press her against Harry's shoulders.

'Hold on tight,' I order. 'Keep your eyes closed and try not to breathe.' Ruby obediently wraps herself around Harry like a monkey.

He hitches her up with his hands, wincing with agony at the pressure on the deep cut on his skin. 'We can do this,' he says.

I nod.

He tears out of the bathroom. I take a deep breath and follow right behind, my hand on Ruby's back. The smoke on the landing is dense now. The stairs are barely visible. Harry feels his way towards them. I have to let go of Ruby in order to find the bannister. I lose them both on the stairs. My eyes sting as I inch my way down. A low fire flickers through the smoke. Harry's right. It's still passable. My chest feels tight, like I can't breathe. I jump over the flames, the heat licks at my legs but I'm through.

We're on the first-floor landing. Harry is just ahead of me, Ruby on his back, her face buried in his neck. They reach the top of the flight of stairs down to the ground floor. Smoke billows all around us. I stumble, my feet catching against something solid. I look down as the dense mist parts for a second. It's Uncle Perry, his pin-striped leg bent awkwardly underneath him. Coughing, I bend down and reach for his neck, his wrist. There's no pulse.

He's gone.

My fingers trail over his clenched fist. A small USB stick is clutched in his hand. This must be the film that shows Dex killed Mum. Numb, I take it then hurry down the stairs to the ground floor.

Thank goodness, the air is definitely clearer here. Harry is already at the front door. Ruby has slumped sideways on his back. My stomach lurches into my mouth. Has she fainted? Is she unconscious? I pelt after them.

And then something out of the corner of my eye catches my attention. It's the reflection of flames in the living room mirror. Has Lucy set another fire here? I glance inside the room and what I see will stay with me to my dying day.

My sister stands in the middle of the room, arms outstretched. Flames radiate from her chest and back and hair.

'Hail Mary, full of grace. Our Lord is with thee.'

'Lucy!' I scream.

She sees me and closes her eyes. 'Blessed art thou among women, and blessed is the fruit of thy womb, Jesus. Holy Mary, Mother of God, pray for us sinners, now and at the hour of our death. Amen.'

'Fran!' Harry is on the doorstep, Ruby in his arms. 'Come *on*!'

I stare at Lucy one last time. Her whole body consumed by fire. As she crumples to the ground I turn away. I try to take a step to the doorway and the outside world and the cool, fresh, night air.

But before I can move a huge gust of smoke envelops me. Giddy, I stumble. Sickness in my stomach. And I am falling, falling, the world dissolving around me.

'Fran? Fran?' Harry's hoarse whisper filters through the fug in my brain. My eyes flicker open. I feel heavy, like lead. The lights are bright, outside flashes blue. A blur of uniform and grey hair moves in front of me. A light shines in my eyes. A calm voice murmurs reassurances. I'm in an ambulance. It's not moving. Harry's face appears above mine: covered in grime, relief in his eyes.

'I thought you were ...' He leans closer. 'Are you okay?'

'I think so.' My voice is as hoarse as his. 'Where's Ruby?'

'The first ambulance took her. They wouldn't let me go with her but the paramedic was nice, she was smiling when they shut the—'

'Is she all right?' I struggle onto my elbows.

'I think so.' Harry wipes a grimy hand across his face. 'She was conscious, alert. But she was coughing a lot. They wanted to check her over properly. I promised her I'd make sure you came straight after her.'

I clutch his arm. 'Did you tell them about the Rohypnol?'

'Yes,' he says, 'and I told them and the police Dex kidnapped her and gave it to her *and* that he admitted to murder. They promised they'd keep Ruby safe. And the police are looking for Dex now.'

'Good,' I say. An image of us charging through the fire and smoke ... and of Lucy, her whole upper body on fire, flashes into my head. 'What about ...?' I gulp. 'What about everything else?'

'I didn't say anything about Lucy and all the doctors who died,' Harry says. Our eyes meet. 'I promised I'd let you decide.'

I nod.

'They found a USB stick in your hand,' he goes on. 'The police took it. They were asking me about it ...'

'It shows Dex killed Mum.' I lie back on the hard board in the ambulance, too dizzy to speak further. Outside sounds chaotic, but in here all is quiet. The grey-haired paramedic jumps in and I open my mouth to tell him to take me wherever Ruby is, but before I can speak Harry is already speaking, making the same request. The ambulance engine starts. An oxygen mask is slipped over my face and, suddenly exhausted, I close my eyes.

It's dark when I wake up. I'm in a strange room: cream blinds drawn down a small window, the smell of disinfectant in the air. I turn my head. Everything feels heavy and sore. My throat is tight. There's a drip beside me, one end fastened in my arm.

I'm in hospital.

With a terrifying jolt I remember the fire: Lucy's burning body, Uncle Perry on the landing. Ruby's arms and legs wound around Harry's back.

Where is Ruby? Is she all right?

I turn further. A shadowy figure sits, head bowed, in a chair by the bed.

'Dad?' The word comes out as a whisper.

He looks up. Tears glint on his cheeks. I have never seen my father cry before.

'How do you feel?' he asks.

'Okay, I think.' My voice is hoarse. 'Sore.'

He nods. 'The doctors have run every test. They thought they might have to intubate but ... they say you've been lucky ... you're going to be fine.'

'Ruby?' I sit up. 'Can I see her?'

'She's okay. She's asleep in the paediatric ward upstairs.'

I try to swing my legs out of the bed but they are too heavy. I grunt, frustrated.

Dad leans forward. 'Easy. I was just in with her, she's going to be fine too. On a drip like you.'

'I want to see her.' I'm still struggling to raise myself.

'Okay, okay. Wait there.' With a tsk, Dad goes to the door and calls a nurse. She comes in, fusses over me for a few minutes, then promises she'll organise a wheelchair so I can go up to see Ruby.

The nurse bustles off. Relieved, I lie back. The exertion has left me breathless. Dad eyes me anxiously.

'They want to keep you all in overnight for

observation. Ayesha's got Rufus.' Dad's mouth trembles. 'But ... but oh, my darling, Lucy and Perry ... in the fire ...'

He shakes his head, a gesture of helplessness.

'I know,' I say. 'Dad, I'm so sorry.' A deep sob wells inside me. Although I'm relieved I don't have to break the news to my father that his daughter and brother are gone, I can't bear to see the agony in his eyes.

It doesn't feel real. I roll the words in my head: Lucy is dead, my sister, my shadow. There's no one I've fought with harder or protected more fiercely. I can't get my mind to bend around everything I found out about her tonight: what she did. Why she did it. Who she really was.

The fact that she has gone.

'Is Harry here? Is he all right?'

'Yes,' Dad says, a sharp edge to his voice. 'Things he told us ... they apparently back up that film you were holding.'

I jerk upright. I'd forgotten all about the film. 'Did you see it?'

'No, but I understand from Harry it shows Dex and ... your mother ... how she really died.' Dad folds his arms. 'They've arrested Dex at the airport.'

I nod. I know this should be good news. But I feel numb.

'What about the house?' I ask. It's easier to talk about bricks and mortar.

Dad waves his hand as if it hardly counts. Which of course it doesn't. 'Destroyed,' he says dully.

'I'm so sorry,' I say again. 'About everything.'

Adjusting to the dim light, I can see that Dad's skin is grey and lined, as if he's aged ten years overnight.

'I can't believe it . . .' he says. 'What Dex did . . . your mother . . . Caspian . . . and setting the house on fire with all of you inside.'

'That wasn't Dex,' I say.

'Thank goodness you and Ruby made it out . . .' Dad trails off, not listening. He shakes his head, lost in his own misery. 'What was Perry doing there? I can't understand why he lied about your mother's death. And . . . and my poor, precious, fragile Lucy . . . why would Dex want to hurt her?'

I frown. Doesn't Dad know? Doesn't he realise that Lucy was behind everything? That it's been Lucy all along?

Harry's words in the ambulance come back to me:

I didn't say anything about Lucy and all the doctors who died or your mum's murder . . . I promised I'd let you decide.

I feel sick. Does that mean I have to tell Dad that his own daughter was behind a horrific series of murders? How can I add to his grief? My guts churn and I watch him, his face buried in his hands.

'Oh, Dad.'

He looks up. 'I've spoken to Graham and Sheila. They're very upset at what Dex has done, terribly concerned for you and Ruby. Well . . . Sheila is. She's in pieces over the whole thing. Jacqueline's with her right now and one of the priests.' He pauses. 'Graham is furious with me, of course. Told me that if Dex has gone off the rails it's entirely my fault.'

'It isn't, Dad,' I say, a lump in my throat. He looks so broken, so miserable.

'You'd think that losing one brother might make him value his relationship with the other a bit more,' Dad muses. 'But Graham's too full of bitterness ... I can't take it all in ...' He trails off.

Lucy dead. Dex arrested. Murderers. My childhood torn apart.

My father devastated.

'We have to speak to the police,' I say timidly, unable to bring myself to tell him the truth.

'About the fire?' He nods, still looking dazed. 'Do you know exactly how it started? Did you see what Dex did?'

I gulp. Now he's asking, I can't lie. 'It wasn't Dex,' I say. 'That is, he drugged me and Harry and Ruby and kept us tied up, but he didn't try to kill us.'

He stares at me. 'What are you saying?'

There's a long, terrible pause.

'It was Lucy.' My voice cracks. 'She set the fire. She wanted to die in it herself,' I say, realising as I speak that this must, indeed, have been Lucy's plan from the start.

'No.' Dad covers his eyes with his hand.

'It goes back to before Mum,' I say gently, leaning against my pillows. I'm starting to feel sick from the effort of talking, but I have to get this out. I have to tell him. 'It goes back to when Lucy got pregnant.'

'What?' Dad frowns as I tell him everything I have

found out, a brief, fact-based version. It takes just a couple of minutes. His eyes widen as I speak. 'No ... no ...' he keeps saying. 'No, it can't be true.'

'So Lucy blackmailed Uncle Perry to cover up that Dex killed Mum, then later blackmailed Dex himself to carry out these ... revenge killings on abortion doctors. She believed it was all justified because of her rape and ... and abortion.'

Dad slumps back in his chair, his head in his hands. Am I a terrible daughter for having added to his pain? Should I have kept quiet?

'I had no idea,' he whispers. 'I can't believe Perry would have kept the truth about your mother's death from me ... I suspected he might be gay years ago, but he always denied it so strongly and ... and as for Lucy.' He shakes his head.

The door opens and I look up, hoping for a wheelchair that will ferry me up to Ruby. Instead, Harry walks in. My heart skips a beat to see him. He looks exhausted, his jumper grimy with smoke and his hand enveloped in a thick bandage. Otherwise it's the same magnetic presence, the same kind eyes, full of life. He glances at Dad, who hasn't looked up, then comes over and kisses my forehead.

'You're awake.' He smiles.

'Are you okay?' I clutch his hand, wanting to be sure.

'I'm fine and I just saw Ruby. She's fine too. Asleep.' He hesitates, glancing at Dad again. 'The police want to question us. The doctors put them off earlier but they're asking again and we ... we need to talk to them now. They have a fire. Two bodies ...' He looks down.

On the other side of my bed, Dad sighs heavily.

'As soon as I've seen Ruby,' I say. 'Then we'll talk to them.' I swing my legs off the bed. They still feel like lead, but I already feel better than I did a few minutes ago. I test my weight, half standing, half leaning on Harry. Maybe I don't need to wait for the wheelchair after all. 'Let's go to Ruby, I just want to see she's okay, still sleeping. Then we can tell the police everything.'

Harry puts his arm around my waist, helping me shuffle. I have more strength than I thought. I take a proper step to the door.

'Wait.' Dad stands up, his tall bulky presence filling the room. He scowls at Harry, then turns to me, his gaze intense. 'What good would ... I mean, think of their memories ... Perry and Lucy ... they weren't well, they needed help but ... it was *Dex* who did the killings. I can't see how telling the world what—'

'Oh, Dad.' I can't bear this. 'Dex was weak and stupid. Lucy used *him*. Not the other way around.' I hesitate. 'She used us all.'

'No,' he says. 'I don't ... I *won't* believe she knew what she was doing.'

I don't know what to say to him. Perhaps if I hadn't heard Lucy's confession I wouldn't believe it myself. Harry still has his arm around my shoulder. He squeezes my arm, letting me know he is there. Outside a thin grey light creeps across the sky.

'Please, sweetheart.' Dad and I stare at each other. 'It's not too late. Not for Lucy's memory. She wasn't involved in your mother's death. That was all Dex.

The film proves it. And no one needs to know she was caught up in the abortion doctor murders. The police think they're random att—'

'Lucy wasn't "caught up" in anything. It was her idea,' I protest. 'She got Dex to kill my husband, we can't just sweep that under the carpet.'

'We can tell the police Dex forced her to keep quiet about what she knew and that he made her set the fire, even that he bullied her into killing herself ... there's no actual evidence against her so—'

'No,' I say. 'No keeping quiet. Not any more.'

'For fuck's sake.' Dad's fist slams against the wall beside him.

I jump.

Harry draws me closer. 'That's enough.'

'Stay out of this,' Dad orders. He turns to me again, clearly struggling to keep his temper in check. 'I'm begging you, Fran. For the sake of the family,' he pleads. 'To save an investigation that will put you through all sorts of fresh hell.'

I hesitate. Harry's eyes meet mine.

'As I promised,' he says. 'We'll do whatever you want.'

I look from my father to Harry. It's a straight choice: Harry and the future and a whole series of hurtful, hard truths. Or family and lies and never moving on from the past.

'The people who died and the people who loved them deserve the truth,' I say.

'And Lucy deserves your compassion,' Dad snaps.

'I won't lie for her, Dad. I can't.' How ironic that, after all the arguments about morality I have had with my father, this should be where we end up.

A long moment passes. Then, without a word, Dad gets up and walks away. Harry and I stand in silence. I have never felt more alone in my life. For a second I contemplate running after my father, agreeing to what he wants, because if I don't it will change our relationship forever. It may even destroy it.

And then Harry links his fingers through mine and the warmth of his hand is like a lifeline, bringing me energy and strength and hope. Dad will come round. He has to. I'm all he has left – me and Rufus and Ruby.

I take a deep breath. 'I want to see Ruby, then the police.'

'Are you sure?' Harry asks.

'Yes,' I say. And we walk to the door, to face the truth together.

ACKNOWLEDGEMENTS

I'm very grateful to the real Chris Smart for a suggestion that gave me the first seed of an idea for this book.

Thanks also to my agent Sarah Ballard and my editor Jo Dickenson, for all their help and, particularly, their excellent advice on the first draft. Ditto to my fellow writers Lou Kuenzler, Moira Young, Gaby Halberstam, Melanie Edge and Julie Mackenzie for their consistently brilliant feedback.

And, as always, thank you to Eoin, who heard and encouraged me every step of the way.

Read on for an extract from
Sophie McKenzie's
chilling bestseller,

CLOSE MY EYES

CHAPTER ONE

I'm late.

I hate being late.

I'm supposed to meet Art at 5 p.m. and it's already quarter to. I race down the corridor to the staff room. I can't remember the new code for the door, so have to wait outside until another teacher lets me through. I shove my spare photocopies in my pigeonhole then deposit my register in the box. As I reach the exit, Sami, the head of Humanities, reminds me that tomorrow morning's class is cancelled due to building repairs. I make a mental note then fly out of the Institute doors and half run, half jog along Great Queen Street to Kingsway. It's grey and gloomy, the clouds swollen with rain. There are no cabs. I should get the tube to Oxford Circus, but since 7/7 I avoid using the underground when possible. Anyway, I've always preferred the bus. Art hates buses. Too slow.

I charge round the corner to the bus stop, negotiating several uneven pavements and a swarm of Italian teenagers as I run.

Good, I can see a number 8 trundling towards me along High Holborn. That'll take me to John Lewis. I can race up to Harley Street from there.

Inside the bus I press my Oyster card against the pad and lean with relief against a post. The woman next to me – young, straggly haired – is wrestling with a baby in a buggy.

'Sit down, for fuck's sake,' she hisses under her breath. There's so much anger in her voice I have to turn away and move up the bus.

I arrive at the clinic at quarter past five. Art is waiting by the door. I see him seconds before he sees me – smart and suave in his suit. It's dark grey, Paul Smith – his favourite. Stylish and simple, he wears it, as usual, with a plain open-necked shirt and no tie. Art looks good in those kind of clothes. He always has. He turns and sees me. He's tired. And irritated. I can see it in the way he raises an eyebrow as I walk up.

'Sorry I'm late.' I raise my face and he kisses me. A light, swift brush of the lips.

'It's fine,' Art says.

Of course the truth is that I'm not really sorry and he isn't really fine. The truth is that I don't want to be here and Art knows it.

I follow Art inside. He shrugs off his jacket as we cross the entrance hall. The shirt he's wearing has a tiny nick on the inside of the collar. You can't see it but I know it's there, just as I know Art is pissed off with me from the way his arms hang stiffly at his sides. I should feel guilty. After all, I'm late and Art's time is precious. And I'm aware that this is hard for him as well as for me.

Art stops as we reach the waiting-room door. He turns to me with a smile, clearly making a huge effort to overcome his mood.

'Mr Tamansini was here a minute ago. He's very pleased we're back.'

'You've spoken to him?' I'm surprised; the consultants rarely leave their rooms during appointments.

'He just happened to be in reception when I arrived.' Art takes my hand and leads me into the waiting room. It's classic Harley Street: a row of stiff chintz armchairs and a matching couch. A fireplace with dried flowers on the mantelpiece and a terrible piece of modern art above. Certificates, licences and awards are positioned in glass frames all around the walls. I catch sight of my reflection in the mirror in the corner. My jumper is creased andnmy hair looks like it hasn't been brushed for a week. It really needs cutting: the fringe is in my eyes and the ends are split and dry and curling shapelessly onto my shoulders. Before Beth, I had highlights and a trim every couple of months. I straighten my jumper and smooth out my hair. My eyes shine bright blue against the pink of my cheeks, flushed from running up the road. I used to go to classes at the gym as well. Now I never seem to have the energy.

'He's on time, but they sent the next couple in ahead of us as you weren't here.' Art's tone is only faintly accusatory.

I nod again. Art runs his hand up my arm.

'Are you okay? How was your class?'

I look at him properly. His face is still so boyish, despite the fact he turned forty last week. I don't know whether it's the soft curve of his jaw or the dimple in his chin or the fact that his eyes are so big and eager. I stroke his cheek. The skin is rough under my fingertips. Art has to shave twice a day but I have always liked the shadow on his face. It gives him a rougher, sexier edge.

'The class was fine.' My throat tightens. I *so* don't want to be here. 'I'm really sorry I was late. It's just ... being here again.'

'I know.' Art puts his arm around me and pulls me against

his chest. I bury my face against his neck, squeezing my eyes tight against the tears I don't want to let out.

'It's going to work this time, I know it is. It's our turn, Gen.'

Art checks his watch. He's had it years and the face is scratched and worn. It's the watch I gave him – my first present to him on his birthday, three months after we met. That evening Art let me buy him dinner for the first time; I'd insisted, seeing as it was his birthday. It was a mild, spring evening – the first warm night after what felt like months of winter and, after dinner, we'd walked along the Embankment and across Waterloo Bridge to the South Bank. Art told me about his plans for Loxley Benson ... how all his life he'd been searching for something to believe in, something worthwhile to put his energies into, something to drive towards.

'And your business means all that?' I'd asked.

Art had taken my hand and told me 'no', that *I* was what he'd been looking for, that our relationship was what he wanted more than anything.

That evening was the first time he told me he loved me.

I pull away now and wipe under my eyes as discreetly as possible. Quite apart from Art, there are three other couples in the waiting room and I don't want them to see. I sit down and close my eyes, my hands folded in my lap. I focus on my breathing, trying to take my mind away from the turmoil raging through my head.

Art still loves me. I know he does. If he didn't, he wouldn't have stayed with me through the long, terrible year after Beth. Not to mention the six failed IVF attempts since.

But sometimes I wonder if he really listens to me. I've tried to explain how tired I get of these visits to the clinic. The highs and lows of IVF. It's been nearly a year since our last attempt. Back then I insisted on a break and Mr Tam – as he's known on the online infertility forums – supported me. Art agreed – we both hoped I'd get pregnant naturally. There's really no reason why I shouldn't – at least not one that anyone's found. Just as there's no reason to explain why every single attempt at IVF has failed to produce a pregnancy.

Art's been angling for me to undergo more treatment for the past few months. He even made this appointment for us. But I can't bear the thought of another round, and the physical side effects and psychological battering it will bring. I've been there too many times: starting a cycle, wasting an opportunity to start one because you're away, going to the clinic every day to be tested, taking the drugs at specific times on specific days – all only to find your follicles aren't big enough or plentiful enough, or else that the embryos don't survive. Then resting a cycle or two, obsessed with when you ovulate, when you menstruate, before you start again. And on and on. And none of it, none of any of it, can ever bring her back.

Beth. My baby who was born dead.

I want to tell Art all this, but that means talking about Beth and she's shut up in my head in a safe place along with the pain and the grief and I don't want to go in there and start raking it all up again.

'Mr and Mrs Loxley?'

Art leaps to his feet. The nurse smiles at him. It's hard not to smile at Art. Even before he appeared on *The Trials* on TV people smiled at him. All that boyish charm and energy. I'm sure that's half the secret of his success with Loxley Benson, that way he looks at you, his eyes blazing, making you feel special, as if nothing matters more than what you're about to say or do.

The other half's a different story, of course. Art's smart. Shrewd. And completely driven. Mum saw it when she met him.

Before he'd made his fortune, when he'd just set up his business – an online ethical-investment company – with no money and no security. 'That one,' she said. 'That one's going to set the world on fire.' Then she'd given me that wry smile of hers. 'Just make sure you don't get burned while you're trying to keep up.'

Mr Tamansini's desk is as big as a ship – all embossed brown leather with brass studs around the edges. He looks lost behind it – a small, olive-skinned man with a pointy face and delicate hands. He's pressing his fingertips together, which he always does when he speaks. He gazes at me and Art sitting next to each other on the other side of the desk.

'I'm going to suggest you try ICSI this time,' he says slowly. 'That's where we inject sperm *directly* into the egg.'

'See?' Art nudges my arm like we're in the back row of a classroom. 'I told you there'd be something new.'

I stare at Mr Tamansini's fingers. Weird to think they've been inside me. But then the whole idea of being a gynaecologist is weird. On the other hand, I like Mr Tam. I like his stillness. The way he stays calm even when Art is at his most forceful.He was my consultant for four of the six failed IVF attempts. I guess you could say we've been through a lot together.

'ICSI's not new,' I say, looking up at Mr Tam. 'Why that? Why now?'

Mr Tam clears his throat. 'ICSI is often used in cases where the sperm is of poor quality. Of course, that isn't the case here, but ICSI is equally useful when couples present with low rates of fertilization and a low yield of eggs at egg retrieval, both of which do apply to you.'

'Won't that cost more than ordinary IVF?' I ask.

At the mention of money Art stiffens. It's a tiny movement, but I recognize it well. It's like when an animal pricks up its ears, listening out for warning sounds. I stare back at Mr Tam's desk. The brass studs around the edge are gleaming in the light. I wonder, idly, whether somebody actually polishes them.

'It *is* more expensive,' Mr Tamansini acknowledges. 'But it will undoubtedly increase the chance of a viable pregnancy.'

'So what does ICSI involve?' Art says. His tone is neutral, but I can hear the steel in his voice. He's not going to let himself – or me – get taken for a ride.

Mr Tam smiles. 'As far as the two of you are concerned, there's really very little difference from standard IVF.' He starts talking about the procedure. I tune out for a moment. I already know about ICSI; it was one of the options I pored over several years ago.

'. . . which works like a cleaned-up software platform,' Mr Tamansini finishes. 'All ready to program a new computer.'

Art laughs. He loves Mr Tam's metaphors.

'So what do you think?' Mr Tam asks.

'Absolutely.' Art looks at me. 'We should go for it.'

For a second I'm furious that Art is speaking on my behalf. And then I remember that I agreed to come here, that he thinks I'm up for this, that I haven't talked about how I really feel for ages . . .

'I don't know,' I squirm. 'I mean . . . I don't know about IVF any more. Let's face it, in a few months I'll be forty which . . .'

'. . . is *not* too old.' Art turns to Mr Tam. 'Tell her, please. It's not too old.'

Mr Tam takes a deep breath. His face remains calm and professional, but underneath he is surely wondering why I'm here at all if I've got such doubts. 'Of course, Mrs Loxley, you are right. There are no guarantees. But you became pregnant once before, which is a positive sign. And forty is not that old in IVF terms. Indeed, one might say it is not as old as it used to be.'

I stare at him, at his soothing, gentle smile.

'I don't think ...' My voice trembles. 'I'm not sure I can cope with ... with going through it all again ...' My voice breaks and I look down at the carpet. There's a brown stain by the far desk leg in the shape of a kidney bean.

Why is it so hard to say what I want? How I feel?

Art's voice is low in my ear, as intense as I've ever heard it. 'Gen, we have to keep trying. Don't you see? If you like, I'll do a full risk assessment on the ICSI stats, I promise, and I'll work out the odds, and if that pans out then we'll make it work together, just like we always make everything work.'

I look up. Mr Tam has walked across the room, to the intercom by the curtained-off area. He is talking to someone in a low voice. Giving me and Art a moment to pull ourselves together.

I turn to Art. His eyes are dancing with this new hope. I hate myself for not feeling it too.

'I know that it's hard for you, all the drugs and the appointments and everything,' Art continues. 'And I know we've been through it before five times ...'

'Six,' I correct.

'... But it would be worth it,' Art presses on. 'Don't you think it would be worth it?'

I shake my head. I thought that once, maybe, the first few times we tried IVF after Beth. But the pain of trying and failing *wasn't* worth it.

Art frowns. 'I don't understand why you don't want to try again,' he says. He's trying to sound sympathetic but there's a note of impatience in his voice. 'If the percentages pan out, I mean.'

I take a deep breath. 'It's not the percentages and the risk factors and the drugs.' I look into his eyes, hoping I'll see that he understands. I lower my voice to a whisper. It's still so hard to say her name out loud. 'It's Beth.'

His eyes express confusion. 'You mean it's being disloyal to her memory to try again?'

'Not exactly ...'

'Oh, Gen. This isn't being disloyal. If anything, it's a testament to how much we loved her ... that we want so much to ... to replace her.'

Replace her?

Mr Tam is back at the desk now, fingertips pressed together.

Art's words are still ringing in my ears. I stare down at the kidney bean stain again, blood drumming at my temples.

'I guess we need a bit more time to think about all this,' Art is saying. His voice sounds dull and distant.

'Of course.' Mr Tam is smiling. I can hear it in his voice, but I'm still staring at the carpet stain. 'At this stage it's just a suggestion. I think we should take it one step at a time.'

I look up. 'That's a good idea.'

Art puts his arm around my shoulders. 'Absolutely.'

A few minutes later we're outside the clinic and heading home in a taxi. Art refuses to travel any other way. He could have a driver if he wanted one, now that Loxley Benson is so successful, but he hates any appearance of elitism. I tell him taxis are just as elitist but he says they're a practical solution – public transport being so slow and Art's time being money.

We don't speak. I'm still reeling. Suddenly I realize he's speaking to me.

'Sorry?'

'I wish you wouldn't do that.' He takes my hand and holds it between both of his.

I look down. The nail on the first finger of my left hand is bitten right down and the skin around the nail is chewed and red raw. I curl it over, out of sight. I hadn't even realized my finger had been in my mouth.

Art's fingers exert a soft pressure. 'Why did you let me make the appointment if you were so sure you don't want any more IVF?'

Through the taxi window, the sun is low above Regent's Park. A perfect burning orange disc against a clear navy sky with no sign of the earlier clouds. I turn back to Art. His eyes glitter in the soft light and my heart lurches with love for him. For all his ruthlessness in business, Art's fundamentally the kindest man I know.

'I'm sorry about the appointment,' I say. 'I know it's not fair ...' I tail off, wishing my thoughts weren't so confused.

'You know you're nuts, don't you?' Art says affectionately.

We stare at each other for a moment, then Art leans forward. 'Can you at least explain to me what you're worried about, Gen? Because I only want ... that is, everything I do, it's all for you, you *know* that. I just want to understand, because I can't see how *not* trying again is the right thing.'

I nod, trying to work out what to say. How I can explain what feels so muddled and fragile in my own head.

'I can't think in terms of "replacing" Beth,' I say.

It hurts to use her name. But not to say it denies her existence, which is worse. My stomach twists.

'I didn't mean *replace*.' Art dismisses his previous word with a shrug. He sits upright. '*Obviously* we can't replace her. But we *can* have the experience of being parents, which her dying cheated us of.'

'I don't know.'

Art fingers his collar, feeling for the hidden nick in the cotton. 'Then let *me* know for both of us.'

'What about the money?' I frown.

'We've already spent so much.'

Art waves his hand. 'That's the least of our problems.'

It's true, though I still can't quite get used to how much

Art is earning. It's not that we were struggling before: Loxley Benson has been doing well for a long time, but it's really taken off this year. In fact, right now, it's one of the fastest-growing small businesses in the UK.

'I don't mean the amount,' I say. 'It's the whole thing of sending good money after bad and—'

'Jesus, Gen, it's not *that* much money. Just a few grand. And me doing *The Trials* is getting us more work every day. A woman at a client meeting the other day, she's involved in some government initiative and she wants to talk to me at the Brussels meeting tomorrow about bringing me in. We're doing really well, Gen, like I told you we would. We're about to go *massive*.'

'But . . .' I stop, unable to say what I truly feel, which is that Art's business success makes me feel inadequate. It's not fair, when he works so hard for us, but being pregnant made me his equal. Like I was making a proper contribution to our marriage at last. And now, the reminder that he makes money hand over fist highlights how I have failed to keep my end of the unspoken deal between us.

'You *have* to want this, Gen. We can do it. I will find a way.'

The words, the set of his mouth, his whole body . . . it's all utterly convincing. And, I know from experience, virtually impossible to resist.

'You really want to try, don't you?'

Art shrugs. 'What's the alternative? Adoption?'

I shake my head. That's one thing we've both always agreed on at least. If we're going to have a baby, it should be *our* baby.

'Exactly.' Art leans forward. 'I do want this, Gen.' He pauses and his mouth trembles. 'But not unless you want it too.'

For a fraction of a second he looks vulnerable, like a little boy, and I see how afraid he is that I will never move on from

Beth dying and that our love will slip away from us because of it … because one day I will have to choose between letting go of Beth and letting go of Art.

'I want to do this *with* you, Gen,' he whispers. 'Please try and see that.'

The taxi slows to a halt at the traffic lights separating Camden High Street from Kentish Town Road. Art and I met in Camden, fourteen years ago at a big New Year's Eve party I'd gone to with my best friend, Hen. Art was twenty-six and in his first year of running his own business. He'd blagged his way into the party with a bunch of his colleagues because he thought there'd be useful people there. I was just up for free drinks and a laugh.

We met at the bar, when one of Art's colleagues – Tris – bumped into Hen and it turned out they were old uni friends who'd lost touch. Of course, Hen introduced me to Tris who, in turn, introduced me to Art. Art bought a round of drinks, most of which I knocked over onmy way back from the Ladies. He was sweet about that, immediately buying another round, even though – I found out later – he could barely afford to eat at the time. We got chatting. He told me about Loxley Benson, how he'd set up the business with a good friend just months before, how he wanted to ride the new wave of online trading, how passionately he felt about making sure the investments his company supported were ethical and socially and environmentally responsible.

I told him how I worked for a boring homes magazine, writing about kitchens and paint schemes, but how one day I wanted to write a novel. I remember being blown away by how driven he was.How he was prepared to take any risk and suffer any setback to get where he wanted. How it wasn't so much about making money as making a difference.

Even then, I knew that whatever Art wanted, he was going to get.

Including me.

'Gen?'

I bite my lip. It's dark outside now, the street lamps starting to glow as the taxi drags its way past the dreary shops and crowded pavements of Kentish Town High Street. If he wasn't married to me, Art would probably have four kids by now. He should have this. I shouldn't stop him from having this.

'It's the hope,' I say. 'I can handle anything except the hope.'

Art laughs. I know he doesn't really understand what I mean. But he loves me and that's enough.

'Why don't you check out the ICSI stats,' I say. 'See what you think. Then we can decide.'

Art nods enthusiastically and reaches into his pocket. A second later his phone buzzes and I realize he must have had it turned off for most of the last hour. I can't remember the last time he turned it off for more than a few minutes.

He's still talking on the phone as we reach Crouch End and walk into the house. Lilia, our Slovakian cleaner, is just leaving. As I shut the door behind her I notice the post piled up by the hall radiator. I pick it up and wander into the kitchen. We don't use the other downstairs rooms that much. It's a big house for just two people.

I flick idly through the mail. There's a postcard from my mum, who's on holiday with her latest boyfriend in Australia. I set that down on the kitchen table, then take the rest and stand over the recycling pile, chucking the junk mail on top of it. I put aside two bills and an envelope bearing the logo of Art's solicitors. More junk mail follows: magazines, takeaway flyers ... How can we receive so many pointless bits of post in just one day?

Art is still talking on the phone. His voice – low and insistent – grows louder as he passes the kitchen door, then fades again. As I throw a couple of catalogues onto the recycling pile, it teeters and finally collapses.

'Shit.' As I pick everything up, Art reappears.

'Gen?'

'How on earth is it possible for us to generate this much paper?' I say.

'They've brought forward tomorrow's Brussels meeting, so Siena's booked me onto an earlier flight.'

'When?'

'The meeting's at ten. I'll be leaving here just after six, so I was wondering about an early night ...' Art hesitates, his eyebrows raised. I know what he's thinking. I smile. At least it should mean the subject of IVF gets dropped for the rest of the evening.

'Sure,' I say.

We have dinner and I watch some nonsense on TV while Art makes a couple of calls and checks various spreadsheets. My programme segues to the *News at Ten*. As the first ad break starts, I feel Art's hand on my shoulder.

'Come to bed?'

We go upstairs. Art drops his clothes on the red-and-orange-striped rug and shakes back the duvet. He gets into bed and grins up at me. I lie down and let him touch me.

To be honest, I like the idea of Art wanting to have sex with me more than the sex itself. Our conversation about the IVF is still running through my head, and it's hard to let go and relax. I move a little, trying to be turned on, but it's just not happening. Art approaches sex pretty much like he approaches everything else – when he wants it he goes and gets it. Not that I'm saying he's ever been unfaithful. And I don't mean he's *bad* in bed, either. Just that he didn't have much idea when I met him, so everything he does now I taught him to do. And he's still doing it, exactly like I showed him fourteen years ago.

'Gen?' Art's propped up on his elbow beside me, frowning. I hadn't even noticed he'd stopped touching me.

I smile and take his hand and put it back between my legs. I will myself to respond. It works, a little. Enough, anyway. Art's convinced I'm finally letting go and eases himself inside me.

I let my mind drift. My focus turns to the pile of recycling downstairs. All that paper. I know that what really bothers me is the reminder of all the written words out there – the endless magazines and books competing for space on shop shelves. And that's before you include the internet. I used to be part of it all: I wrote and published three books in the time between marrying Art and getting pregnant with Beth. Sometimes the amount of published material in the world feels suffocating – squeezing the air out of my own words before they have a chance to come to life.

Art moans and I move again to show willing.

It's not just the paper stuff either. Art's 'Mr Ethical' and insists we are ultra-green, with separate boxes for everything: aluminium, cardboard, glass, food waste, plastic ...

Sometimes I just want to chuck it all in a black bag like we did when I was growing up. My mind slides to a memory from childhood. I'm struggling to carry a bin bag across the back garden, the grass damp under my feet. I'm hauling it towards Dad, who's on a rare visit home between tours. The grass smells sweet and fresh. Dad has just mown it and now he's making a compost heap with the cuttings. I want to help. That's why I'm carrying the contents of the kitchen bin out to him. He laughs and says most of the contents won't rot so we make a bonfire instead. I can still remember the smell of the fire, my face burning hot while the cold wind whips across my back.

Art's kissing my neck as he thrusts harder in to me. I just want him to get on with it ... get it over ... As soon as we're done he'll fall asleep and then I'll get up and have a cup of tea.

Art's breathing is heavier now, his movements more urgent. I know he's close, but holding back, waiting for me. I smile up at him, knowing he'll know what I mean. A minute later, he comes with a groan and sinks down onto me. I hold him, feeling him slide out of me and the wetness seeping out onto the bed. I love the way he feels so vulnerable like this, his head on my chest.

I wait ...

Art nuzzles into me, sighing contentedly, then rolls off, leaving just one arm draped over my chest. His breathing deepens and I slip out from under his arm. It's one of those things that I know, but don't want to face: our sex life has got into a rut. Unsurprising after so many years, I suppose. And it's certainly a lot better than during the years when I was obsessed with getting pregnant. I know Art felt under pressure then, having to do it at the right times, and I hated how trying to conceive took all the fun and spontaneity out of it. I stopped checking when I ovulate ages ago but maybe all that history has taken its toll. Or maybe it's just classic, married sex: predictable, comfortable, safe. I'm not complaining, though. One day I'll talk to Art properly about it. He'll listen, I know he will. He'll want to make it better. Which means he will. I've never known Art fail at anything.

Art's iPhone rings from his trouser pocket on the floor. He wakes with a start, then sighs as he reaches over the side of the bed to retrieve it.

As he starts talking, I get up and go downstairs.

*

I wake up. The bed beside me is empty. Art is long gone, headed to Heathrow. A damp towel lies across his pillow. Irritated, I push it onto the floor.

Half an hour later I'm dressed and spreading butter and Marmite on my toast. The day stretches ahead of me. My normal Wednesday morning class has been cancelled and I have no appointments. Not even coffee with Hen. But I have this niggling sense that there's something I'm supposed to do today.

You could write, says a voice in my head.

I ignore it.

The doorbell rings and I pad to the front door. I'm not expecting anyone. It's probably just the postman. Still, you can't be too careful. I hook on the chain, open the door and peer through the crack.

A woman stands on the doorstep. She's black and plump and middle-aged.

I instantly assume she's a Jehovah'sWitness and brace myself.

'Are you Geniver Loxley?' Her voice is soft, with a hint of a Midlands accent.

I stare at her. 'How do you know my name?'

The woman hesitates. It seems unlikely that a Jehovah's Witness would have this kind of detail, so I'm now assuming some kind of invasive mailing-list scenario. Still, the woman lacks the bravado of the sales-trained. In fact, now I'm looking closely at her I realize she's nervous. She's wearing a cheap suit made of some kind of nylon and sweat stains are creeping out from under the armpits.

'I ... I ...' she stammers.

I wait, my heart suddenly beating fast. Has Art been in an accident? Or someone else I know? The door is still on its chain. I open it properly. The woman presses her lips together. Her eyes are wide with fear and embarrassment.

'What is it?' I say.

'It's . . .' The woman takes a deep breath. 'It's your baby.'

I stare at her. 'What do you mean?'

She hesitates. 'She's alive.' The woman's dark eyes pierce through me. 'Your baby, Beth, is alive.'